THE FOURTH WATCH OF THE NIGHT

A Mystical View of Scripture

By

Carter Gregory

ISBN: 1-4107-4194-X (e-book)
ISBN: 1-4107-4193-1 (Paperback)
ISBN: 1-4107-4192-3 (Dust Jacket)

This book is printed on acid free paper.

1stBooks – rev. 07/14/03

TABLE OF CONTENTS

ILLUSTRATION CREDITS

Grateful acknowledgment is made for permission to reproduce the following:

Front Cover: the Storm on the Sea of Galilee, 1633 (oil canvass) by Rembrandt Harmensz van Rijn (1606-69)

CREDIT: Isabella Stewart Gardner Museum, Boston, Massachusetts, USA/Bridgeman Art Library

Page 188: The jaws of Hell fastened by an angel, made for Henry, Bishop of Blois (d.1171), Winchester, Psalter of Henry of Blois, (1140-60)

CREDIT: British Library, London, UK/Bridgeman Art Library

INTRODUCTION

If Dr. Robert M. McNair of the Philadelphia Divinity School had not used the word "riddle" during a lecture and then invited me to his home to discuss the riddle, I would have had no reason to write a book. He was speaking about Mark's Gospel, and at the end he said, "The text is the despair of its expositors—it is full of riddles."

One evening later that week he invited me to his home and over coffee he confided his sense of wonderment about the gospels. "Listen to this," he said, opening the Marcan text to the eighth chapter: "We read that Jesus crosses the Galilean Sea and the disciples in the boat complain they have only one loaf of bread. Jesus then thrusts a riddle upon them; he asks them how many loaves they gave out and picked up during the two miraculous feedings in the wilderness. The disciples recall the numbers, but fail to understand the Lord's meaning. What do you make of that?" he asked.

He took pencil and paper and outlined the first part of the Gospel narrative. "Another thing," he said: "Look—Jesus tells the parable about a sower who scatters seeds of grain, and he tells us that there are three reasons why the seed may not bring forth grain—birds, shallow soil, and thorns. Then, when the seed grows in fertile soil, he measures its yield by three terms—thirtyfold, sixtyfold, and hundredfold. There! Do you think the number three might be important?" I stared at his outline. The parable fell in the area of Mark's first pattern of three: three disciples are surnamed on the mountain, three great healings take place, and the three disciples just surnamed serve as special witnesses to the third (5:37). He put his text down and looked directly at me: "What do you think about that?" he asked.

"The ancient world was impressed by numbers," he added. "The bible is no different; it is studded with numbers; sometimes given right out, sometimes hidden. You have to dig them up, as I did. In the New Testament, three, four, five, and twelve are everywhere. They must mean something. The question is, 'What?' Have you ever wondered?"

At the time, no; but now, yes. That evening at Bob McNair's home, I was hooked.

v

That 8th chapter of Mark was only the beginning of riddledom. Why, I wondered, does Jesus administer loaves on two occasions? Or—a more sophisticated question—why does Mark twice tell us about one feeding? And why does the storyteller, the author of riddles, tell us that twice the disciples cross the sea, both times at night, and when high winds threaten to sink them? Or does Mark twice tell about one crossing? And why does Jesus call the first four disciples in pairs? Many things appear to happen twice; I was getting *deja vu*.

> Before long I was staring at this collection of doublets:
> Jesus calls the disciples two and two (1:16,19); the four go to Simon's house.
> *and*
> three disciples are surnamed (3:16) and the three go to Jairus' house (5:37).
>
> Jesus sends the disciples on mission two and two (6:7),
> *and*
> three disciples witness Jesus' transfiguration on the mount (9:2).
>
> Jesus sends the disciples two and two ahead to prepare the feast (11:1; 14:13) and the four witness his revelatory discourse on the Mount of Olives (13:3).
> *and*
> Jesus calls the three witnesses apart for a revelation in Gethsemene (14:33).

My interest in pairs turned into a passion for the number three, which began to emerge from the shade. The four thousand pilgrims who follow Jesus into the desert wait three days before Jesus feeds them: the world had to wait three days before the buried Christ arose on Easter Day. And when Jesus riddles the disciples about the number of loaves, he is crossing the sea a third time.

I didn't realize it at first, but my observations and the questions that followed them cut deep into the fabric of standard opinion. Scholars regard Mark's Gospel as irrefragable testimony to the historical Jesus—the best record we have. Its simple vivid style, with details, seems like the work of a sharp-eyed witness. This opinion is supported by a first century tradition that the Apostle Peter is the witness, and that he passed the facts on to Mark. And, since two of the other gospelers incorporated large blocks of Mark's text into their books, the literal accuracy of Mark is a vital matter. Therefore we ought not ask questions that imply that something is odd.

But it *is* odd history, if history it is. Others found it odd, too—scholars who knew more than I, and who braved ridicule when they published their ideas. Austin Farrer's book *A Study in St. Mark* was new to me when I stumbled upon it in the 60's—Farrer, an Oxford don, wrote it in 1951, but it was a hushed up scandal for years. This scholar unearthed patterns in Mark's narrative, and finally a ground plan that supported an elaborate numerology. I was elated: at last it made sense that Jesus calls twelve men to be his followers, gives twelve loaves of bread to an anticipated twelve thousand in the desert, and heals exactly twelve suffering Jews of their afflictions. If this is history, Jesus is beyond rational comprehension; if it is a literary device with a method, let us have the method.

(Would it help to note that Matthew, when he wrote his gospel, doubled the number of suffering Jews? Twenty four. Luke did the same. They knew what Mark was doing, and improvised on his scheme.)

One might object: "If Mark had some point to make by all this, why didn't he hand it to us, plain and simple? Why make us count and look for numbers and patterns and the like?" The answer is that Mark wrote for a select readership, members of an esoteric school, perhaps—we do not know—who understood how scriptures are written and how they should be read. Mark knew his readers and they knew him. Perhaps they met together for study and worship; if they had questions about his gospel, they could go to him for answers. They would understand the symbols, the types, the numbers, the sacred images from the past that Mark revived. Mark had no notion that people like us, in subsequent centuries, would read his book.

The first readers would have recognized the images and patterns because they knew the old scriptures; they would have known *The Book of Daniel*, for example, which dates from the second century B.C.E., and they would have noted its pattern:

Four heros are introduced and undergo a mild temptation together (i). Daniel's three companions undergo a severe temptation (iii) and we are left expecting that Daniel himself will undergo one equally severe. He does so (iv). The first temptation is followed by a dream (ii), the second by a dream and a vision (iv, v), the third by a dream and three visions (vii, viii, ix-xii).

Farrer, *St. Matthew and St. Mark, p. 18*

Such is Farrer's hypothesis: Mark, fashioning his phrases after earlier models, composed an epic narrative that involves a patterned exposition, a numerology, and a far-reaching typology by which Jesus is seen to be a "new" Daniel, a "new" Moses, a "new" Joshua, and so on. His hypothesis became known as "*that* hypothesis" by his critics, of whom there were many. But calm has been restored; it is acceptable now to speak of Mark as a "redactor" (an editor; but more than an editor—an author in his own right).

Most scholars now admit that Mark was influenced by *Daniel*. A most obvious point in support of this is the emblem "Son of man," whose only *Old Testament* location is in *Daniel*, and is much used by Mark. But not so obvious is the allusion in Mark's passion narrative to *Daniel's* story of the hero in the den of lions. Even the amateur Randel Helms, in his *Gospel Fictions*, spots the hidden lions among the allusions Mark wrote into his narrative of Jesus' suffering and death on the cross, as well as his third day rising.

Danielic lions in the Holy Week liturgy! The notion stimulated a psychological reflection on my part. In the late 60's I signed up for some psychology courses at the University of Pennsylvania, which was close by the theological school, and I contemplated a dual career—the Ministry of the Episcopal Church, and Psychotherapy. Theology, scripture, liturgy, Teilhard deChardin, Sigmund Freud, and Carl Jung all impacted my imagination. It was Freudian psychology that led me to suspect that the beasts lurking in the background of the passion-resurrection narrative had meaning beyond what the author of *Daniel* or Mark would have admitted: I wrote a paper on the subject "The Subterranean Beast" in which I asserted that the "beast" was the libido that Jesus struggled to suppress by his ascetic life and bodily denial on the cross. (But now I have a different mind on the subject.)

But it was also the patterns and the numbers that impressed me. A psychologist looks for patterns in his neurotic clients: by means of the patterns he uncovers the images, obsessions, and fears that show up in their bad dreams and spill over to ruin their lives, and he traces them back to their origins; he brings them to the surface where they can be exorcized. I suspected, in the course of my studies, that things tend to spill over—that the images of scripture, and the wellsprings of human behavior, and all human history and culture, are fed by some deeply hidden reservoir; and from that source that Carl Jung knows so well, come the patterns (archetypes) and numbers.

The study of numbers and biblical images led me to the riddling mystery of "the fourth watch of the night." One of the most ancient of mental images is the night sea journey. When Mark tells us that Jesus sends his disciples to sea during those dark nights and exposes them to peril, he makes sure we know that these night sea journeys are fused (6:52) with the riddle of the numbers of loaves, a riddle that is told in a boat scurrying a third time across the Galilean Sea– this time by daylight, when dark sayings should be exposed to the light of human understanding or divine explication. But in the text, the disciples do not comprehend—nor did I. My most respectful readings of Farrer and others left me in a perplexed state of mind. I failed to find the inner sanctuary where mysteries and their answers have common root.

But the actual sinking of a ship— I should say, a poem about it— has brought me closer to that inward place. The poet, Gerard Manley Hopkins, like Austin Farrer, was an Oxonian and a priest, unappreciated in his time. Hopkins could not have known Farrer, but he had his own instincts to trust. He was shattered one morning to learn that during the night a storm had driven a ship against the shoals of the Thames, the "Kentish Knock," as it was called, and that five nuns lost their lives. The nuns were fleeing persecution in Westphalia and were seeking a new life in America— in St. Louis, where their order was engaged in health care among the poor—but they perished in the waters of the Thames that dark night. Hopkins composed a long ode as memorial to the nuns, *The Wreck of the Deutschland*, in which he indicates that the nuns perished on December 7, just before dawn. But the ship was driven onto a shoal by the storm at about 5 A.M. on December 6; it foundered all day and into the next until a tugboat pulled alongside the submerged stern at noon on the 7th to rescue the few who remained alive. The bodies of the five nuns washed up on the shore during the following week. It cannot be said exactly when the nuns perished. But Hopkins needed to say that the nuns perished in the hours before dawn.

THE WRECK OF THE DEUTSCHLAND
Gerard Manley Hopkins
To the happy memory of five Franciscan Nuns, exiled by the Falk Laws drowned between midnight and morning of Dec. 7th 1875

Why? Hopkins could not have known when the nuns perished...*or could he?*
Hopkins, like Mark, wrote for a select readership, people who understand poetry and its powers. The truth, for Hopkins, was in the images and the numbers that he discerned in the disaster at sea, that helped him struggle with it and finally accept it. He was a priest as well as poet, and the images best known to him were those of his bible—*The Book of Job*, and the books of the *New Testament*. In stanza three of his poem, for example, he speaks of himself, and claims his right to boast, for he has endured much and achieved a safe haven at last for his heart; his allusion is to the Apostle Paul, who also found safe haven—following his shipwreck and near death in the Mediterranean. Then the poet cries "Gennesereth!"—the port to which another ship was driven by strong winds: Jesus' disciples, crossing the Galilean Sea in a small boat, are driven from their intended port, Bethsaida ("house of provisioning" i.e. bread) to a strange place, Genneseret, far from their safe haven. Hopkins must have meditated deeply upon this text in Mark whenever his mind turned to the death of the five nuns who were searching for safe haven and new life across the sea. Certainly it caught his eye that in Mark's text, the crossing - the second, in the sixth chapter—takes place during the fourth watch of the night, and that in the dark night the disciples see Jesus walking toward them atop the waters. Here, in this text, Hopkins found the salve for his soul: he believed that the five nuns, too, in the hours before dawn, saw their Lord coming to them atop the waters. Having determined this, the poet's mind turns to another number—a number that Mark knows, too—and he announces "Cinquefoil." It is the five-leaved emblem of the Christ, his dying Lord.

He struggled with the ode. The writing occupied him inordinately. He developed a unique stanzic pattern and a difficult rhyme scheme. Form and pattern were vital; in a note to the poem he stated that stress and meaning are one. The poem is autobiographical in the first part; he reveals his pain. God, he says, is his Master; God created the world's strand and all the forces that bring man down upon it. The sinking of the Deutschland provoked his long-standing feelings of despair and hopelessness. It was a crisis of faith. Yet in this crisis he encounters the God who brought him to the crisis—a paradox. For answers he searches the scripture. Enigma and paradox abound there too, but its images begin to move him: the sea especially, the sea that engulfed the five nuns, he comes to believe, is a redeemable image. He has read in the gospels that his Lord was baptized in the waters of the Jordan River, that he called up fishermen from the Galilean Sea, that he began healing people by the sea—people who were victims of the universal deluge—and he relieved them of their ills and restored them to health and faith. And he must have known the prophet's oracle that said living waters shall flow from a new temple and all who come to these waters shall live.

What did Hopkins know about the nuns and their deaths? In the poem, the nuns died in the early hours before dawn—the fourth watch of the night. Hopkins would have been asleep during the fourth watch of the night. So were the disciples of Jesus in Mark's 14th chapter: Jesus, greatly agitated, takes three witnesses aside and three times tells them to "watch" while he goes off alone to pray. Three times, after he has prayed, he comes upon them and finds them asleep. Finally, he says to them, "Arise..." That is the scene at Gethsemene, in which Jesus says that all things are possible. *How could the sleeping disciples - witnesses, allegedly—know what Jesus did when they were asleep?* Hopkins knew. And I believe I know.

The first chapter, "The Fourth Watch of the Night," is creative non-fiction, in which I extend the Marcan stage to make room for my psychological and theological ruminations. My hand was guided by Austin Farrer and his disciples— Dr. Michael D. Goulder of Hong Kong, in particular, whose various writings taught me to understand the Marcan and Lucan texts in a new way and enabled me to discover the mystical element in *Acts of the Apostles* and compose my second chapter. (Dr. Goulder, unlike Dr. Farrer, lost his religious faith at the end of his life because, I am told, he dug up too many historical roots in his search for numbers and types.) The first two chapters, therefore, will differ from established views of these texts.

During my undergraduate years at Hunter College I met the Catholic Chaplain Fr. Herman Heidi. During one of our many conversations, we got onto the number 666—it came up during a stir on campus among some Protestant students. The number is "the mark of the beast," and it is infamously used by some preachers to arouse fantasies of the Devil's works, particularly the anti-Christ, when the "end time" comes upon us. Heidi quietly mentioned that something "unusual" had happened in St. Louis along those lines. I quizzed him for more details, and I got an earful. About fifteen years ago, he said, in 1949, a young boy had been assaulted by the Devil himself, and it took three priests to save him. I gave little credence to his story, but I remembered the discussion, and I remembered something else: Heidi said that he sent a gift to the chief exorcist, one William S. Bowdern; the gift, he said, was a record album of Handel's oratorio *Messiah*, Columbia records, ML 666. I filed the discussion away for future use. In 1973 a movie came out of Hollywood called *The Exorcist*, based on Peter Blatty's book by the same name. I got hold of the book, and soon realized that it was taken from the incident related to me by Fr. Heidi. There was little in the book to stimulate my interest in patterns and numbers, but in 1993 a book came out written by a journalist, Thomas B. Allen, that covered the actual experience of Bowdern and his helpers. (*Possessed: The True Story of An Exorcism.*) Allen had access to a notebook kept by one of the three priests. In that same year, I happened to meet The Rev. James J. LeBar, of Hyde Park, New York, an exorcist attached to the Archdiocese of New York. My reading of Allen's book and its revelations, and my discussions with Father LeBar, gave impetus to the fourth chapter of my book. More recently I have had the pleasure of meeting Michael Cuneo, the author of *Exorcism in American Culture*, who provided further enlightenment. That 1949 exorcism, I came to realize, was full of patterns and numbers—the same numbers I find in scripture, poetry, mystical experiences, and the dreams of my clients.

The sections of Chapter Four that I call "The Trap" and "The Sign" are meditations inspired by the 1949 exorcism. I have not made an attempt at investigative reporting—Allen's book has done that perfectly well; readers who want "just the facts" without my theoretical trappings should turn to him. My work is a meditation: its literary genre, I believe, is called "creative non-fiction." In other words, I put my thoughts into the mouth of the chief exorcist, Fr. William Bowdern. The word "theory" is perhaps too grand—let's say I wrote this chapter with a speculative premise in mind. The three priests became characters on the stage of my imagination. But my meditation, like all good theological meditations, rests upon a bed of fact. Again, I must credit Allen's book, which added clarity to some issues that were unsettled in my mind and provided factual information that was unknown to me: the precise dates of Bowdern's visits to the victim's home, the words of the "Demon," the markings on the victim's body, the role of the Alexians and the incident at the Retreat House. I structured my meditation around these facts. (Fr. Heidi told me about the Archangel's presence over the high altar at Bowdern's church: I take it as credible, for the Jesuits present in the church at the time are to be trusted. Of course, I permit myself to interpret the angel's epiphany as a fact of the mind, a soterial archetype projected from or through the mind of Bowdern.)

My intent in Chapter Four has been to erect an interpretive scaffold around the reported events, that will incite interest in the mythic proportions of the forty day ordeal. The interpretation is mine and mine alone; none of the above cited persons or authors are responsible for my opinions; in fact, at least one would fiercely disagree with me. Finally, I add that present day revelations about pedophile priests lend an element of realism to my speculative premise.

The Fourth Watch of the Night is about *muein*, "night vision," literally, "to shut the eye." The Greek word is the root of mystery, mysticism. Mystical vision is "seeing with the (outer) eye shut." Hopkins, in his poem, tells us what he saw when the light of his faith had grown dim, when he closed his (outer) eye in despair. In Chapter Two, many persons tell us what they saw when their inner eye was opened to the light of a new day.

The title *The Fourth Watch of the Night* is metaphoric; it suggests a journey of the spirit through remote chambers of the unconscious mind in search of its origin and its destined end. In this journey the spirit has for its guides certain images and stories that issue from these chambers. I will give a few examples: the cross, the circle, the cube, the globe, deep water, dark night, magical numbers, the stars, the virgin water birth, the night sea journey. I have found these images and stories in the pages of Scriptures. *The Fourth Watch* is about these images and stories. Some of them are familiar to us; others are not recognized for what they are. They all call to us from a distance; in ages past they had power to move and inspire, but they have become old and worn, and they have been trivialized by shallow repetition. We fail to recognize in them the voice of mystery. Yet, if we hear and respond to their call, they will guide us to our life's goal. Mariners at sea followed a polar star that charted their course; wise men of Scripture followed a night star to a divine Child hidden in a manger; we may follow our night star until we come to the manger of our new birth. If we fail to recognize our journey, we die a spirit-less death.

The wise men brought to the manger three gifts from their treasure house: gold, frankincense and myrrh. Their journey too was inward and psychic; the number three testifies to this truth. Numbers arise in our conscious minds when the ego plunges into the deep waters of the unconscious mind. Poets know this: just as they know the right word or metaphor that yields infinite overtones, they know the right number that resonates in the cavernous mystery that is life. The title of my book, *The Fourth Watch of the Night*, recalls that the Romans divided the night into four "watches" of three hours each, and the last is the "dark before the dawn." "Three" often means the dawning awareness of divinity, following the plunge into utmost dark, the Galilean Sea of the Unconscious, where Jesus has sent us and where he awaits us—he who, together with the Father and the Holy Spirit, is one God, world without end.

Theologians who tear down established views of the sources invariably challenge those of us who have built our hopes and carved out our prayers on those views. The disciples in the boat were challenged by Jesus: they asked him about the one loaf, how it could provide for their journey. He riddled them; he riddled them because their established views were no good. They complained they had no bread; they failed to see they had all the bread in the world. *The*

Fourth Watch of the Night explores Scripture and mystical experience, not so as to tear down, but to reveal that which cannot be torn down; not to rob people of faith but to strengthen faith, so it will be a fit vessel for that great journey.

It is customary for an author to acknowledge and thank people who have helped him with his thinking, his manuscript, his life. There are many, and my fear is that I may offend by my inability to acknowledge all. But I think it best that I thank those who most need to hear it from me, because in their modesty they know little what their intelligence, goodness, and spirituality have meant to me. I begin with Dr. McNair; he warned me never to preach "this stuff" from a church pulpit, especially not a mainline pulpit. I took his warning to heart. I wrote this book instead.

I dedicate the book to my parents, Flavius Hammett ("Hamm") Gregory and his beautiful wife — my mother, Mary Virginia Guion Gregory; and to their grandchildren—my two "little ones," Mary Jeanine Gregory and Christopher Gavin Guion Gregory. I honored my children when they were young by not imposing religious instruction upon them; they have rewarded me by their shining faith and love. The Lord lives in them, truly.

I wish to honor Alma Murchison, my tenth grade English teacher, who tried her best to teach me to write. She never did (not her fault), but she did teach me to sit still while she tried.

Now, words fail. Two persons I cannot tell how much they have meant to me and the manuscript of this book. Yvonne Tierney I cannot tell, because she is where words cannot reach— only love reaches so far. But the three years of her life that she gave to me, and the three years I gave to her, will be a part of eternity. In this life, she was noble and good, until her mind was ravaged by the disease that took her. She now rests with the One who gave her to us.

Following her loss, the manuscript of this book fell to the floor of my study and gathered dust for seven months. How I came to write again seems a miracle—how do I find words to describe *that*? This much I can say: the poet Hopkins suffered seven years without being able to complete his works, until the faith of a woman—the brave nun he saw in his vision—inspired him to pick up again and write his great poem. A young woman's face did the same for me. Her pure smile put an end to seven months of depression, and I began to write again. That was in late June, 2001. Adrienne Ann Selle continues to be an inspiration, even into the beginnings of a new manuscript. She is simply a rare person who brings out the best in me.

* * *

PREFACE TO CHAPTER ONE

On December 6, 1875 a steamship bound for America from Brehmen struck a sand bar in the Thames River during a violent ice storm. Seventy eight persons died that night as the Deutschland went down, including five Franciscan nuns. The nuns had been driven from their home in Germany by anti-Catholic laws and were seeking safety in a new land. Instead of safety their flight brought them nature's fury. They heard and saw things they could hardly bear: children crying in the hold where they were trapped; a sailor trying to rescue the children, lowering himself by a rope, disappearing from sight, then his headless body hanging loose—a hideous sign he had failed to reach them. Everywhere they saw men and women crying, consoling one another, cursing God; all were beyond human help. Finally the bulkhead cracked. The nuns held hands and prayed their last as they were swept away by the rushing waters.

The ship had entered the Kentish Knock before dawn and struggled against the wind all day and into the night, when the nuns uttered their last. As the ship sank lower into the sea, a Roman Catholic priest at St. Beuno's theological college many miles to the west recited his last office of the day and then took refuge in his bed: it was his only refuge—an affliction of the spirit so troubled him that he often sought it early. Parish work had proved too demanding, and so his bishop permitted him to live at St. Beuno's, where his duties were light and he had time for his poetry. But even at the college he was troubled by dark spells and visionary flights that robbed him of his will to write, even the will to pray. He had not composed a poem in seven years. In his earlier years he had written a few poems—fragments, mostly—but his father, a marine insurance adjuster, distracted him with stories of dangerous seas and disasters. But his spiritual nature prevailed: he took holy orders and composed several poems that revealed a rich and probing mind. The writing and the praying stopped, however, when the affliction came upon him. For seven years he wrote nothing and his prayers were perfunctory.

When he woke up on Tuesday the seventh he heard that the Deutschland had gone down and taken five nuns with her. At once he went after the facts. He asked his mother in London to send him the *Times* and the *Illustrated News*, in which he was able to read reports from survivors and eyewitnesses. As he read he imagined himself a witness: He stands at the water's edge and hears the cries of those about to drown. He sees a sailor take pity on the children below and come down from the rigging at the end of a rope, only to lose his life when the breakers dash his head against the raised keel. He feels the terror of those who are blown into the water. He follows the ship's agonized turning from about midnight to just before dawn. Always his eye is upon the five nuns: their head is a tall lioness of a woman, strong and brave; she leads the others in prayer and keeps up their faith. Then, a cracking sound beneath them...they cling to a rail as the ship pitches sharply and the stern sinks into the sea. The tall nun shuts her eyes against the slashing wind. Her lips move in prayer— her last. Her head rolls portside. Suddenly she calls out

CHRIST, O CHRIST, COME QUICKLY

When he heard the words of the nun, he must have recalled the last words that St. John the Divine, the seer of *The Apocalypse*, spoke to an army of martyrs: "Come, Lord Jesus, come." Then he turned his head and gazed at the dark shapes of souls in the water, their arms flailing, their hopes fading. And he saw— could it be?—what the nun saw. Her eyes were closed, yet she called out. Yes, he saw it too.

When he finished the newspapers, he rose and made his way to the college chapel. On bent knee he offered his prayers for God's mercy upon the souls of the five who perished and the many other souls who were lost. Then he went to his room and shut the door. If he could pray he could write. He picked up his pen. After seven lean years, the words began to come. Images and symbols rushed into his head as he pondered the last five words of the tall nun. He saw her again in his mind's eye, joining hands with the others like Christian martyrs marching to their death in the gladiatorial arena. Then he wondered if the nun had merely recited a text from her daily devotion—it was the eve of Blessed Mary's Holy Day; how admirable; she was loyal to the end. A cynical thought came upon him: the nun merely prayed for a speedy end to her ordeal. No: he rejected these thoughts.

His lean years had taught him much. In his deep abyss he learned to see when the outer eye is shut. That night he saw what the nun saw—Jesus walking over the water to the Deutschland.

The poem that began to form was a thicket of images, allusions, numbers, and sacramental metaphors. He was searching even as he wrote. He saw Jesus. But the Lord's presence atop the waves deepened the old mystery and roused fears of his childhood, when his father told him stories of storms and wrecks in the deep. He no longer doubted the presence of Jesus in the midst of human need; his gifted vision assured him of this truth. No:—the mystery was the Deutschland itself. Who brought the vessel to the foundering shoal and buried its cargo in the brine? Who made the cold winds to snap at the rigging and turn the ship upon its side? Who made man and pitches him into the abyss? And the dark...who made *that?* He turned to the Scripture and pondered "life's dawn," when there were "endragoned seas," and all manner of evils. He remembered how Cain and Abel sucked at the same mother's breast: he studied good and evil; life and death; light and dark. All from the Maker. The cold is God's cold; the wind is God's wind; the wreck of the Deutschland is God's harvest.

As he wrote he suddenly exclaimed, "Gennesereth!" There was another storm at sea: he turned to the sixth chapter of Mark's gospel: the disciples of Jesus are making a night journey across the Sea of Galilee to Bethsaida, which lies on the east shore. Contrary winds rise up to buffet them and they are helpless in the cold and the dark; the winds turn them toward Genneseret. They look out into the dark and they see a figure walking toward them over the water. "It is a ghost," they cry. But it is Jesus: "Have no fear," he says, "it is I." Yes, another dark sea journey—he meditated upon the text until he saw what he had not seen before: it is the old mystery, for the cause of the disciples' distress at sea is Jesus himself. The text is clear: Jesus sends them out upon the dark sea in their frail barques while he watches them from a hilltop.

When he came to pen the nun's vision, he had the disciples' night sea journey I mind. "Strike you the sight of it," he wrote, "look at it loom there...the Master, Ipse, the only one, Christ, King, Head: he was to cure the extremity where he cast her."

Hopkins composed an ode of great depth and intensity; the dark spells that stunted his powers proved an asset, even became the substance of the ode, which has to do with the dark night in which the

Deutschland sank. It is a difficult poem, but one thing emerges clearly from the study of it: Father Gerard Manley Hopkins, his eyes closed in sleep, saw and heard a figure upon the waters that multitudes, their eyes open, have only prayed to see.

CHAPTER ONE

The Fourth Watch of the Night

i. The Mystery of the Sea

The Jews had always been afraid of the sea. Their ancient sages said that some unruly substance existed before the world was made, something that resisted even the Primal Light that issued from the mind of God. This unruly substance was the sea, the deep waters that they feared along with the desert and the dark. Even after God set in place the sun and the moon and the stars to guide human feet, the sea remained a dark place and a curse settled upon it. Demons lived in it, they believed, and ghosts had been seen moving upon its moonlit mists. The author of Psalm 69 prayed, "Let not the deep swallow me up; and let not the pit shut her mouth upon me." The sea meant death and the pit of hell: Jonah cried from the belly of the whale, "Thou hast cast me into the deep, in the midst of the seas; and the floods compassed me about; all thy billows and waves passed over me." The Jews were not alone, for the ancient Babylonians believed the same of the sea; they spoke of Tiamat, an ugly goddess of the sea who was murdered by the other gods who hated her, and whose carcass was cut up to form the several layers of creation. In the Hebrew Bible, when God made man, He cast not an eye toward the sea, nor to the land; rather, He made man "in His own image," that is, from his pure creative will, so that this creature, man, would be fresh and pure from the start.

It was the land, rather, that they trusted—safe and solid, it was theirs, God had given it to them. It was His gift, to save them from the sea and its terrors. But they could not escape the sea. Set deep in a pocket of the northern desert was the Sea of Galilee, thirteen miles north to south and eight miles wide. From the high land that surrounded it one could often see the west wind stir up storms that harassed fishermen. Fishing was esteemed, for necessity required that men go out upon the sea to fish, but it did not redeem the sea itself or diminish its terror; places near it had an unclean aspect, as if the curse had risen up and contaminated the land. Saphoris and Tiberias, for example: Jews detested these cities because they were on the wrong side of the sea, and pagans had built them. (Actually, the Jew's own King Herod built Tiberias; he did it to honor a pagan emperor. And he built it over a gravesite sacred to Jews. He could at least have put it to the east, where the pagans lived; both Tiberias and Saphoris were west of the sea, which Jews claimed as their own.) Even villages to the west were suspect, however: Capernaum stood near the sea; the Jews kept it free of pagan influence, but demons from the sea had come up to afflict the synagogue there—Jesus denounced the place. Chorazin and Bethsaida he denounced for stubbornness and hardness of heart. (Bethsaida was actually to the north and west, near the mixed territories where Jews and pagans tried to live together. Jesus healed a blind man there but it rejected him.) And Magdala: Mary Magdalene had lived there—she was possessed by seven demons. No good came from the sea, not the one side or the other. The author of *The Book of Daniel*, who wrote about the pagan kings who threatened his people, depicted them as awful beasts who came up from the sea when mighty winds blew over it; and they may come again to devour the godly nation.

ii. *Jesus Sets a New Temple by the Sea*

Jesus, fresh from the waters of the Jordan where he was purified by John the Baptizer, has come to the sandy shore of the Galilean Sea to find four fishermen who will drop their nets and answer his call. In the distance, in the dim light of the setting sun, he sees the forms of four men. Can these be the ones? He comes upon them and studies them closely; they are sturdy looking men, well fit for their work. But he will demand more of them than a fisherman's skills. A prophet of old had said that in the day of the Lord's coming the great temple will be restored: a healing and life-giving stream will flow from the center of it, he had said; fishermen will stand beside it and spread their nets for a great catch. But, Jesus thinks, they will not be ordinary fishermen and they will not spread their nets for fish. They must be fit for a greater work. And they must not be fearful, like many who go out to sea and ask for signs and portents. For Jesus has no signs or portents to give—yet.

He looks at these men. Will they trust him? Men do not easily give up their life's work to follow a stranger. He calls to the men by name: surprised, they lay down their nets and listen to what he says. They speak of the sea and its dangers; then they speak of the people who live about the sea, Jews and Gentiles alike. These men love their own people but they detest what they have heard about their leaders, that they are arrogant and corrupt. They fear such men more than they fear the sea; they have mastered their fear of the sea, but how can they master fear of evil men, men who have great power that yields no good? The sea yields fish; what does Herod yield?

As they share their thoughts about Herod, Jesus remembers the strong words John the Baptist had uttered against the House of Herod. He had been attracted to the Baptist for that very reason, and submitted to his water Baptism in the Jordan. That was when he heard the Voice, when he came up from the water. He believes it is the Voice that brought forth the world. "You are my beloved son in whom I am well pleased," it had said. No one heard the Voice but him. The Voice has brought him here, now, by the sea, searching for these men, whom he will call to a work more dangerous than the sea.

Their names are Simon and Andrew; James and John. They decide to leave their nets for a time and follow him. It is the only way they can learn about him and his need for them. He himself knows no more than what the Voice requires of him, that he should leave his own work and follow the call. This is how matters stand, then: he has called these four men with his voice, just as the greater Voice has called him. He has been baptized and tested; they will be baptized and tested, but in other waters and at another hour. He knows no more. But he believes the world has made a new beginning.

When Sabbath comes, he takes the four with him to attend synagogue in Capernaum, near the sea. For devout Jews this is a day of rest—no work is permitted. The day begins at sundown, and a large congregation has assembled. He attended the synagogue several times in his youth, but he doubts anyone will recognize him, for he has changed. (Even his parents say he has changed— "He is beside himself," they say, not understanding that he has heard the Voice.) He stands and speaks to them about Scripture. They are astonished as the wisdom of this young man—he speaks like a great sage, they exclaim, and such authority they have not heard even from the scribes who come up from Jerusalem. He knows, however, that a foul spirit is in their midst who listens to every word. The spirit may have been here for a long time; or Satan just sent him—for Satan witnessed his baptism and tried to tempt him from his destined journey. Satan is stalking him—he has followed him and his companions to this place. A man stands up in the midst of the congregation and curses Jesus and God. Again, the congregation is astonished; the man had not done that before. Jesus knows that the foul spirit entered the man and makes him speak thus. The man cries out again: "What have you to do with us? Have you come to destroy us? I know who you are, the Holy One of God." Jesus knows he is being tempted. Satan wants him to accept the title of "God's Holy One." Jesus will not accept this from anyone; hardly will he accept it from foul spirits. "Be silent," he commands. The foul ones flee at the sound of his voice. He has done his first great work.

His four companions are awed by the spectacle of their master driving out the demons. He must be an exorcist, they think. They had taken him for a rabbi—an original and splendid rabbi, to be sure—but he is more. Is he messiah? When they have left the synagogue and are on their way to Simon's house where they will be staying, the men

turn to their master and question him: "Are you messiah?" they want
to know. He is hard put to answer their question. He knows no more
than what the Voice has told him and the Voice has not called him to
be messiah to his people. But the Voice has said things that make him
believe he has existed from the beginning of the world. He has
meditated about another kingdom that is not of this world—a paradise
where Adam and Eve had their bower. Man's true home. If it is the
Voice that has inspired these meditations, then the Voice has set him
on a course that requires him to be not a messiah, but more than a
messiah. Messiah is expected to raise an army against Caesar and
restore the Kingdom to the Jews. But his thoughts are on paradise.
He does not answer his companions' question. For now, he will be a
man with secrets—secrets that in time he will tell—and he will let
men judge him by his works. When he arrives at Simon's house, he
learns that his companion's mother-in-law is down with a fever. He
puts out his hand to her and lifts her up. She is instantly well enough
to serve them a meal. The four men are astounded; their master is
more than an exorcist, even; he makes the sick rise from their bed.

As they walk back to Capernaum, his friends ask him again if he
might be messiah. It is a fearful thing to contemplate; what good are
four fishermen up against Caesar's legions? But he must make them
understand that there are worse enemies that Caesar: Caesar is mortal;
the spirits are not. And the spirits are stirred up. They were waiting
for him in the synagogue and they followed him to Simon's house.
Like their master, they will tempt him to take a worldly course...*to
become like them.* And they lie:— they will deceive people about the
Voice. They will even try to deceive him about the Voice. He knows
the truth: — the spirits shudder at the sound of the Voice. They first
heard the Voice when it cast them and their master from God's
presence, and they have feared it from that day. They dwell now in
the darkness of the sea where the Voice does not reach. However,
when their master seduced God's new creation, Adam and his wife,
they all came up from the sea in packs and went about the land
seducing Adam's children. They attack him now because their master
fears the Voice that has spoken to him and what the Voice has said to
him and the power that the Voice has already given him. Full of spite
and malice toward the children of men, they will try to hold their
power over them, lest God restore the children to paradise and cast

6

them back into the sea. These are Jesus' thoughts as he and his friends enter Capernaum.

A large crowd comes out to see him and soon a man calls to him from a distance; the crowd splits in order to let the man pass; they seem afraid of the man, and soon Jesus knows why—he is a leper, an untouchable. His friends try to shield him from the man but too late––the man is upon him: "I know you can heal me if you will," he cries. Jesus is stunned: the man has raised the question of power and will. Who ordains him to go about exorcizing and healing? The scribes who come up from Jerusalem will want to know this. And they will give their own answer: Jesus does the work of Satan, they will say. He decides he will leave the issue for the morrow; today he will act out of pity; he reaches out to the man and heals him. Then he says, "Go show yourself to the priests." This will get attention soon enough. He takes his companions away to a private place where they await the scribes and their judgment.

The private place is an abandoned shepherd's hut that stands on a slope of land and overlooks the sea. It will serve as his temple for a while, pathetic though it may be, for he hears the Voice clearly here and he is able to speak to his chosen four. But soon the crowd is upon him; they assemble about the door and call for him to come out and answer their questions. Who is he? they ask. The spirits have gathered too—outside, for they fear to enter what they cannot corrupt. Jesus comes to the doorway and speaks to them all: a power greater than Moses banished the son of the serpent from the synagogue, he tells them. When his friends hear this they shudder; their master has blasphemed—what will come of this when the priests hear of it? A power greater than Moses? Only God is greater than Moses. Suddenly the crowd notices what Jesus has seen for some time: four men are approaching from beyond the sloping hills; they bear some burden. Now they see what it is—the men carry a paralyzed man on a pallet. The crowd is not minded to let the men get through to Jesus. After a brief commotion the four men withdraw. But soon Jesus hears a noise above his head. The bearers have gone to the back of the hut, climbed onto the flat roof and carved an opening. In a moment he sees the paralyzed man being lowered by ropes into the house. The man's need is obvious—he is prone, unable to move or speak. Jesus speaks: "Your sins are forgiven you," he says to the man. The crowd, peering through the door, is silenced by these words, so strong and clear. Then he says: "By the authority of the Son of man I say to you, rise, put away your pallet and walk." Instantly the man is on his feet. Now, Jesus thinks, the scribes will say that I blaspheme because I forgive sins, and that the demons obey me because I am the prince of demons.

Later, he and his companions describe this event as a funeral procession: the man, speechless, flat on his back, carried by four bearers, is lowered into his grave where he hears the voice of Jesus say, "Your sins are forgiven." Again the men press Jesus for a word: "Are you messiah?" they ask, and "Does messiah forgive sins?" They talk about the four wonderworks he has done before their very eyes. His deeds have made some people angry, they say. Even the first, on a Sabbath, riled the scribes, who argue that a good Jew does no work on that holy day. The four men find humor in the thought of the offended scribes: their master does his best work on the day God rested, he should let them know. More and more, Jesus appreciates the simple valor of these men; they can joke about sacred things and they shrug off piety and great learning. And they eat without washing their hands—a defilement, the scribes would tell them.

These scribes, Jesus fears, will soon gather like vultures. He enjoys the image of the high flying bird that has a sharp eye for small prey; for the scribes, lesser rabbis who assume greatness for themselves by picking at little things, fine points of the law—they are without pity or any feelings at all. The main thrust of their attack on him, he tells his friends, will not be a point of law; rather they will quarrel about his identity and attack him on this point. Jesus has now raised the question before his friends in a new way. He had called himself *Son of man* when he healed the paralytic. He did that knowing that some scribes were among the crowd and they would report his words to Jerusalem. The title had danced on his tongue— did the Voice place it there?

He recites to them the text from the *Book of Daniel* where a celestial being called *Son of man* sits on a throne next to God. This being is the one speaking to them now, he says to his friends, and who called the four of them to share a new work with him. No: he is not messiah, not in the way the nation thinks of messiah, a warrior-king who will raise an army of rebels and go up against Caesar. His friends are as speechless as the paralytic. He keeps to himself,

8

however, his reason for sending the healed leper to Jerusalem. He sent the man there as evidence of his power to heal. He wants to test the godliness of the priests. If the priests rejoice with the man over his healing, then they are men of God, shepherds of the flock, and they will rein in the suspicious scribes. He suspects, however, that the sight of the man will sting like the bite of an asp, for no one in Jerusalem or elsewhere heals the sick and drives out demons as he does. If God is not in their hearts, they will boil with jealous passion, and instruct the scribes to keep close watch while they consider what to do. He will know: if the scribes return with hatred on account of his good deeds, then Satan did not enter *him*...he entered *them*.

In a moment of peace, when the four have left him for a time, he looks at the flat-topped roof with the hole in it. His thoughts go back to his childhood in Nazareth, when he and his family slept on roofs like this when the trapped heat of the day drove them outside, through the central court, and up the common stairs to the tops. The rooms were small, he recalls, with windows so high he could not see out, but they admitted light. He recalls the oak forests and olive groves that made Nazareth a supreme spectacle, the glory of Palestine, for elsewhere all was cold stone and desert brush. From nearby hills he could look down on the Via Maris—the sea route—upon which caravans linked Saphoris with other parts of the region. Saphoris was anathema to his family and countrymen, as was Tiberias. Things were said there that Moses never taught. He knew...he had been there, and to Tiberias, too. He went with his father and other laborers who went about looking for work with the construction crews that built those cities. During these visits he discovered the sea. That was when he first heard voices and sensed mystery. He wondered about beginnings—the world's, the nation's, his own. He met people in Saphoris who taught him to pray...not as the Jews pray, but to seek and to find. They even taught him something about his own religion, the mysterious *Son of man*. It meant something that this creature, some said, had his beginning in the sea.

He returns to the sea often. He watches fishermen go out in boats upon the deep water where wind comes up suddenly. Fishermen are laborers, too, as he and his father were. These men work to feed themselves and others. Does the Voice want him to feed people? The Voice does not speak with words, but the Voice places words on the tongues of those to whom He speaks. Jesus sees images before he hears himself utter the will of the Voice. In this way, the sea and the fishermen reveal to him how he is to obey the Voice. It has to do with the sea. Over and over in his mind the image of the sea intrudes and gives him no peace. His gaze is drawn to a helmsman seated on the high afterdeck of a large boat, safe from the splashing waves. On this journey he must take to feed the world he is the helmsman, and his four companions will come with him. He must keep them safe. Yet, at sea, men know that the apprentice must suffer the hardships their masters have overcome. *As goes the master, so goes the disciple.* He thinks of the four men now as disciples, not companions only. For, in truth, when he called them up from the sea, that was their baptism. He had not realized this before; now it is clear to him; they were baptized when he called them up from the sea and spoke to them. To be baptized is to go into the deep and rise up at the summons of a Voice. The sea is death, in the minds of his people; and the source of demons and treachery and all manner of evil. This is what he has called his friends up from. Now they will face these evils on land. He must pray for them.

He is disturbed by a noise; people are shouting, cursing. The sea is no refuge; the crowd has found him. They are angry at an older man who has tried to get through to him. "Back off, leave the master alone," they shout. Others pick up stones to throw at him, yelling "Gentile pig, get back!" Jesus calls out over the din and rebukes the crowd, who reluctantly permit the man to pass through. The man is no Gentile, he sees. It is Levi. He has seen Levi before; the man goes about collecting taxes from the fishermen. People call him "pig" because he works for Caesar, taking Jewish money and giving it to the Gentile tyrant. That makes him a "pig," like all Gentiles.

The man is clearly frightened. What great need does he have to speak to him, that he risks the worse the crowd can do? He guides the old man away from the crowd and they talk. Levi is cynical and bitter. He used to be a good Jew, he says, but he ran afoul of the rabbis who made religion a heavy burden. Jesus asks, "What is the heart and soul of the law, do you think?" He answers, "Love the Lord your God with all your heart, with all your soul, with all your mind, and with all your strength, and love your neighbor as yourself." The words were spoken with conviction. No wonder the man is bitter; he is wiser than those who would condemn him. It is his heart that is

10

wise. He knows that burnt offerings and sacrifices do not turn the soul to God. Could he make a follower of this man? No: —a fifth man would ruin the beauty of the numbers that it has pleased the Voice to provide. Or is it his own preference? As a builder he and his father built foursquare from the ground up. Four is the fundament. Five...that is the number of books of the law. He can taste the irony in his mouth. Levi a disciple? His heart is right, but he is old and the work will be dangerous. His instinct is to shelter him. But Levi has come to him from beside the sea. This is how the Voice calls people to be with his beloved Son. He goes to the old man's home and they talk deep into the night.

Levi a "pig," an outsider, unfit for the kingdom? No—those who tried to stone him, they are unfit for the kingdom. Levi is a man of faith; his bitterness is not toward God, it is toward man. As for the crowds, Jesus turns a critical eye toward them: they have followed him about Galilee for many days to hear his words and see his deeds. But what is the fruit of their devotion? They will not move aside to allow the paralytic to reach him. They are perpetually astounded—to the point of brute stupefaction. And they would have killed Levi had he not stopped them. Love of God and love of neighbor? He has been preaching love of God and love of neighbor: truly, what have they heard? They see but do not perceive; they hear but do not understand. He will call Levi to follow him, and he will teach his five friends the mysteries of the Kingdom of God. To those who are without all things will be parables. If any of them should prove to be "good soil" for his words, they will rise up and follow him. His heart is not hardened—he has compassion for the people; they are like sheep without a shepherd. He will feed the sheep, as many as come to him and are eager for his words.

He goes up into the hills to seek peace, taking with him the four, Levi, and some others who have heeded his words and have goodness in their hearts. But when he climbs to a high mount he finds no peace. He thinks of Moses, the great lawgiver, who climbed a high mount that smoked and quaked amidst thunders and thick clouds. It must have been an angry God, Jesus thinks, who thus dinned his will into the nation. And the woes inflicted upon those who disobey...the scribes will advise about that. He wonders, did Moses hear the same Voice that he heard? How could it be?...unless God has two faces and two voices. The God who called Moses and his family into Egypt and attacked him in the night lodge—that was the Angel of Death. The same Angel came at paschal midnight to kill the firstborn among the Egyptians—from the firstborn of Pharaoh to the firstborn of the maidservant behind the mill to the firstborn among the cattle of the fields. The Angel took away Enoch and demanded sacrifice of Abram's son Isaac. Behind every nocturnal cruelty a divine demon? He remembers as a boy he would hide his face and cover his ears when the Passover story was read and his people rejoiced in the slaying of the Egyptian firstborn. His father chided him for that; he said it was not manly for him to behave so. But he could never share Passover joy with his people.

The rabbis teach that God is good to his people; He brought His children out of captivity in the land of the Pharaohs. In older days He warned His people of the flood, so they could build an ark and be saved. Yes: —but the Angel of death struck down Moses before he reached the promised land. And whose wrath was it that sent the waters of doom over the land in Noah's day? The Angel of Death was God's wrath, even before the law. Now he must ask: What does the Angel require of him? He knows only that the time of his Passover will come when it will come.

iii. New-born Christians See Life-giving Waters Flow From the New Temple.

In the year now known as 70 C.E. a small group of Christians gathers at the home of one of the members, John Mark, a devout Jewish scholar. They come together often, especially on the first day of the week, to pray, break bread together, and study the sacred books of the Jews. Mark is the right person to help this largely Gentile group understand the conflicts that led to their Lord's death, because the roots of the conflicts run deeply through these sacred books of the law that Mark knows so well. Also the group has been pouring over scrolls that Mark has brought from Galilee, written by people who lived about the sea and may have been in the crowds that saw the Lord. They are excited by what they have begun to read.

Moreover they have a visitor: John of Ephesus. He is much younger than Mark and less learned; but he has vision that runs in a deep current. He leads the group in a meditation on the First Day of the week, the Day of Light, when God's spirit moved upon the waters. As they listen they feel the same spirit among them, the spring wind that brought the world to be and has brought them born anew into this holy fellowship. From the winepress of his imagination John brings forth images of the divine work in those first days: How the spirit drew back the flood waters in the mystical fluvial valley—whether it be of the mind or time or space they cannot know—allowing the earth and its seas to be formed; how the spirit lifted Noah to safety over those same waters when they raged; and how the spirit parted the Red Sea waters for Moses and the Israelites when they fled Egypt for a new land. John tells the group that he too wishes to compose a gospel, as Mark has set about to do. It will be a book of signs: the Lord's work will be chronicled under the sign of bread, the sign of water, and other spirit-images. He points to the scrolls from Galilee and tells them that he sees already the sign of water: the Lord himself is the restored temple from whom flows healing and life-giving waters. Look at the healings, he exclaims—they give life. You shall see. Then he reads to them the story of the Lord healing the leper and sending the man to the priests in Jerusalem. The Lord gave a sign to the priests and to the nation. The priests consider that they "cure" lepers by a water ceremony. The Lord cured the man by the spirit. You see, says John—first the water; then the spirit. So it was ordained at the beginning: the spirit hovered over the waters and invested creation with its shape and its history. The Lord creates anew: at Cana, when he attended a wedding, he took jars of water that the priests use for their purifying and changed the water into wine—a symbol of spirit. In his gospel, John says, he will show how each great miracle turns on the sign of spirit-filled water.

John's preaching has been inspiring to the small group that thirsts for more knowledge of their Lord and his message for them. But when John returns to Ephesus they are left with a sense of mystery, of a story yet untold. Most compelling are the Lord's words in the scrolls that require them to *understand*. But the crowds to whom he spoke did not understand; he grew weary of trying to reach them; he resorted to parables and showed great reserve. And the disciples—they were fearful and unreliable; in the end, one of them betrayed him. A more chilling thought is that the demons did understand—but the Lord silenced them. If the group is to understand what the Lord meant, they will have to find the answer in the scrolls...but the scrolls come to them from the very crowd whose eyes and ears the Lord deemed unfit for the kingdom. They can only hope that men like John and Mark and others will guide them through pools of mystery into the light.

Mark knows their fears very well. He must give them faith that the Lord cares for them, as he cared for the first four men who gave up all to follow him. He recalls for them what John of Ephesus had just said: the miracles are signs. He reads to them from the scroll: Jesus entered the home of a disciple, Simon Peter, and raised his sick in-law from her bed. The moment she got up she began to serve food. What does this tell us? Marks asks. Think—the Lord entered the home of a disciple. Mark reminds them that he himself—by God's grace—is a disciple, and they are in his home where they often break bread together, feed and comfort one another in the Lord's name. So, when the Lord entered Simon's house he gave a sign that he will enter this house and raise us up when the hour comes for that. And while we wait we must serve one another as he bids us to do.

But the great disciple Simon Peter is dead—crucified upside down. They have heard this from friends of Mark. They are shaken.

Peter, into whose home the Lord entered, whose home is the mother-church for all Christians, is a victim of cruel persecution. Everywhere they hear of danger. The Jews have finally rebelled against Rome, but things are going badly for them. They are being taken from their beds and slain in the streets. The temple has been torn down—only one wall still stands. Many Jews blame the Christians for this trouble; Christians follow a false messiah, the Jews say, and God has sent his punishment. But more: Rome has reasons of its own to hate Christians. The Emperor Nero, when a fire broke out in Rome, scapegoated Christians by blaming them for it; and Rome regards Christians as seditious; after all, Christians refuse to take part in the cult of emperor-worship and do things in private that Rome forbids. So, while no law prevents someone from becoming a Christian, it is dangerous; magistrates believe Christians are enemies of the state and they exact severe punishment. It is rumored that Nero has impaled Christians on a stake and set them on fire to amuse guests at his dinner parties. And here is Mark's house-church under the very nose of the emperor.

When, as companions and disciples of the Lord, they are taken from their beds, condemned by the magistrates, and thrown to the lions, will the Lord come and rescue them? He did not rescue Peter. Or any of the others. Many Christians have despaired— especially those who had believed the Lord would quickly return to earth and vindicate his followers. Some had even thought the Lord would establish a thousand year reign on earth, trampling Satan underfoot and binding him in a fiery pit, along with the world's evils. But the Lord's own words should have discouraged that: "My kingdom is not of this world," he had said, when he himself appeared before the court that condemned him. Why then should he return? And those dark sayings he left behind, and the parables...what good are they? And the repeated exhortations to see and hear...hear and see what? And the strange emblem *Son of man*: What does that mean? They fear that before they find answers to the questions, Peter's fate will be theirs.

What can match the terrible power of the Caesars? is the question in their hearts. Mark knows, therefore, that he must speak to his flock about power before he can speak to them about faith and vision. He reads to them from *The Book of Daniel*:

I saw in the night visions,

15

and behold, with the clouds of heaven
there came one like a Son of man
and he came to the Ancient of Days
and was presented before him.
And to him was given
dominion and glory and kingdom
that all peoples, nations and languages
should serve him;
his dominion is an everlasting dominion,
which shall not pass away,
and his kingdom one
that shall not be destroyed.

Mark explains: God, the Ancient One, gave dominion over the earth to a divine being about whom nothing more is known—not his origin, not his name—than that he is divine but has the form of a man and that God gave him power. To us Jews, power means that someone will be able to rid us of our enemies. We lost our power years ago when invaders overran our land and made slaves of us. At one time our fathers were force-marched to Babylon where we wept and sang bitter songs by the side of a river. Much of our poetry and prophecy comes from that exile. Our hearts still ache for our blessed freedom. In our hearts we imagine how we shall be saved. First, we look back to our heros whose deeds are in the sacred books. David, the shepherd-king, is much honored among us—some believe God will send us a new king like David, of the house of David, who will save us; we speak of such a one as *messiah*. Then we think of Moses—in older times he brought our fathers out of Egypt and gave us a law to keep—perhaps God will send us a new Moses. But there is an older and greater—Adam. God gave Adam dominion at the very start, a dominion that covered the face of the earth and the waters. Adam was placed in Paradise; he was God's offspring, he was divine. And in the form of a man. The *Book of Genesis* says Adam sinned and was cast out of Paradise; he died and turned to dust. But our prophet Isaiah foresaw a new heavens and a new earth; this new creation will require a new Adam to rule over it. Adam, the head of our race, will be raised from the dust of death. He will be called Son of Adam, or simply *Son of man*—for in our tongue, "Adam" means "man."

Mark will teach them more about the Jew's religion; for now, he warns them to watch for lightening flashes in dark places, echoes in deep caverns, shapes and forms moving in the night— for God moves among his people in mysterious ways. They must watch or they will fail. Numbers, especially, they must watch for; sometimes the numbers are given, sometimes they must look for them. Learn to count, he says. Again, he reads from the prophet Daniel:

Behold I saw in my vision by night...the four winds of heaven strove upon the great sea. And four great beasts came up from the sea.

We imagine our enemies as beasts, he says. Daniel's message is that four times these beasts will come upon us—but the fourth must be the last. Why? Because, in our way of speaking, there are four winds that blow; from the north, east, south and west—and no more. When the fourth beast has come up from below, the *Son of man* will come down from above and claim dominion over the beasts. Mark then turns to *Genesis* and reads that God's spirit moved over the waters, bringing up the sea monsters and creating the world. God then laid his command upon—not the sea or the land but upon himself, his own creative will, and brought forth Adam. To Adam he gave dominion over all the world, to the four corners. "Now then," Mark says, "what do these scrolls say?"

They read in the scrolls that the Lord went down to the Galilean Sea and laid his command upon it. He called up four fishermen, who obeyed his call and followed him to witness four great wonderworks. You see, says Mark: God has begun a new work. He is restoring the old creation.

Mark holds up the *Book of Genesis* and announces he will read the two stories that relate God's creating man. Two? they ask...why two? Mark notes their surprise: Some of you are Gentiles, he says, who use logic, who strive for a perfect finish to things. But we Jews are different: we love rhythm in our lives and poetry in our souls; we need things to count—there's the rhythm—and things to ponder all our days. Nothing is finished; we have no home on this earth, we are always seeking. He then reads from *Genesis* how God made man in his own image and ended his six day work with a Sabbath rest. He then set about making man again—this time from the dust; in one day he did this, breathing spirit into man's nostrils. The difference? The first act was chaste, for it came from God's pure will. But the second act brought us up from the dust. Pure will could not do that; spirit was needed.

Now, says Mark, let us read what a great prophet made of these two stories. He tells them how Ezekiel was led by the spirit to a valley of dry bones, where he saw the dust of death. That is the second act of creation. Listen to the prophet's words: "Thus says the Lord God; Come from the four winds O spirit, and breathe upon those slain, that they may live." The second creation, says Mark, is a foretelling of a great thing that is to happen. He recites for them the remainder of the second creation story: after bringing man up from the dust, God set him in a garden called Eden, out of which runs a river with four heads, and God made this man king of the garden. The group exclaims—"the number four is Paradise, is it not so?" Mark agrees, and adds that the second creation and the rising to Paradise is resurrection. This is what the prophet spoke of in his vision—the resurrection of the dead and their ascent to Paradise. It is a rare thing in our scriptures, he says, but when you find it, watch out. It ranges far and wide, to the four corners of the earth. And consider the inevitability of it: Daniel spoke of four winds—no more. What comes next can only be from above. When our Lord stood amidst his four disciples he was *Son of man*, Adam, living again. He has come to call us all from the sea, which, for us, is death. The spirit is within him; he has the power to do this. You must remember, you Greeks, that you have great thoughts and you aspire to high places: But we Jews have suffered long and lived in the valley of the shadow of death. We know that we need our God to send for us and take us home.

The Ancient of Days gave dominion to the Son, who at once was tempted by Satan, as was the first Adam. But the new Adam proved worthy and did not yield to the serpent. He went on to assert his dominion over sickness and evil spirits: the people in the synagogue felt his power and were awed by it; the demons felt it and fled from it. And more: dominion means the power to judge—to judge the nation, and to forgive sins. Our Lord first declared this power to forgive sins when the paralytic was lowered through the roof of his shepherd's hut. Mark's group has read the four miracle stories and they have not forgotten to count. The fourth miracle, they exclaim...the dead man lowered into his grave by four bearers, witnessed by four disciples...Four! The man has entered Paradise. Now, their guide tells them, they have learned how to read scripture.

Yes—they can see that the Lord revived the Genesis story when he undid Adam's misdeed. Where the old Adam gave in to Satan, the new Adam prevailed. Bearing the full power that God gave Adam to rule in Paradise, the Lord made this power manifest as he went about Galilee giving the land and the sea a foretaste of Paradise by healing the sick and driving out Satan's minions. His power was such that soon tongues began to wag in Jerusalem—a hint that the Lord's power is destined to cover even that bastion of evil. Mark's group sees this power clearly in the miracle stories: when the Lord banished the demon in the synagogue the congregation was awed by his power; when he healed the leper, the man asked about the Lord's will and the scribes questioned the power behind it; when he pronounced forgiveness to the paralytic, he declared himself to be *Son of man* and gave a promise of Paradise.

Mark looks again at the fourth miracle—it is also a third. In those three miracles the Lord asserted his power, and in the last of the three he pronounced title upon himself, a title that proves his right to the power he has used. Mark knows that three is a sacred number among believers, for it signifies the Lord's rising from the tomb on a third day. He is a Christian because he has accepted this story from truth-telling men. Now, as he and the others read from this scroll, they see that the Lord's healing of the paralytic signals his power over death itself.

Yet—doubt stalks them. If the Lord had all the power that God gave Adam, why did the Lord give in to his enemies and suffer a criminal's death? It is strange. Are they deluded to believe in him, risk their lives for him? If so, they of all men are to be pitied. Mark tells them to be patient and heed the mystery, let it speak to them, give up its secret. They must remember that, if the Lord does the works of Adam, then the Lord *must* die—for it was in God's plan that Adam die.

The fourth is also a third...what magic or art made it so? They now know that for the Jew, numbers are alive; they are not the static

cubes or lifeless theorems of Pythagoras; they are signs of a drama
that has a beginning and a destined end. They feel the pull of the
drama as they look intently at the four miracles. Again...they see
something: the paralytic's healing is a third in another way. The Lord
healed first in a synagogue, then in a disciple's house, then in a
shepherd's hut that was his home. The Lord offered the shelter of his
home to those who are the symbolic dead. Mark explains that the
flat-topped hut must have reminded the Lord of his childhood in
Nazareth, where all the houses were flat topped. It would have been
simple for the four bearers to climb up, dig a hole in the roof and
lower the man into the Lord's home—under the sign of the four and
the three. Who ordained the sign? The Lord himself...or the God
above? This God of the Jews—he has a poem in his heart that he
would teach the world if they would but learn from these miracles by
the sea. God lays out his poetry not in words but in deeds.

It is late, past midnight. The group has been studying by
candlelight. They know it is dangerous to stay so late; a suspicious
neighbor might speak to a magistrate who would investigate. But
they need Mark to explain something about Jewish religious practices.
Those four seaside miracles...they have a rhythm; *they are paired.*
The pattern of pairs was set when the Lord called two pairs of
brothers to follow him: the brothers Simon and Andrew, and the
brothers James and John.

FIRST MIRACLE	SECOND MIRACLE
Evil spirit in synagogue. An exorcism, a type of purification.	Simon's in-law in her home. A restoration to health.
THIRD MIRACLE	FOURTH MIRACLE
Cleansing of a leper, who is sent to Jerusalem for his purification.	In Jesus' home. A restoration to health (to life itself).

The pairing is an echo—they have heard it before. Where? They
ponder it: the Lord purifies, the Lord restores to health; the Lord
purifies, the Lord foretells the raising of the dead. Like the two
creation stories, the second is greater than the first. The Son does the
work of the Father, cleansing and restoring the fallen world.

Ezekiel's vision of the dry bones and the raising of the holy dead is before them, as they read of the Lord's miracle that he performed in his shepherd's hut by the sea.

But only spirit can raise the dead. The pairing is really water—spirit, as John of Ephesus had said. And where does this leave the priests?...they will have no place in the kingdom of the spirit. This will be as clear to them as it is to Mark and his friends. The priests claim status under a covenant that goes back to Moses and Aaron. The Lord's covenant goes back to Adam but the priests will not care about that. They and their water washings go back to the *Book of Leviticus*, which was given by God to Moses; it is the Law. At the mention of *Leviticus*, the group is startled: who is this Levi, here, in the scroll? The Lord has called him to be a follower. What new thing will happen, if there is a fifth man?

Whatever they may think of it, the Lord has called a man named Levi. Levi is called up from his work by the sea, just as the four were called up from their work by the sea.

They go on reading: the Lord did a fifth miracle. He healed a man whose arm was withered; and he did it on the Sabbath. His critics now are members of the Pharisees. They are not the most strict party in the nation, Mark explains: but they would not tolerate the Lord's behaviors when it comes to fasting and Sabbath rules. The Lord has offended them on these counts and they are wrathful. The Lord made his response: he told the story of King David's brash act when he and his companions broke into the house of the high priest and made off with five of the twelve loaves of holy bread that the priest was entrusted to keep. The Lord has said that human need is more important than rules, even more important than sacred objects; for David and his men were simply hungry—that is why they took the bread. And the Lord's words took on a new tone—he spoke of seething new wine that bursts old wineskins. He told parables that seek fresh rich soil for the seeds of his words. It is as if his call of Levi has shaken something hidden deep inside him.

The Lord's words strike home to Mark's group: the bread and wine...they eat bread and drink wine as a memorial to the Lord on each Lord's Day; and they recall what John of Ephesus said about wine when he preached about the wedding at Cana and how the Lord changed the water into wine, a sign of the spirit. But here, the Lord's signs caused bitter argument: the Pharisees conspired with the Herodians to do away with him.

About the bread—where, they wonder, is the story of the Lord's feeding five thousand men who followed him deep into the wilderness? They have heard Mark tell the story often; but they do not yet see it in the scrolls. And what happened to Levi? They read that the Lord took twelve men into the hills and appointed them disciples; Simon and Andrew, James and John were among them; but not Levi. Be patient, says Mark: the other scrolls will tell the story of the bread, and help us understand Levi. Yes, his absence seems strange, for the Lord went into his home and supped with him, just as he went into Simon's house. Now they see it...a mother church for outcasts. For Gentiles, Mark adds. Levi was called a Gentile pig by his countrymen. He is the first of many, for this house church, were they are gathered, springs from the Lord's supping with the Gentile. They do not need Mark to remind them that the crowd would have stoned Levi—his danger is now theirs.

In the next scroll the group reads that the Lord, after he appointed the twelve, engaged the scribes in argument—they say that he must be Satan himself because he has power over demons; then he retreated to the sea where, from his perch in Simon's boat, he began to instruct the crowds that followed him. He spoke darkly of secrets and buried seeds. The first parable sets a mysterious tone: A sower goes forth to sow seed: some seed falls by the side of the path where birds devour it; some seed falls upon rocky soil—these spring up but are fragile, the sun scorches them and they wither; other seed falls among thorns which choke them; but other seed falls into good soil and yields grain, increasing to thirtyfold, sixtyfold, and an hundredfold. The Lord finished his parable by saying "He who has ears to hear, let him hear."

The Lord's sermon disturbs the group. Parables, riddles, and numbers...a new number, five, is a puzzle; what do they tell us of our death, they ask, and what will become of us? Mark has the answer, though he fears they are not ready for it. The parables tell of the Lord's own death, as do the seeds and the numbers, he tells them; and his death will be ours. Why parables and riddles? The Jews suffered to get answers to their deep questions, and they buried the answers in their suffering. He holds up *The Book of Daniel* again. This book was written at a time of great suffering and its message was hidden so that the enemy could not find it. It is for those who persevere. Others will read but not understand. The group begins to understand the need for parables, and the Lord's words that parables are for those who are without.

Parables, secrets, ciphers—in these signs the Jews bury their souls; if others want to discover the secrets they must suffer on their own or be guided by the signs the Jews have given to the world. Mark tells them that the number of the Jews themselves, as a nation, is twelve: by itself it is no mystery; it is simply taken from the *Genesis* story of the twelve patriarchs, sons of Israel. Jews honor the number. In these scrolls from Galilee, Mark says, the Lord called twelve men to assist him in his work. This they have read already. Soon, they will find that he healed twelve Jews of their various miseries; five so far have come forth. And that is not all: he has twelve loaves of bread to give to the thousands who follow him to a special place in the wilderness. Soon they will read of this special place in the wilderness and how he gave five loaves to the great crowd that followed him. The Lord's intent was to minister to twelvefold Israel, the entire nation. So much is clear: the presence of Levi is not so clear.

His students clamor to know what the Lord meant by "He who has ears to hear, let him hear." It means understanding, he answers, a special kind of understanding. As the Lord spoke those words by the Galilean Sea, he had in mind not Gentiles who fail to understand the ways of Jews; he had in mind those among the Jews who fail to see the hand of God in the works that the Son does in their very midst. Mark urges his students to listen and learn: they have studied the first four great healings; what have they learned so far? The Lord purifies, the Lord restores...yes. But look again. The message is hidden in yet another way: the fourth healing enabled a man to get up and walk; the fifth enabled a man to use his arm. Pairs again: feet and arms. When all twelve sufferers have been studied, Mark adds, the Lord will have restored all the powers of a man, making him fit for heaven. But as he did so, he aroused the hatred of those who should have called him blessed. But he was not afraid; he was doing a divine work. The psalmist gloried in this work when he wrote of the heathen gods.

> they have mouths but they speak not:
> eyes have they but they see not;

23

> they have ears but they hear not;
> noses have they but they smell not;
> they have hands but they handle not;
> feet have they, but they walk not...

Worshipers of dead idols become like dead idols; they do not see or hear, they do not rise up and walk. But those who trust in the Living God will see and hear, rise up and walk, says the psalmist. The Lord does God's work, says Mark. He makes people stand and walk. Soon he will make us see and hear so we will not be like dumb idols.

Mark and his students ponder the difficult sermon that the Lord gave to the crowd from Simon's boat. The scroll gives no hint that the crowd said a word in response; they were mute. At evening, the Lord left them standing on the shore and put out to sea with his disciples. A great storm came up, but he slept. Waking him, the men cried out, "Do you not care if we perish?" Mark's students hear these words as if from their own lips: *"Do you not care if we perish?"* The answer comes. The Lord awoke and rebuked the wind and waves: "Silence," he said, "and be still." At once the elements obeyed his voice. The sea was calm.

"He has purified the sea," exclaim Mark's students. They remember the Lord's words when he exorcized the foul spirit in the synagogue: *epetimasen*—he *rebuked* the foul spirit and silenced it; *epetimasen*—he *rebuked* the wind and silenced the waves. Then they note the words of the disciples, who ask "Who is this, that even the wind and sea obey him?" The disciples have just heard the Lord's parables and the exhortation to be fertile soil; their response, though a question, could become a hymn of faith. Indeed, the Lord had said to them "Why are you afraid? Have you no faith?" The group is awed, as were the disciples in the boat. They begin to understand that the Lord, having shown a power greater than priests and kings, extends this power to the sea itself, the source of all evil.

When the Lord and his four disciples got out of the boat that had carried them to the far side of the sea, they were in the land of the Gerasenes; the group does not know exactly where this is, but in the scroll they read that there is a cliff there, by the sea, and a burial place nearby. They read that a wild man had been living among the tombs, crying day and night and bruising himself with stones. No one had been able to bind him, for he broke the chains. At the sight of the Lord, he dashed toward him, shouting as if the howling winds of the sea had entered him and were roaring in his throat. Yes, says Mark: it is the old, well trod path: the evil ones come up from the sea and infest those who live on land, turning them against God and those who come in God's name. The Lord demanded to know the name of the evil spirit that inhabited the man. "My name is Legion," it cried, "for we are many." At that, the Lord banished them. They fled and entered into a large herd of swine that had been grazing close to the cliff; the swine then stampeded over the cliff into the sea, where they all disappeared.

Mark comments that the evil ones failed to subdue the Lord when he sailed over their dominion in the sea; they failed again when they assaulted him among the tombs. The group now understands an oracle that the Lord had uttered when the scribes had accused him of being Prince of Demons because he had power to cast them out: "No one can enter a strong man's house and plunder his goods, unless he first binds the strong man," the Lord had said. The oracle has been put to the test: the Lord has entered the strong man's house—Satan's––to bind the man whom no one could bind, by words that set the man free but sent the evil ones plunging into the sea from whence they came. So the Lord is not head of the house of evil; he is the one who plundered it— that issue is settled. The powers of evil are thwarted: the sea, that could have been the Lord's burial place, becomes instead the burial place of the evil ones who perish in its purified waters.

The farmers who lived nearby were astonished to see their swine drowning in the sea, and the wild man in his right mind, fully clothed, and perfectly calm. Mark's students know that the Lord who slept on his cushion in Simon's boat bestowed his own calm upon the man and upon the sea. This is the calm, lying on the deep, that guides the church across the sea. They hope this calm will last forever. John's words ring in their ears, that the spirit moved over the waters—what miracles have come from the spirit! they exclaim. Moses led his people to safety through the Red Sea waters, in which their enemies perished. Mark tells them that their house church must yet pass through dangerous waters, and they may panic; but the Lord's calm will go with them and abide with them.

But mystic calm dissolves by harsh light of day, when fears and doubts prey upon the mind. Their faith, which has been nourished by reports that the Lord lives beyond the grave, is not sustained by reading the scrolls. The refrain of purification—restoration, promise– –fulfillment, wears thin. They will want something firm, some evidence, lest they come to think a dead man is at the helm of the ark of faith. Mark understands this. Faith is not belief, he tells them. Belief is a knowing state of mind. But faith, knowing nothing, is a motion of the spirit that is within a man. The spirit makes a journey; if it is pure and honest it finds its object and is greatly rewarded. But until then, uncertainty is its grace. Mark goes on to tell of men like Noah, Abraham, Isaac, Jacob, Moses, and others, who answered the call of their inner voices and made journeys in the spirit, not knowing the end. And, he adds, faith means growth. Belief does not make a man grow; faith does. A man grows in ways he cannot know and becomes what he cannot know. If he knew at the beginning of a spirit-journey how it would end, he would grow heavy with the knowledge of it; he would not strive, not hope or pray. He would only wait, and then nothing would come to him.

They will have to wait. An hour will come when faith will prove itself or be lacking: a dark hour—not the dark of despair, but a dark like the soil in which the sower plants seeds that will increase manyfold. This dark is the intent of some eccentric cults who would "baptize" a man by holding his head under water until, near death, he sees the risen Lord. Mark has heard that such visions give a lasting faith that a man may take with him to the martyr's arena. But the Lord never ordained such a way—though he comes to greet those who take it. Mark will not baptize in this way; it is dangerous. No: – –his friends must abide by the parable of the sower and the seeds, and know that what is planted needs time and dark in which to grow. They have been baptized in purified waters; they must wait for the baptism of the spirit which comes when a man passes through the true baptismal portal, the waters of death. Then they will have left their enemies behind drowning in the font, while they exchange madness and mortality for robes that are immortal. For now, then, they must study the scrolls. Soon, he believes, they will ask the right questions: Why did Daniel see the Son *in his night visions*? What secret intent did the Lord have in mind when he put out to sea?...and why at night?

Mark plans for his friends a liturgy of worship and the breaking of the bread for the next Lord's Day. He does not know how many of his friends will attend; their numbers have been dropping; last week, no more than a dozen came for the liturgy and only a handful for the evening study of the scrolls. He understands: they have fears; so does he. But they must persist in the study of the scrolls. On Sunday he will preach to them about the seventh miracle; it is the greatest since God brought up Adam from the dust. Yet, it will end badly.

At the liturgy he tells the story as if it were happening before their very eyes. The Lord has returned from across the sea and is standing on the shore by Simon's boat. A man makes his way through the great crowd that has gathered and calls out to him urgently; his daughter is dying. Will the Lord come quickly to save her? The man's name is Jairus — it means *God awakes*—and he is the ruler of the synagogue; probably, says Mark, the one where the Lord banished the foul spirit. Yes: —the Lord sets out for Jairus' house and the disciples go with him. But on the way, he is stopped by a woman whose flow of blood has made her impure, as the custom of the Jews would have it. The Lord heals her, biding her to go in peace, for her faith has made her whole. When the Lord starts off again to Jairus' house, word arrives that the girl has died—no need to disturb the master, it is too late. But the Lord tells Jairus not to fear. He goes to the man's house, taking with him only three disciples—Simon, James and John. When he enters the house he says "Why do you make a tumult and weep? The child is not dead but sleeping." The three disciples, the child's parents, and some others can only gaze upon the cold body on the bed. The Lord takes the child's rigid hand and says *Talitha cumi*— "Little girl, I say to you, rise." Instantly the child gets up and walks about. The Lord turns to leave the room, but has a few words for the parents: give her something to eat, he says to them. He leaves the place and returns to his home in Nazareth, where his countrymen fall upon him with sharp tongues and harsh words. Miracle worker or no, they reject him—his teaching is not that of their fathers and the teachers of old. How could he, the son of people known to them, stray so far from the olden ways? Besides, does he not know, what good can come out of Nazareth?...no prophet had ever foretold a good thing from their village.

Mark's students are not surprised to hear of the Lord's rejection; it has happened before, even in the synagogues. But they sense that an even greater rejection is being foretold; the whole nation, its leaders at least, will see to it. One leader, they think, will *not* reject him; they speak of Jairus, the ruler of the synagogue, whose daughter the Lord saved from death. Was she actually dead, they ask? If so, why did the Lord say "she only sleeps?" Mark answers: when Jairus came up to the Lord, he made a play on the Lord's name, Jesus, which means "God saves." For Jairus had said, "Come and save her." The Lord, in turn, made a play on words: Jairus means "God awakes," so what unfolds is that God awoke when his Son was called upon to save one who slept the sleep of death. But something else is worthy of notice, Mark says, that foretells not only the Lord's rejection, but also his rising from the dead. God will not sleep when his Son sleeps in his tomb. Look at the numbers: the raising of Jairus' daughter is a third in a series of three miracles that began with the man among the tombs. The fact that it is a third is hidden, almost, by its linkage with the bleeding woman; the woman's healing is the second in the series, then comes the raising of Jairus' daughter. It is a third; and it is witnessed by three disciples.

So then, they say, the seventh miracle is not a seventh; it is a third...and an eighth. Both three and eight signify the Lord's rising on Sunday, which is the third of three saving days that begin with his death and entombment on Friday, and carry through to his rising on the third day, and the eighth day of that week. Yes, says Mark: Jairus' daughter only seems to be the seventh miracle, for the Lord meets Jairus before he meets the bleeding woman; at that moment Jairus is seventh. But the woman is seventh to be healed; Jairus' daughter therefore is eighth. As the number seven is sacred to the Jews—it is the day God rested after his labors—the number eight is sacred to Christians. It is the symbol of the eight day week, a week that begins with Sunday and ends with Sunday:

1.SUNDAY GOD SAID *LET THERE BE LIGHT*
2.MONDAY
3.TUESDAY
4.WEDNESDAY
5.THURSDAY
6.FRIDAY
7.SATURDAY GOD RESTS (sleeps)

8.SUNDAY GOD AWAKES: THE LORD ARISES:

THE LORD SAVES. EASTER and ETERNITY.
A NEW LIGHT ENTERS THE WORLD.

When the Lord rose from his three day entombment on Sunday, that day could no longer be simply the first day in an endless series of seven day weeks. Sunday is Easter; it is Eternity.

A divine rhythm sounds through these miracles—they hear it, they feel it. The Lord purifies and restores; he promises and fulfills. The rhythm is everywhere. They see now that when the Lord entered the house of sickness and healed Simon's in-law, he promised a greater healing; he entered the house with his special witnesses—four, at the time—and extended his hand to her, so that she rose up and fed them. That the Lord made a promise becomes clear when it is renewed: he forgave the sins of the paralytic, a necessary and godly act—before the four witnesses—and prepared the man for blessedness when he is raised to newness of life. The promise was fulfilled when he entered the house of death with his special witnesses—three, now—and extended his hand to the child, raised her up from death, and ordered that she be fed. The raising of Jairus' daughter is a promise kept; and it is a promise made, for it foretells the Lord's own rising—they see this also, it is part of the rhythm. And this is not all. The promise extends to them. The Lord's rising proves that they too will rise.

In the shepherd's hut by the sea, where he made his home, the Lord promised blessedness to the man who was lowered into his home. He promises the same to all. The inside of that hut was a dark secret to those without—for "those who are without" hear only parables. In that dark he was the light of the world for those who came to him. He called four men to witness the light. When he went to Jairus' house he made that his home for a time, leaving many outside, but admitting a chosen few. There he extended his hand to the child and raised her to the life immortal. Upon leaving, he spoke to the parents and, like the Good Shepherd he is, provided for her to be fed as if she were a guest in his own home.

About the inner three who went inside the chamber of death...why three? the group asks. Is it that three is the emblem of the Lord's three day ordeal and his rising to glorious new life? Yes, says Mark; but it is also true that Jewish law requires the testimony of three witnesses in court; truth is secured by the word of three men. What they testify must be the truth. The three testify that on the third day the Father's hand reached down and lifted up the Son. Three tells of Paradise and our return to it, past the two cherubim whose flaming swords guard the east gate to frighten off those who try to make it back. Numbers—they make our spirits sing: two cherubim, three witnesses, three days, four winds, four rivers, five loaves...five loaves? What is this, five loaves? Mark knows that they have not yet studied the miracle of the loaves. They will come upon it soon enough; for now, he knows their minds are on witnessing. Those of the group who have been brought up on charges and taken away did not have the benefit of truth telling witnesses; they were convicted by the words of gossipers and grudge-bearing neighbors. The group members, those who are left, have this question: what if a Christian should lie before a magistrate who demands to know, "do you burn incense before the Emperor's shrine?" Or, "Are you a Christian?" When they were pagans they would have had no issue with this—they would have lied; but now they are Christians and loyal to the God of the Jews who sends to them a savior. And this God requires truth.

Witnesses, before they testify, must watch. The three were told to watch. It was a heart-stopping piece of news when the group heard that the three holy disciples, Simon Peter, James and John, that night in Gethsemene, when three times their agonized Lord came to them...*had slept!* Unforgivable: even though the men had risked much and were weary, they should have remained awake—they were sentries for the Lord. The Lord's last words to them, "It is enough," sting with contempt, as the Lord hears the clanking metal of the guards who have come to take him away. The disciples scatter and flee. But, says Mark: —were they on sentry duty? After all, the Lord took the men to the garden at night knowing they would be weary and might sleep; he knew that Judas and the temple guards could find them easily and he made no effort to evade his enemies. What, then, did the Lord mean by asking the men to watch? What is watching? Now, with the Galilean scrolls, the students begin to study the Lord's last days in light of his early works by the sea. They begin to see that in Galilee he was girding and testing himself for his greater work in a deeper sea of death, Jerusalem, and testing those who followed him. At the beginning of his work, he called four men; these four men were

30

with him when he gave a private teaching on the Mount of Olives. The three disciples...they go with the Lord into the inner chamber where he raises the child from death—they are an inner three, it is now clear. A strange unfolding, however, remains for them to study: the seeds planted in Galilee sprout up in Jerusalem in ways they could not have foreseen.

iv. Galilee to Jerusalem (Mark's chart)

GALILEAN MINISTRY   JERUSALEM MINISTRY

Crisis in the synagogue; the scribes conspire against the Lord.	Crisis in the temple; the priests conspire against him.
Four persons healed; four men called as disciples.	
Fifth person healed; Levi called.	
Secret teaching from the boat: parables etc. for those without; the kingdom for those who are insiders. Need to hear and understand.	Secret teaching from the Mount: more parables; need to watch four times uttered to four disciples. Need to persevere
A storm at night over the dark sea; the Lord is calm, the disciples panic.	In garden, three times the three are told to watch and pray. They panic and flee into the night

THREE SAVING MIRACLES   THREE SAVING DAYS

The man among the tombs and death at sea, where the demons would have buried the Lord.	Friday. Passover; the Angel of Death comes for the Lord. He dies and is buried in a tomb.
Ritual impurity: the woman touches the Lord's garment.	Saturday. Impurity of the corpse entombed in new garment. Body to be anointed by three women. The shroud.
The Lord raises Jairus' daughter; witnessed by the three disciples.	Sunday. God raises the Son. Three women witness the Angel who wears the Lord's new garment.

All eight healings take place under the sign of Easter, the Eighth day: the five, the three, yield an eight. This numeric strain is not lost on the group. Nor is it lost on them that the Lord, as shepherd of his flock, goes to his slaughter taking the flock with him. He crosses the sea into the mixed territory where Jews lived uneasily with their Gentile neighbors. He is not buried in the sea; the demons are—but when he takes his flock to Jerusalem, Caesar's legions, who have conspired with the priests, will take the Lord's spiked and lanced body and bury it, while the disciples flee. The Lord dies on the first of three saving days.

The second of the three healings: an impure woman imposes herself upon the Lord's person. She has four counterparts in the Jerusalem ministry. In Bethany, just outside the holy city, the Lord is at supper in the house of a leper named Simon when a woman tries to anoint his body with an alabaster cruse of spikenard. This act would honor such a fine guest as the Lord, Mark explains. The Lord does not check her action—but he gives it an unexpected meaning: she has anointed me aforehand for my burial, he says. Suddenly the matter of impurity is to the fore again: the second woman herself is not impure, but she lives in the house of a leper, Simon, who is. The earlier miracles are recalled, and they are ominous; the Lord has all but pronounced himself impure, for Jewish law regarded corpses and their tombs unclean, along with lepers and bleeding women. After the Lord's body is actually buried, three women come to anoint his impurity—but they cannot touch it; it is gone.

The third healing: the third day. After the Lord has been touched by the impure woman, he goes into the death chamber where Jairus' daughter lies upon her bed. The Lord says, "She only sleeps," arousing the ridicule of the crowd. But Jairus grasps the Lord's allusion to his own name —"God awakes." The meaning of the allusion is now clear: after the third day of the Lord's own "sleeping" he awakes and departs his tomb like a God issuing from his temple.

It must be that as the Lord purified and raised up others, he could see ahead to his own mortal end and the divine hand that would lift him up. He acted with a sense of purpose; everything that happened came from his will. Mark's friends need to know this: the Lord was not a simple healer and misfit who was done in by the priests. He had something greater in mind; he set a course and finished it. This truth quickens their faith. They remember what their guide said about faith: it is not at home in the world and it knows nothing, but it becomes wise in ways the learned are not, as it looks for the path home. When its eye is sharp, it sees, even from a distance, specks of light that draw a man closer to the Lord. Faith sees, for example, the Lord's purpose in his words to Jairus and his spouse that they feed their child.

The Good Shepherd feeds his sheep. He extends his feeding hand even in the midst of betrayal and rejection. Mark's friends take heart at this sustaining truth. They already know from the scroll that soon after the Lord raised Jairus' child and took care that she be fed, he was rejected by his countrymen. And now they read what happened to the Baptist when Herod got hold of him: how he was murdered and his headless body placed in a tomb—a story that conjures memories of other prophets, how they met their deaths, and that darkly foretells the Lord's own death ("Jesus must be John the Baptizer risen from the dead," Herod said—as if the whole affair would have to be repeated). Mark's friends must hold to their faith, even though they shudder to read how the Baptist died. They read on: suddenly they are transported to a paradise where a saintly shepherd cares for them and guarantees against every want. The Lord leads a multitude—some five thousand men, the scroll says—to a place of pastoral solitude in the wild, and, when they grow hungry and perplexed ("How shall we feed them, having only five loaves and a few fish?") He commands that they sit down on the green grass. When the five loaves are given to the five thousand, many basketfuls of crumbs are left over. It is, as the prophets foretold, the blooming of the desert in the Day of the Lord.

They want to linger over the miraculous feeding and what it seems to say to them—it reminds them of the blessed and broken bread they eat every Lord's day. As they read on, however, their eyes fall upon Simon Peter's boat. Again, it is as if they are witnesses on the hill above the Galilean sea; they look down and realize that there is going to be another crossing. As before, it is dark. But this time Jesus sends the disciples out to cross the sea without him. They recall Mark's words that a Jew can scarcely imagine anything more fearful than being lost upon a dark sea. "What an act of faith," they exclaim, "that they obey him." But they wonder why he sent them. Why is it necessary for them to cross the sea, and at night? He is the Good Shepherd...he must not leave the sheep when they need him. And he created their need, did he not?

34

Mark, having read all the scrolls and the Jerusalem story, tells them that three times in this gospel the Lord prays for his disciples and each is a time of crisis. So he prays for them...but what is that? He is safe on shore. They are out upon the sea, buffeted by the winds; they cannot make their way to safety; they are weary, they cannot see or hear their Lord. It is the fourth watch of the night, the deepest dark before dawn. Finally they see a figure coming to them over the waves: "It is a ghost," they cry. They are terrified. But they hear the figure speak: "Fear not," he says, I AM WHO I AM." It is the Voice of God who spoke to Moses in the wild and said I AM WHO I AM. The Lord calms the sea and soon they are able to put in at Gennesaret. Mark's group dwells upon this second crossing, marveling at the Lord's words. Mark bids them remember the words the disciples spoke when first they crossed the sea with the Lord and saw him purify the waters: "Who is this that even the wind and the sea obey him?" they had asked. Now they have their answer, out of the dark, upon the waters.

v. *Two Crossings of the Sea (Mark's Chart)*

Who is he? Mark's friends know: he is the glory of God and the God of glory; and he is a mystery in the flesh. He purifies, restores, raises up and feeds...and places his followers in grave peril at sea. He is an enigma to his disciples; he is an enigma to Mark's students. Yes, they believe what they have heard—that the Lord died and on the third day God raised him up, and that he lives on in the hearts of his faithful followers. But what does it mean that he "lives on in their hearts?" Mark tells them they are close to grasping this when they study the sea crossings and the sleeping disciples in the garden of Gethsemene. He points to his chart; the parchment is on a wall for all to see:

FIRST CROSSING	SECOND CROSSING	IN THE GARDEN
Late; storm at sea; the Lord sleeps while the disciples panic; he calms the waters	The 4th watch of the night. The Lord sends them to sea, prays for them at a distance, then comes to them like a "ghost." Identifies himself as God of Moses, Lord of history.	Between midnight and cockcrow he leads them to the garden, tells them to watch; they sleep; he comes to them as they sleep. The hour has come.

They study the chart and ponder again the pattern of the Lord's promising and fulfilling. The crisis in the synagogue is a promise that he will cleanse the temple. The secret teaching in the boat is a promise that he will open the ears and eyes of his disciples when the time is right. The parable of the grainfield is a promise that he will break Eucharistic bread to feed the world. And the "ghost" seen in the dark is a promise they will see the risen Lord coming to them with "Fear not" on his lips. When, they wonder, will this promise be fulfilled in the gospel? When will it be fulfilled for them?

And the raising of Jairus' daughter promises the Lord's own rising. Now then, says Mark, why is this child twelve years old? It must mean that she is the daughter of Israel; she stands for twelvefold Israel waiting to be fed. Twelvefold Israel will be fed when twelve loaves have been given to the symbolic thousands whom the Lord draws to his sanctuary in the wild. Five thousand of this appointed number have been fed. The age of Jairus' daughter betokens that all Israel will be fed.

A group member stands to unroll a new scroll which he places upon a podium; he begins to read from it, and soon the group perceives that something is wrong. A scribe's error? It has to do with a brief comment about the disciples and the fact that a non-Jewish woman comes to the Lord demanding a miracle. The strangeness of it compels them to read it again, carefully. At sea, when the Lord quieted the wind and entered the boat, the disciples—so says the scroll—were astounded because they had not understood about the loaves. What do the loaves have to do with the quieting of the sea? Does this remark mean that if the disciples had understood about the loaves, they would not have been astounded that a ghost would enter their boat and reveal itself as their Lord and quiet the wind? What is it about the loaves? And the scroll will not let them forget the question: a woman boldly steps forth and demands that the Lord heal her daughter who is possessed of an evil spirit. The woman is Gentile, a Syrophoenician by race and tongue. It is a troubling moment for Mark's students; they know that never before has the Lord been asked to heal a non-Jew. But here he is on Gentile soil, where his fame has spread about among the nations. Why, they wonder, has he gone to Gentile soil in the first place? Twice he and the disciples have sailed across the sea to the other side: first, to visit the Gerasenes; then to go to Bethsaida—although the wind swept them to Gennesaret instead. And now he goes, by himself, among the villages of Tyre and Sidon. Is he running from Herod's threats? Or is he looking for someone among the Gentiles? In their hearts they hope he is looking for them. But if he is looking for some particular person, it is not this woman, for he speaks abruptly to her: "It is not right," he says, "to take the children's bread and give it to the dogs." So, the Good Shepherd feeds sheep but not dogs. This is why the group is troubled—they themselves are Gentile dogs. But the woman's answer leaps off her tongue: "Yes, Lord, but even the dogs

37

eat of the crumbs that fall from the children's table." At that the Lord declares her daughter healed. The group is instantly relieved. Yet, they are aware of trouble ahead: news of the Lord's reaching out to non-Jews will not sit well in Jerusalem when the priests hear of it.

Instantly they see that the two daughters are paired—the Jewess and the Syrophoenician, united, just as in Mark's group Jew and Gentile are fed by the Lord when they break bread together at the same table. For the Lord provides—indeed, he commands—that the two daughters be healed and fed. And look:—he heals the Gentile child at a distance; his mere word leaps across space to the child's sick bed and banishes the demon that had possessed her. Gentiles have a place in the kingdom—this proves it. But there is more: a member points to the papyrus and exclaims that the Gentile child is healed of a demon; she is exorcized; this is exactly how the Lord began his work among Jewish sufferers—he banished the foul spirit in the synagogue. They take delight in this discovery: if the Lord were to heal an equal number of Gentile sufferers, they believe, the next would have been a restoring to health, then a lifting up, and so on. It is the rhythm again, and it inspires them to find it among their own kin. The Lord is shepherd to sheep and to dogs. Is there any the less bread for the Jews, now that the Lord has promised bread to the nations? For a moment they are puzzled. In their worship there is no lack of bread. But what do the scrolls say? They recall the Lord's sermon from the boat: grain planted in good soil will yield its increase thirtyfold, sixtyfold, an hundredfold. As the royal psalmist had said, they whose shepherd is the Lord shall not want. The Lord has fed five thousand with five loaves and a few fish: the increase is a thousandfold. Mark unrolls the next scroll and they all read from it. The Lord again calls thousands into his sanctuary, where he holds back nothing; his heart and hands are full of heavenly manna for the children of Israel who gather as if in tribes for their bounty. Seven loaves he offers to them; he has now offered twelve in all. The granting of crumbs to Gentiles makes for no loss. But not all the children come to the table. Of seven thousand called, only four thousand come. The desert does not bloom.

After many hours with the scrolls, Mark lights candles and leads his friends in evening prayers. Soon he will give a blessing to all and they will leave for their homes. As always, he senses danger when they linger into the night. His house is shielded from prying eyes by a terraced wall, but leaving has to be planned carefully, for a large group going out into the public street at night would draw attention. One of the members is a magistrate who, with his wife, has been with Mark from the beginning; they leave first. Then a soldier—he must report to his duty post. Others leave one by one or in pairs. They have often discussed what they would say if questioned about the meetings: it would hardly be credible for them to say they were attending a dinner party at Mark's home—the Jewish scholar, even with his Latin name, could not pass as a toga-wearing Roman citizen who invites magistrates for dinner, along with soldiers, women and slaves. No: — they are a group that can be no other than what they are and what they do. And even if they had a credible story, would it be right to lie? Their Lord, before his accusers, told the truth. Yet, it is right to be cautious: next week they will meet in the home of a new member, a rich Roman citizen, a friend of the magistrate, who often holds dinner parties—that will be their lie, if they need it. It is an ugly thought, that they take refuge in a man's riches. Mark will never be comfortable breaking bread over a table with pure ivory legs, on a grained marble floor among alabaster columns, and among many servants. But he is shepherd of this small flock, and he has made a good decision. Even so, he wonders about the servants...can they be trusted? Always, something to fear. What kind of shepherd is he, leading his flock from one danger into another? But that is what the Lord did; he led his followers to their paschal midnight.

Mark brings with him the last of the scrolls; it is not safe to bring them all here tonight; nor is it safe to leave them at home. He has asked a trusted friend to take them to his mother in Jerusalem, who will pass them to John of Ephesus. If trouble comes, the scrolls, at least, will be safe. At the meeting he unrolls the one scroll, praying silently that its contents will give his friends the gift of faith. He knows what is in the scroll: the Lord's final miracles, the blazing light on Mount Hermon, and the Lord's resolve to go to Jerusalem and die. He asks a lector to read briefly from the scroll, translating the Aramaic to Greek, as he prepares for the Eucharistic rite. How many times has he broken bread for his friends? Yet, they fail to hear its heartbeat. Jews are closer to broken bread, for death has been their meat and drink. His Gentile friends, especially the rich, are shielded in their minds from the drinking of this cup. Yet again he performs the fourfold mystery: he takes the bread, thanks God for it, breaks it, and gives it to his friends. They eat it, and they drink from the cup. Do they know what they have taken upon themselves?

When the liturgy is done Mark's host leads them all to an inner room far from the servants' ears. Mark studies his new student: he needs to trust the man, but he wonders what the man thought when he heard the lector read the Lord's words about the cost of following him—"If any man would follow me let him deny himself and take up his cross..." The man would have heard the Lord three times predict his death. What must he think of a savior who does not save himself, who gives himself over into the hands of his enemies? What will the man think when he comes upon other words the Lord spoke about the danger of riches? Mark's worries spill over quickly into the evening's lesson, the last scroll, and how the Lord braces his followers for the Passover pilgrimage into Jerusalem where he will suffer and die.

When they are settled, Mark picks up the scroll, unrolls it, and begins the lesson. He reminds them first of the tribal symbol. The Lord comes to twelvefold Israel: he heals twelve Jewish sufferers, he appoints twelve Jewish men to assist him in his work, and he gives twelve loaves to the tribes whom he has called to his sanctuary in the wild. It is a simple plan, really. But the plan goes awry when the Lord meets Levi. A thirteenth shatters the symbol by going outside the nation's boundaries and religion: a thirteenth "disciple," —Levi; a thirteenth sufferer—the Syrophoenician daughter; and a thirteenth loaf. Mark knows that the students have not yet studied all twelve of the healings—they will get to that. Nor are they ready to understand the thirteenth loaf.

He reads to them again the story of the second feeding; he reads slowly and carefully and encourages them to close their eyes and let their mind's eye see the Lord as he offers the seven loaves to the four thousand. They close their eyes—there! Now they see him again. He offers the seven loaves to the four thousand, and soon after he gets into the boat with his disciples to cross the sea a third time. They set out for Bethsaida—no storms prevent them—and as they sail the disciples complain that there is only one loaf in the boat. How can one loaf suffice to meet their needs? they wonder. The Lord's response is a riddle: he presses them to understand and chides them for their hardness of heart, for having ears and eyes yet not understanding.   Mark puts down the scroll and meditates for a moment, he then speaks to his friends. It would be a pity, he thinks, if the magic of the numbers were to be lost on his friends as they were on the Lord's first disciples. He reminds his friends that the Lord and his disciples were making their way to Bethsaida, the House of Provisioning; under this sign, the sign of bread and fishes, the Lord gives his riddle: five loaves fed five thousand; seven loaves fed four thousand; and many basketfuls were taken up. To understand the riddle, they should recall the Lord's parable from Simon's boat, when he spoke of the increase of yield in good soil—thirtyfold, sixtyfold, an hundredfold...*a thousandfold*. Surely they must have faith that the Lord, who can feed a thousand with one loaf, can feed the small band in Simon's boat as they cross over to Bethsaida. Yes, faith is needed. With faith, they may see that Bethsaida is their destiny, their safe haven. His friends must never complain that they have no bread. *They have all the bread in the world.*

There, in the bottom of the boat, is the thirteenth loaf; to the disciples, it is of no account; to the eye of faith it is the salvation of the world. It will be multiplied like grain in good soil over and over to the end of the age. Mark's friends have been eating of it. Yet, he knows they understand neither the riddle about the bread nor the bread itself. Not yet. Their eyes are smitten by ivory legs, marble floors, and alabaster columns.

Levi must have been the first person on earth to understand the Lord, Mark thinks. With his inner ear he heard the Lord's silent call from a distance and he parted the crowd in his haste to greet the one who called him. This is how a man understands the Lord—with the inner ear he hears words not spoken, words that leap across a gulf. Mark heard about the Lord's power to reach a man this way from John of Ephesus, when he visited: John related how the Lord called a man named Nathaniel: at a distance the Lord saw him meditating under a fig tree, and, at the very moment the Lord came upon him, the man rose to his feet and acclaimed him "Rabbi, Son of God, King of Israel." It is as if the Lord passes through a man's head and plants understanding there: hard hearts are melted and ears unstopped and eyes opened at last. Mark wonders—silently; he does not share this with his friends—if he has found the true meaning of the seaside parable about the sower and the seed, how seed needs good soil in which to grow and then it yields great increase. If he is right, Mark thinks, then the seeds, the bread, the feedings, calling disciples, are all the Lord's efforts to come to a man, enter his very soul, take possession of his life and lift him up to the heavens. As he did for the paralytic. As his mind turns to the paralytic, Mark begins to wonder: How did the paralytic and his four bearers come to know the Lord? The man must have been called from a distance. That nameless, speechless man—he was the next to understand. He heard the Voice that made the world and raises the dead.

His thoughts have wandered. His friends are waiting to hear the solution to the Lord's riddle: why does the Lord, during his third crossing, riddle his disciples about the numbers of loaves, thousands, and even basketfuls of crumbs? Mark is at a loss. They are at the knife's edge of mystery; how can he tell them what words cannot grasp? That is the Lord's dilemma—he speaks not with words but with loaves, healings, signs. Mark can only speak about the Lord's signs and invite his friends to meditate and pray, that they too may be called to the feast and heed the call. Well, then: —he tells them that the Lord's miracles in the wild are more than the feeding of hungry men. This is clear from the three day fast. They have overlooked this. Returning to the scroll, they read that the crowd that answered the Lord's second call had no food for three days.

The great banquet therefore was a third day miracle. With this in mind, Mark says, they must ponder the Lord's riddle. How many thousands were fed with the seven loaves? They answer, four thousand, only. What has happened to the missing thousands? Perhaps the missing thousand never answered the call—they stayed home. Or perhaps they came out, but fell away because they could not endure the three day fast. Like soil that is shallow, the seed sprouts but it is scorched by the sun. Mark's students need to grasp the riddle. Israel has rejected the Lord, many of them. They rejected him because he went to Gentile lands and fed the pigs, and did other things to offend their leaders and law-givers. Yes: —and then they killed him. Three days the world waited for him to rise and open the gates of heaven.

The feedings are more than feedings, but how can he tell them? — he has no words. He can talk about the sanctuary in a blooming desert, or he can talk about the desert that withered when the children failed to come to the feast. He must speak about falling away, to warn

42

them. He looks into their tired eyes; he cannot bear to lay evils upon them, but it is his duty. He tells them that their numbers are decreasing; that, even with a new member, they are fewer than before Passover. He knows they all live in fear—he does, too—but fear is their friend if they fear what is evil. He warns them not to lose faith and fall away, as did those whom the Lord called into the wild. Be steadfast in faith, he urges them, and be rewarded a thousandfold. It is the demons who tempt men away from the Lord, and their numbers seem to have increased since the Lord told his seaside parables—as if they came up from the sea at once to torment the Lord and his followers: they came at him in the synagogue by the sea; they multiplied two-thousandfold when they entered the swine and perished...or did they perish? If not, they have multiplied again: they entered Herod's palace when the Baptist was murdered; they hardened the hearts of the children who failed to come to the banquet; they entered the temple to turn the priests against the Lord. Now, Mark wonders, have they entered this rich man's home? If so, he may never see his friends again.

Mark and John had burned candles long into the night sharing their thoughts about the grassy sanctuary and how a man comes upon it. The scrolls say a man is called into it; the call is planted within a man by the shepherd, the priest of the sanctuary. He calls all men, but not all men hear; and not all who hear answer. The shepherd calls them many times, in many ways: in their sleep, in their dreams, their night visions, and finally in their dying. That is why, every time Mark has talked to an evangelist or a wise student of the scrolls, the story of the feeding is prefaced by a symbol of death. John says that when he writes his *theologoumenon*, he will preface the feeding with the Lord's speech in Jerusalem in which he speaks of the dead—how the voice of the Son will call them up from their tombs. Mark, in the scrolls, reads the lengthy story of the Baptist's death before he reads the story of the feeding of the five thousand. First, death; then the banquet.

The sanctuary is the garden Paradise. Mark has thought deeply on the scripture that says God banished his children from their heavenly home for their sin. Mark knows wise men, Jews and Greeks, who think otherwise: God banished no one. Rather, men turned away of their own accord to pursue the devices and desires of their own hearts. But there was no place to go, no world outside the garden, where they

43

could do as they willed; so they made up a world of their imagining, a godless place despite its memories of glory, and came to be at home in it all the while they feared it. The truth, Mark thinks, is that Adam and his children live still in the garden and know nothing of it, except that sages and seers hint at it, and at rare moments a man's outer eye dims, the inner eye opens, and there!...he sees it, the garden and the Lord in the midst of it.

John of Ephesus is one of those sages; he told Mark that on the first Easter Day Mary Magdalene went to the Lord's tomb weeping; when she could not find the body, she turned to a man she supposed to be the gardener and asked where the Lord was taken. The gardener called her name: "Mary," he said—and she knew it was the Lord. In her ignorance she spoke the truth. Men often speak in ignorance and sometimes hit upon the truth; the disciples at sea mistook the Lord for a ghost; he is a ghost indeed, for a ghost cannot be contained in its tomb. More:—Mark has long meditated on the Christ-like patriarch Joseph, whose brethren believed him dead and were astounded to behold his apparition when they saw him as viceroy of Egypt dispensing the bread of life to the nations. Joseph's mission is a promise fulfilled when the Lord strides forth to embrace his trembling brethren when they need him. Only one returned from the dead can feed the fainting multitudes with the bread that sustains life in the sanctuary that is above.

It grows late, past midnight. Mark had intended to finish reading from the last scroll, but he may have time only for the Lord's glory on the Mount and one of the miracles. He will read these, then study the faces of his friends to see how willing they are to remain till dawn. He begins to read about "Ephphatha" —not the man's name, but Mark has come to think of him by the words the Lord uses to make the man's deaf ears to hear and his tongue to speak; "Be opened," the Lord says. Another miracle? The group says. What miracle can fittingly follow upon "Talitha cumi," when the Lord raised Jairus' daughter? Mark says that "Ephphatha" *must* follow Talitha cumi, so that the Lord forever will not be mistaken for a ghost. What happened in Jairus' secret chamber must be heard and proclaimed to all. "Ephphatha" is first of four miracles that signify to Mark the hidden powers of a man to see and hear what has not been seen or heard since Adam's day. Mark bids his friends close their eyes and meditate as he reads from the scroll: they see the Lord returning from Tyre and making his way through Sidon to the Sea of Galilee when a man is thrust at him by the crowd that lines the coastal strand. The man is deaf and has an impediment in his speech. The Lord takes him aside and speaks to him privately: EPHPHATHA he says to him. Instantly the man hears every word and speaks plainly. And the onlookers—heretofore stupefied and mute—proclaim that the Lord has done all things well, just as if they were praising the God of *Genesis* for having made the world fresh and new.

Only an hour before dawn; they are weary. Soon Mark will send them to their beds, where they would be now had they not insisted on reading more of the scroll. But first, he will read the story of the blind man; for ears and eyes are a natural pair. His own eyes are heavy and the scroll is hard to read in the poor light, but he is able from memory to tell them what happens after "Ephphatha." First, he reminds them that the Lord in Simon Peter's boat had laid upon the disciples the rule that ears must hear and eyes must see. That was during the third crossing, when they went to Bethsaida. They have heard of Bethsaida before. When the Lord sent the disciples to sea and he came upon them as a ghost, they were sailing to Bethsaida, though the wind took them off course. In Hebrew, Bethsaida means "House of Provisioning," Mark reminds them. Now they grasp his point: *he sent them to Bethsaida, just as he called them into the wilderness, to be fed.* Yes: —they recall, after the feeding he set out to cross the sea to Bethsaida. He provides for them at sea and in the wild—both places of death. And what he feeds them with is his very presence. So then, eyes must be opened so that they may not only hear the Voice that calls them but see who calls them, that it is the Lord himself, I AM WHO I AM. Quickly, then, Mark tells of the blind man of Bethsaida: the man is cured in three stages. First, he is blind. Then, after the Lord lays hands on him, he sees, but darkly—men look like trees walking. Third, he sees clearly.

Thus it is with Simon Peter, Mark says, who is brought to his vision of the Lord in three stages. On the way to Mount Hermon, soon after the Lord cures the blind man, Peter rebukes the Lord. An astonishing thing, that a disciple should rebuke the Lord. But Peter could not bear the Lord's words, that he must go to Jerusalem and suffer and die. Peter's eyes are shut, Mark explains, he does not understand. But when the Lord takes the inner three disciples to the

Mount, Peter begins to see, though darkly. A mysterious dazzling light coming from the Lord's person causes the three men to lose their senses; they look upon the Lord's body but can hardly recognize his features or even his garments, which are glistening white, such as no fuller on earth could have made them. The three men think the Lord has changed, but it is they who have changed. Blinded, they begin to see. Peter enters upon the next stage of his restoration; blinded by the light he witnesses the Lord's divinity but he confuses him with two ancient prophets, Moses and Elijah. He must await a third stage. It will come when the three witnesses come to Gethsemane and beyond. There they will see the Lord a third time.

Light opens eyes. The blind man's eyes are opened on the plain as the Lord journeys to the Mount; the three witnesses' eyes begin to open when they reach the summit and see the light and hear the Voice. This is spiritual seeing—the group knows this. One of them, a Jew, tells them that as a young man he lived in the region about Bethsaida and the Mount. At the foot of the Mount, he says, there was once a village occupied by a scrappy warrior tribe, the Danites. The most famous Danite was Samson, the hero who slew thousands with the jawbone of an ass—until his enemies got hold of him and blinded him. Now, the man explains, Jewish tradition has it that Dan, the tribal founder, was a great moralizer who often preached about spiritual blindness. Mark agrees: the Lord has taken up the theme, he says, as he cures blindness among the Danites and then ascends the Mount to open the eyes of his chosen three so they may witness spiritual truth.

vi. The Angel of Death

Jesus misses the finer air at the mountain top. As he makes his way down from the peak of Mount Hermon the air becomes thick and hot and his step heavy as he nears the desert floor. And for another reason he would have stayed atop the Mount: the ecstasy of the Presence that welled up within him reminded him of his heavenly home. His three friends, too, would rather have stayed, even though they were blinded by the light. They wanted to build booths for him and the two prophets to lodge in; they would have slept next to each prophet's booth, the three of them...was that their plan? If they understood the ordeal that lay ahead, they would have built six booths and slept forever.

His body has returned to its natural color, but the eyes of his friends are still dimmed by the shock of the great light. He knows this shock can last for days; he has seen it in others. He lets them hold on to his robe lest they bruise their feet against the stones or fall by the way. At length they come out upon the plain. A scorching sun has risen, though it is only mid-morning; it is no pity that his friends cannot see its glory, for they have seen a greater glory. He himself was not surprised when the light shone forth and the Voice spoke; the light has restored his memory of the first day. The light and the Voice vibrate from the same source: God said "Let there be light" when he brought the world to be.

The villages of Caesarea Philippi are dead ahead; they must find a place to rest before the villagers are upon them. They have come far, and they have far to go. He will need strength for his ordeal. Even a drunken man is entitled to the peace of his bed, but he has had no place to lay his head since he first heard the Voice. The Voice now demands that he and his friends go to Jerusalem. "This is my beloved son; listen to him," the Voice had said. They heard the Voice: they are closer to the Father's heart. They hear, but do they understand? He has told them that he must go to Jerusalem and die—did they listen to him then? They are too tired to listen. They find a place to rest under some small trees, but their rest is cut short by villagers who come upon them and ask for Jesus. All the world, it seems, looks for him. They press upon him their needs and hosannas. One of them tells him a story that moves him to pity. He is the father of a young boy—his only son—who is possessed by a foul spirit that casts him down and makes him foam at the mouth. Even worse, he says, the boy is deaf and dumb. Will the Master come? Jesus forgets his tiredness and goes with the man.

The boy has been like this since he was a child, the man explains. Sometimes the spirit picks him up and throws him into water or fire to kill him. If Jesus can do anything, will he have pity? Jesus recalls the words of the leper in Capernaum who questioned his power and will before his critics; he sent the healed leper to Jerusalem to testify to the power that healed him. If this man goes to Jerusalem for Passover, will he also testify? It matters not: —soon enough he will himself stand before his accusers and testify to his power and title. Healing this man's son ought to be an act of purest pity. Still, he is struck by a thought: whether or not this man goes to Jerusalem, they both are pursued by the Passover Angel that metes out death; the Angel throws the boy into fire and plans to throw Jesus into gehenna where Jerusalem burns its rubbish. Jerusalem is the destiny of all; for all are pursued by the Angel and will be slain like lambs at the Passover. But the man's belief inspires Jesus to think that he and his son will drink from a different cup this Passover: "I believe; help thou my unbelief," the man says, as they walk together to the man's house. The man quivers between two opposing powers: Jesus, who may have power to heal his son; and the evil spirits who inhabit his son and also inhabit the powers in Jerusalem whose spies have been nosing about asking questions. Jesus comes upon the boy in front of his house. He rebukes the spirit, and it leaves immediately, but the boy falls upon the ground like a corpse. He is dead, say the onlookers, and the scribes judge that Jesus failed. But Jesus gives another sign—the boy must not only be healed, he must be raised to the heavens and given the power to understand what has been done for him. He takes the boy in his arms and carries him into the house, far from unbelieving eyes. In the presence of the father alone he touches the boy with healing hands and the corpse returns to life.

He has healed a father's only son; he himself is the Father's only Son. He takes this healing as a sign from the Father that he be raised again and lifted to the life above. He does the Father's works; he is a loyal son. But his work is not done. He must obey to the end so that men may have faith. He knows that men seek faith by going to the priests for washings and teachings. In Jerusalem there is a pool of water near the sheep gate where a mass of people bathe every day in the hope that it will heal them of their pains. He has heard of a man who for many years has begged for someone to help him into the pool at certain times when the water has healing power, but no one has ever helped the man. The priests are at the root of the idolatry; they control the nation's worship—and it serves no good except their own. With this thought in mind he sees a fig tree by the side of the road; it is barren; its roots must have withered away, he says to his friends. Like the nation itself, he thinks, it bears no fruit. The nation's roots are the priests; they are withered—and so are the people. How then can men have faith? He turns to his friends and tells them that faith in God can remove a mountain and cast it into the sea. He would take the whole mass of those gathered about the pool and cast them into the sea of his own healing. He has healed a man whose hand was withered; he has healed a paralytic whose body was withered; he has healed many whose bodies and spirits were withered. Thus he gives a sign to the nation that he does the Father's works—for the law said that miracles are from God—and gives men faith. When men have faith, he can carry them to the waters that flow from the four-headed river of Paradise.

It is midday; he and his friends are passing through Jericho, suffering the hazy heat lying on the village and the hills that surround it like prison walls. He thinks of his namesake, Joshua, who made the sun to halt and brought down the walls of the ancient city with a mighty shout. He can hardly put a foot on the ground without arousing a prophet's dead voice or a dead hero's deeds. He, like Joshua, will tear down walls, the walls of the temple, and rebuild it in three days. He will be misunderstood when he says that, but let it be. He sends his friends to fetch an ass upon which he may ride into the city. But he is hindered by the crowds, Passover pilgrims and others, who surround him and touch him and call out to him—they acclaim him messiah. He hears a strong voice rise above the din: "Son of David, have mercy," someone calls out. Odd. He has not yet been called Son of David—why now? True, he is of David's lineage, but this is not known. The man who called to him can know very little— he is blind. Yet, he must know much; he has heard the crowd cry, "Look! Here comes Jesus of Nazareth." The blind man is a diviner;

he hears *Nazareth* as if it were *nassar*, which means branch, a word used by the prophet Isaiah when he spoke of a branch from David's tree, a royal shoot, upon whom the spirit will rest. Who is this man who knows this of him? He walks over to the man and speaks to him. His name is Bartimaeus. The man, upon hearing Jesus' words, casts off his mantle and repeats, "Son of David, have mercy." Jesus rewards the man's faith—or his divination—by healing him. The crowd roars mightily at this miracle. Jesus takes the man aside, as he once stepped aside with Levi, and they talk about many things. Before long the man has put on the mantle of a disciple and will follow him into Jerusalem. He knows the danger; Jesus has told him that he is a Joshua who will tear down an old kingdom and a David who will start anew. If Bartimaeus wants this for himself, yes, he may follow along.

Putting Jericho behind them, Jesus and his band move west across the River Jordan and into the mountains of Moab where they seek rest before they enter the holy city. They find a small cave and sleep for several hours. Jesus then, for the third and last time, tells them that in a week he will be dead. They are no more ready to hear it than when he first told them.

The next day they are up before the sun. If they were closer to the temple, they would have heard three trumpet blasts proclaim dawn. Each day a dedicated levite climbs to the highest pinnacle and looks to see if the sky is lit up as far as Hebron, which is twenty miles south and west, in a basin on one of the large Judean ridges. When the sun lights up Hebron, it is a new day. The levite cups his hands and calls his *yes*! to a priest below who claps his hands to signal the three priests with their long silver trumpets; they lift the trumpets to their lips and pierce the dawn with their call to prayer and the day's work. As clouds of incense rise from the temple precinct, Jesus, a few miles away, has completed his plans and is ready to begin his journey into the city. The royal ass is waiting, and his disciples have found an upper room where they may observe the feast without being seen by their enemies.

The people on the road into the city are as numerous as locust in a grainfield. They are pilgrims who will be looking for lodging in or near the city or joining their families in time for the feast that beings in a few days. They have heard of Jesus of Nazareth, many of them;

they think of him as messiah, and if he comes to the city at this time he will add greatly to their Passover joy. Will he appear on the pinnacle of the temple, as some rabbis have said? If so, it will be a new day for his people who have suffered so long under foreign rulers. Messiah will loose the shackles from their ankles and restore the royal splendor of days past when they were ruled by kings like David and Solomon. Then, they think, they will be free.

As Jesus waits for his friends to bring the ass, he takes Levi and Bartimeaus aside. Do they really want to go into the city with him? They risk their lives. They say they already owe him their lives. They will go with him. It is good, Jesus says, because there is much they can say to each other. He trusts them with his thoughts about the Galilean works. As he speaks, pieces come together to form wholes, like a simply woven garment that conceals the art of its maker. God's Voice called him and guided him along a path that becomes clearer the longer it gets. The crisis in the synagogue: —that sharpened his wits for contending with the evil spirits he may find in the temple. His teaching from Simon's boat: —that sharpened his wits for another sermon he must give, perhaps on the Mount of Olives, a place where Bartimaeus says he has often gone for solace. The tempest at sea: — he slept then while his friends panicked; soon, he believes, they will sleep while he faces his enemies. Let them sleep, says Bartimaeus: for when these eyes close—he points to his own eyes—inner eyes and ears begin to see and hear. Yes, Jesus thinks: he will come to his friends a third time, as they sleep, and he will reveal himself to them. He will plant himself in their heads like seeds in good soil, so that when their hour comes they will understand and—yes—they will see him and not take him for a ghost.

The ass is at hand: they speak quickly in the little time they have left. Jesus speaks of the rabbis and prophets who spoke of this hour. Some rabbis said that messiah will inspect the temple and take charge over it and cleanse it—if that need be. This he will do but not as messiah; rather, as one sent by God to reveal the true temple, the one not made with hands. Other rabbis said messiah will appear with a host of angels and occupy the highest pinnacle of the temple, where all may behold him. This he will not do; he has not come for the sake of the crowds, or to seek high places—he will leave that to the levite who reports the daily rising. Then he speaks of the prophet who said that messiah will come to his people humble and mounted upon an ass. This he will do. And he hopes the crowd will sense the rebuke. But as he looks down upon the road he sees all Jewry, it seems, gathered and waiting for him. They will not suffer rebuke. Many have cut palm fronds to wave at him as he passes. Already they begin to sing Hosanna—an act of praise or a signal to revolt. If the levite is still watching from his pinnacle, Jesus thinks, he will have something more interesting to report than the rising of a routine sun.

As Jesus mounts the ass, Bartimaeus thinks to guide the beast by the halter. This may not help, Jesus thinks, when we enter the flow of the crowd; we will be carried along like a twig in a stream. But Bartimaeus' gesture tells him something of the man. He has lived long in the dark. Who did he have to guide him and allay his fears? And he must have learned much in the dark. He went to the Mount for solace, he said? He went there—but for a different reason.

From the beginning Jesus has had trouble with crowds; they cry out but never listen; they make demands but give nothing. Today they shout Hosanna, which on their lips means *Revolt Now*—it is a battle cry. They call up the name of David—as Bartimaeus foresaw? — to provoke him to battle, to be a David against Caesar's Goliath. But he will enter the city as a royalty who is not a David but a royal offspring, a scion of his Father, and he comes in peace. He wonders who all these people are. Bartimaeus reads his thoughts: many are devout pilgrims hurrying to find lodging before the feast begins, he says; others are merchants, thieves, beggars, flatterers—and some are spies. As a blind man, Bartimaeus had spied on those who now spy on them. No doubt, he says, guards at this very moment are looking down from the Fortress, peering into the crowd, looking for messiah. They are nervous; and the priests are nervous. As Jesus listens to his new friend, he realizes that Bartimaeus has been looking for him all his life, and in the dark was able to find him. But he has no time to explore this memory; the crowd is raucous, they push him ahead, they ask petty favors and want places of honor in the new regime. Finally they come to the Mount of Olives; they go up the eastern side and down the western. The crowd is even thicker: they clutter the road, they are backed up the slope of the Mount; fathers lift their infants high over their heads so they may see the temple, the procession, messiah's march to victory. Gethsemane is in sight: normally it is a quiet garden but not so today. Bartimaeus tells Jesus that this is the place he has in mind for them later, after they have escaped the crowd.

The moment they pass through the Golden Gate his friends lift their master from the ass, throw a cloak over him, and take him quickly through the narrow streets before the crowd grasps that he is gone. Soon they are in an upper room on the far side of the city, a place they have rented for the week and where they can keep him safe from throngs and priests. Later in the day, however, close to evening, Jesus takes Levi and Bartimaeus with him to the temple. He wears a new garment that conceals his features, and with his beard he looks like any Jewish male pilgrim come to gaze at the temple and its marvels. As they enter the temple grounds through the eastern gate, they mingle with the thousands of worshipers who have poured into the precincts. Still, they know that the temple hirelings will be watching. They must be wary.

The throngs jam the stairs that lead to the several courts, making it hard to move about. However, they make their way to the great columns that support the edifice: four rows that form three isles, and each column so large that three men would not be able to encircle it. Jesus stares at the columns and whispers to Bartimaeus: What a spectacle it would be if these columns came crashing down. They are not overheard, but they feel unholy eyes upon them. Then Jesus sees large tables placed where bankers do their trade. He has heard of them. So has Bartimaeus, who whispers to Levi that he, of all people, should appreciate this business: Levi used to take Jewish shekels and give them to Gentile lords; here, bankers take Gentile money and purge it so shekels can be offered to the God of the Jews: a job like this might redeem him, Bartimaeus says to his friend. The joke is chilled by the sight of two priests standing by a portico. Bartimaeus has the right words for this, too: the priests must be searching Scripture to see if any good thing can come out of Nazareth, he whispers. Hearing this, Jesus knows how the blind man endured his years of darkness: in his mind he ridiculed those whom he detested. The two priests have a scroll and are holding it to the light. If they search Scripture and find him not, thinks Jesus, where indeed will they look? At that very moment the priests stare at Jesus. They then walk over to temple guards and glance toward Jesus and his two friends. Jesus doubts that the guards will try to take him in a public place; but they might have him followed back to the upper room. He will not let that happen. Quickly and without a word to his friends he moves to the tables and upends them. Coins litter the floor. The bankers leap to their feet and stare at Jesus. Who is this wild man? they wonder. As priests and guards rush to the scene and begin picking up the scattered shekels, Jesus disappears into the crowd and is gone.

The next evening he takes his original four followers— Simon and Andrew; James and John—together with Levi and Bartimaeus, to a grassy slope on the Mount of Olives. In the distance the temple stands out in the dark, lit by a thousand lamps. They hear the voices of pilgrims singing Passover hymns, praising God and hailing messiah. Jesus turns his back to the temple and speaks to his disciples about last things. (He calls them disciples—a title they will soon earn.) What do they think of the temple and its worship? he asks. Bartimaeus is outspoken: if the temple should be burned down by the heathen, it would be no great loss, he says; it is the abode of evil. Levi agrees. The four disciples, simple fishermen from the north, are thoughtful men: their simple wisdom tells them that the slaughter of bulls and goats cannot do for people what they have seen their master do many times over—he heals the sick, he drives out demons. Bartimaeus, at the mention of demons, has a thought: when Jesus overturned the tables of the money-changers, he exorcized the temple; he purged it of their greed. More: his rebuke was aimed at the entire nation and its demonic ancestor worship—the patriarchy, the priesthood, the monarchy, all of it. Jesus completes these thoughts: the nation has a new temple, he tells them; it has existed from the beginning of the world—he is the temple, his body; the voice of God is within him. His body can be destroyed—and it will—but it will be restored in three days. This is the third time he has told them this. It is a hard saying, but they are disciples now and they must hear it and understand. They press him for signs of the end of the age and the coming of the new kingdom. But Jesus was not speaking of the end of the age and a new kingdom. He listens patiently, as they speak of empires that come and go, of heros and kings who come and go, of each person's end of days. How all must die—how *he* must die. They still do not understand.

God will raise him on the third day? The Voice did not say this. He has made an act of faith that his end will restore his past. He has memory of his past; but it serves as no surety of his future. He has scripture; but it is a mix of God's Voice and the babel of men. So he is not unlike men—he must strive for faith, as they all must. And, like his fellow Jews, he turns to scripture to find his future, veiled in symbol though it may be. He has meditated on the symbols "three" and "four." The prophet Hosea said that God will raise up his people in the person of messiah after three days. *Daniel's* author said that the *Son of man* will be seated on his throne on the fourth day. The numbers resound in his memory like an oracle, a distant certainty now lost. Four and three? A seven day week? His people say God did a six day wonderwork and rested on the seventh. But his memory fixes upon the first "three days" of the seven. Those three days were in the Light—but no ordinary light. He himself has lived in that Light and he was that Light and still is that Light. God had said, "Let there be Light" on the "first day." This Light can still be seen by men. At Saphoris he knew some men who had been lifted up and seen the Light—a few only. He himself, on Mount Hermon, had seen it, and known it to be inside himself; this is why he speaks of himself as a temple; temples should be flooded with great light. During those "three days" the earth was in darkness, for God had not yet placed the lamps in the sky to guide the feet of men and beasts. This He did on the fourth day: the sun, the moon, the stars—ordinary light. Now he must speak to his disciples and tell them of the greater Light, the Light that is best seen in the dark.

He points to the starlit sky. "When the sun will be darkened and the moon will not give its light; and the powers in the heavens will be shaken, you will see the *Son of man* in the clouds with great glory, who will send his angels for you." He looks directly at them: "You four have been with me from the beginning. Many times I have tried to tell you who I am and why I have come. Here, do you see this man?" —he points to Bartimaeus— "Let me tell you, when he was blind he learned to see without light from the sun or moon or stars, and he came to know me before he ever saw me. I tell you, there is great wisdom in the dark." Even so, they do not understand; they think he prophesies that the great lamps will fall down from the sky. He tries again: "When I sent you out to sea and I came to you out of the dark, over the waves that terrified you, you saw me...but only as a ghost. I pray that when the power of darkness comes upon you, you will see me again, and I will not be a ghost."

He knows what they think: there are no answers in the dark, they will say. Bartimaeus tries to explain: "When a man's lights are dimmed, he may see a light that is greater than what he lost." But the disciples can think only of the *Book of Daniel*, where the *Son of man* is expected to light up the skies in the last days. Jesus leads the disciples in a meditation about the four winds, the four beasts, the four ends of the earth; and how the seer, in his night vision, saw the triumphant *Son of man*. He asks the four men what they understand the seer to mean by these visions. "The *Son of man* will come in the last days to save us from the evil ones that frighten us," they say. "Yes," Jesus answers "he comes after four days—a half-week of suffering. We begin these four days now. And when the four days are done, pray it will be the first day of a new week." He recites for them the great passage from *Daniel*, in which the author's night visions reveal to him the *Son of man* in glory. He tells the four men that when the four dark days are done, a disciple may look up or he may look down. If he looks down, he will see the harrowing of hell as the Son calls up the holy dead. If he looks up he will see the Son in clouds of glory. He says to them, "Watch—for you do not know when the Master of the house will come; in the evening, at midnight, at cockcrow, or in the morning." He prays they will understand these words, when the four days become only three, and they will be left with only his words to comfort them. For now, it is late— the fourth watch of the night, as the Gentiles reckon it.

The next evening all Jerusalem prepares for the feast. Jesus knows the priests will be too busy to worry about him until they are done with their chores in the temple. At Passover the priests work in relays; they pour the slain lamb's blood into large basins which they then throw over the altar and the heads of the worshipers; they believe this brings God and the nation into covenant. The lamb's fat will be burned and the carcass dressed for the meal as choirs of Levites sing from the psalter in honor of the feast. Jesus leads the disciples to a secret upper room of which he is sure the priests are ignorant and prepares for his last supper.

While Bartimaeus and Levi remain below to warn of danger, Jesus stands before his twelve disciples and realizes that he is a thirteenth among twelve. He has brought one loaf with him and he holds it up before them, a thirteenth loaf—for it is like the extra loaf in the boat when he and his companions crossed the Galilean Sea a third time, toward Bethsaida, among the Gentiles. He riddled them at the time to make them aware of the sign of bread and what it means to the world. If he could feed them in the wild, he can feed them in this upper room. His eyes favor the original four companions as he begins to reveal himself in a fourfold liturgy. He takes the loaf from the midst of them, where he had placed it: by taking it from them, he takes the full measure of their life and the life of the world; he is the one loaf that will suffice for Jew and Gentile alike. He blesses the bread: his words assert that life comes from God and life returns to God; he comes from God and returns to God; they all come from God and return to God. He breaks the bread: he himself is the broken loaf, he tells them, and they shall see how he will give himself to them. Then he leads them out.

Making sure they are not seen they move quickly through the narrow streets, out the Golden Gate, and toward the small garden of Gethsemene, a half hour's walk from the city wall. A stream runs close by the garden, which lies in a valley called the Kidron. When they come to it they turn and look back at the walled city and the temple. Even Levi is breathless at the sight, his cynical nature for once overcome by the beauty of the moonlit edifice and the sounds of many harps and voices lending their lush harmonies to the night. Other lights combine to make an eerie spectacle: lanterns hanging from the porch of Solomon and embers of campfires all about the city from pilgrims unable to find room within the walls, all bewitch the eye. Aromatic smoke rises from censers placed about the temple altar, forming great white clouds against the night sky. Bartimaeus too is moved—to cynicism: Who says Jews do not worship vain idols? He says. He does not believe—nor does Levi—what the pilgrims are chanting inside the temple: "God is good to us." He believes the words of this man they have followed to the garden tonight, who has said that he is the true temple and the light from him is the true light of the world. Enough of the city and its deceits and its sights and its sounds and smells—let Satan have it all. He pities the pilgrims who think God's goodness is to be found in the temple and that messiah will join them there. Jesus, they believe, will soon show them all of God's goodness a man's heart can hold. Those stones over there, the temple, let them fall down. The temple is a whited sepulchre. They turn from it and take in the beauty of the garden.

Jesus beckons to Levi and Bartimaeus. He tells them they must return to the city. They have already tasted God's goodness, he reminds them—now he must be alone with the three. Andrew must return also, and Judas, and some of the others. Last night, on the Mount of Olives, he was alone with the four; tonight he will be alone with the three. Little time remains: it is between midnight and dawn––in a few hours the trumpeting priests will call up the new day and, if the priests have their way, he will be dead by the end of it. He takes the three to a dense part of the garden near the stream. They can hear the water moving softly, singing a nocturnal song of peace. With a motion of his hand he invites them to sit with him, their backs to a clump of trees, and he studies their faces. Did they understand his words? About the four ends of the earth? the four days? the four horsemen? the collapse of the temple and the world's dark when the sun and the moon fail to give their light? No: they ask for signs. How can they understand?...they are men of the day... how can they understand the dark? He had spoken about the state of a man whose light grows dim. The light of day deceives a man, he had said to them—it has no power to save. But they think of days that come and go, of what has been and what is to come. He would have them understand the world's soul and their own—what is deep and true. Not what the future may bring. The future holds nothing that the present lacks. They wanted signs...he gave them signs, signs for the outer eye. Earlier, in the upper room, he held up the broken bread— that was the first sign. Now it is paschal midnight and the Angel of Death soon will cross the stream and take him—the second sign. Later, when the cock crows up a new dawn, his friends will not find him— the third sign. And the fourth sign—only the inner ear will hear it for what it is: he will stand before his accusers and speak the plain truth about himself.

Jews ask for signs, it is their way. He has given signs; even before he understood his own calling he was hearing signs from the Father and he enacted them for his followers. Wherever he plants his feet he sets a sign that makes the earth a paradise. Even in the walled city he gave signs; three times he supped within its walls—but the city was no place for him to set his feet. He called the first four of his friends to join him on the Mount, but they did not see or hear his message. That was last night, when only four days remained to the rising of his sun. And four times he told them to watch. Again, they did not know what he meant. Watch for what? they could have asked —they did not even know to ask. Now, tonight, three days remain to the rising of his sun. He will speak to the three a third time. He has intended this from the first: when he took them to Jairus' home, when he took them to Mount Hermon to see the light shining in the true temple, and now, tonight in this private place. He has prepared them: he took them to Jerusalem to see that it has no light that compares to his. Tonight, outside the city walls, he will finish the work he began by the sea.

He knows how weary they are. He tells them to rest for a time; they fall asleep almost at once, so heavy are their eyes. He too is weary, but he cannot lay down his head. He leaves the sleeping men and goes to a far corner of the garden. The spring grass is cool to his feet and he feels the earth's peace beneath him. Adam may well have stood upon this spot as he felt the evening balm and called his bride to come lay down with him. But Jesus' brow turns hot and moist as he kneels beside a rock and prays to his Father that this cup may pass. He prays as a Jew— passionately, with all his humanity. But the cup will not pass. The Voice has brought him to this hour. He must drink of it. His limbs tremble and his mouth is dry. Cold fear grips him as he senses the Angel of Death. He fears the agony that will soon be his. But more: he feels the ancient fear laid upon him—Adam's curse. When Adam turned his back to the garden gate he lost his way and death became his lot. The sickly fear of all Adam's children is now his; it is the burden that the ancient prophet saw but got wrong— the oracle said messiah will bear the *iniquities* of all men, but messiah, here in the garden and by the rock, bears the *grieving* of the world that has lost its home. Salty sweat breaks out on his face and runs down his beard onto the rock where he can see it. It is the color of wine. It clots his beard and his robe, staining it blood red. At this moment he does not know if the Father will call him home on the third day.

But if he is not to be raised on the third day, what irony! The Father gives him power to raise Jairus' daughter but leaves him in hell. Did the Father barter with the Evil One?—his life for hers? The thought strikes him: his life for all Adam's children? He a ransom for all? He will know on the third day. Today is Friday, just before dawn. He will do for his friends what he intends to do.

59

The night air is still; a low western moon reveals the garden's short trees and shrubs and he can see in the distance the silhouettes of his friends lying where he left them. He remembers how once he slept while they faced danger; he sent them to sea, weary and fearful, while he stayed on the hill slopes and prayed for them. He sent his spirit across the waters and calmed their fears. He prays for them again—not as a Jew prays, but as he learned in Saphoris. He prays with wings to his prayers that soar through the night, across the gulf between him and them. His spirit calls to them in the dark, just as his spirit had called to Levi, and the paralytic, and Bartimaeus, and they heard him and saw him within. In the spirit he is lifted up; he looks down upon his body, collapsed upon the rock; he no longer feels the sting of the sweat. He goes to his friends. He has prepared them well: they are watching. Three times he calls to them, to remove the scales from their inner eyes. In their night vision they see the *Son of man* in clouds of glory. When they awake they will not remember his visit. But the hour will come when they will remember—and that will be enough.

He knows now why the Voice sent him to find these men and call them up from the sea. These are men of the world, good hardy men, not prone to dark spells or visions. If he can remove the shells from these three, he will make of them a sign to all the world, that all men can be opened to the Father's love. He has taken the three to the inner chamber where life rules over death; he has taken them to the Mount where he began to open the inner eye; now he has brought them to this garden, where he is the gardener who makes all things new. Tonight he has made the inner eye open wide.

Will he be able to open other shut eyes? When he is lifted up on the cross he will be able to see a far distance; the whole world will be within his ken. His friends and his mother...they will be somewhere among the crowd...he trusts that they will be there. They cannot come too close; the centurions who guard the base of the cross will not permit it. No matter: he will see them. His mother will be there, and the other Mary, and, he believes, Salome. The three women will open their eyes more quickly than his disciples. He knows that he can come to them, even when he is in pain, even when they are grieving. Yes, they will be standing afar...but he will go to them.

All men are at a distance from me, he reflects. Yet, if it is the Father's will to raise him on the third day, he will be able to reach out to them all. But not all will see him. Few, in fact, are willing to eat his bread and drink from his cup. Judas is such a one who will not eat and drink. Judas, who just hours ago supped at his side. Judas, who at this moment betrays him to the high priest.

Men like Judas can be seduced by silver and the praise of those in power. But even men like Judas, at times, or at the end of their days, may come to wonder Where is God? And why does God hide his face from me? Jesus himself has felt bereaved of God's presence—even now, in this garden. He has learned what it is to be human, to feel bereaved of comfort, peace, and the bliss of heaven. To have to struggle for faith. It is too easy for men to give up—to fear the loss of the world more than the loss of God. If he were in Saphoris now he would debate this subject as a Greek among Greeks; but tonight he is a Jew, and Jews know about suffering. How odd: —men and their God are like angry lovers who come to enjoy silence between them: yet the silence causes suffering and sorrow. Men hide from God but curse him for his absence—again, like lovers who have much to learn about love. Men who do this will suffer until they are delivered by a merciful death. Suddenly he looks up—he hears footfalls and voices from across the stream. It will be the guards and soldiers, and—he thinks—Judas. He has thought about how the priests will go about killing him without the people knowing. He will not hide; he will let them take him at a time when the worshipers are in the temple or asleep, and lead him to an inner court where the High Priest will condemn him. Early in the morning they will take him before Pilate, who will give the order to crucify him. How then will they get him to the mound of death? for at all hours the city is crowded with pilgrims and others who are looking for him. The priests will be clever: messiah must not look like messiah. They will beat him about the head until his face is covered by blood. And they will find other ways to disfigure him. When he is led out to the gallows he could be hidden among other criminals—two thieves, perhaps, there are plenty of them about. An onlooker will shrug at the sight of three thieves being carried off — so much the better for all. And if he should stumble on the way, and be unable to carry his cross, they will compel some stranger to carry it. No act of mercy, this: the onlooker will shrug again; some stranger is being carried off, an offender of some sort—so much the better for all. Yes:—how clever of the priests to think of this simple plan: hide the face of the man who has seen the face of God.

He hears the voices coming closer; they have crossed the stream and are in the garden, an unlikely cadre of soldiers, temple guards, priests and scribes. They are led by Judas, who, as usual, will greet him with a kiss. Soon they will be upon him. Bearing tapers and torches they have come looking for the light of the world.

He walks back to his sleeping friends. Another irony: they are close to the temple where, if a priest were caught sleeping, he would be stripped of his robe and sent away disgraced. Soon, he will be stripped of his robe and wrapped for burial in a tomb where a linen shroud will be his priestly robe. He prays to the Father that, after a three day sleep, He will send an angel to him bearing a glistening white garment, such as no fuller on earth could make. If the angel comes, the world will know that the true priest and mediator between God and man lives in his bodily temple. And his robe will never be taken away from him.

vii. Epilogue: "The Sun Shall be Darkened and the Moon Shall not Give Her Light"

The tall head nun does not know how much she can endure. The ship has been foundering for hours. She looks to land for help but sees only the abysmal dark. It is the fourth watch of the night, the deepest dark before the dawn. No stars, no moon—only the primordial darkness that never heard the Voice of God. Her prayers weigh heavy with the repeating but she prays on: she asks God to forgive all her sins, then she recites the rosary—"Holy Mary, Mother of God, pray for us sinners now and at the hour of our death." In the convent, in Brehmen, she had thought that her death, when that time came, would be a quiet grace, lighted by candles and lifted by the words of a priest. But this? The ship turns sharply portside as a sudden burst of wind and sleet take hold of it and the bulkhead cracks. She grabs a rail, she and the other four. A thought comes to her out of the deep ignorance of the night: they are five...the Lord's wounds were five, *the stigmata*...four spikes and a lance. He suffered and died. Never before had she understood that. She is weary; they all are weary. They have seen despair and death. The cries of the children are no more. The battered corpse of the sailor hangs and sways upon its rope, dashed again and again into the ship's keel. Another burst of wind whips the sleet into needles against her face. She closes her eyes and begins again to pray—her last prayer, for she has breath for no more. She sees him...there! Close to port, he comes. She calls out with all her strength:

CHRIST, O CHRIST, COME QUICKLY

At last she understands. He has come to take her home.

APPENDIX A. DR. FARRER'S TABLES (*The Patterned Exposition*)

TABLE ONE

Call of four disciples, 1:16-20	Call of four extended, 1:36-39	Call of Levi, 2:13-14
	Contact with leper, 1:40-42	Contact with publicans, 2:15-17
New teaching and		New "wine" of Gospel, 2:18-22
Sabbath exorcism		Sabbath "harvesting," 2:23-24
Contrast Christ and the scribes, 1:21-28	Christ and the priests, 1:43-44	David and the priests, 2:25-26
	Powers of the Son of man shown by	Powers of the Son of man, 2:27-28
Raising of woman from sick bed, 1:29-31	Raising of the paralytic in face of opposition, 2:1-12	Withered man healed in face of opposition, 3:1-6
Many healings and exit, 1:32-35		Exit and many healings, 3:7-12

TABLE TWO

NOTE:This second table includes material covered in the previous table. Each table shows how the material is arranged with reference to certain healings, which are arranged in "handfuls," that is, a group of five, a group of five, and two over. See Farrer's explanation in his Chapter Two, "The Marcan Pattern of Healings."

Call of four, 1:16-20	Call of Levi, 2:13	Call of Twelve, 3:13
They left their father, 1:20b	Feasting and fasting, 2:18-20	No leisure to eat; mother and brethren dismissed, 3:20-35
Exorcism with new authority	The power of the new teaching, 2:21-22	By what power does Christ exorcize, 3:22
and new teaching	Cornfield episode 2:23-27	Teaching from boat: cornfield parables, 4:1-34
in episode of demoniac, 1:21-28		Exorcism of storm; exorcism of Legion, 4:35-5:20
Raising of woman in Simon's house, 1:29	Healing in synagogue, 3:1-5	Raising of Jairus' daughter in ruler of synagogue's house, 5:21-43
Many healings 1:32-34	Rejection in synagogue: many healings, 3:6-12	Rejection in synagogue and not many healings, 6:1-6

TABLE THREE

Call of twelve, 3:13	Mission of twelve, 6:7	
No leisure to eat, supernatural power behind Christ's acts said to be Satan, 3:20-35	Supernatural power behind Christ's mighty acts said to be John redivivus	
	No leisure to eat, 6:14-32	
Cornfield parables, 4:1-34	Five loaves for 5,000, 6:33-44	Seven loaves for 4000, 8:1-9
Stilling the storm, 4:35-41	Walking on water, 6:45-52	Return by sea, 8:10
Tombs, demons, swine, Gentile soil	Clean and unclean; pharisaic opposition and disciples' incomprehension, 6:53-7:23	Pharisaic opposition and disciples' incomprehension, 8:11-21
in the exorcism of Legion, 5:1-20	Gentile exorcism, 7:24-30	
"Talitha cumi," 5:21-43	"Ephphatha," to the deaf, 7:31-37	Cure of the blind, 8:22-26

APPENDIX A

TABLE FOUR

Jesus comes near to lose his life for saving life. He admonishes the demons who confess him to be silent, 3:4-12	Opinion of Herod and others concerning what Jesus is. The Baptist's passion prefigures that of Christ, 6:14-29	Opinion of Herod and others quoted. Peter confessing is admonished as Satan. Jesus predicts his passion. Saving and losing life, 8:27-9:1
Jesus ascends mount with three surnamed disciples and nine more, 3:13-19	Jesus ascends mount to pray and descending amazes his disciples, 6:46-52	Jesus ascends mount with three disciples and descending amazes the nine and the crowd, 9:2-15
Jesus' exorcism discredited as demonic. He warns his critics of everlasting sin, 3:22-30	Dispute with Pharisees about disciples. Exorcism of child for parent. Healing of deaf stammerer, 7:1-37	Dispute of Pharisees with disciples. Exorcism of deaf mute for parent. John discredits strange exorcist as schismatic; the rebuke of Jesus warns of everlasting death, 9:16-50
Jesus turns from mother and brethren and declares that his faithful hearers are his kindred, 3:31-35	Pharisees tempt Jesus with request for a sign, 8:11-13	Pharisees tempt Jesus with marriage question. He says, "Leave father and mother..." 10:1-16
Parable: cares and riches choke the word. But good soil bears a hundredfold, 4:1-20	The disciples may rely for bread on the power that fills 5000 with 5 loaves, etc., 8:14-21	Rich man turns back. The disciples who have made sacrifices are promised a hundredfold, 10:17
Jesus's sailing companions terrified and amazed, 4:35-41		Jesus's traveling companions terrified and amazed. Request of James and John, 10:32-45
	Healing of the blind, 8:22-26	Healing of the blind, 10:46-52

APPENDIX A

TABLE FIVE

	Disciples confess Messiah, 8:27	Disciples prepare messianic entry, 11:1
Christ as a new David, 2:25,	Christ in glory: "Let us make three tabernacles," 9:2	Ovation as at Tabernacles; hailing of David's Kingdom, 11:7
who, hungry, overrides the priesthood, 2:26	Jesus expels demon from boy 9:14-27	Jesus comes hungry to Jerusalem and overrides the priesthood when he expels the bankers from God's house, 11:12
Healing of withered hand, 3:1-5	Power of prayer, 9:28	Withering of fig reveals the power of prayer, 11:20
	Discussion on greatness and authority; only Christ's name authenticates. Failure to receive in the Name is damnation, 9:33-50	Christ's authority is questioned. He acts in God's Name. Rejection of God's representatives brings final overthrow, 11:27-12:11
Pharisees and Herodians, 3:6		Pharisees and Herodians, 12:13
	Marriage question, 10:1	Marriage question, 12:18
	The commandments of the One Lawgiver, 10:17	The commandments of the One Lawgiver, 12:28
	God to be served in Jesus, 10:21	Messiah shares God's throne, 12:35
	Snare of riches, 10:22	Abuse of riches and power, 12:38
	Those who give all receive a hundredfold, 10:28	Poor widow gives all, 20:42
Withdrawal of Jesus: Peter, James, John, Andrew, etc. on the mount: parabolic discourses, 3:7-4:34	Question of James and John, 10:35	Withdrawal of Jesus from temple to mount and question of Peter, James, John, and Andrew answered by apocalypse, 13
	Christ hailed as Son of David, 10:46	Christ anointed, 14:3

APPENDIX A

TABLE SIX

Mission of two disciples to prepare festal entry, 11:1-6	Mission of two disciples to prepare festal supper, 14:12-16
Entry to the festival. The hunger of "David." Old rites reformed, 11:7-18	Entry to the feast. "David" plotted against, gives "shrewbread" to his companions; new rite instituted, 14:17-25
The power of prayer, 11:20-25	The power of prayer, 14:26-42
High Priests march upon Jesus, 11:27	High Priests' servant and men march upon Jesus, 14:43-52
Debate of Jesus against High Priests and scribes. He maintains against them the session of Messiah at God's right hand, and predicts the fall of the temple, 11:29-13:2	Trial of Jesus by High Priest and scribes. His prophecy of the fall of the temple is twisted against him. He maintains the session of Messiah at God's right hand, and is condemned, 14:53-65
Warning to Peter and his companions that they stand fast before Sanhedrins and Governors, 13:3-13	Peter denies in the court of the Sanhedrin. Jesus stands before the governor, 14:66-15:5
The Abomination of Desolation and the agony of the saints, 13:14-23	Crucifixion and agony of Jesus, 15:6-47
The Son of man appears and sends his angels to gather the elect. Jesus receives "burial anointing" from woman, 13:24-14:9	Message, summoning disciples to see the Son of man, given by angel to women who come to anoint Jesus after burial, 16:1-8

APPENDIX B

THE WRECK OF THE DEUTSCHLAND
Gerard Manley Hopkins

To the happy memory of five Franciscan Nuns, exiled by the Falk Laws drowned between midnight and morning of December 7th, 1875.

PART THE FIRST

1

THOU mastering me
God! Giver of breath and bread;
World's strand, sway of the sea;
Lord of living and dead;
Thou has bound bones and veins in me, fastened me flesh,
And after it almost unmade, what with dread,
Thy doing: and dost thou touch me afresh?
Over again I feel thy finger and find thee.

2

I did say yes
O at lightning and lashed rod;
Thou heardst me truer than tongue confess
Thy terror, O Christ, O God;
Thou knowest the walls, altar and hour and night:
The swoon of a heart that the sweep and the hurl of thee trod
Hard down with a horror of height:
And the midriff astrain with leaning of, laced with fire of stress.

69

3

The frown of his face
Before me, the hurtle of hell
Behind, where, where was a, where was a place?
I whirled out wings that spell
And fled with a fling of the heart to the heart of the Host.
My heart, but you were dovewinged, I can tell,
Carrier-witted, I am bold to boast,
To flash from the flame to the flame then, tower from the
grace to the grace.

4

I am soft sift
In an hourglass at the wall
Fast, but mined with a motion, a drift,
And it crowds and it combs to the fall;
I steady as a water in a well, to a poise, to a pane,
But roped with, always, all the way down from the tall
Fells or flanks of the voel, a vein
Of the gospel proffer, a pressure, a principle, Christ's gift.

5

I kiss my hand
To the stars, lovely-asunder
Starlight, wafting him out of it; and
Glow, glory in thunder;
Kiss my hand to the dappled-with-damson west:
Since, tho' he is under the world's splendour and wonder,
His mystery must be instressed, stressed;
For I greet him the days I meet him, and bless when I
understand.

6

Not out of his bliss
Springs the stress felt
Nor first from heaven (and few know this)
Swings the stroke dealt
Stroke and a stress that stars and storms deliver,
That guilt is hushed by, hearts are flushed by and melt
But it rides time like riding a river
(And here the faithful waver, the faithless fable and miss).

7

It dates from day
Of his going in Galilee;
Warm-laid grave of a womb-life grey;
Manger, maiden's knee;
The dense and the driven Passion, and frightful sweat;
Thence the discharge of it, there its swelling to be,
Though felt before, though in high flood yet—
What none would have known of it, only the heart, being hard
at bay,

8

Is out with it! Oh,
We lash with the best or worst
Word last! How a lush-kept plush-capped sloe
Will, mouthed to flesh-burst,
Gush!--flush the man, the being with it, sour or sweet,
Brim, in a flash, full!—Hither then, last or first,
To hero of Calvary, Christ's feet—
Never ask if meaning it, wanting it, warned of it—men go.

9
Be adored among men,
God, three-numbered form;
Wring thy rebel, dogged in den,
Man's malice, with wrecking and storm.
Beyond saying sweet, past telling of tongue,
Thou art lightning and love, I found it, a winter and warm;
Father and fondler of heart thou hast wrung;
Hast thy dark descending and most art merciful then.

10
With an anvil-ding
And with fire in him forge thy will
Or rather, rather then, stealing as Spring
Through him, melt him but master him still:
Whether at once, as once at a crash Paul,
Or as Austin, a lingering-out sweet skill,
Make mercy in all of us, out of us all
Mastery, but be adored, but be adored King.

PART THE SECOND

11
'Some find me a sword; some
The flange and the rail; flame,
Fang, or flood' goes Death on drum,
And storms bugle his fame.
But we dream we are rooted in earth—Dust!
Flesh falls within sight of us, we, though our flower the same,
Wave with the meadow, forget that there must
The sour scythe cringe, and the blear share come.

12

On Saturday sailed from Bremen,
American-outward-bound,
Take settler and seamen, tell men with women,
Two hundred souls in the round—
O Father, not under thy feathers nor ever as guessing
The goal was a shoal, of a fourth the doom to be drowned;
Yet did the dark side of the bay of thy blessing
Not vault them, the million of rounds of thy mercy not reeve
even them in?

13

Into the snows she sweeps,
Hurling the haven behind,
The Deutschland, on Sunday; and so the sky keeps,
For the infinite air is unkind,
And the sea flint-flake, black-backed in the regular blow,
Sitting Eastnortheast, in cursed quarter, the wind;
Wiry and white-fiery and whirlwind-swivelled snow
Spins to the widow-making unchilding unfathering deeps.

14

She drove in the dark to leeward,
She struck--not a reef or a rock
But the combs of a smother of sand: night drew her
Dead to the Kentish Knock;
And she beat the bank down with her bows and the ride of her
keel:
The breakers rolled on her beam with ruinous shock;
And canvas and compass, the whorl and the wheel
Idle for ever to waft her or wind her with, these she endured.

15

Hope had grown grey hairs,
Hope had mourning on,
Trenched with tears, carved with cares,
Hope was twelve hours gone;
And frightful a nightfall folded rueful a day
Nor rescue, only rocket and lightship, shone,
And lives at last were washing away:
To the shrouds they took,—they shook in the hurling and horrible airs.

16

One stirred from the rigging to save
The wild woman-kind below,
With a rope's end round the man, handy and brave
He was pitched to his death at a blow,
For all his dreadnought breast and braids of thew:
They could tell him for hours, dandled the to and fro
Through the cobbled foam-fleece, what could he do
With the burl of the fountains of air, buck and the flood of the wave?

17

They fought with God's cold
And they could not and fell to the deck
(Crushed them) or water (and drowned them) or rolled
With the sea-romp over the wreck.
Night roared, with the heart-break hearing a heart-broke rabble,
The woman's wailing, the crying of child without check
Till a lioness arose breasting the babble,
A prophetess towered in the tumult, a virginal tongue told.

18
Ah, touched in your bower of bone
Are you! Turned for an exquisite smart,
Have you! Make words break from me here all alone,
Do you!--mother of being in me, heart.
O unteachably after evil, but uttering truth,
Why, tears? Is it! Tears; such a melting, a madrigal start!
Never-eldering revel and river of youth,
What can it be, this glee? The good you have there of your own?

19
Sister, a sister calling
A master, her master and mine!--
And the inboard seas run swirling and hawling;
The rash smart sloggering brine
Blinds her; but she that weather sees one thing, one;
Has one fetch in her: she rears herself to divine
Ears, and the call of the tall nun
To the men in the tops and the tackle rode over the storm's brawling.

20
She was first of a five and came
Of a coifed sisterhood.
(O Deutschland, double a desperate name!
O world wide of its good!
But Gertrude, lily, and Luther, are two of a town,
Christ's lily and beast of the waste wood:
From life's dawn it is drawn down,
Abel is Cain's brother and breasts they have sucked the same.)

21
Loathed for a love men knew in them,
Banned by the land of their birth,
Rhine refused them. Thames would ruin them;
Surf, snow, river and earth
Gnashed: but thou art above, thou Orion of light;
Thy unchancelling poising palms were weighing the worth,
Thou martyr-master: in thy sight
Storm flakes were scroll-leaved flowers, lily showers—
sweet heaven was astrew in them.

22
Five! The finding and sake
And cipher of suffering Christ.
Mark, the mark is of man's make
And the word of it Sacrificed.
But he scores it in scarlet himself on his own bespoken,
Before-time-taken, dearest prized and priced--
Stigma, signal, cinquefoil token
For lettering of the lamb's fleece, ruddying of rose-flake.

23
Joy fall to thee, father Francis,
Drawn to the Life that died;
With the gnarls of the nails in thee, niche of the lance, his
Lovescape crucified
And seal of his seraph-arrival! And these thy daughters
And five-lived and leaved favour and pride,
Are sisterly sealed in wild waters,
To bathe in his fall-gold mercies, to breathe in his all-fire
glances.

24

Away in the loveable west,
On a pastoral forehead of Wales,
I was under a roof here, I was at rest,
And they the prey of the gales;
She to the black-about air, to the breaker, the thickly
Falling flakes, to the throng that catches and quails
Was calling 'O Christ, Christ, come quickly':
The cross to her she calls Christ to her, christens her wild-
worst Best.

25

The majesty! what did she mean?
Breathe, arch and original Breath.
Is it love in her of the being as her lover had been?
Breathe, body of lovely Death.
They were else-minded then, altogether, the men
Woke thee with a we are perishing in the weather of
Gennesareth
Or is it that she cried for the crown then,
The keener to come at the comfort for feeling the combating
keen?

26

For how to the heart's cheering
The down-dugged ground-hugged grey
Hovers off, the jay-blue heavens appearing
Of pied and peeled May!
Blue-beating and hoary-glow height; or night, still higher,
With belled fire and the moth-soft Milky Way,
What by your measure is the heaven of desire,
The treasure never eyesight got, nor was ever guessed what for
the hearing?

27
No, but it was not these.
The jading and jar of the cart,
Time's tasking, it is fathers that asking for ease
Of the sodden-with-its-sorrowing heart,
Not danger, electrical horror; then further it finds
The appealing of the Passion is tenderer in prayer apart:
Other, I gather, in measure her mind's
Burden, in wind's burly and beat of endragoned seas.

28
But how shall I...make me room there:
Reach me a...Fancy, come faster--
Strike you the sight of it? look at it loom there,
Thing that she...there then! The Master,
Ipse, the only one, Christ, King, Head:
He was to cure the extremity where he had cast her;
Do, deal, lord it with living and dead;
Let him ride, her pride, in his triumph, despatch and done with
his doom there.

29
Ah! there was a heart right!
There was single eye!
Read the unshapeable shock night
And knew the who and the why;
Wording it how but by him that present and past,
Heaven and earth are word of, worded by?—
The Simon Peter of a soul! to the blast
Tarpeian-fast, but a blown beacon of light.

30

Jesu, heart's light,
Jesu, maid's son,
What was the feast followed the night
Thou hadst glory of this nun?—
Feast of the one woman without stain.
For so conceived, so to conceive thee is done;
But here was heart-throe, birth of a brain,
Word, that heard and kept thee and uttered thee outright.

31

Well, she has thee for the pain, for the
Patience; but pity of the rest of them!
Heart, go and bleed at a bitterer vein for the
Comfortless unconfessed of them—
No not uncomforted: lovely-felicitous Providence
Finger of a tender of; O of a feathery delicacy, the breast of
the
Maiden could obey so, be a bell to, ring of it, and
Startle the poor sheep back! is the shipwrack then a
harvest, does tempest carry the grain for thee?

32

I admire thee, master of the tides,
Of the Yore-flood, of the year's fall;
The recurb and the recovery of the gulf's sides,
The girth of it and the wharf of it and the wall;
Stanching, quenching ocean of a motionable mind;
Ground of being, and granite of it: past all
Grasp God, throned behind
Death with a sovereignty that heeds but hides, bodes but
abides;

33
With a mercy that outrides
The all of water, an ark
For the listener; for the lingerer with a love glides
Lower than death and the dark;
A vein for the visiting of the past-prayer, pent in prison,
The-last-breath penitent spirits—the uttermost mark
Our passion-plunged giant risen,
The Christ of the Father compassionate, fetched in the storm
of his strides.

34
Now burn, new born to the world,
Doubled-natured name,
The heaven-flung, heart-fleshed, maiden-furled
Miracle-in-Mary-of-flame,
Mid-numbered He in three of the thunder-throne!
Not a dooms-day dazzle in his coming nor dark as he came;
Kind, but royally reclaiming his own;
A released shower, let flash to the shire, not a lightning of fire
hard-hurled.

35
Dame, at our door
Drowned, and among our shoals,
Remember us in the roads, the heaven-haven of the Reward:
Our King back, oh, upon English souls!
Let him easter in us, be a dayspring to the dimness of us, be a
crimson-cresseted east,
More brightening her, rare-dear Britain, as his reign rolls,
Pride, rose, prince, hero of us, high-priest,
Our hearts' charity's hearth's fire, our thoughts' chivalry's
throng's Lord.

CHAPTER TWO

A View of the Heavens

i. Dr. Bucke's Illumination

Richard M. Bucke, M.D. was a many-sided man: a youthful outdoorsman and adventurer who almost lost his life in a fight with the Shoshone Indians; a lover of poetry, who enjoyed meeting with friends and reciting poems for endless hours; and a man of science who attained prestige among his fellows, who in 1888 elected him President of the Psychological Section of the British Medical Association, and in 1890 President of the American Medico-Psychological Association. One might say he was a complex man, or paradoxical even. But more: he was controversial; and to this day, among the few who have heard of him, something of a miracle.

On a visit to London in the spring of 1872 he had spent an evening with two friends reading poetry—Wordsworth, Shelley, Keats, Browning, and the American, Walt Whitman. The three men parted at midnight and the doctor got into a hansom for the long drive to his lodgings outside the city. His mind was intent upon the poems he and his friends had been reading; he was in a state of quiet, passive enjoyment of the evening, as he later recalled. Suddenly he saw an intense light. The city was on fire, he thought. But the flame colored cloud was closer to him than that—it was within him. What happened next is described by Dr. Bucke in the Proceedings and Transactions of the Royal Society of Canada:

> Directly there came upon him a sense of exultation, of immense joyousness, accompanied or immediately followed by an intellectual illumination quite impossible to describe. Into his brain streamed one momentary lightening flash of the Brahmic Splendor which ever since lightened his life. Upon his heart fell one drop of the Brahmic Bliss, leaving thenceforward for always an aftertaste of Heaven.

He was thirty five when this happened—a fact he later would consider significant—and his life was changed forever; he said so himself and so did those friends who knew him best. Not a change of character—he was always high-minded and idealistic—but something lofty and impossible to put into words. That was always a problem, to find the right words; yet as a medical man he wanted to explain precisely what had happened to him. He first made it known publically when he made it the subject of a paper he read to the British Medical Association in Montreal. His colleagues must have been stunned by the doctor's revelation, for he became controversial. Yet his prestige among them was not weakened; to the day he died he was respected as a man of science. Controversy was to be expected in that day and time—on this subject, it is always to be expected, for the doctor's experience fit no known category of human knowledge—not science surely, and not religion either. No one knew what to make of it. He himself struggled to understand it: What caused it? Is it supernatural? Will it happen again? Will it happen to others? The result of his study is the book, "Cosmic Consciousness," which first appeared in 1901 and is now in its twentieth edition.

In the sixteenth edition an admiring editor, George Moreby Acklom, reveals something of Dr. Bucke's background; more than a *pro forma* biography, it is a search for causes. What set the doctor apart from most men? What opened the heavens for him? Acklom begins by telling us that the doctor hailed from sturdy farming parents who lived at Creek Farm, near London, Ontario, to which they had migrated from England where his father had been a clergyman. The Bucke family brought with them a large library which proved an inspiration to young Richard, who spent hours among the books teaching himself to read and to enjoy poetry. He was not long content with this life, however; at seventeen he set out on adventure. He did odd jobs in various places, including a stint as deckhand on a Mississippi River steamboat. Not satisfied for long, he turned his back on the river and latched onto a wagon team headed for Salt Lake; from there he decided to push on for the mountains and the Pacific. In the dead of winter, he and two friends struck out on foot. Evading hostile Indians they made their way from camp to camp. Luck almost ran out on them when, after crossing the Rockies by the south pass, their food and supplies ran low. Reduced to eating flour mixed with water they came upon a mining camp and were saved. But again they set out, still in deepest winter, hoping to reach the Pacific. This time they were not so lucky: one of the men died of hypothermia; as for young Bucke, both feet were frozen. When a mining team came upon him they had to amputate all of one foot and part of the other. Having told us all this, Acklom draws no conclusions. We are left to wonder: Is this how the young Bucke conceived his career as a doctor? Is there some key that unlocks the secret of his sublime experience many years later?

The coming of the light—did it give him euphoria? Or did it confer knowledge? It is one thing to feel; another to know. Bucke begins by describing euphoria: "Directly afterwards came upon him a sense of exultation, of immense joyousness..." Euphoria is the keynote. But then he describes the intellectual illumination: it is a revelation of content, a knowledge of something new and unheard of. Eventually he comes to speak of the experience as "cosmic consciousness," for it is "a higher form of consciousness than that possessed by the ordinary man...the prime characteristic...is, as its name implies, a consciousness of the cosmos, that is, the life and order of the cosmos." Clearly, Dr. Bucke's analysis tells of a manifold revelation; along with the intellectual gift comes a quickening of the moral sense—the person rejoices in nature's goodness and rightness, and evil is a word that can be banished. And a blessed sense of immortality streams into his brain—death, too, is a word that can be banished. Dr. Bucke implies that all this is a gift: God threw open a window and let in the light. No one could earn or deserve the cosmic sense...those are a theologian's words, and Bucke does not use them; he merely states that the light came into his life while he was riding in a cab.

The light truly gives a view of the heavens, says Bucke: direct sight into the inner workings of the cosmos, things that have been secret from the beginning of the world, that no science can discern. He learned in a flash the meaning and drift of all life:— not a belief, in the sense of a proposition or dogma, but rather it is a sight; he sees and hears the ultimate mystery unfolded before him. He sees that "dead matter" is alive with intelligence and will, while men (he means men who are merely self-conscious) are pockets of dead matter in the midst of bounteous and plentiful life. Men are not, he says, "patches of life scattered throughout an infinite sea of non-living substance," but are "specks of relative death in an infinite ocean of life." He means that the self-conscious person is "dead" to the greater life that is all about him, while the cosmic-conscious person is "alive" to it. The life of man is eternal. All life is eternal. Man's soul is immortal, as is God's; the universe is so built and ordered that "all things work together for the good of all; the foundation of the world is love; the happiness of each person is in the long run absolutely certain." The cosmic sense confers a vision of the whole, an immense whole that dwarfs all conception and makes all scientific rational efforts to comprehend it seem petty and useless.

Not long after his vision, Bucke turned to the books in his library––the ones from his father, and others he had acquired, including much poetry. He turned over familiar pages again and again; words and phrases leapt to life, as if he had never seen them before. He found in the writings of certain poets and philosophers evidence that they, too, possessed the cosmic sense. Above all, Shakespeare. Bucke was convinced that the bard was endowed with the great gift: for example in the thirty-third sonnet he read;

> Even as my sun one early morn did shine
> with all-triumphant splendor on my brow;
> But out, alack! He was but one hour mine
> the region cloud hath masked him from me now.

Suddenly these words seemed no longer the conceited language of the poet's day. Bucke's notes on the sonnets state his opinion that "sonnet thirty-three refers to the intermittent character of illumination, which holds true in all cases of cosmic consciousness, in which there is more than one flash of the divine radiance. It treats of the cheerlessness and barrenness of the intervals as compared with those periods when the cosmic sense is present.." He notes also the many references to spring in the sonnets: it was a fine spring evening when the cosmic sun lit up his life, and as he poured over the writings of those who he believed had this sense, he found time and time again that spring is the season for the cosmic sun to light up the dark sky.

> Thou that art now the world's fresh ornament
> And only herald to the gaudy spring...

Sonnet One

Bucke came to believe that Shakespeare's genius derived from the heavenly gift and that in his plays and sonnets the poet alludes to the sense in subtle ways, both concealing and revealing at the same time. For there is a great need to express the new sense, to make of it a gift to others; yet it is unspeakable due to its nature. It is like a lamp that must be hidden under a bushel lest it burn the eyes that fall upon it. Admittedly, it is a long draw of the bow to make these assertions about Shakespeare: but then, Dr. Bucke, as Acklom reminds us, was no conventional mind. Indeed, those who have the cosmic sense see things that others do not see. (They are not infallible about all things and a modern scholarly judgment would hold that Bucke is wrong about the poet's intent. Yet, some scholars can be found who regard *McBeth* and *Lear* as religious allegories. Who can say?)

Bucke is on firm ground, however, when he turns to philosophers and mystics such as Jacob Behmen. Jacob Behmen, a simple shoemaker from Gorlitz in the sixteenth century, one day was sitting in his room when his eyes fell upon a burnished pewter dish; the dish reflected the sunshine with such intensity that he succumbed to a marvelous ecstasy and was enabled to see into the deepest heart of things. In his words,

> The gate was opened to me so that in one quarter of an hour I saw and knew more than if I had been many years in a university, at which I exceedingly admired and thereupon turned my praise to God for it.

A second time the light came to him: he was outdoors, walking through the fields to the green before Neys Gate, at Gorlitz, when the light flooded his senses and he beheld the creation as a whole and in all its fine detail, which gave him a great measure of joy. He attempted to write about his knowledge in a manuscript entitled, "Aurora, or the Morning Redness," and later in another book, "De Signatura Rerum."

Bucke says of these experiences that they were not complete; the dawn but not the day, he says. Ten years later, in 1610, the fullness of it entered him; his early biographers say that what he had seen previously only chaotically, fragmentarily, and in isolated glimpses, he now saw in perfected outlines; he saw things more as a whole, like a harp with many strings. What he saw, says Bucke, was no propositional truth, no logical deduction; he *saw* the reality behind all thought, the "Urgrund," (original ground) behind all things. He saw the three worlds of mystical discovery: the divine (angelical and paradisaical); the dark (internal); and the external visible world which proceeds from the first two. This joyful knowledge causes old illusions to fall away: the sense of mortality, sin, and the dread of death. The loss of sin means, not that sin is forgiven, but that the sense itself is faulty—there is nothing real about it. A person endowed with the cosmic sense has no need to escape what exists only as an illusion of the merely self conscious individual.

The coming of the cosmic sense greatly enhanced Behmen's mental abilities, both on the normal and psychic plane. He had no education but suddenly he could write profound essays that amaze us to this day. As for his psychic ability, the description of his death, quoted in Bucke, will attest to it:

> On Sunday, November 20th, 1624, Behmen called his son Tobias to his bedside and asked him whether he did not hear beautiful music, and then he requested him to open the door of his room so that the celestial song could be better heard. Later on he asked what time it was and when told that the clock had struck two, he said, "This is not yet time for me, in three hours will be my time..." He gave his wife directions concerning his books and other matters...and told her she would not long survive him (as indeed she did not), then...when the correct time came, he said, "Now I shall enter Paradise." He then asked his eldest son, whose loving looks seemed to keep Behmen's soul from severing the bonds of the body, to turn him round, and, giving one deep sigh, his soul gave up the body to the earth to which it belonged and entered into that higher state which is known to none except those who have experienced it themselves.

Bucke quotes the words of an editor who produced Behmen's writings: it is from "The Three Principals" in the quarto edition of 1764:

> A man cannot conceive the wonderful knowledge, before he has read this book diligently through, which he will find to be contained within it. And he will find that The Threefold Life is ten times deeper than this and the forty questions to be tenfold times deeper than that...

The number <u>three</u>, again, again: —the sign of mystery, infinity; the soul's return to Paradise from whence it came. But why <u>three</u>? "Three worlds," says the inspired shoemaker of Gorlitz, "are revealed to the enlightened eye." He means, first, the angelic world, Paradise; then, the inner dark of man's nature; third, the outer world known to the senses, which is an exterior birth out of the angelic and the human. And not only are there three worlds, there are three flights of the spirit that seeks Paradise. Dr. Bucke reflects on Behmen's words: he who would approach the world of angels must throw himself for a moment where no creature dwells, then he will hear and see who dwells there. A paradox. But such a place is to be found within, says Bucke, again studying Behmen and others. In that dark, the seeker stands apart from the thinking and willing self and discovers a greater thinker and willer, his deep and true self. Finally, it is God's mind that works through the seeker in a mystic bond.

Behmen is close to the threefold path known to western ascetical theologians: first, the seeker must change his habits and character— this is called purging, sloughing off the heavy weight of worldly attachments. (Bucke and others are quick to add that the moral life cannot usher in the new life in God—but its absence is a barrier.) Fr. Augustine Baker, the author of "Holy Wisdom," calls this first stage a time for "acts of the will," by which a person begins his journey— "forced acts," he calls them, repeated strokes of will that sustain the effort to conform to the moral life. Others have said of this stage that one acts *as if*—"Act as if you have faith and faith will be given you." The second stage Fr. Baker calls "proficiency": it is the "affective" stage, calling for mastery of will and emotion by high prayer and contemplation; acts of love and joy and desire are fused in a passionate quest for the Divine. The third stage: the seeker aspires actively to his goal—not by acts of will, for the will could only till the soil for the new growth; will and emotion are taken up to the heavens; a higher self takes over. Fr. Baker says that the Holy Spirit of God joins with the seeker in his seeking; God himself is within the seeker as he seeks and finds.

Of the forty three persons whom Bucke studied in his book, no two could be more different than Behmen the mystic and Walt Whitman the poet. Behmen was a shy mystic; Whitman a robust, outspoken American of the late nineteenth century, whose fierce and limber words were unlike any poetry ever penned, and who would seem to be worlds away from a mystical experience. But Bucke believed otherwise; he knew Whitman personally, and he became the poet's first biographer. He included him in his book because he considered him to be "the best, most perfect, example the world has had so far of the cosmic sense..."

Bucke first heard of Whitman in 1867 when a visitor to his home quoted some of Whitman's poems; from that moment on, Bucke confesses, he was "under the spell" of this unique man. When, in

1872, Bucke was reading poems in the company of two men, Whitman was one of the poets they were reading—and shortly after, that evening, on his way home, the splendor came upon him. Bucke went to Camden, New Jersey in 1877, when Whitman was living there, and the two men met. Bucke found what he had been looking for. Later, when Bucke wrote the introduction to Whitman's "Calamus," he described his feelings upon meeting the poet: he was "spiritually intoxicated," he said, in the man's presence. A new sun had burst in his sky.

When Bucke says that Whitman is the most advanced instance of the new faculty, and that he is the man who in "modern times" has written distinctly and at large from the point of view of Cosmic Consciousness, and who also has referred to its facts and phenomena, Bucke is expressing a theory that the cosmic sense is a new faculty that biological evolution is gradually dispensing to the human race. Those few who have received it are as advanced beyond merely "self conscious" individuals as these latter are advanced over the higher animals. And, Bucke claims, as self consciousness must have appeared sporadically—an individual here and another there—so the new faculty is appearing among a "chosen few," who are best qualified by moral and physical endowment to receive it. This theory would imply, then, that Whitman was more "advanced" in his appropriation of the new faculty than others, even Jesus or Paul.

Bucke's estimate of Whitman and his poems is more credible than his estimate of the non-living subjects in his book, for he spoke at length to the poet and came to know him thoroughly well. We can only guess at the conversations that must have taken place: two men who loved poetry, and who had (according to the doctor) the same exalted experience. And more: —they were seekers, men who had made the symbolic journey as youth and then come to a sudden maturity while in the prime of their manhood (Bucke at 35, Whitman at 31). But first, let us sample the poet's "Leaves of Grass" and the doctor's commentary:

WHITMAN'S LEAVES	BUCKE'S NOTES
I believe in you my soul...the other I am must not abase itself to you, And you must not be abased to the other. Loaf with me on the grass...loose the stop from your throat, Not words, not music or rhyme, I want... not custom or lecture, not even the best, Only the lull I like, the hum of your valved voice. I mind how we lay in June, such a transparent summer morning; You settled your head athwart my hips and gently turned over upon me, And parted the shirt from my bosom-bone, and plunged your tongue to my bare stript heart. And reached till you felt my beard, and reached till you held my feet. Swiftly arose and spread around me the peace and joy and knowledge that pass all the art and argument of the earth; And I know that the hand of God is the elder hand of my own, And I know that the Spirit of God is the eldest brother of my own.	He was at first in doubt what the experience meant, but then became satisfied and said: I believe in its teaching...but it is so divine, my old self must not be abased to it, neither must the new sense be overridden by the more basic organs and faculties. He goes on: Loaf with me, instruct me, speak out what you mean, what is in you...He then turns back to tell of the exact occurrence...it came upon him one June morning and took (though gently) possession of him, at least for the time...his outward life became subject to the dictation of the new self -- *it held his feet.*

Another text states matters admirably:

> As in a swoon, one instant,
> Another sun, ineffable full-dazzles me,
> And all the orbs I knew, and brighter, unknown orbs;
> One instant of the future land, Heaven's land.

Again, a pity we do not know what transpired in these conversations between the two men. We may guess, however, that they discussed how their lives had changed dramatically at about the same age—in their thirties. Whitman, like Bucke, had left home at an early age: he had been a journalist in Huntington, Long Island, but left abruptly for New Orleans and other places; finally after years of foundering mediocrity he became the inspired genius who wrote

"Leaves." Bucke attributes this change to the arrival of the cosmic sense.

Leaving home, making a journey...these are the necessities of growing up, achieving adulthood. They may also be necessities of achieving a higher plain of consciousness. Jesus and Paul separated from their past and made journeys—Jesus to Jerusalem, Paul to Damascus. Bucke educated himself, left home at seventeen, and went mountain climbing on his way to the Pacific. And, like the others, he returned from his journey bearing a great gift for mankind. This is archetypical heroism. The hero wrests himself from the confines of his past. He does not know why he does this; he does not know where he is going. If he persists and wins out against all manner of snares and dangers, he comes to a new place. It is a spiritual realm where golden seeds from within rise up and make him a new creation. The hieroglyph of this journey is often a mountain—mankind's most lofty natural image. The hero returns with a gift: Whitman gave us his "Leaves of Grass"; Bucke, his "Cosmic Consciousness." Of course, climbing mountains will not induce the cosmic sense—this is not the point. Rather, those who have made the spiritual ascent express it, even prolepticaly, in the sacred symbols. It is the spirit that ascends a mountain.

Bucke saw Paradise. Not another world, but this one, its glory unveiled at last. He is not alone in this discovery: it is a staple of religious mysticism and visionary experience that we live and breath in a paradise of indescribable beauty and festivity, but are normally blind to it, and in this blindness is our evil, depravity, and banality. It is when we approach the holy, that nature is aglow with inner life. In the Parsifal legend, the hero-knight, at the end of his spiritual quest, performs his first sacred office; he is stunned to see nature transfigured before his very eyes:

> How fair seem the meadows today.
> Once I came upon magic flowers
> Which twined their tainted tendrils about my head;
> But never did I see so fresh and charming
> The grass, the blossoms and flowers, nor
> Did they smell so sweet of youth
> Or speak with such tender love to me.

Bucke and Whitman epitomize the inner journey and its revelations; we might imagine they spoke about their early years and their experiences, when each drifted about for a time, seeking but not finding. Surely Dr. Bucke experienced the loss of his two feet, and added that—as we know from Acklom—he lived in constant pain following the amputations. Suffering is a dimension of the archetype: the hero separates from his past, he faces dangers and sufferings, and he returns a new creature. This is the mythic view. A scientific view, however, would point to the suffering and tell us how the body and mind respond to chronic suffering. The brain is a wild thing, capable of virtuoso improvisation; it conjures fantasies, delusions, hallucinations, and seduces the wisest of men into folly. It is susceptible to malfunction; it becomes ill, it takes medications that deceive it all the more. In recent times, we have discovered a class of analgesics that the brain produces at times of stress and pain; these are the endorphins—they kill pain and make opium eaters of us all. They can send us to a neuropeptide nirvana, where there is no sorrow or pain. Is this where Dr. Bucke went? And the others? For centuries, religious ceremonies in certain parts of the world have had as their central sacrament a natural psychotropic, mescaline, which sends its worshipers on ecstatic journeys to far places. All of which proves that we have a need to escape our work-a-day selves by some means or other. We must question these visions of heaven and starry flights into the emphyrean. Has Dr. Bucke bewitched us into believing a fool's paradise?

In such matters, we ought not to draw conclusions; instead, we must take the mantle of pioneers and make the journey ourselves or listen to those who have. Aldous Huxley is such a one. His "Doors of Perception" (a phrase taken from the poet William Blake, one of Bucke's studies) describes his experiences with mescaline. He says that at last he saw things as they really are; ordinary vision is illusion, he concluded. Objects about him—chairs, tables, flowers and gardens—became luminous, real; his only reservation was that he feared being addicted to this giddy state of being real and true. He might never want to do anything else, he remarked. His words resonate. Huxley himself realized the point to his words. It is not practical to stare too long in the face of reality—and dangerous (Moses could not long abide the sight of God's epiphany in the burning bush: "Man cannot see God and live."). Huxley points to the philosophy of Henri Bergson. The human brain has evolved, Bergson said, as a sort of "reducing valve" precisely to shut out reality in its full aspect. We might use the analogy of a filter; the brain filters out the divine aspect of reality so that we are prevented from knowing the world as it truly is. The striking implication is that the brain is an instrument of ignorance. On account of it, we are confined to a world of practicalities, a world that is of our own making. Mystics, of course, are pleased with this doctrine; they have long suspected such a thing; for them, when the heavens open, it is as if the filter has for a moment slipped out of place and behold—Paradise!

The filter may slip...or it may be removed. This is precisely what some ancient and modern schools of meditation try to do; they thrust aside the veil from the face of God. Even certain ascetical practices have the same goal; they strive to mortify the flesh—not because it is evil, but because by doing so they cause a shift in focus, in consciousness itself. (Fasting for example can induce visions.) An excellent analysis of this method is offered by Daniel Brown who wrote in *Transformations of Consciousness* that the mediator "dismantles the coordinates of ordinary perception and gains access to non-ordinary or extraordinary structures of consciousness that do not operate by ordinary psychophysical laws." Consciousness, he goes on to say, has three stages or levels; when the last of these has been stripped away, illumination will occur. Brown's analysis of this ascetical tradition reveals the commonality of the innumerable practitioners and mystics of the day. (Jacob Behmen comes to mind, whose "threefold way" resonates with many others who take or analyze the inward journey.) Brown has studied the Mahamudra discipline from the Tibetan Mahavana Buddhist tradition; some co-authors with Brown, Ken Wilber and Jack Engler, discuss related disciplines, such as the Visuddhimagga from the Pali Theravada Buddhist tradition, and the Yoga Sutras from the Sanskrit Hindu tradition. They conclude that these models, in spite of vast cultural and linguistic differences, are quite similar, and that those who master the art of these mental disciplines are "maestros of the mind's inherent music."

Consciousness, then, is a crime of sorts—and it has been called that. It shields us from paradise and spawns all sorts of egotistical ugliness. All the world's troubles spring from this original crime. Some would call it the original sin.

Evolution, however, knew what it was doing. As we indicated earlier, too much divinity would have been a disaster for the race. Our hominid ancestors had the necessity of surviving in tiger infested savannahs...awesome creatures, whose remains tell us that one tiger needed to consume a hundred pounds of meat each day. Our ancestors had no time for dreaming of divinity. They invented a religion, of course, consisting of gods to whom they could pray to help them with their survival issues; but these gods were only symbols of peoples' needs, not true Divinity. The pressure of everyday survival put a sharp point to the brain's development; we needed an edge in the game of life; we became more and more conscious and calculating...and farther from Paradise.

As consciousness evolved farther and farther from Paradise, some part of the brain—we speculate—may have retained a memory of primal divinity; or, perhaps compensating for its criminal tendencies the brain created a dark room, an underground, where roots could take hold and, when nourished by some sacred potion or drug, these roots push through the surface and achieve the true light of day. Some researchers, like Dr. Eugene d'Aquilli of the Pennsylvania Medical School, have investigated many such instances of "transcendent perception" and wonder if the phenomenon has to do with the dichotomy between the right brain and the left brain. He thinks that sometimes messages from one side to the other, which are normally routed through a band of nerve fibers called the corpus callosum, may under certain circumstances be routed through an area within the right brain called the limbic system. Powerful emotions would do this. The result would be, he believes, that the artistic and creative right brain could slip something past the analytical left brain; the experience would go uncensored, and seem like a "transcendent perception." This of course is a reductionist neurobiological explanation that fails to satisfy those who have had the experience, for whom it is a foretaste of heaven or even heaven itself. Even lesser glimpses provide a respite from our survival obsessions, and nourish us greatly by giving us a new sense of immortal worth. We feel restored, exalted—we know *that we are where we have always been;*

we have discovered ourselves as we really are and the world as it really is. We know naked being...no garments, no veils.

Many religions have at their core a means to attain the Light. The Zen Buddhist disciple, for example, tries to "trick" the conscious self into letting go its authority; this he does by giving it some impossible command such as "Listen to the sound of one hand clapping." The conscious self can be overwhelmed by an intense bombardment of nonsense and be shut down for a moment. The disciple aids this shut-down by drawing psychic energy down into his abdomen. After much practice, suddenly a "window" opens and he makes his way like a blind man through a passage that is bordered on all sides by psychosis. The journey takes only moments but the disciple travels far. Finally, the *incognita terra* behind him, he comes to the goal of his seeking: Sartori—the Light. He sees himself and the world for the first time. He may even claim to see God himself. Like another mystic, Meister Eckhart, he can say "the eye with which I see God is the same with which God sees me."

When we look at the Christian religion, it is hard to discern who among the many saints and eccentrics are the true seekers. One might wonder, for example, at St. Simeon Stylites, an early fifth century anchorite who built a pillar forty cubits tall and lived atop it until the day he died. Why? He was a type of flesh-despising hermit who wanted to escape the temptations of the flesh, and the pillar seemed well suited to the purpose. But, apart from his aversion to the flesh, he may have had also the intent to escape the confines of his conscious self. We cannot know, of course; but it can happen that those who mortify the flesh undergo as a secondary consequence the shifting of the self; for conscious states and physical conditions are related. Another instance that may seem more appropriate is St. Thomas Aquinas, the thirteenth century theologian whose *Summa Theologica* has become the official theological statement on doctrinal matters for the Roman Catholic Church: near the end of his days, Thomas was blessed by an ecstatic vision— unexpectedly—that moved him to pronounce all his intellectual accomplishments to be as nothing compared to his vision. Then there is the composer, George Frederick Handel, who did not mortify the flesh, nor did he study theology; he was a worldly businessman who made a living from his music; but when he lost his sight he saw the heavens open and tears of joy streamed from his blind eyes.

Having a religious or moral disposition, it would seem, does not usher in exalted visions. Nor does evolution bring it on; Bucke's theory that the cosmic sense is a new faculty that is being dropped on our doorstep by a kindly evolution on the march seems too much a product of the liberal progressivism that appealed to intellectuals of Bucke's day. Some lesser form of the sense can be induced by drugs. The Russian philosopher P. D. Ouspensky experimented along these lines, and was able to duplicate some of Huxley's visions—that was in 1920, and the widespread use of psychedelics proves that the brain can be manipulated quite apart from the spiritual state of the person who takes them.

Yet, Bucke has his points. The lack of a moral or spiritual disposition would seem to militate against the spontaneous rise of the cosmic sense. Also, his observation that so many of his cases were healthy specimens, their average age about thirty to forty, is worthy of more study: is this the time of life when the endorphins are most active? Moreover, in a tentative way he pointed to a type of experience induced by drugs—ether and chloroform; he considered these "minor and incomplete" instances of the sense, and not to be compared with the full splendor of the spontaneous experience. But, most valuable to some of us, the doctor calls our attention to the New Testament and challenges us to read it in a way we have never read it before.

Jesus, he asserts, spoke of his illumination under the figure "the kingdom of heaven," which is a "pearl of great price" that one should seek above all else, even though narrow is the way. And, believing that the new faculty is rising up among us to give new life to the race, he quotes Jesus on the subject of "You must be born again," and he points to a parabolic saying in which a woman takes and hides three measures of meal till it was all leavened. The cosmic sense first leavens the individual, he explains, then it will leaven the world. As for the Apostle Paul, he considers that Paul's words about "being in Christ" and other statements refer to the cosmic sense.

Most scholars would consider Bucke's scriptural exegesis to be perverse and willful. This is to be expected. The doctor was that kind of person—controversial.

ii. The Hero's Journey

Three times in Jesus' early ministry he goes up into the hills and gives cause to his disciples and others to wonder who he is and what will become of him and them. The first time (*Mark* 3:13) he goes into the hills and appoints twelve disciples to be his followers; when he returns home his friends exclaim that he is "beside himself" and his enemies accuse him of being in league with Satan. The second time (6:45) he goes into the hills he has sent his disciples out to sea in a small craft, then he amazes them by walking toward them upon the water. They take him for a ghost. The third time he leaves behind all his disciples save a chosen three and meets with two great heros from the nation's past, Moses and Elijah, both of whom ascended to high places themselves, and there at the summit he is transfigured by light; his awed disciples are afraid; when Jesus comes down from the mount, people are amazed at the very sight of him.

The third time, on Mount Transfiguration (Mt. Hermon) he crosses a spiritual divide, a threshold. Before this ascent he engaged in ministry, but without mission. After the transfiguration, his pace quickens, he sets his face toward Jerusalem and marches toward a fourth and fifth ascent, which will be revelatory and decisive. Before he ascended snow-capped Mt. Hermon he came into Caesarea Philippi, on the Sea of Galilee. The Greeks who lived there spoke of a sacred cave that gushed spring water into the Sea, one of three springs that nourished that body of water. The cave was a portal into the underworld, they believed, and they built a temple over it. Jesus came upon this place and soon he began to speak of his identity and mission. On the Mount he startles his disciples by saying that he must go to the underworld himself—such is his destiny. His ascent to the Mount, therefore, is a spiritual crossing, a threshold event, that turns him around and sends him marching off to Mount Calvary.

It is a universal experience of our great men and heros that they leave us at the foot of a mountain, as it were, while they aspire to adventures in lofty and fabulous places, are transfigured, and return to astound us. In western religion this experience takes its most familiar aspect when we assert that Jesus was lifted up onto Mount Calvary to die, placed in a tomb, and on the third day broke forth from the tomb to astound the whole world.

Joseph Campbell, who has studied mythic heros as few others have, states the matter thus: a hero ventures forth from the world of common day and enters a world of supernatural wonder; he encounters dangerous forces and wins out over all; he then returns from his mysterious journey with great powers and he bestows gifts and blessings to those whom he had left behind. Campbell cites the example of Prometheus, who ascended into the heavens, stole fire from the gods, and returned to earth with this gift so necessary to civilized life. Aeneas is another example: he went to the underworld, crossed the fearful river of the dead, threw a sop to the three-headed dog Cerberus, and came to the place of departed souls; he conversed with his father, learned the destiny of all souls, and finally returned home through an ivory gate to inspire his fellows with his new wisdom and courage for the future.

This experience is defined as the monomyth: Campbell credits James Joyce with the coining of the term in his *Finnegan's Wake*. The myth has three stages: the hero separates; the hero is initiated into some mystery; the hero returns home.

As Jesus is the great and central myth in the west, Guatama the Buddha is the central myth of the orient. Campbell sums up the story for us: let us listen with a keen ear for something that Campbell does not notice:

> The young prince Gautama Sakamuni leaves his father's home secretly on his steed Kanthaka. He passes through the guarded gate and rides through the night attended by torches of four times sixty thousand divinities. He crosses a river that is eleven hundred twenty eight cubits wide and he journeys to the acclaim of woodland creatures and music that fills ten thousand worlds. At last he comes to the Bo Tree, the Tree of Enlightenment, on the Immoveable Spot, whereupon he sits under it and waits.

> Soon comes Kama-Mara, the dangerous god of love and death; he rides upon an elephant and carries weapons in his thousand hands. His army comes with him, extending twelve leagues to the right and twelve to the left. In fourfold darkness the god assails Gautama. But the prince is unaffected by the assault, for the goddess earth came and dispatched Kama-Mara with a hundred, a thousand, a hundred thousand shouts. Victory is to the young prince.

It is sunset. In command of his spot, the prince now begins to study the mysteries. In the first watch of the night he learns of his previous existences; in the second watch he sees the divine eye of all-seeing; in the third he learns the chain of causation; finally, by dawn, he obtains perfect enlightenment. For seven days, he sits enraptured; for seven days he stands aside and gazes at the spot whereupon he had sat; for seven days he paces between the two spots; for seven days he lives in a pavilion given him by the gods; for seven days he sits under the Tree while the girl Sujata brings him rich-milk in a golden bowl. He goes to another tree while a storm rages seven days; finally he enjoys the fruit of his liberation as he sits under a fourth tree.

He decides, at length, that he must return to tell men of his discovery—the god Brahama so persuaded him, for at first he did not want to return. He does: he goes about speaking to his fellows of "the way" that leads to enlightenment. This is his gift.

The magic is in the numbers. Of course, we must allow for a certain exaggeration typical of oriental stories of this sort; but the numbers adhere to the basic elements of the myth. Gautama does not merely sit under a tree—he sits under it for seven days. No ordinary tree, we are to believe. And in fourfold dark there are three watches that precede the dawn and the coming of the great light; this is the universal dark in which the mystic contemplates the divine presence—no ordinary nightfall, to be sure. The use of numbers such as three, four, seven, twelve, a thousand, is almost universal among myths, legends, fairy tales, hero stories, and in descriptions of origins. Moses, according to Jewish legend, came to God's holy mount three months after he departed from Egypt; at the mount he passed through four portals of fire, earthquake, storm and hail, and was thus empowered to return to men bearing the gift of God's holy law. The numbers give us a sense of the numenous—we expect miracle and revelation.

We even find the numenous in comic guise. In Mozart's opera *The Magic Flute*, which is based on Masonic themes, the hero Tamino has left his home and come to a strange land. He is attacked by a serpent but rescued by three women archers who are in the retinue of the Queen of the Night. Tamino is persuaded by the Queen to rescue her daughter Pamina from the temple of Sarastro who, the Queen says, is an evil man—he kidnaped Pamina and holds her captive.

Tamino goes forth in the hope that he can rescue Pamina and make her his bride; he is guided on his way by three young lads who protect him from dangers. When Tamino arrives at the temple gate he enters into a dialogue with Sarastro's High Priest. The Priest's words are set to a sublime melody of four measure duration. Moments later, when the Priest has left, Tamino meditates on the Priest's words as an offstage chorus repeats the four measure melody, this time punctuated by solemn chords from three trombones. Tamino learns that Sarastro is a noble and high-minded being—over the Queen's objections—and that he must himself enter into this ideal fraternity of the temple. His arrival inside is announced by a blast from three horns. Finally, Tamino and his bride are purified and released from the dark powers of the Queen by a fourfold testing by air, earth, fire and water. Mozart was a Freemason and knew the symbols; what they actually meant to him we can only guess (the opera's libretto was written by someone else). Mozart speaks to us through his music, so we shall confine our conjecture to his use of the orchestra and vocalists. This harried composer almost always wrote in a hurry; might not unconscious forces have come into play as he wrote under the influence of the text and the Masonic ideals? He begins the overture with three great chords, which will recur at dramatic crises—for example, when Tamino is summoned to his fourfold trial. Indeed, the threefold chord itself suggests the square and its doubling in the Masonic esoterica. But finally we are left to guess how much of this numerology is art and how much is a revelation from the misty dawn when all images were born.

If Tamino, the character on Mozart's stage, is a mythic person, so is Mozart himself. As a young man he painfully separated from his father in Salzberg and went to Vienna, where he struggled against jealous competitors and creditors but triumphed and gave the world an immortal gift. His journey to the cultural center outwardly was a shrewd move toward celebrity and financial reward; but it was also a psychological journey that placed him in the company of past heros who went to great cities like Thebes, Troy, Jerusalem, Rome. The city is the outward sign of the inner center where the hero discovers himself. Vienna drew others—Haydn, Brahms, Beethoven; Bach had gone to Leipzig; later Chopin and Stravinsky and others would go to Paris. In the new city they all took on a new *persona*; they represented themselves to the world by new names: Mozart called himself "Adam"—Adam, the primal man, the first to leave his home, and the emblem that Jesus applied to himself. The young Brahms fantasized about himself as "Krisler." Beethoven was so intent upon a new identity that he added *van* to his name; he was to be known in Vienna as Louis *van* Beethoven, a nobleman, and he tampered with his birth records in Bonn to disguise his true parentage. His first composed song, while a boy of thirteen, long before he left his home, was called "An einen Saugling,"— "to an infant,"—the text of which contains the thought that a child can never be certain who his father was; he may therefore be some occult figure, a noble person, or a god, even. Beethoven's entire artistic and personal life revolved about the themes of heroism, idealism, transcendence, and the conquest of new artistic worlds. Journeys brought out the mystic dreamer in him. He wrote the following letter describing a journey he made in 1812 from Prague to Teptitz to meet a woman who aroused his passions but a union with whom would have been crippling to his personal freedom and creative artistry; he would have had to accept a "steady quiet life." His inner conflict made him ill. He described his journey to Teptitz in these words:

> The journey was a fearful one... the post coach chose another route, but what an awful one; at the stage before the last I was warned not to travel at night; I was made fearful of a forest, but that only made me the more eager— and I was wrong. The coach must needs break down on the wretched road, a bottomless mud road... Yet I got some pleasure out of it, as I always do when I successfully overcome some difficulties.

This letter, says Maynard Solomon, describes no ordinary ride in a mail-coach. Solomon is a psychiatrist who has written an analytical biography of the composer in which he says that this letter resonates with a hero fantasy of grand proportions. Dangerous voyages, he says, are undertaken by ancient heros as they turn from the ephemeral to the eternal, from death to life, from manhood to divinity. Beethoven had not been able to resist the quest: the woman represented for him his immortality—he was to call her his "immortal beloved." He remarks that he should have remained at the last stage, waited out the night until the light of day. But the hero must go on through the night. At last, the composer's fears are mitigated by a sense of triumph.

In all literature, however, there is no more famed a journeyman than St. Paul the apostle— the hero of the *Book of Acts*. How he became so is a mystery. Apostles were those who had been with Jesus during his life on earth and had been commissioned by him to do his work; they were *sent* on their journeys (the Greek *apostolos*: a messenger, one sent on mission; journeying was necessary to their call and duty). But Paul was not among them. When we first come upon his name in *Acts* he is Saul of Tarsus, a Jew, of the tribe of Benjamin (his namesake is the mad King Saul—*I Samuel* 10 ff.). He worked as a tentmaker, although he was well educated, and he was a member of the strictest party among the Jews, the Pharisees. He was also a Roman citizen, possibly because a parent or grandparent had rendered some service to the government. As a citizen of Rome, he would have been required to assume three Roman names—a praenomen, a nomen, and a cognomen. We know only his cognomen, Paul. Luke tells his readers how Saul went on a rampage against the followers of Christ; he hunted them down and reported them to the authorities (Christians were considered subversive by the government.) Luke continues to call him Saul, even when he relates how he was struck down by a vision of Jesus as he journeyed to Damascus. But after the conversion, Luke calls him Paul (13:9). Paul became a fiery preacher of the religion he had once tried to destroy. He traveled about the Roman empire preaching and teaching the new religion; he risked his life many times. He eventually came to Jerusalem where he met Peter, one of the original twelve disciples. Peter's name had been changed by Jesus himself—from Simon to Peter. Peter's story is told briefly by the evangelists: he was fishing with his brother and others when Jesus came upon him. Jesus looked upon him with eyes of far perception, and the look mastered him and won his heart. The two apostles, Peter and Paul, became cornerstones of the new faith. They came to understand what is meant by the saying, "As goes the Master, so goes the disciple."

Just as Jesus won over Simon Peter, he won over Saul. But Jesus was still alive when he looked upon Simon Peter by the Galilean Sea, and dead when he looked upon Saul of Tarsus. The evangelists prepare their readers for this miracle. Mark and John, in their gospels, often tell us that Jesus had the power to know his friends before he met them, and to see them when at a distance from them. In

Gethsemane and at Calvary he was able to see them—though they were not there -- and to imprint his love and will upon their hearts forever. After his death his power to do this was perfect; he could search out the likes of a Saul even as Saul was searching for him, and overwhelm him with the force of his presence deep within Saul's mind. (Saul, of course, was searching for Jesus' followers, not Jesus himself—so he thought.) The evangelist Luke gives us another prefiguring view of Saul's conversion. He tells of Stephen's death— Stephen, the Church's proto martyr, who had a face like an angel's, Luke says, but an angry mob rushed upon him and killed him because he like other converts from the Jewish religion had forsaken the ancient law, so they said. In his last moments his eyes were opened to see what only angels are permitted to see—the glory of God. His garments, Luke carefully points out, were then placed at the feet of a Jew named Saul, who was consenting to Stephen's death. Destiny has prescribed that Saul will convert and become a new Stephen. Stephen in his dying is a model for Saul's new *persona*; as Paul, he too will see the glory of God. Luke tells the story of Saul's conversion three times in his book. Saul saw the Lord in light as he journeyed down the Damascus road. He turned his back upon his past; he struggled with inner demons that would hinder him, and he was aided—not by the succoring angels who aided Jesus after his baptism and temptation, but by the Lord himself, who sent a disciple named Ananias, like a ministering angel, to have Paul baptized and made ready for his new work.

Paul's journey down the road to Damascus was a psychic journey, a motion of the spirit. He was seeking...he knew not what; he found the object of his hatred at the very core of his own self. This journey became the first of many that he would make as an apostle, an ambassador for Christ; it would bring him at last to Rome where (history does not record but Luke implies) he was martyred in the name of Christ. His last journey, therefore, was an ascent to meet the Lord—to use his language for it—in the sky, which too is a psychic center, far more real than any place or object known to the eye or ear. Paul had much to do, however, before he came to this appointed end, and it is the business of Luke's *Acts* to tell the truth of Paul's works; we have also some of Paul's letters that tell us in his own words what trials and ordeals he underwent in Christ's name. In Luke, we may read the threefold telling of the conversion on the Damascus road. In the letters (called "epistles") we may read something of that conversion and what looks like another vision, a very strange journey, that he has difficulty speaking of. We find it in 2 *Corinthians* 12: 1-5:

> I must boast; there is nothing to be gained by it, but I will go on to visions and revelations of the Lord. I know a man in Christ who fourteen years ago was caught up to the third heaven—whether in the body or out of the body I do not know, God knows. And I know that this man was caught up into Paradise - whether in the body or out of the body I do not know, God knows—and he heard things that cannot be told, which man may not utter. On behalf of this man I will boast...

It is related in the third person, as if Paul is not directly involved. But, whether it is someone Paul knew or Paul himself, it is a bold assertion for a Jew to say that he ascended into the heavens; not since *Genesis* had a man glimpsed Paradise—although Jewish lore claimed that Moses and Elijah had been carried up, and, of course, Paul must have heard that Jesus himself was ascended into the heavens. Another aspect of the vision, however, presents a commonplace among occult practitioners and others who have spontaneously received such a vision: they see and hear things that cannot be repeated. These things may be "unlawful" to utter, because to do so would violate a cultic code; or impossible to utter, because there are no mortal words. In literature of mystical visions the one who is blessed by the vision, or who goes to heaven and returns, is rendered blind and speechless. His tongue cannot tell the glories he has seen and heard.

Most scholars believe that Paul, even though he uses the third person in this text, speaks of himself. Why, after all, would he abruptly speak of someone else while he is presenting his own credentials and personal history to the members of the Corinthian Church, where he is involved in a dispute? The context makes it clear that Paul is contending with issues that have arisen among the Corinthians and he feels the need to assert his own authority. He senses that he is boasting too much (12:1) and suddenly pulls a veil over himself—a thin veil, for it is Paul himself who has always presented himself as a "man in Christ." Moreover, Paul has described himself in this letter as a journeyman; chapter eleven is an passionate recounting of his labors on land and sea. Paul must have learned something about journeying from his friend Luke, whom he met at Troas. Luke had things to say about journeying. When he came to write his Gospel history of Jesus, Luke summed up the Lord's life as a journey to Jerusalem; and in his later work, *Acts*, he summed up the church's mission to the world as commencing at Jerusalem. Also, Luke presented a parabolic figure who epitomizes the spiritual journey: "a certain man." This nameless person makes a journey that begins in Jerusalem; he is set upon along the way and left to die; finally he is taken up to a place of refuge where he hears the promise that all will be well. (*Luke 10:29*). At least a few Christians through the ages have seen in the figure of the wounded man in this parable of the Good Samaritan a psychic and spiritual wayfarer. Could he be also the "certain man" whom Paul describes in his account of the ascent to the third heaven—Paul himself?

Scripture offers a vast stage: we as audience sometimes feel as we might when watching Shakespeare's *Hamlet*, a play that begins with the words "Who goes there?" and leaves us wondering during the entire drama who indeed goes where. Hamlet's inner conflict paralyzes him and renders him unable to act decisively—to be himself. We hear him cry, "To be or not to be; that is the question," and these words become our own. To wonder about identity is the nature of our being in the world.

The journey is necessary because we do not know who we are or what we must do. If we are to learn who we are, we must make the journey of discovery. Adam, standing at the head of the race and in the first pages of the Scripture epic, marks the beginning of our journey. In the *Genesis* story Adam sins and is expelled from his garden home bearing a curse that will pass to his children; and the gates to the garden are guarded by two terrifying cherubim whose flaming swords tell us that if we want to return to the garden we must lay down what we take to be our lives and put on garments more acceptable within the royal precincts. The original story of Adam the First Man is more complex than the moralistic rendering we find in *Genesis*; Adam bears a rich connotative background in the history of ideas; he is a mythic royal Primal Man who is of the earth but breathes divinity. We his children are like him; we have this ambivalence within us; we can never be at home in the world. We say "Adam is dead," but we read in Scripture that his dust will be raised up. We should never take these words literally; instead, we should let them resonate within us until we hear them call us to our primal estate. In the New Testament Christ stands as the new Adam, the divine *Son of man*, who promises to lead us back to the source of all life. This is the essential journey; it is told again and again in many variations: Noah, the patriarchs, Moses— they all wandered, as did the nation as a whole, over waters, the desert, through the wilderness. Jesus' words to his disciples were "Follow me." He did not say simply "hear me." He said "*Follow* me." (And sometimes *he followed them*: Luke tells how certain disciples, the third day after Jesus' death, were making their sorrowful way to Emmaus, a seven day journey from Jerusalem, when a stranger took up with them; when at last they came to a place of rest and sat at table with him, they discovered who he was, when evening was far spent.)

They come to know who he is...*but who are they*? Indeed, *who are we*? We read the New Testament to learn about Christ, and we hear his words "...who do you say that I am?" to Peter, but we forget to ask about ourselves. What does the New Testament say about us? We might look again at "a certain man" who leaves on journey from Jerusalem but is set upon by robbers who leave him as dead; but a stranger lifts him up from the dust, takes him to a place of rest, feeds him, and promises him a future. In biblical language, the "certain man" is Adam, mankind, who is in the pit of death and needs to be taken up into the heavens from whence he came. A "stranger," a third among three, delivers him. The victim is the old Adam; the "stranger" is the New Adam, Christ. Luke, the evangelist, and friend of Paul, told his parable in his gospel (Luke 10:30), and Paul would have understood it.

Scripture, as we have said, presents the journey as an elite image; again and again within its pages we come upon the journey in one or another of its variants, and often in counterpoint with other images such as eating, fleeing, going under water, seeking a new home, facing dangers, taking on a new persona. In the Passover festival these images are joined. The people flee their home in the slave camps to escape Pharaoh's armies, they eat bitter herbs and unleavened bread, they pass through the waters, they rise up as a new nation in a promised land, and, on a mountain top their leader hears the very word of God. In the New Testament, Paul turns to the Passover images when he thinks of Christ: "Christ our Passover is sacrificed for us," he says, "therefore let us keep the feast." Jesus journeyed through baptismal waters, left his home and family, faced his enemies, and came to Jerusalem where a new Pharaoh crucified him while the nation ate bitter herbs. Christians in Paul's day had to flee this same Pharaoh. These images are fixed in the minds of the evangelists, especially Paul and Luke, who composed their literary works to incorporate them. They tell us of the mythic journey that leads through dangers and confusion, a symbolic death, and a turning toward one's true nature and destiny. Luke prefaces his "certain man" parable with the cynical words of a lawyer who asks of Christ "What shall I do to inherit eternal *life?*" Jesus responds: he tells of a "certain man" who while he journeyed came near to *death*. The lawyer's literal mind misses the deeper point made by this parable. (See "A Certain Man," Chapter Three of this book.) A man who wants eternal life must make this journey, face its dangers, and pray to come upon a mysterious stranger who lifts people up and carries them to the inn of salvation. The journey from Jerusalem to Jericho leads through death to eternal life. (Jesus died in Jerusalem; his namesake, Joshua, triumphed in Jericho.) Luke tells of another journey. Two disciples journey from Jerusalem to Emmaus. It is the third day since Jesus died. The two men are soon joined by a third man, a mysterious stranger, and the three men continue their journey into the night.

Paul, when he made his Journey from Jerusalem, wore the mantle of the parabolic "certain man" and the others who began in that holy place and underwent a holy death. On the road he was struck down by a blinding light and the voice of the Lord. The voice told him to rise (*anastas, Acts* 9:6) and go into the city. He rose up and was led into the city where for three days he remained blind and could not eat or drink. The Lord then sent Annanias into the city to lay hands on Saul: "Brother Saul," he said, "the Lord Jesus, who appeared to you on the road by which you came has sent me that you may regain your sight." Immediately something like scales fell from Saul's eyes and he was able to see. Thereupon he rose (*anastas,* v. 18), was baptized, fed and strengthened. It is a third day resurrection for Saul—now Paul—followed by eucharistic nourishment for his new life in the spirit. Later, in his hastily written letter to the Corinthian congregation, Paul described a companion piece to the conversion vision that Luke relates in *Acts*—the ascent journey to the "third

107

heaven." Paul's journey, that began in Jerusalem, finally transcended Damascus and all cities of the earth, and made of his life a Passover mystery.

We may now return to Paul's ascent to the "third heaven" and study it as a Passover journey that carries Paul to Christ himself, who lifts him up and takes him to a place of refuge and salvation. *Fourteen years* ago, Paul writes, a man was taken up to the third heaven. Why fourteen? Why any number? Numbers in the New Testament are rubrics, signposts, that point the way. This is as true in Paul's letters as it is elsewhere in Scripture. In *Mark*, Jesus heals thirteen suffering persons of their ills with the anticipation that they will be raised from the dead—Jesus himself to be raised from his own suffering as a fourteenth. Moreover, fourteen is seven doubled: seven recalls creation week and man's first home, the Paradise garden; Paul says he ascended to Paradise in his vision. (Doubling and multiplying were commonplace among the rabbis: four becomes forty; forty days becomes forty years.) Turning again to *Mark*, we find that the evangelist "doubles" his list of sufferers by arranging them in parallel cycles: a series of seven sufferers ends with the raising of Jairus' daughter from her death bed, and the next series of seven sufferers ends with the raising of Jesus himself from the tomb. "Fourteen" signifies ascent.

Paul, we know from his writings, prefaces his ascent vision with a recounting of his own sufferings. This is the pattern: three days ordeal, then resurrection. Three times, Paul says, he was beaten with rods (2 *Corinthians* 8:25), and three times he was shipwrecked. Consciously or not, Paul regards his ordeals as sacred and he confers upon them the sacred number: three times he suffered, and, as Luke will say, he suffered *in the darkness*, as if in a three day tomb. Paul believes that his vision of the Lord on the Damascus road was like a resurrection, and he believes the same of his second vision—both follow a kind of dark. Yet Paul does not consider his life's journey complete; he has merely begun, and more sufferings await him. He mentions his "thorn in the flesh," which three times he prays will be removed from him. He closes his letter by saying he will come to his friends in Corinth a third time.

Such highly wrought thinking...did Paul expect his Corinthian congregants to understand his allusions and the structural organization of Mark's Gospel? Mark had not written his Gospel when Paul wrote his letters. But if Paul wrote twenty years before Mark, it is also true that he wrote twenty years after the Lord's death—time enough for him and other Christian sermonizers to meditate on the relation between the old and new religions and conceive a typology and a numerology. We know Paul was capable of typologizing and allegorizing (*Galatians* 4:24). Why not a numerology as well? And, as for Mark and the others, Paul traveled about with Mark and Luke, and he met with the church leaders in Jerusalem: they differed on certain things, but surely they refined each other's thoughts on the issue at hand. Could they, for example, have decided that Christians needed a "sacred seven" to oppose the idolatrous seven of the pagan world—five planets, the sun and moon? The fear of these elemental forces (*stoicheia*) lay heavy upon many pagans, who believed the seven starry bodies to be world-rulers, for good or evil. Paul, in *Galatians*, says that Christians who revert to pre-Christian practices have in fact given in again to these world rulers from whom the gospel rescued them (4:8-10). A godly seven that would prevail against these rulers might have been a thought. What is more certain, however, is that they spoke about Passover: "Christ our Passover is sacrificed for us." And Paul as a doctor of law would know that a certain number was associated with Passover; it is found in *Exodus* 12:6-18, which describes the institution of the Passover rite, as the children are set to begin their pilgrimage to a new home. They are to take a lamb without blemish and on the *fourteenth* day of the first month, in the evening, they must slay it. And "In the first month, on the fourteenth day of the month, ye shall eat unleavened bread...seven days shall there be no leaven found in your houses." The number cannot be used at random: Luke, describing Paul's midnight sea journey (*Acts* 27:27, 33), twice brings up fourteen, and makes a point of it that Paul was adrift in the dark of night.

In *Acts*, Luke places Paul and his journeys in a symbolic setting that makes theological sense of his ordeals. Paul becomes the perfect manifestation of the dictum "*As goes the Master, so goes the disciple.*" Luke tells how Paul was called, tested, made to suffer on his journeys, and finally brought before the same secular powers that put his Lord to death. Luke quotes Paul's very words: "I am ready not only to be imprisoned but to die at Jerusalem for the name of the Lord Jesus." (21:3) Paul is accorded the same mythic treatment that

109

Jesus was given in the gospels: the call, the separation and journey, the suffering, death and rebirth. The pattern is stated or implied at many points in Luke's book: we might look at Paul's third speech where, for the third time he speaks of his call by a Voice from the heavens; he describes it as if it were a Transfiguration—a light seen at midday and brighter than the sun. As Jesus, after his transfiguration, turned his face to Jerusalem and announced his passion three times, so too Paul in *Acts*, having a third time told of his transfiguring vision, begins his final journey, a journey that will take him to Rome and his martyrdom. Luke encloses this last journey within mystic rubrics, telling us that "after three days" Paul calls the leaders of the Jews and speaks to them from morning to night, but they remain unmoved, just as Jesus faced his accusers and they remained unmoved. And, of course, Luke has already presented Paul's four missions, the last prefaced by the sacred number three; and Paul's four sermons (Antioch, Athens, Miletus, Rome); Paul's four miraculous healings; and Paul's denunciation of four false disciples who are unworthy to follow the Lord. Paul himself may not have thought of these numbers (he has thought of other numbers, certainly—not Luke's literary scheme); but Luke has, and he knows exactly what they mean.

Luke's book, it has been observed, consists of four parts; it is not always observed, however, that the fourth part itself consists of four parts. Luke traces the growth of the new community through Jerusalem, Samaria, Judea, and brings history to the eschaton—this as being the fourfold re-enactment of Christ's life during the course of Paul's ministry, leading to his martyrdom. The total of these parts is seven, the hallowed number based on the hebdominal week. Luke, as he writes, has an eye to *The Book of Daniel*, whose author displayed the fortunes of the nation on a numeric scale: four heathen empires have persecuted his people, he said, and in the final week of history the nation will suffer terribly; but God mercifully will shorten this week by half, then his kingdom will come and a new history for his people will begin. Luke adopts this scheme: he presents the church's history during his time as a "half-week" of persecution, and it is the final half day, the fourth that will be most dire for Christians. Luke discovers this pattern in the sacred history of the Jews, beginning with Abraham; Abraham answered the call to get up and go to a strange land, where his children suffer four hundred years (*Acts* 7:6. Luke treats four hundred as the equivalent of four). Journeying is at the very beginning of the national saga. And suffering. Luke tells us that Christians, as true sons of Abraham, must suffer, too, and this suffering is defined by four periods of persecution until the coming of Christ. But Luke has not forgotten Moses. The greatest of heros, Moses' life was divided into three periods of forty years: when he was forty years old, an angel came to him and promised that his people would be delivered; four decades of persecution followed his visit to his people; then, the third period, Moses lead the children through the wilderness of their forty year sojourn. Luke relishes these numbers and the tradition: he places the recital of it on the lips of the dying Stephen, the martyr who receives a vision of the *Son of man* — *Daniel's* heavenly being—moments before he is slain. Stephen stands out as the type of the church's four periods of persecution as she journeys through the wilderness of the world seeking a vision of the heavens.

When Paul, as a new Stephen, begins his sojourn he thinks back upon Moses' sojourn through the wilderness. In his first sermon, at Antioch (*Acts 13-16*), Paul preaches about how the nation's greatest hero had defeated the hostile tribes that inhabited the land and gave it to the children for four hundred and fifty years. The number four hundred and fifty is a novelty, and in context it requires us to meditate upon it. Luke, it seems, has inserted the number into Paul's speech (which Luke himself authored, of course) as a reminder of the *Book of Daniel* and its author's conception of history: four heathen powers followed by a fifth power from above—the last being a divine intervention that saves the nation. Luke has already introduced a fifth power into his narrative: the Pentecost story (*pente*, five) when the holy wind came down from above—a fifty following a forty day time when the risen Jesus lingered with his fellows and told them they would be baptized by the Holy Spirit (*Acts* 1:3-5). Five predicts triumph: the national history celebrated Moses' four decades in the wild followed by forty five decades until Samuel the prophet—forty nine decades; in the fiftieth decade comes David the King and true type of Christ. (Over against all these promising fours Luke sets the recollection of Saul, whose wicked reign lasted forty years.) Luke has Paul looking back to meditate upon the nation's fortunes and its destiny in order to understand his own destiny. Paul, in *Acts*, if not in his own mind, is the hero representative of the New Israel founded by

Christ; he has inherited the mantle from those who went before. He will have his own threes and fours, then a final triumph.

Luke's typology conveys his belief that the series of four in the sacred history, followed by five, signify a final exodus, a deliverance of the church from all earthly afflictions. He begins his book with a five: the harvest festival, Pentecost, when the Holy Spirit came down upon the disciples. This festival itself is a type, for it prefigures the harvesting of all nations at the final coming of Christ. Luke devises a basis upon which the formula for deliverance should rest secure; he ascribes a period of forty days between Jesus' resurrection and the Pentecost festival—a four followed by a five. So then, we have forty days to the ascension, followed by five periods of ten days until God's Spirit descends like a mighty rushing wind: four periods of humiliation for the saints, then, in the fifth, a final Pentecost when all the saints will be gathered in. The numbers bear witness: Luke tells us that three thousand souls were added to the church "on that day"— Pentecost —and, at a later time, five thousand hear and believe (2:41, 4:4). Three seems to be an equivalent of four, as evidenced when Peter heals a lame beggar at the temple gate: it is revealed that he is "more than forty" years old (3:-4:22): four decades he is crippled, then in his fifth, he leaps up to praise God.

The number four, along with three, five and other numbers, attests to the journey that leads to a vision and a revelation of history's end. In Mark's Gospel, four disciples are called up from the sea, tested, proved and made the basis of the new community: then a fifth, Levi, is added, to show in what direction the community must grow. Luke, in *Acts*, wants to show that nothing is worse to the life of the community than a four that fails. In *Daniel*, four empires are depicted as beasts because they are not the true people of God, and they perish. With the Danielic story as a model, Luke proceeds to castigate Theudas, whose messianic pretensions bring upon him the judgment of the wise Galaliel (5:33), who relates that the pretender and four hundred of his followers were justly slain. Luke mentions others who fail: Elymas, and Simon Magnus the magician, whose falsity is exposed by the disciples (8:7). Given the fact that many fail, Luke is keen to prove that Paul is tested and proven. When Paul is bound in chains and brought before the authorities, a centurion mistakes him for a certain Egyptian who caused a revolt that cost the lives of four thousand men (21:38). Paul's "revolution," in contrast, is a peaceful one: when he, like his Lord, is brought before the council, he stands fast—Luke places on his lips one of only three references to resurrection in his address to the council members. Later, Paul survives an attack of forty assassins. Those who hold fast to the hope of resurrection, Luke proclaims, even when brought before the world's hostile powers, will survive as the church passes through the fourfold wilderness to her foretold end.

Four is the marker of a journey undertaken; it is also a premonition of journey's end— *anastasis*, a Greek word used often by Luke. It means "rising up." In *Acts*, it is used together with its opposite, *thanatos*, "death." Death and resurrection mark the climax of Jesus' earthly life; they serve to define his disciples' lot as well. *As goes the master, so goes the disciple.*

When Paul comes to the end of his last journey, he stands in the presence of the very ones who had condemned his Lord and sent him to Calvary; we presume the same fate for him. His fitness for the role has been tested, and Luke allows us to trace this testing through the four phases of his narration. The first of these four parts is prefaced by the word of an angel, the angel who set Peter free from his chains and allowed him to escape the four fours of Herod's soldiers: *anastas*, the angel had said, "Rise up." Peter's bondage in Herod's prison was a notional death. In the prefigured sense, Peter died and was called up from his dust by the angel's summons (*Acts 12:7*). An angel has presided over Stephen's martyrdom, as well has Peter's; it remains for Luke to press the pattern upon Paul as their successor. Paul's first journey, to the Galatia province, is described; Paul gives his first sermon there, Luke tells us, in a synagogue; Luke need not remind his readers that Paul's Lord preached his first sermon in a synagogue, the one in Capernaum. Before long Paul stirs up opposition, as did his Lord. Christ lives again in his disciple. But Paul's discipleship is marked by far more than rejection; he has the power to heal, as did his Lord—*anastathai*, he says to the cripple at Lystra, who gets up and walks. Christ acts through his disciple. And the number four, assigned to him by Luke, follows him everywhere: in all, he visits four provinces of the Empire; he delivers four great sermons; he heals four infirm persons, he puts to shame four false prophets; he suffers persecution in four cities, he is in peril at sea and four times rescued by God. In the course of all this, he becomes more and more like his Lord: his farewell sermon at Miletus (20:18) sounds like his Lord's discourse in *John 17*. As Luke describes how Paul nears his end, he heaps up the fours, to impress us that Paul nears his apotheosis—being like God. When Paul lands at Caesarea (and the reader must recall that Jesus passed through Caesarea Philippi on his way to Calvary), he visits the home of Phillip the evangelist, one of the seven deacons and father of four unmarried daughters; and there he makes plain utterance of Luke's doctrine, saying "I am ready not only to be imprisoned but to die for the Lord's sake." When he arrives at Jerusalem he meets four Nazirites and with them he enters the temple—again, as did his Lord—but whereas his Lord escaped to die another day, Paul is seized in it and taken to the barracks, where he addresses the crowd. He states his case four times: before the crowd, before the Sanhedrin, before Felix, before Agrippa. Following his speech to the council, he is attacked by forty men. He is befriended by four, but nearly outdone by the forty—until four hundred infantry come to rescue him.

The numbers convey inevitability: every good work begun must be finished; every deed of the Master must be imitated by his disciples. In *Acts* Luke relates Paul's vision three times; we are left to expect that Paul will be granted a consummate vision in the near future. Luke's numerological plan spans both his writings, the earlier *Gospel* and the sequel, *Acts of the Apostles*: the two books are a diptych, showing in two panels that what the Lord began must bear fruit in the lives of his followers.

LUKE'S GOSPEL	LUKE'S ACTS
1-2 Incarnation – a descent	1 Ascension – a rising
3 Jesus baptized in water	2 His followers baptized in the Spirit
4 Jesus' message rejected in Nazareth	3-5 Apostles' message rejected in Jerusalem
4:31-9 Galilean works	Parallels distributed
9:10 Feeding of 5000	6 Feeding of widows
9:28 Transfiguration before three witnesses	7:55 Stephen sees Jesus in glory
9:51 Samaritan village	8 Phillip in Samaria
10 Mission of seventy	6-8 Mission of seven
10-13 Journey begins; Israel is condemned	8-13 Church leaves Israel and goes forth to the Gentiles
13 Herod intends to kill Jesus	12 Herod intends to kill Peter

14-18 Journey continues; the gospel to the downcast	13-20 The gospel to the Gentiles
9-19 Jesus' journey to Jerusalem	19-21 Paul's journey to Jerusalem
20-23 Jesus' passion and four trials	21-26 Paul's passion and four trials
23 Jesus' death	27 Paul's "death"
24 Jesus' resurrection Jesus' ascension	28 Paul's "resurrection" Paul's arrival at Rome, his expected martyrdom and final (fourth) vision

That Christ's incarnation is a descent is implied by the Angel's announcement ("the Holy Spirit will come upon you and overshadow you..."); at the beginning of *Acts* Luke tells of Jesus' ascent to the heavens from whence he came. The two panels of the diptych are bonded by the number four: forty weeks from the Angel's annunciation to the nativity; forty days from the resurrection to the ascension. The ascension serves as end to the Lord's earthly ministry; it stands also as the beginning of a new story to be told; it is the first panel of a new diptych. Two angels announce another ascent (1:11) when the Lord's followers will be united with him in the heavens where he has gone on ahead. Luke has conveyed this expectation with such force that for centuries Christians have taken the Lord's ascension as a surety of the ascended life for all. St. Augustine, a doctor of the church (354-430 C.E.), has said that Christ our Head has entered into glory and will draw all his members after him. And the reformer John Calvin in the sixteenth century wrote "Since our soul and body are appointed to heavenly life and immortality...we must therefore exert ourselves to see that they are kept pure and blameless until the day of his appearing." They built upon Scriptural foundations. The author of *The Epistle to the Hebrews* called Jesus the "pioneer" of our faith; a pioneer goes ahead so others may follow. And the biblical image of first-fruits implies a Pentecostal harvest; we will be harvested by a heavenly hand and gathered up to a new home in the skies.

Luke's book is certainly about the ascended life and how disciples ascend to the heavens by becoming more like their ascended Lord: he did miracles, so do they; he aroused opposition, so do they; he suffered, so do they; he died at journey's end, so will they; he ascended, so will they.

The disciple's journey is depicted by another Lucan literary symbol: the Apostolic Day. So often in the book is the time of day

115

made known, and by quarters, that it draws our attention. At the beginning, Pentecost, the holy wind descends in the morning—the third hour of the day, as Jews reckon it. A proper beginning, for the day begins at sunup. But the point is supernatural. Christ is the dayspring from on high, the Light of the world, who comes up like a sun after his night of death. Thus begins the Day's journey. As the Light reaches its zenith, it begins to decline and it passes again into the night. Those who follow the Lord will accompany him on this journey from sunup to dark of Day's end; a night of death and a rising anew. Luke projects this symbol onto the life of the new community. The Lord's rising commences the new Day, at daybreak; the holy wind sweeps in at the third hour—the Light is in its ascendant, and the disciples are "of one accord," and have all things in common. The meridian is reached at noon, and its divine unity is untroubled. Paul's vision at noon confirms the meridian. But come the ninth hour, Peter and John go to the temple, where they heal a man, thus giving cause for complaint to those whom Peter offended by his speech; the church moves past its apostolic meridian. At the end of the Day that began with Peter and John praying in the temple (4:3- "...it was already evening...") a crisis besets the disciples; they are taken into custody of the priests and temple guards—the same ilk that took Jesus away after his appearance in the temple. But at the end of their four-quartered Day, their labors bear fruit, for the number of those who hear them and come to believe is five thousand.

The Day of course is rhetorical and literary; it is based on a numeric symbolism that is used elsewhere in Scripture; it draws the apostolic labors into the stream of destiny as the Apostolic Day runs from the Lord's rising to the rising of the tested and true disciples. We come upon the climax (5:19) when we read that "...at night the angel of the Lord opened the prison doors and brought them out and said 'go stand in the temple' and when they heard this they entered the temple at daybreak and taught."

At night the angel came. What night is this? If the Day is no ordinary day, the Night can be no ordinary night. It is the Night in which Paul faces four crises and his entire nocturnal journey. Luke does not fail to tell us of the dark. In a night vision Paul sees a man call to him from Macedonia; he goes there and falls among enemies (16:25). So much in Paul's life is shrouded in darkness. In prison, he and Silas are praying when an earthquake strikes - - midnight, we are told. But Paul seeks always to redeem the night's evil—when he and Silas are released from prison they offer spiritual counsel to the jailer, who then feeds them. On another occasion, Paul is preaching a Sunday evening sermon in an upper room; his words prove too heavy for a young man named Eutchyus, who is overcome by a deep sleep and falls from a third story to his death—whereupon Paul raises him to life and leads the congregation in the breaking of bread. These nocturnal miracles and sacraments—the escape from prison, the upper room, the First Day, a threefold death and resurrection, the breaking of bread, feeding—take us back to the spiritual world of the gospels and the works of the Lord. As for the Night—it is the Night of the Lord's apocalyptic discourse, when he spoke of the sun, how it will be darkened; and the moon, how it will fail to give its light; and the stars, how they will fall from the heavens (*Mark* 13:24 and *Luke* 21:25); and it is the Night in which Jesus burst his three day prison. It is our Night, too...the dark Night of our souls in which the Christ will appear in bright clouds of glory.

The dark was sometimes a literal dark for Paul, before Luke saw its potential as a symbol. For the Romans dug deep into the ground when they built their prisons and they favored locations near public sewers; a more convincing symbol for death could hardly be imagined. Each time an apostle was imprisoned, Luke must have seen him being lowered into his grave, just as Mark had seen the image of death when a paralyzed man was lowered through a roof into the Lord's presence. When Luke wrote his book he saw in his mind's eye the descent of the apostles into a tomb; he may also have seen the angel who brings them up. In *Acts* the arrests begin early on: three times apostles are seized and thrown into prison (4:3, :17, 5:40). The story of Peter and John being arrested is capped by the number five as five thousand souls come to believe in Jesus' resurrection. At the second arrest the Lord's angel springs open the prison doors and the apostles come forth to enter the temple at daybreak. The third arrest leads to a beating; the Jews intend to kill them but they are saved by the saintly Gamaliel, who was Paul's mentor at one time. The beating calls to mind Paul's words in his last Corinthian epistle: ... "far more imprisonments, with countless beatings, and often near death," he wrote, "and five times received I the forty lashes save one. Three times beaten with rods, once was I stoned, three times shipwrecked... I must boast... I knew a man who fourteen years ago was taken up into the third heaven..." It is as if Paul has completed Luke's thoughts for him: descending into prison, like a death...then being called back to life as if by the angel who announced his Lord's resurrection. *Thanatos, anastasis*; death and resurrection.

Or does Luke complete Paul's thoughts? The two were companions on the sea crossing over to Rome; as they spoke, what was on the mind of one must have been on the tongue of the other and eventually in the writing of both. We ought not be surprised, therefore, if Paul's ascent to the third heaven finds typological expression in *Acts*, where Luke relates their adventure at sea. "When the fourteenth night had come," Luke writes, "as we were drifting across the sea, about midnight...fearing we might run aground..." (27:27, 33). He repeats the fourteen, lest the reader miss it: "As the day was about to dawn, Paul urged them to take some food, saying 'today is the fourteenth day that you have continued in suspense and without food...' " Our mind turns again to 2 *Corinthians* and the number fourteen. We have stated that fourteen was to signify twice seven, the sacred week that God ordained in *Genesis*. In *Acts*, the number seven and its double allude to *Exodus*, the story of the journeying Israelites, where fourteen takes us to paschal midnight (Ex. 12:18). On the fourteenth of the month the children ate their Passover bread and made their exodus, coming at length to the waters of the Red Sea. They bore with them the obligation to observe the feast and abstain from leaven for seven days. So then, as Luke and Paul make their exodus through the waters they are observing a spiritual Passover, pilgrims who seek safety in God's helping hand who will again part the waters for his chosen ones, as they sail at a dangerous time, the equinox, when winds and currents are most treacherous, and they are sailing where the waters are already parted in two (the ship goes where two seas meet and there it strikes ground). In the mind of the apostles, it is paschal midnight and they look for their deliverance in the midst of waters. They think of Moses, for whom God split the sea in two so that the children could walk on the sea bottom with unmoistened feet and rise to safety on the shore of the promised land. And they are saved, they and the entire ship's company, and Paul's words of encouragement suggest the Christian Passover and unleavened bread. They are saved from death: the sea, to the Jew, was death itself; they sang liturgical praises to God whose hand had drowned their enemies as He saved their fathers from it. Now, in a new Exodus, God has acted again, leading his chosen ones through parted seas to a risen life in the promised land beyond the seas.

Going down into the sea, being cast into prison—these are the dangers that the apostles face as they journey to their destined end. Each is a death: merely a symbolic death, we might think; but we do not easily comprehend the Semitic experience of life and what it takes to lose it. Death is in the midst of life, the apostle Paul has told us often; it is an experience that the living have when they suffer or fall into unbelief. We think of death as a status—we are dead or we are not. The Semitic mind, however, thinks of the wilderness or the sea as a place of death and if a man enters upon it he has entered death's portal. A man walks out into the wilderness: he may perish today or the next, it matters not, for he dies the moment he sets foot outside safe boundaries. In Luke's parable of the Prodigal Son, the younger son is pronounced "Dead" by his father. ("This my son was dead, but is alive; let us kill the fatted calf.") To be lost is to be dead; to be sick is to be dead; to be in prison or at sea is to be dead. Paul died, he tells his readers, when he was beaten, and stoned, and lost at sea: "We despaired of life: yes, we had the sentence of death within ourselves, that we should not trust in ourselves but in God who raises the dead, who delivered us out of such great death, and will deliver." (*2 Corinthians 1:8-10*) Death is in the midst of life.

When the apostles are set free from their prisons they are signs of the resurrected life. The angel who breaks open the prison doors testifies to this truth (5:19-20—the angel tells the apostles to go forth and speak the words of *this life*, which they do *as soon as day breaks*). They are set free at night, we read. We have spoken of this Night—it is the mystical dark that shrouds the hero's journey. Luke has written his book in four parts, we have noted, and the last part is in four parts; this last part is particularly darkened by Paul's journeys and his sufferings—and his "deaths." As we read of the apostle's sufferings, we recall his Lord's sufferings, and the three times he predicted his passion; Jesus too entered into his death even as he contemplated it. In the dark of Olivet and Gethsemane (*Luke 21:37-38; Mark 14:17-15:1*) Jesus speaks of the darkening sky in which the heavenly lights will fail, men will faint, the sea and the waves will roar, and, Jesus adds— he who will burst his three day prison at night -- men will look up and see their redemption draw nigh.

When we return to Paul's ascent-vision in *2 Corinthians*, we shall study it against the darkened sky of Luke's fourth cycle in *Acts*. In this epistle, Paul spoke first of his sufferings then of his ascent to the third heaven. We have seen already how Luke describes Paul's vicissitudes in the dark of prisons and in the deep waters at night, followed always by the break of day. It is dark, Luke points out, when the sailors who guide Paul's ship let out four anchors from the stern and pray for the light of day. It comes, and when it does they find themselves in a new and strange land. And we, too, sense that we have come to a new and strange land when we read that angels deliver apostles from prisons, and that Paul rouses a young boy from his fall into death, and the apostle escapes persecution by the Sanhedrin by fleeing during the third hour of the night. Luke speaks of the Day that is at hand when the night is far spent. Paul, in his ascent-vision, wrote of the Day into which he entered when he emerged from the dark into the Lord's light.

But first we must appreciate Paul's concern for his Corinthian congregants and his reason for telling them about his ascent-vision. Paul had opponents in Corinth. We do not know as much about them as we would like, but Paul makes it clear that they preached a gospel that he considered strange and contrary to what he had taught when he was there in person. First, as we read his letters (we can identify four letters in all), he mentions an eloquent and learned Alexandrian Jew named Apollos, who must have arrived in Corinth shortly after one of Paul's visits. When Paul speaks of Apollos, he reveals his humanity; he sounds jealous of this charismatic leader who replaced him. Over against the Alexandrian's brilliance, Paul asserts the merits of suffering. Suffering, Paul says, comes before the glory and the dark comes before the light. The disciple must follow in the way of the Master, who took upon himself the suffering of his rejection and crucifixion. Paul goes on the speak of his "deaths" on land and sea, then he tells of how he was raised to glory. His authority is thus sealed by Jesus himself, who called him, sustained him through his sufferings, rescued him and granted him a view of the heavens. What better authority can there be? Apollos cannot make such claims, Paul implies. But what claims did Paul's opponents actually make?

Again, we do not know, but we may guess that they, too, claimed to have visions. We may assume this since Paul seems to set his vision over against them. Paul's point then is that the vision without suffering is sham. It is also possible to wonder if the opponents induced their visions by artificial means. If so, Paul would not have approved. Perhaps they claimed to have brought on their visions by means of their sacraments and liturgies; perhaps they ignored the importance of the body when they spoke of the ascended life (were they having "out of body" experiences?). Again, Paul would not have approved. (He seems to chide them when he says in his account that he does not know if he was in the body or out of it—only God knows such things.) For their edification, therefore, he describes his ascent-vision as a model of what a Christian may aspire to as he contemplates his journey's end.

Having considered Paul's relationship with the Corinthians, we must consider the larger world of Paul's time, and what others thought of mystic journeys. If anyone went into a barbershop in, say, Athens, around the time in question, he would hear the latest story of a cult leader or ecstatic who claimed to have visited the highest heaven, whether that be a third or a seventh. Local debate would focus on this person's credibility, and his worth relative to other voyagers or mystery religions. The world Paul lived in and preached to was full of stories about people who had ascended into the heavens. Most of these stories concerned Gentiles, but Jews told such stories, too. In a typical report, a person is so honored because he has led an exceptional life, or he has magical powers that he will not divulge to outsiders; he ascends into the heavens for a brief but glorious moment, having been challenged on the way by hostile beings who resent this intrusion into their realms. In the oldest literature on this subject, the man who ascends does so as an invader from below; his true abode is on earth, he has no destiny above; following his brief moment of glory, he must return to earth and never ascend again. What, we wonder, is the purpose of such an unnatural event? The answer seems to be, in some cases, that a man was deemed exceptional.

By contrast, the Jews viewed an ascent as a seal, a warranty. As *Exodus* says of Moses, God's intent was to impart a revelation so special that ordinary dreams or angelic messengers would not dignify it. Moses, therefore, is called to the top of a fiery mountain to receive the revelation that he must give to his people; the ascent certifies to the nation that this revelation is from God and is to be honored. There is no hint that Moses is divine and has a future in the starry heavens. On the contrary, Moses, like all his fellows, belongs here on earth, a three-tiered creation that has at its center a flat disc surrounded by chaotic waters. The disc is the earth; below roam the dead–this is sheol; above is the vault of heaven where God dwells. Man's lot is to live here on earth in obedience to God's laws and be content with it.

But in the Greek world, things began to change; a new cosmology came to regard earth as the bottom rung of a cosmic ladder that extends up through seven planetary spheres, all of them alive with supernatural beings, and Divinity presides at the very top. This shift in world-view made for profound changes in the way men regarded themselves: a man could think of his destiny as above; he ought to be looking up; he is a stranger on earth and should strive to ascend through the spheres into God's very presence. This new attitude made its way into late Judaism. *First Enoch* contains a fantasy based on a figure from the *Book of Genesis* (4:17;5:18), Enoch, who is both a third from Adam and a seventh—highly qualified for a mystic journey. According to the fantasy, Enoch was taken up through the seven heavens where he learned many secrets and was glorified before God. His flight to the heavens foretells a divine future for himself and his fellows. Man is a stranger on earth, this fantasy seems to say; his true home is above where an immortal destiny awaits him. It is possible, therefore, for an individual to risk danger and aspire to heavenly places; in so doing he will stand apart from his fellows and his nation in order to assert his true status as a citizen of the heavenly realm. In other literature the earthly life is depicted as a prison; souls long for release so that they may soar to the beyond. Those who do escape may return to inspire their fellows: this is the story of Ur, a slain warrior mentioned by Plato; he wandered outside his body for twelve days, Plato says, during which time he was entrusted with knowledge of rewards and retributions in the hereafter, and he saw a gathering of deceased spirits in a meadow, who, after seven days began a four day journey to a place of light where they were given to understand the mysteries of the spheres; Ur returned to earth and advised his fellows how to live so as to obtain the blessed hereafter. Another Greek story relates how one Aridaius fell from a great height and was dead for three days; but he revived during his funeral to astound his friends; he underwent a noble transformation of character and edified his friends by telling of his celestial journey. In these stories we have the type of ascent-vision that may be called *proleptic*; a man is blessed by a vision that gives him foreknowledge of his future state and the future of his fellows. The aforementioned 1 *Enoch*, in a section called *The Parables of Enoch*, expands the legend: the hero of *Genesis* tells how...

> ...in those days a whirlwind carried me off from the earth,
> and set me down at the end of the heavens,
> And there I saw another vision, the dwelling places of the holy,
> And the resting places of the righteous.
> Here mine eyes saw their dwellings with
> His righteous angels,
> And their resting places with the holy.
> There I wished to dwell,
> And my spirit longed for that dwelling place.

The garments of glory had been prepared for him and awaited him besides God's throne. Scholars like Carol Zaleski have noted this point; she draws the comparison to Paul's doctrine of the resurrection body that the mortal body will inherit. It is as if the new garments and the body that will wear them have always existed—*it is exactly like that, for it is man's immortal nature that is identified here, body and all*. The text suggests another Pauline doctrine, that in the highest heaven the person sees himself *as God sees him*. These are suggestive notions only, but consistent with the experiences of many others. The clear doctrine behind 2 *Enoch*, however, is this: God has prepared many mansions for His beloved saints. Enoch, when he returned to earth, offered this message to his fellows: he put it in writing, an effort that required thirty days and nights and filled three hundred and sixty books; he told his fellows that his cosmic tour lasted sixty days; and, upon completing his writing, he handed his books to his sons and, after thirty days of preparation, ascended into the heavens a final time, whereupon he donned his heavenly garb and dwelt eternally with God.

Garments of glory are described also in a Christian text from the first or second century C.E. called *The Ascension of Isaiah*. This fantasy concerning the Old Testament great has him taken up through the seven heavens; at the second heaven the prophet was overcome by the splendor he saw and fell down in worship, but was told not to worship yet, for such worship is proper only in the seventh heaven where he will be given a crown and new garments befitting his status as an immortal. The prophet rejoiced greatly to hear that his exalted status will in time be enjoyed by all the faithful. His ascent prefigures theirs; all will be arrayed in garments of glory. As he ascended from height to height toward the seventh heaven he saw other heros from the nation's past, like Abel, Enoch, and many righteous men, all clothed in glory like unto the angels.

The righteous live in this heaven; it is theirs, their home; and Enoch will join this company of immortals, the sons of God, all transfigured and shining as lights.

> My face was changed
> for I could no longer behold...

He is blinded by the glory of it; his countenance becomes transfigured to resemble theirs. This text is a model of the proleptic ascent: Enoch beheld his own blessed future—he will, when time comes, ascend into the heavens. When this happens, he will not die; he will be taken up "during his lifetime" and join the blessed ones he had visited in his vision.

> And it came to pass after this that my spirit
> was translated,
> And it ascended into the heavens;
> And I saw the holy ones of God.
> They were stepping on flames of fire:
> Their garments were white,
> And their faces shone like snow.

A later text, from early in the Christian era, continues the theme of the hero's ascent (2 *Enoch*): two angels carried him aloft through the seven heavens to see the Lord, whereupon Enoch was transformed. The Lord commanded the Archangel Michael:

> Go take Enoch out of his earthly garments
> and anoint him with my sweet ointments, and put
> garments of glory...

Having been dressed in new garments, Enoch said:

> and I looked at myself and was like one of his
> glorious ones, and there was no difference.

Paul's ascent story, therefore, is not unique. The Gentile world relished such stories, and so did his own countrymen, including, possibly, his opponents in Corinth. But Paul's personal story is unique in the New Testament, for he alone, of all the sacred writers, tells us of Christ as he is known by mystical vision. And it is by mystical vision alone that we can approach Christ.

Based upon what Luke and Paul tell us, we must conclude that Paul's vision is of a certain type: it is not the earlier type, that accorded to Moses in *Exodus*; rather, it is the later type, in which the mortal is called up as if to his proper home and is no alien in heaven, and where he receives a new nature in the form of a spiritual persona and a "resurrection body," and regards his ascent as prefigurative of a general resurrection of all. As we make this claim, we assume that Paul is consistent: that what he learned from his vision taught him— or confirmed for him—the doctrine that we find in his epistles.

In *1 Corinthians* he presents his famous paean of praise to the triadic virtues, faith, hope, and love (*1 Cor. 13:1-13*). The greatest of these, he says, is love; it never fails. *Never*. The implication of *never* is that these virtues are qualities of the ascended life in the heavens where the sense of immortality is gained and all good things are known to last forever. He goes on to speak of knowledge. What kind of knowledge? He speaks first of a knowledge that in this life is imperfect, like the knowledge of a child that is put away when the child becomes mature. This is an analogy: a man's present knowledge is like his image in a mirror, dimly seen. (Mirrors in Paul's day where dim, indeed; the best of them were made of bronze. Paul's analogy is a fine touch, actually, for Corinth was a bronze-working center, where these better mirrors were made.) In the future state, however, there will be true knowledge, for—he implies—it will be based on vision. "Now I know in part," he says, "then I shall understand fully, even as I have been fully understood." *As he has been understood*. Who has fully understood Paul but God? Paul's paean therefore, is based on his ascent-vision, for it was the vision that gave him this self-knowledge as well as knowledge of the triadic virtues that characterize the ascended life. The spiritual aspirant achieves this in the third stage of his progress, as Fr. Augustine Baker has pointed out. In this stage all the virtues are fused into one will by God's act when the aspirant enters His presence. The aspirant then comes to know himself through God's own eyes.

In his Corinthian epistles (*1 Cor. 15*) Paul goes on to state the source of the gospel he preaches. He reminds his friends in Corinth that his preaching is the common gospel of the church, for all have seen the risen Lord: the gospel holds that "Christ died for our sins, that he was buried, that he was raised on the third day as the scriptures had said, and that he was seen by Cephas, then by the twelve; after that, he was seen by over five hundred brothers all at once...after that he was seen by James, then by all the apostles, and finally he was seen by myself..." Paul's liturgical recitation is based on the number seven: seven instances of the perfect tense of the verbs *died, buried, raised, seen, seen, seen, seen*. Three of the visions are to individuals (Cephas, James, Paul himself), three to groups (the twelve first, then the five hundred, finally all the apostles). Paul's use of seven and three may at this point reflect the linking of the world's beginning and end: the seven day creation week, and the three days that, according to some rabbis, would intervene between the demise of the old creation and the general resurrection. Paul speaks, however, not simply as one who has listened to the rabbis, nor as one whose gospel came from those in Jerusalem, (nor as a student who has made a rabbinic interpretation of *Hosea 6:2*, "on the third day we shall be raised"); he speaks as a visionary. A prophet, yes, but more; he speaks as one whose knowledge is perfect; the risen Christ called him on the road to Damascus and then took him up to the third heaven where he saw what Enoch saw—immortal souls clothed in garments prepared for them from the beginning of time.

The garment in which the risen saint is clothed is a body. Is it this *mortal* body, the one we live in and experience "on this side?" Paul, recalling his ascent-vision, is able to speak of such a body...but his tongue is set a-trembling. Those who ascend to such heights are forbidden or unable to speak of the glories they have seen. Paul tries to speak, however, as best he can, for he wishes to give his fellows the gift of this message, that they may have faith and hold steadfast in the face of heretics and persecutors. Besides, they are pressing him for answers to their questions; if he fails to answer, they may be led astray by Apollos or the other false preachers. He does the best he can. "With what kind of a body are they raised?" is a question put to him (*1 Cor. 15:35*). Paul understands the terms in which this question is stated: it is the traditional Jewish doctrine of a literal raising of the dead in the last days. Paul's ascent has taught him that each person is already clothed in a glorious body, but does not know this of himself because he sees reality dimly, through a bronze mirror. How to explain this? Paul is no different from all the others who have been illuminated and perceive the truth about themselves: the "new" body is continuous with the "old"— it *is* the old, but seen at last in its fullness. But he considers it best to explain this to the Corinthians as an analogy: as birds of the air, fish of the sea, and land creatures have the kinds of bodies they need for their present lives on earth, Christians will have the kind of body they will need for the life to come. He speaks proleptically; what he knows to be true now, he asserts, will be true for all when God's trump calls up the dead from their sleep in the ground.

Paul has managed to conflate the Greek and Jewish traditions. Greek philosophers, such as Plato, believed in an immortal soul in man that survives the body's death. The Jewish belief at about the time that Paul lived and wrote is that at some appointed end-time God will raise the dead —bodily—from their graves. Paul could not abide the Greek notion of some spirit that could claim no body for itself; he was a Jew and never departed from this basic conviction. Yet, in spite of his apocalyptic language about an end-time resurrection, his vision conferred upon him a sense of the end in the present moment; eternity now; immediate immortality and a heavenly wardrobe. He speaks in the Jewish idiom and preaches a future resurrection, but his assurance derives from his self-knowledge, which in turn derived from his *being known even as he is known*, that is, being clothed in garments of glory and seeing himself as he truly is, and his Lord as *he* truly is. Consistent with the heroic impulse to give a gift to others upon his return from the high and holy place, Paul conveys the gift in the form of proleptic—we should say, prophetic—assurances that what he has come to know they all will come to know, what has been true from the beginning, since Adam, that man is divine.

Paul insists that his vision of the Lord is the equivalent of the visions vouchsafed to the apostolic leaders of the church. (Luke

127

differs with his friend: he says there can be no sightings of Jesus following Jesus' bodily ascension into heaven.) Paul's words are clear enough; he saw the Lord in the flesh. In light of these words, we are compelled to rethink whatever notion we may have had of the ascension and take it to mean not a separation of the Lord from flesh but the Lord's transmutation of the flesh, as prefigured by the scene on the mount (*Mark* 9); or, in psychological terms, Paul was empowered in his vision to see the truth not only of his own nature, but the truth about his Lord as well. The veil was pulled aside; the seer saw what has been there all along. He saw a man who was dead. As Jew and a doctor of the law, he was constrained to describe this knowledge in terms of a bodily resurrection from the dead. He wishes to tell his friends in Corinth this new truth; he tells them that all will be raised to be with the Lord. The saints, therefore, have no need of further visions—they will be with the Lord soon enough. Hence, Paul tells his friends that his vision of the Lord is the last of all prior to the general resurrection, which is to be expected in the near future.

Paul's ascent-vision proved to him that the dead will live again, and that he was endowed by the vision with authority to preach this doctrine to all who would listen. Yet in 1 *Corinthians 15:8* he says "And last of all He appeared to me *as one untimely born...*" Why this curious phrase? It could be said that he feigns humility, as if to say "He actually appeared to me, this so-called abortion of an apostle." His enemies may well have called him a mal-formed soul, recalling how he persecuted Christians before he became one, and we may guess that Paul alludes to this criticism. And Paul was keenly aware, too, that he was the *last* to have seen the Lord, and therefore his enemies considered him the least of all who call themselves apostles. Paul admits that it took a miracle to bring him into the world, and another miracle to make him live again as an apostle, bearing the authority of the Lord himself in his very words. Paul drives home his claim to authority by his use of the curious phrase *as one untimely born*. For Paul alludes to the fact that he is a Benjaminite, and in *Genesis* we read of an untimely birth, that of Benjamin, whose unfortunate mother's dying words were to name the boy *Ben-omi*—"son of my sorrow." But Jacob, the boy's father, determined to name him *Ben-jamin*, "son of the right hand." What this means in oriental protocol is that one who sits on the right hand of a ruler or deity shares the power of that person. (The Christian creed states that Jesus ascended into heaven and sits on the right hand of the Father.) Benjamin, therefore, can expect to come into power, and he does—when his descendant Paul the Benjamite comes to claim his place among his apostolic brethren. Mark understood this: in his Gospel he made Benjamin a type of the blind Bartimaeus (*Mark 10:35ff*) who comes to Jesus with a request. The name Bar-timaeus means "Son of the honorable one," and in the Marcan context we read that two disciples, James and John, have made an unreasonable request of the Lord, that he grant them places of honor when the Lord comes into his kingdom. The request is denied. But Jesus grants the request of the blind beggar who wishes to regain his sight. Paul alludes to this known incident and applies its significance to himself as a member of the apostolic college, where he asserts his place at the right hand of glory. *He has been to the right hand of glory.* His claim, therefore, is based on his ascent-vision; and his felicitous phrase *as one untimely born* conveys to memory what Paul, we may believe, must have told the Corinthians when he was among them and spoke of his visions—first, the one that turned his life about, gave him a new birth and a new name, and, notwithstanding his late arrival, a place among his fellow Christians; and, second, the ascent-vision that confirmed the first, and assured him, like Bartimaeus, a place in the true Kingdom.

But this is not all: Paul has been speaking of Scripture and he has appealed to it as a warrant for his authority. In Scripture, young Benjamin was taken with his father down into Egypt when a great famine overcame the land and drove the patriarchal family to plead for grain. In that land they beheld the "resurrection" of one whom they believed dead, Joseph, the beloved son of his father, whose blood stained garment had been offered to the father as token of his death, who had overcome treachery, temptations, imprisonment, and great suffering, and finally risen to authority in that land when he was thirty years old, so that he stood at the right hand of the king himself and had authority to administer the life-saving grain. (*Genesis 35-45*). Joseph revealed himself to his father and brethren at a banquet and his authority among them was never again in dispute; his dreams were proven true—his sheaves were greater than his brothers', and the son and moon and stars offered him obeisance. Not only did he prove to be their superior, he proved to be their savior; as a lord risen from the dead he had power to administer the bread of life to all, even to those who betrayed him. Nothing in all Scripture is more clear than that Joseph is a type of the Christ. As for Benjamin, the one *untimely born*, he also is a beloved of his father, and is given to sit at the right hand of Christ in glory and assist in administering to his brethren the supreme gift, the bread of life immortal.

But Paul was not honored as a Benjamite when he met with the successors to Jacob's twelvefold family. The apostles were less than receptive to Paul and his claims; they particularly resisted his mission to the Gentile world. Paul states (*Galatians 2:11*) that he "withstood Cephas to his face." It seems that Luke's doctrine of an original unity was more a matter of pattern than reality. There were power struggles from the start; we see evidence of this in the most sacred scenes: John's gospel offers a piece of theological stagecraft when he tells us (20:4-8) that the "other disciple outran Peter to the tomb, and was the first to believe." Clearly, the evangelist favored the one over the other. Given the reality of these struggles, it is easy to understand why Paul, in *Corinthians*, had to present his credentials; not simply an exegesis of the *Genesis* story, but his ascent to a heavenly court where such matters are decided.

Political conflict caused an eruption of images and numbers in Paul's mind when he wrote *Galatians*—rather, when he dictated its composition to a scribe, for he became so excited near the end that he grabbed the stylus from the scribe's hand and finished the letter himself with bold letters. His ascent to heaven gave him no inner peace, it seems. He struggled against inner demons and black spells––enemies within and without. He always identified with the Lord's sufferings, which began at Passover, when the Lord took bread and broke it and gave it to all— then went into the dark of Gethsemene and Calvary. So, when he wrote to the Galatians and asked who bewitched them? his mind turned to Passover images and those last days of his Lord. We read that "after three years" he went to Jerusalem and met with Peter. He remained there, he says, "fifteen days," then went on mission for "fourteen years." Finally, he went a second time to Jerusalem, along with Barnabas—this is Joseph surnamed Barnabas, which means "Son of comfort." Barnabas, we learn from *Acts 4,* sold his property to help provide relief to Christians in Judea. Luke, in *Acts 11:27-30*, indicates fear of a world-wide famine, (which never materialized), and we may assume Luke contrived with Paul to represent Joseph Barnabas as true to his namesake, Joseph of old, whose oversight of the grain delivered his countrymen from famine, according to the *Genesis* story. Paul's mind, when he wrote of his visits to Jerusalem, turned to the ancient history and its heros, and to recent events—the Lord's own Passover provision for his people, a work that Paul believed he carried on in the Lord's name.

The evangelists often represent the Lord's work under the figure of bread: Scripture provided the history and the image, beginning with the first evening Passover meal, manna in the wilderness, then the Lord's taking the bread into his own hands, first in the wilderness, then in the upper room where he gathered during Passover with his twelve disciples. The bread image is linked with the night and the number twelve. In the gospels, twelve indicates the fullness of Israel– –twelve loaves for twelve thousand—and the mission to the Gentiles– –twelve basketfuls of crumbs left over for their provision. Bread nourishes the growth of the church, we might say, as it embraces both Jew and Gentile. The church, Luke says, grows *day and night*. (Luke offers the lesson of the importunate widow who prayed *day and night*: in his *Gospel 18:3-7)*. Jews enter by day, Gentiles by night. Luke's numbers symbolism makes the point; if three thousand souls are added at the third hour (*Acts 2:41*), then twelve thousand should be added by the end of a twelve hour day. We have discussed Luke's concept of the Apostolic Day. As the day moves into night, Paul's work with the Gentiles enters a symbolic dark, for the twelve night hours are what remains for him. Night, the Passover night, implies death—the Angel of Death, who slew the firstborn in Egypt. Jesus has no bread to give the world apart from his Passover death. Paul understood this. As an individual, he seems to have been naturally inclined to attacks of anxiety; as an apostle, his anxiety was an existential death. How often we find in his writings that in the midst of life he finds death.

As we study Paul's life and mission we realize that in him the monomyth has been projected into the skies. He is the hero who has been called—when he was "converted" on the way to Damascus— then hurled into a three day dark for nurture. He begins his new work, and encounters opposition both natural and supernatural; "powers and principalities," he calls them (*Colossians 1:16*). He finally arrives at his goal—his ascent to the third heaven or paradise where he is initiated into the heart of mystery, things that cannot be told. Like a Passover pilgrim, he has come at last to the Feast in the Promised Land, Paradise. To share the graces of his experience with men he travels about the empire preaching and teaching what he has learned about the Christ who called him.

An analysis of Paul's account of his ascent-vision to the third heaven will help us understand what it meant to him and how he interpreted it to others.

Whether by design or not, Paul's words in *2 Corinthians 12* present a diptych:

I knew a man in Christ	And I know that this man
fourteen years ago	whether in the body or
whether in the body or not	separate from the body
I do not know	I do not know
God knows	God knows
	was caught up into
was caught up into the	Paradise
third heaven	
	he heard words which are
	unlawful to speak

Does Paul, in this text, merely retell the "conversion" vision that came to him on the Damascus road? Or does he mean that he had two visions—first the Damascus vision that converted him, then a second vision some years later? Or, does he mean that he had two visions and the second was a two-staged journey—first, to the "third heaven," then to "Paradise?" (It is even possible to guess that in this text he uses "third heaven" to refer to the Damascus vision, and "Paradise" to the second vision.) As we have said, Paul wrote in haste; he may have assumed that his Corinthian readers would understand his meanings without further explanation. Obviously, the apostle had no consideration for twentieth century scholars.

We will say this: if Paul had two distinct visions years apart, he is in good company. Jacob Behmen, for example, had first a glimpse of glory then years later the glory itself. Of course, we should not judge Paul's words by the experience of others. We have looked at Paul's text already; let us return to it and attempt a literary analysis.

It looks like Paul wrote in the manner of much Hebrew poetry. In the Bible we find many "coupled phrases"—a phrase is given, then repeated. Sometimes the second phrase amplifies the first. Even some prose has this quality: "Through the window she looked/Sisera's mother cried through the lattice; why is his chariot so long in coming/why tarry the wheels of his chariots?" (*Judges 5:28*) *Psalm 59* begins: "Deliver me from mine enemies, O my God/defend me from them that rise up against me; deliver me from the workers of iniquity/and save me from the bloody men." The last verselet amplifies the first; we learn that the poet's enemies are bloody men. Is Paul's text like this? One vision repeated in verse but not in fact? Or were there two visions in fact? It may be impossible to settle the matter on literary grounds: a look at *Numbers* 24:17 exposes the problem—"I see him but not now/I behold him but not nigh; there shall come forth a star out of Jacob/and a scepter shall rise out of Israel." Are star and scepter symbols of the same dynasty? Or does star designate priesthood while scepter designates royalty? We can make a reasonable guess about the *Numbers* text, but what shall we do with Paul?

Is "Paradise" a repeated phrase that means "third heaven" in a parallel literary edifice? Or is "Paradise" something else, different and beyond "third heaven," such as "seventh heaven." The issue may seem academic; but we need to distinguish Paul's experience—*his understanding of it*— from pagan cultic practices: "third heaven" may have suggested some pagan religious practice, so that Paul would have acted immediately to clarify his intent. "Yes, I meant the third heaven," he points out, "...but in the sense of our ancestral home, Paradise, as our Scripture tells us." He would feel the need to do this because the number three related to many pagan notions and practices: very often the ancients believed that three days or months or years stood between the beginning and end of some momentous event—the Egyptian priests, for example, celebrated the recovery of their murdered goddess Isis three days after her death. And the Mithraic religion, which Paul would have known from his youth in Tarsus, tried to induce mystical journeys in their worshipers, and the number three is involved:

> Draw in from the rays, drawing up three times
> as much as you can, and you will see yourself being lifted up and
> ascending to the height so that you seem to be in mid-air.

In the Mithraic worship, priests and worshipers initiate the procedure that send souls soaring into the heavens.

There is much we do not know about Paul, and much we do not know about the pagan practices of his time. But we do know that transcendence is a common theme of many pagan religions as well as at least some early Christian theologies. It is logical that Paul, a strict Jew by heritage and training, would want to separate the practices of the new Israel from those other practices going on among the pagans. The Jews believed in a general resurrection that would be God's action on behalf of mankind, and this same God was, they believed, the author of all messages that people received in their dreams and prophetic visions. In other words, Jews and Christians believed in a revealed religion, one that stressed God's power to act to save; they shunned and abhorred pagan practices that seemed to depend upon humanly devised liturgies or magical doings that would induce some spiritual state. Paul is consistent with his heritage, therefore, when he describes his vision; he says he was "caught up" into the "third" heaven—he does not say that he made the trip under his own volition; he says he was "caught up." He uses the Greek verb *harpazmo*—a word he uses again in *First Thessalonians 4:17*, when he tells us how the dead will be *caught up* together with the living to meet the Lord in the air. God's action— indisputably. No hint of breathing exercises or drugged potions.

Yet, Paul uses the number three, as do other Christian authors, frequently—a fact to which this essay testifies—and in doing so he runs the risk of joining himself to the various religions that also used this number, as well as some of the elaborate astrologies and mathematical systems that were in vogue. Why would he use the number, therefore, if he could be misunderstood? Of course, the number is scriptural and honored among Jews and Christians alike— especially Christians, who would honor the Lord's passion, entombment and resurrection. But there may be another reason. Paul's vision or visions took him to the heart of things, the secret center of all life, where the number Three resides.

Many persons who experience illumination—ancient and modern—feel the force of the number three. We have seen many examples of this. The experience is called "illumination" precisely because it enlightens the deepest aspect of the personality, the hidden source of the psyche, which, when held to the light, is seen to be the center and ground of all being. The number three presides like a deity in this inner sanctuary, according to many who have seen this place. The poet Gerard Manley Hopkins said, "Nature itself echos man's inner triad, which in turn is a forepitch of the real self." Paul, we may believe, when he wrote his epistles, in his haste did not censure the reality of his illumination; he could not hold back as much of the truth as he found to be utterable. The number three—which eventually came to stand for the Christian religion's entire conception of God: Father, Son, Holy Spirit—appeared on Paul's lips and in his dictation. He simply spoke the truth. And to whom did he speak it? To his friend, Luke.

What do we know of Luke? His name is mentioned only three times in the New Testament— unless he is the "Lucius of Cyrene" named in his own *Acts* at *13:1*. The three references are in Paul's epistles: *Colossians 4:14*, where Paul mentions "Luke the beloved physician," *Philemon 24,* and *2 Timothy 4:11.* A second century tradition claims that this person is the author of the third gospel. (The "threes" here are non-symbolic.) Of course, such secondary attributions cannot be trusted, but nothing challenges it. In *Acts*, Luke's second book, he claims to be Paul's traveling companion and seems to reveal himself in the "we" passages that begin at 16:10 and read like a travelogue. He met Paul at Troas and presumably was converted to the new religion by the apostle himself. Scholars have considered him an educated Gentile of literary habits, who gives evidence that he knew the Old Testament (in its Greek form) and wrote in the Hellenistic style of his time. But a few among us suspect that he was no Gentile. He knows a great deal about the Jewish religion. His second book is in large part a typological re-working of the Old Testament. Scholars generally have not appreciated the extent to which Luke utilizes the heros and events of Israel's history. His books may have been written, not to edify Gentiles, but to impress the authorities at Jerusalem who gave Paul such a difficult

135

time when he journeyed there. From this angle he comes across as a Christian rabbi. Let it be granted for argument's sake that he was a Jew and that Paul confided in him as a Jew.

We can imagine that the rational, scholarly Luke had never met anyone like the fiery tempered Paul, who claimed to have mystic transports that made him the like of Moses and Elijah. The first meeting could have taken place at Tarsus, where Luke, if he was a physician, may have studied medicine, and which is Paul's home. Or they may have met at Troas, as Paul was making his second missionary journey. Paul, we must believe, converted Luke to the new religion; Paul's story of his ascent to the heavens must have been the cornerstone of the argument that persuaded Luke—whether he be physician or rabbi (we favor the latter)—to join him and travel about the world as a believer. As Luke listened to his new friend speak of his vision, he must have meditated upon the ancient Scripture, where Jews looked for answers. The elements of Paul's vision and ministry were to be found there: the voice, the call, the separation, the journey, the light...and the number three. Abraham the patriarch was the first to heed the call; he took his family and his flocks to a strange land and began a new life. Then Moses: Israel's greatest hero as an infant was cast out by his parents after a three month nurture and hid among the bulrushes; in time he led the children to safety and heard God's command that the children multiply (*Exodus 2:1-3*). Luke would recall the numerous threes and fours (such as *Exodus 3:18b*), that punctuate Moses' life, and how Scripture divided it into three periods of forty years; and of course, Luke would dwell upon the Passover night and how God wrought his people's deliverance, guiding them through their journey by his presence, manifested in the glorious cloud, God's effluence, and the joy of Israel *(Ex. 40)*. Luke's first thought, no doubt, upon hearing Paul speak of his vision, was that Paul had seen the *skekinah*; after that, the typology fell into place.

When Luke set about composing the speeches of *Acts* he saw Glory everywhere; what Paul saw in the heavens, the Voice, the Light, Luke put on the lips of his heros. In Stephen's speech, the Glory is there at the beginning (7:2) when the dying martyr rehearses the call of Abraham; he goes on to speak of Moses, how the people prospered in Egypt, how the infant Moses was nurtured three months in his father's house then cast out; how Moses' life is divided into three periods of fours; and how, at the end of Stephen's life, when his enemies rush upon him to kill him, he speaks of the tabernacle in the wilderness—he has not time to describe the Glory, but the Glory he cannot describe is his to behold in his vision wherein he sees Jesus, the Son of man, at God's right hand. And Luke does not let us forget that Paul was there witnessing; his vision is next.

When Luke contemplated Paul's zealous efforts to win converts to the church from far and near, he may have recalled God's command in *Genesis*, "Be fruitful and multiply." (1:28) Those words were taken by Moses and the Israelites as a divine sanction: a blessing upon their growing numbers and a promise they would thrive and enter the Promised Land. Luke applied these words to the New Israel: God wills that the church should grow and thrive; Paul is perhaps a new Moses who will be God's agent in leading the people to their new Promised Land. Luke thereupon set out to sanctify the church's growth by designating numbers and symbols that would prove the divine intent. He starts out with the number one: at Pentecost, the church's life constitutes a perfect unity. (Luke wants his readers to understand that the symbol of The Apostolic Day covers not only the work of Peter and John but the work of Paul as well, and lays God's command to be fruitful upon the church's work to embrace Gentiles.) When the apostles go into the upper room, they devote themselves with one accord to prayer *(Acts 1:12-14)*. And when the day of Pentecost comes, they are together in one place, having all things in common and continuing daily with one accord. When the peoples come to Jerusalem from the length and breadth of the known world they are understood as if they speak one language (2:7-8), a portent that the church will grow as these peoples hear the words of God spoken through the apostles. Later, when Peter and John are set free from prison, their fellows lift up their voices to God "with one accord" and are of "one heart and soul." (4:32) When Gentiles come into the church, the unity is not sundered; rather the church grows in strength and numbers as the ministry of deacons serves both Jew and Greek at the same table; the two groups thrive in harmony. Soon the deacons are assigned to a second ministry, preaching the word to Greeks; two ministries now preach to the two communities beyond the center in Jerusalem, and a second order ministers to the two communities within Jerusalem. Stephen and Phillip, both deacons, are prominent in discharging this ministry; the two men work separately, but Luke treats them as outstanding among all those appointed to be deacons. Stephen's death (6:8-7:59) becomes the first Christ-like martyrdom, and Phillip works miracles in Samaria, where the multitudes, with one accord, give heed to him (8:6). After the pair of deacons is no more, Phillip only remaining, Luke's text moves from the ones and twos into the realm of three. Saul, Aeneas and Dorcas are raised up, the first of these, as we have noted, being struck blind for three days. Then Cornelius has a vision in the ninth hour— the third quarter of the day— and the story of his vision is three times told; he sends three men to Peter; three watches later the following day Peter goes to a rooftop and has a trance; he sees a threefold vision. We shall have more to say about Peter's vision; suffice it to say that these events enable the church to grow numerically and spiritually into the divine community. Luke then, as he composes the last section of his book and nears the completion of his purpose, relates the fourfold works of the apostle Paul and his sufferings on behalf of the church. Luke proves that the church achieves a universality of purpose under its apostolic leadership. Luke's intent, of course, is not limited to the church's obedience to God's command to be fruitful and multiply (*Genesis 1:28*): he intends to reveal the purpose behind God's command, that was withheld from those of old, but to be revealed now in the time of the Christ. The purpose is revealed in the word *anastasis* and its kindred word, *apokatastasis*; rising up, being restored. Both words are used by Peter in his speech (3:21-22), which is in the "unity" section of Luke's scheme. (Early church fathers were impressed by this thought that at the end of time all things will be restored to their original state—Origen, for example, said this.) Paul states God's purpose plainly: the saints are to be "heirs of God and fellow heirs of Christ, provided we suffer with him that we may also be glorified with him."

The linking of beginning and end, creation and redemption, was to become a familiar theme among later theologians. Here are its sources, in the typology that joins great events. In Mark's Gospel, for example, we read that as Jesus begins his Ministry in the baptismal waters the heavens are split and the spirit-dove comes down; at the end of his earthly life, as he expels his last breath, the veil of the temple is split from top to bottom. Mark brings these two events together by his use of the rare verb *skizomenous* at 1:10 and 15:38—

138

the beginning and the end, both spirit-filled events; as the Lord dies, his breath (spirit) goes forth into the world, entering first the centurion who witnesses the splitting of the veil as God goes forth from his temple prison, then entering all Jesus' followers. Jesus' body was the true temple, we learn. (The historian Josephus records that the outer veil of the temple was a tapestry on which was depicted images of the starry skies above; is this what was split top to bottom, the same heavens that opened above Jesus at his Baptism? Can we say also that as Jesus came up from his Baptismal waters, so too the Centurion and other converts will come up from their immersions and find heaven waiting for them? Converts proclaim Jesus as Son of God— this is their salvation; the Voice that proclaimed Jesus out of the split sky, God's own Voice, is heard from the mouths of Gentile converts as the temple's starry veil is split.)

The beginning-end linkage is paralleled by a descent-ascent motion—so Jesus' rising from his Baptismal waters would suggest. Mark describes other ascents: three times, Jesus goes up to a high place, and it is on a mount that he is transfigured in the presence of three witnesses—is the centurion now a holy fourth, as he witnesses the Lord's fourth ascent? (On the Mount of Transfiguration, Jesus, descending, speaks to the three about how he shall rise from the dead.) Mark also tells of a paralytic who was lowered in Jesus' presence through a rooftop then ordered to rise, take up his pallet and go home. All the raisings in Mark's Gospel look forward to the raising of all the dead from their graves. In Luke, as we have seen, Jesus ascends into the heavens as two witnesses forecast his return to earth—which begins to happen as the Spirit descends at Pentecost. The pattern is that the Lord descends from the heavens in order to raise and restore his followers to their heavenly home: *apokatastasis*. In John's Gospel, too, we read that the Word was made flesh—the descent—then that Jesus, the Son of man who descended, will ascend again, when he is "lifted up." (3:13-15) Jesus is the bread of life come down from heaven (6:51) and he will raise the dead (6:39). When Jesus says it is not yet time for him to *go up* to the feast at Jerusalem, John uses the verb *anabainein*, a verb that has two meanings—*go up* to the feast on Mt. Zion, *and* ascend into the heavens. To go up to a high place, in the evangelist's mind, is to ascend into heaven: at 20:17 Jesus states plainly that he will ascend to the Father—*anaibainein*. John's point is that any talk of Jesus ascending to the Father is premature until he is actually lifted up upon his cross at Mount Calvary, his true Glory. These evangelists, we may believe, were influenced by their friend, Paul, who was "caught up" into the third heaven—Paradise. The meaning of the New Testament is this: whereas the Jewish religion could speak of God's Voice coming down upon a Moses on Mt. Sinai, heaven and earth never meet. The gulf is not bridged; God is above, man is below. But Paul was "taken up," and allowed to return, as did his Master, to proclaim the unsearchable riches of the heavenly life.

Yes, the Lord's death is an ascent to glory and he wins for us a restoration to Paradise. But, Paul reminds us, we must not forget the suffering. Paul felt the Lord's suffering as if it were in his own flesh. And, along with others, he meditated on the fact that Israel's rejection of the Lord and his consequent suffering became the portal through which the restoration was brought about, and through which the Gentiles entered the new community. The Lord's death is fertile; new life springs from it, and the church prospers. And, as the old community flourished under Moses, the new community flourishes under Paul who, like his Master, is a new Moses. But Paul is a Moses in a way his Master was not; Jesus was rejected not by the nation as a whole but by a cadre of corrupt leaders; Paul, however, finds himself being rejected by the nation—the model for which, he believes, lay in Israel's perversity when Moses tried to lead them through the desert to the Promised Land; they complained about everything and took to worshiping an idol. Or, in Luke's view, Israel as a nation rose up against Christ by persecuting Christ's disciples; in fact, this is the argument he places on Stephen's lips as he dies. The pattern—that we call monomyth—here assumes a variant form: a separation or parting from the past, involving rejection by his kindred and kind; then a period of nurture or strengthening as he prepares for heroic deeds to be done. Luke assigns the number three to this aspect of the hero's journey. Jesus, Luke tells us, was thirty years old when he completed his nurture at home and then left to begin his new work; he was rejected by his own, then after a longer period of being tested by outsiders, he achieved his true goal and identity. (*Outsiders*: a topic of great interest to Luke. See the essay *A Certain Man.*) The infant Moses was hidden three months by his mother then placed in an ark of bulrushes by the river bank; he was taken up by Pharaoh's daughter, then the entire nation of Egypt, where he attained prominence. Paul fits this pattern, as we have seen: after a three month stay at the synagogue in Ephesus (19:8) the people become "stubborn" and speak evil of him so that he must leave the place and take up preaching in the hall of Tyrannus—a Gentile—for two years. The pattern repeats when he lands on the island of Malta (28:1-11): he is nourished there for three days in the home of Publius, the chief, and treated like a god—this, too, implies the pattern—because he does great miracles; he leaves the island after three months, sailing in a vessel that bears the figurehead "Twin Brothers." Next, he arrives at Syracuse where he puts in for three days, then goes to Phegium, Puteoli, and—finally—Rome. In the great city people come from as far as the forum and Three Taverns to hear him speak. But after three days he calls the local Jewish leaders and begins to preach to the Jews in the city; they become dissatisfied and Paul is moved to denounce them as Isaiah had done in his day. We are told, as Luke's book nears its end, that Paul remained in Rome two years, extending welcome to all.

Luke expects that Paul will die in Rome. He trusts his readers to believe, from what he has related so far, that Paul's death will be a glorious martyrdom like unto his Lord's and Stephen's. Three times Luke has predicted Paul's death—as Jesus three times predicted his own death—and Luke adds that Paul picked up the mantle of the dying Stephen. Paul has undergone many "deaths" already, including death at sea; these are proleptic and set forth by Luke's cyclic method so that the reader can draw no conclusion but that Paul will die a martyr's death. It will be a glorious death because Paul will see Glory, as did Jesus and Stephen. Paul will come to the *shekinah*, God's own dwelling. He has lived out the monomyth; he has broken away from his past and taken on a new persona; he has been given nurture and guidance as he matured in his new calling; he has been tested and afflicted, and experienced rejection; he has gone down into the sea—a death—and risen to new life in Rome. He sees two visions during the course of his journey; the two prefigure a third, which is to be granted in Rome when he suffers his glorious martyrdom. As Luke writes, Paul awaits his end, having come like a hero of old to his Thebes, his Troy...his Jerusalem. (An early legend says that the evil Emperor Nero, who ruled in Rome about 67 C.E. and stained the city with the blood of Christians, had Paul beheaded, and that Paul's head, when it fell from his body, bounced three times, and each time a fountain of sacred water flowed from it. This happened, says the legend, at a place called Ad Aquas Salvias, just three miles outside the city. In honor of the legend, it was renamed Tre Fontane. Paul was buried at S. Paulo fuori le Mura nearby.)

Apotheosis marks the end of the journey, and it was the goal from the beginning. Luke places the motif at the very beginning of his *Acts*: Jesus is taken up into the heavens where he is received by a cloud that fits him like a royal garment. He is a king who has come to his throne. Paul agrees: Christ is the royal master who has overcome the hostile powers of the world, Paul states, as he alludes to *Psalm* 8 saying "For he must reign 'till he has put all his enemies under his feet (*I Cor. 15:25*). This is a messianic proposition; Jesus is hailed as messiah-king. But it is not normative Jewish thinking that the messiah is divine. Messiah is God's agent, but that is all; he does not transcend his human limits. Clearly, then, the new religion breaks with the old—Jesus has gone up into the skies and he calls his friends to follow him. Stephen is first to follow; then, in *Acts*, Paul is the last:

	PAUL'S TWO VISIONS	
ASCENSION OF JESUS (*Acts 1:9*)	(Three times Luke relates the conversion; Paul himself provides the second ascent-vision in *2Cor. 12:1-5*	PAUL'S ASCENT (Anticipated)

Paul's ascent-visions are definitive; they prevail over all other ideologies and religions and underlie the many levels of theological reflection we find in the New Testament, including even the literary structures. Wherever we read in the gospels we hear Paul's ecstatic cries. Luke in particular allows us to hear him; he enthrones the great visions with the numerology of the heavens, the threes and fours, and the relentless repetitions of the risings. These, and the restorations (3:21), come from the same psychic source—Paul's triumphal procession to the third heaven and Paradise. Those who come to this heavenly place feel like kings and lords, as indeed they were born to be.

The Lord's ascension to heaven is represented as a literal and bodily ascent, from earth to sky. Luke, of course, must have understood the Lord's ascension as literal; we are not obligated, however, to share his world-view. We of the twenty-first century cannot imagine a bodily levitation into a localized heaven in the cloud cover. Nor should we have to. We may take heart in the fact of Paul's ascent-vision and consider it a true ascension, an elevation of the mind and spirit, an opening of the inner eye. We may, therefore, agree with Joseph Campbell, whom we mentioned earlier in this essay, when he speaks of myth and defines it for us. Myth is factual truth, he will tell us; the facts inhabit a landscape of the mind. Miracles and ascensions are not the less true for this; they are all the more so.

Therefore we study symbols, for they reveal the mythic element. We find symbols in Paul's epistles, even though his writings are unstudied and the symbols are scattered about; Luke's writing, however, is refined and we can read in his two books this evangelist's understanding of what occupied Paul's mind. When Paul told him about the light that came to him at midday, for example, Luke thought immediately of *Genesis* where God said "Let there be light," and there was light on that first day. When Luke met John the evangelist, these two lyricists of the spirit, whose writings so curiously echo each other, would have meditated on the symbol of light; and soon Paul's subjective light would have found its way into the majestic prologue of the fourth gospel, where the words "In the beginning..." tell of a light that lit up creation week and has the power to shine in the dark. And when John speaks of history's witness to that light and comes to speak of Christ who *is* the light, he can speak of those who, like Paul, beheld the light and are therefore creatures "born not of blood nor of the will of the flesh, nor of the will of man, but of God." The evangelists have objectified Paul's inner world of light and made it history's goal for all believers. John' prologue conjures up our deeply buried and dimly recalled memory of Paradise, the wall-girt scene of God's labors, where He stamped upon us His own self-image. Luke, too, in the first pages of *Acts*, arouses in us this memory; the images of wind, fire and judgment bring to mind the words of the prophet Isaiah (*Isaiah: 65:8, 66:15-22*), who envisioned a new heavens and a new earth, God acting to make all things new—*apokatastasis*. Luke reminds us again of *Genesis* and the prospect of new birth when he pictures the peoples who come to Pentecost as born anew—the list, which makes no sense to scholars except on the proposition that it is a list of the world's peoples as the world was known to the authors of the *Book of Genesis*. They have come to Jerusalem to be restored to their original state. And, of course, in a piece of irony that would have made John proud, Luke points out that the disciples at Pentecost were accused of being drunk; indeed they were, Luke would say— drunk with the new wine of the spirit. His actual words: "For these men are not drunk, as you suppose, *since it is only the third hour of the day.*"

Paul referred to Jesus as the new Adam, reflecting his own theological ability—which must have been considerable; and he is consistent with this theme throughout his writings, most obviously when he described his illumination as an ascent to the gates of Paradise. The Scriptural terms "born again," "being in Christ," "receiving the Spirit," while they may serve various arguments and expositions, have as their origin the daylit journey through the night and the birth of the new man in the heavens. The opened mind is the portal through which these blessed ones pass into the ancient, true, and only real world, for which we have only the feeble word "Paradise." It remains a question to ponder, however, whether Luke and John—or Paul himself, for that matter—have rightly presented the nature of the revelation at journey's end. We have said that Luke and John "objectified" it, making it pertain to this world and its history. By using the language of Scripture, these evangelists and others have explained the vision as a goal of the national history; thus they speak of rising up to be with Christ, greeting him in the air, worshiping Christ as the new Adam. In so doing they are in a position analogous to that of Dr. Bucke, who could only explain the cosmic sense according to the Darwinian theory of evolution. Essentially, they all do the same thing: they assert that the cosmic vision is the result of an historical process; the evangelists speak of a sacred history from Adam to Jesus and an eschaton to follow; Dr. Bucke speaks of a secular history from simple forms of consciousness to cosmic consciousness. Paul may have shown the greater wisdom when in his *2 Corinthians* text he said "...only God knows."

The "new man," who, like Paul, is "born again," has certain attributes. Sometimes Paul speaks of the "fruits of the spirit," certain virtues that the pilgrim acquires along the way; these prove to be the virtues, mainly love (*agape*) which enables the gifted aspirant the power to "bear all things, believe all things, hope all things, endure all things." Paul speaks easily of these powers, for he himself has had the vision; the vision enables a man to see life in its true perspective, its infinite depth, and it lifts up the heart, even when faced with a martyr's death. The vision also beautifies human relations: far from being isolated, the cosmic sense makes a person loving, generous, and radiantly so: Bucke felt this in Whitman. And the English priest who in the 14th century composed *The Cloud of Unknowing* speaks of a cloud "that shrouds God's presence, and when a man enters the cloud he becomes beautiful in the sight of his friends, and has a most pleasing disposition toward all—and a sublime deference toward his detractors, those who will never understand the contemplative life."

Paul's list of virtues also includes the power to heal and the power to work miracles. (*1 Cor.* 12:27-31), and these too are attributes of mythic hero. Luke states that Peter and John performed miracles, but Luke makes it clear that Peter was a laggard in his acquisition of this power, for the "prince of the apostles" was not converted until his mind was filled with new wine. Peter's conversion was a problematic issue; Luke dwells upon it at length.

Luke's account begins in *Acts 10*. Peter has come to Joppa, a busy seaport on the Mediterranean, where he lodges with a man called Simon, a tanner. At the sixth hour Peter goes to the rooftop to pray and falls into a trance. He sees the heavens open and a great sheet is let down by its four corners, in which are all kinds of animals and birds and reptiles–creatures that Peter's religion forbade him to eat. He hears a voice that says, "Rise, Peter, kill and eat." He answers, "No, Lord; for I have never eaten anything that is common or unclean." Three times the sheet is lowered in his sight, then taken up to heaven. Peter of course is inwardly disturbed by his vision. At this moment, three men arrive at Simon's gate asking for him. These men have been sent at the behest of an angel. The story of the angel's sending the three men to Peter, by means of Cornelius, a Gentile centurion of Caesarea, is three times told (10:3; 10:30; 11:13). As Peter is still on the rooftop, the Spirit instructs him: "Rise," the Spirit says, "go down and accompany them without hesitation..." Peter speaks to the men and agrees to go with them to see Cornelius. The next day Peter rises and the men begin their journey—they are ten men in all, three groups of three (some of Peter's group join in: 11:12) and Peter himself. When they come to Caesarea, three days after Peter's vision, Peter enters the house of Cornelius, who falls at Peter's feet and worships him. "Stand up," says Peter, "for I too am a man." The fact that Peter is willing to enter this Gentile's house signifies a change in the apostle; he states to the centurion (10:28-29) that Jewish law stands against him, a Jew, entering the house of a Gentile; but, says Peter, God has shown him that he should not call any man common or unclean. He has learned from his vision.

On the surface, this incident seems to confirm that Peter has come around to Paul's position about admitting Gentiles into the new community. And indeed, this is true of Peter...he did come around, eventually, and this was a triumph for the new community. But Luke knows there is more to this than a change of disposition. When Jesus reached out to the Gentile world and entered their homes, it brought him to his gallows—this fact was always on Luke's mind, as it was with Paul. So, Peter's trance-vision at midday is a true conversion, like unto Paul's, at least in some certain respects, and conversions lead to discipleship and martyrdom. Luke does not regard Peter's tutelage under Jesus as decisive for his discipleship, for Peter's heart was plagued by his adherence to the law. He must, therefore, be converted by the Spirit, as was Paul; and, as the Lord sent Ananias to be with Paul and nurture him in the company of the disciples at Damascus, so too, the Spirit sends men from Cornelius to nurture Peter, in preparation for his ordeals to come.

Three times we are told of Cornelius's inspiration to send men to Peter. At the ninth hour (the third quarter of the day) Cornelius receives his instructions to send the men; he sends three men and, three watches later—at the sixth hour of the following day—Simon Peter goes up onto the rooftop to pray. (Luke calls the apostle *Simon Peter*, whereas he elsewhere calls him Peter only. Luke has a point to make about this: Simon is a tanner, a fact that Jews could hold against him, for he worked with the hides of unclean animals that Peter is not allowed to eat; he is like Levi the seaside tax collector in *Mark* who spans the gulf between the Jews and their Gentile neighbors. The same is true of Cornelius, who is a Roman soldier, yet he revered the God of the Jews. When Simon Peter enters Simon's house, the apostle is identified with those who cross the gulf.) Luke uses the decisive word *anastas*, and its companion *egeiro*—Stand up, Rise. Three times *anastas* is heard during the Peter-Cornelius narration; but the word had already passed Peter's lips—when the apostle went to

Lydda and Joppa (9:32-42) he performed miracles. In Joppa itself, the apostle came to the house of a woman named Tabitha, who was dead; in the upper room of that house he spoke the word that raised her—that word was *Anastasthi*, from *Anastas*: Rise. Peter has the power, like his Lord, to do wonderworks; and we recall that Peter's Lord died and rose on the third day—a fact that is on Peter's lips in his speech to Cornelius (10:40).

In the narration of Peter's vision, we hear the word three times: "Rise, Peter, kill and eat" and the apostle addresses Cornelius with the words "Stand up"—*egeiro*. The Holy Spirit falls upon all who listen to the apostle's words; the men are called, therefore, to Rise up, and the Spirit descends upon them; the ascribed divinity of the holy apostle mediates a vertical motion between heaven and earth (Peter's divinity has been all but stated at 10:26—these words imply that divinity has been imputed to him. We are in Luke's "Three" section, where we have read of three resurrections—Saul's, Aeneas' and Tabitha's.) The command Rise is addressed to all: the entire cast is brought forth in this mystery-play. All men will someday hear the Voice command that they come out of their graves. Luke, like Mark, prefers to use *anastas* to describe the Lord's own rising—as in *Luke 24:7*. Elsewhere in the New Testament all the third day and resurrection statements take the word *egeiro*. However, Luke will use *egeiro* in speeches that summarize resurrection events, and Paul will do the same, as in *1Corinthians 15:4*. We suggest that *egeiro* is a lesser *anastas*; it is indirect, less impressive. It is a long shot of the bow—but an irresistible thought—that *egeiro* stands in relation to *anastas* as "third heaven" does to "Paradise" in the Pauline diptych. Certainly, when Luke wishes to convey the full force of his doctrine, he uses *anastas*: "Rise, Peter..." Peter is destined for the ascended life: he has crossed the gulf that separated Jew and Gentile, he has crossed the gulf that separated man and God.

Luke's doctrine of Jesus—his Christology—is that Jesus was an ordinary man until he was taken up by God's hand. At the Ascension, this man was raised to the heavens and crowned as a king above the clouds, a sun god, divine in his own right. Here, in Luke's narrative of Peter's vision, Peter is a man; but he is a man that will be lifted up. Peter asserts his manhood in the presence of Cornelius—and rightly so; but Luke's intent is to show that Peter as a disciple goes the way of his Lord, who died and rose on the third day. Luke has Peter

147

remind Cornelius that he too is a man; for he is not yet risen; we are reminded of Jesus' third day warning in *John*—that no one should touch him, for he is not yet ascended to the Father (20:17). (In *Acts 2:36* we read "Let Israel know that God has made him both Lord and Christ, this Jesus whom you crucified." Scholars call this *adoptionism*; God the Father adopted Jesus as his son; it is an acceptable term, so long as we understand the underlying truth, that the Spirit summons a man to behold his own divinity; in metaphysical terms, we *are* divine.)

Peter's vision on the rooftop represents a necessary step in his ascent; the apostle's mind must be cleared out; he must turn from old ways and start anew. He is at the seaside house of Simon the tanner. (Two Simons: Luke finds in this more than the bridging of the gap; he senses destiny—it is written, so to speak, that Simon Peter will come to Simon the tanner.) The house is close to the water, close enough for Peter on the rooftop to look out over the busy seaport. He can see at a distance the great sails of ships approaching the harbor—a breakwater of reefs through which the ships must pass slowly. Many of the ships are full of cattle. The animals will be taken from the ships wrapped in sails, then slaughtered and their carcasses sold for food; their hides will be turned over to men like Simon who will make garments from them. It is noon and Peter succumbs to a trance. Images come before his bewildered mind. He sees a large sheet being lowered from the sky, much like the sails he has just seen entering the harbor. The sheet is full of animals, much like the animals he has just seen—and they are forbidden to him. Suddenly he hears the voice: "Rise, Peter, kill and eat." Three times this happens. Then the sheet is taken up. The voice is the voice of his Lord, who had pronounced that all things are clean and thus abolished the dietary laws. But Peter had repressed this new teaching—it was too much for him. His repressed state plagues his heart and deadens his spirit; he is unfit for an ascent to the heavens.

Since the problem of relating to Gentiles involved eating with them, the matter of Jewish dietary restrictions had to be removed in order for the church to go about its mission. And Peter, as an individual, had to overcome his resistance to the new teaching in order for him to grow in the spirit. The Spirit takes over, says Luke; it brings to mind what the Lord had taught but his followers had forgotten. Peter finally is able to say, "Then remembered I the words of the Lord..." (11:16: and what is Pentecost but the removing of inhibitions? When the Spirit came down, the disciples were able to speak in other tongues—2:4. Later, when Peter speaks to Cornelius and his Gentile friends, a new Pentecost enters the world, and Gentiles speak in tongues—10:44-46). Luke's doctrine, and John's as well, is that the Spirit opens the mind to truth. Peter heeds the voice and turns to the Gentile world—he understands that this is his mission. More important, however, is the need to recognize the Voice as that of the Lord God who spoke at creation and called to Adam, whom He set in a Paradise garden.

Peter's conversion and mission dominate the third section of *Acts* and his life is wreathed in the sacred number. Three recalls the Lord's passion and resurrection, which in the gospels was announced at Caesarea Philippi. Peter, reenacting the Lord's life, rises (anastas) in response to the spirit that calls him down from the rooftop and he goes with the three men to Caesarea where Cornelius awaits him. As we read through this third section, we see Peter enter upon his *thanatos-anastasis* destiny as a preparation for Paradise. His journey to the heavens began when he was called from his work by the sea—a story that was told by Mark, but not by Luke, for Luke tells the story in this transfigured way, the seaside summons in Joppa. When Peter and his fellow fishermen came up from the Galilean waters, that was their baptism, and the first symbol of their ultimate rising to glory. In Joppa, Peter is called from his seaside vision to stand before men like a god and to command that they, too, be baptized. The apostle is now a fisher of men, as the Lord said he would be. One must first know one's own destiny; then he may preach to others of theirs.

Peter's destiny requires him to go down into the pit of death. A disciple does not escape this destiny; Paul did not; neither will Peter. All the apostles were arrested and imprisoned in Jerusalem; this sets in motion a chain of events that seem to have been ordained:

Arrest of the apostles (4:1-5:17)	Arrest of Stephen (6:11)	Arrest of Peter and James (12:1)
Trial of apostles (4:5; 5:27)	Trial of Stephen (7:1)	(No trial for Peter and James)
Punishment of apostles (5:40)	Martyrdom of Stephen (7:54)	Martyrdom of James by Herod (12:1)
Apostles delivered by angel (5:19)	Stephen's face like an angel; he beholds glory like the angels in heaven (61:5; 7:54)	Peter delivered from Herod by an angel (12:7)
Peter strikes Ananias dead (5:1)	Peter confronts the evil Simon (8:18)	Angel strikes Herod dead (12:20)

All the apostles are arrested, then Peter and James are arrested. James is murdered— testimony that prison is a death. To go down into this prison is indeed to go into the pit from which only angels can deliver a man.

Prison is not the only sign of death, however. We must not forget the sea. Peter at Joppa looks out over the same sea that swallowed up the prophet Jonah. Luke has Jonah in mind, we are sure, for in his Gospel (*Luke 11:30*) Jonah is commended in that he was sent to preach to the Gentiles at Ninevah. Jonah at first fled from the Lord's call, however; he went to Joppa and set forth from there to cross the deep. A great tempest overtook him, and he was tossed into the water whereupon a great fish consumed him. He spent three days and three nights in the belly of the great fish. Joppa, therefore, was a place of encounter with God's spirit, where one heeds the call or one does not. Jonah fled God's call; Peter forgot it. But Peter, then Paul, are like Jonah in that they, too, go down to the water—Paul more so than Peter—and rise up to convert the Gentiles to the Lord God. More: the call that they answer is the Holy Spirit of God, who both casts man into the pit and raises him to the life above.

Stephen's martyrdom is the apogee of the *thanatos-anastasis* motif in Luke. Paul's symbolic death and rising are modeled upon it, and that is true of Peter as well. But Luke does not let us forget that Jesus' death and resurrection stand behind Stephen's and are the ultimate model. In his *Gospel* Luke has Jesus proclaim his high status before the High Priest, "You shall see the Son of man sitting on the right hand of power..." (*Luke 22:69* and *Mark 14:62*). In *Acts*, Stephen stands before the High Priest and proclaims that he sees the heavens opened and the Son of man standing at the right hand of God (7:55-56). Stephen says the Son of man *stands* at the right hand of God. Jesus stands because in *Acts* standing is the posture of those who raise up others to the immortal life. (The High Priest, by this logic, will neither raise nor be raised; for Matthew records that the Priest had been sitting, standing only to condemn.) Luke, when he sees spilled martyr's blood, thinks of Calvary and the Lord's saving deeds. Lest we miss his point, he draws detailed comparisons between the Lord's death and Stephen's: offended accusers imitate one another as Ciaphas rips his clothes upon hearing Jesus, and the Sanhedrin grind their teeth and stop their ears as they rush upon the martyr; both Jesus and Stephen are led out of the city to be executed; both speak of forgiveness for their tormentors and both speak of their spirits—Jesus offers his to the father, Stephen offers his to Jesus.

Peter's fate was determined when he heard the two prophets atop the Mount of Transfiguration speak of how Jesus would die in Jerusalem and then he heard Jesus say "Let these words sink into your ears." (*Luke 9:44*) The import of these words was not immediately clear to the apostle; but soon enough he comes to *his* Passover; he is arrested, like his Lord, at Passover (*Acts 12:3)* and must wait out the feast before he is brought out to face the people (compare *Mark 14:2* and *Matthew 26:1-5;* Luke omits this in his gospel, but brings out the force of it when he relates Peter's arrest). Jesus prays in Gethsemene before he is seized, and when he is on the cross the two Marys and others watch from a distance; Peter has been the object of prayer at Mary's house (12:12), into which he enters upon his release. (The three women who watched the Lord's passion are identified in *Mark*; Luke reports that the church that prayed for Peter included Mary, the mother of John Mark, who authored the first gospel.) Luke draws upon *Matthew* for another detail: the angel of *Matthew 28:1-10*, who makes the guards tremble but comforts the two Marys by announcing that the Lord is risen (*egeiro*), appears to be the same angel who "awakes" (*egeiro*) Peter from his sleep in prison, saying to him "Get up quickly" (*anastas*), and who leads him past the prison guards who, come morn, cannot find him and are put to death. Peter, like his Lord, has risen from his sleep and he goes forth, fresh from his tomb, to greet his astonished friends, who at first doubt but come at last to rejoice that he is with them. He is risen from the pit of death; the iron gates, like the stones that entombed his Lord, having been opened by the power of God.

Once the apostles are delivered from prison, they exemplify the risen life. This pattern of arrest and escape is the *thanatos/anastasis* theology and, as expected, Luke gives it typological support from Jesus' last days. The apostles are three times arrested, imprisoned and released in chapters 1-5 of *Acts*; even in their arrest they demonstrate the pattern, for they are arrested for preaching the resurrection (4:1-4). Those who arrest the apostles are paired with those who arrested Jesus (4:5-7 and 5:17). The apostles are delivered at night, recalling dark Gethsemane (5:19; 12:6), and when Peter is arrested he is guarded by four squads of soldiers, recalling not only the soldiers who brought Jesus from Gethsemane to the temple but also the general use of the number four in Luke, beginning with the four weeks of generations that lead up to Jesus (*Luke 3:23-38*), and concluding with the four divisions at the end of Acts, which define the mission of the Lord's greatest apostle, Paul, who also escaped from prison and was lifted to the very gates of Paradise.

To be risen is to be endowed with God's own powers, says Luke, and he shows us this in the deeds of Peter and Paul and the others who, like their Lord, heal the sick and raise the dead. This is *apotheosis*,— a man in this life achieves his rightful status as a child of God and an inheritor of the kingdom. These powers persist into eternity, for divine beings cannot be confined to the pit of death— angels burst open prison doors to deliver them. The highest heaven is within reach. For Jesus, Jerusalem was the site of his rising to the divine life and it is forever the symbol of his rising to the highest heaven. For Peter and Paul, and the others, Rome symbolizes destiny—the eternal city. As *Acts* closes, Paul is there, his martyrdom imminent, his future secured.

Paul—Peter's virtues notwithstanding—is the true *alter christus* in Luke's theological world-view. And he is the successor to Stephen, more so than Peter, and his vision and obedience to the call make him the true bearer of the Christ-spirit. What does Luke hold against Peter? Peter had a vision, too—Luke knows this—but Peter's vision did not lift him to the gates of this Paradise, whereas Paul's did. Peter's vision was only a trance, in which the Spirit summoned up what the apostle had forgotten. But there was also a political aspect to Luke's view: Peter often spoke in favor of the stricter party, those who hindered the growth of the new religion among gentiles, and his reputed stubbornness may have been held against him. The story of Peter's rooftop vision indicates that his attachment to the old prejudices was profound. Yes, Peter's rooftop vision was powerful— Luke describes it in detail and relates that three times Cornelius was sent to Peter by an angel. But Peter's vision lacks the solid realism that Luke attributes to Paul. It is not only the number three, but also the number four that envelops Paul's ministry and last deeds. Paul ascended to the third heaven and to Paradise itself. There is no greater reality. Peter is not so honored.

There were power struggles in the early Christian communities. Primacy was based on the leader's presence among the original followers of Jesus, those who had known him in the flesh. This fact favored Peter over Paul. And the party that eventually gained the power to define orthodoxy looked to the past, to those who claimed knowledge of the Lord during his time on earth. Paul struggled with this orthodoxy. He says in *Galatians* that he confronted Peter in Antioch and withstood him to his face. Not everyone agreed with the orthodox party, therefore, and Paul did not stand alone—the evangelist John, in his gospel, seems to throw his weight against Peter when he writes that in a foot race to get to the empty tomb, Peter was beaten out (*John 20:4*). These others, beginning with Paul, did not look to the past. Instead, they looked to discern God's word for them in the present moment. Visions and revelations counted; arguments based on the law did not. (When Luke states that even Peter, when he defended his change of heart before the circumcision party—the orthodox, that is—appealed not to the teaching of Jesus but to a vision. A decisive point in debate—no wonder Luke makes much of it.)

In time, the party that looked to the past prevailed and eventually they set the church on course for its future. Of course, they relaxed the old traditions, and agreed to admit Gentiles into the Church without having to obey the strict laws. But they were skeptical of visions; they preferred objective historical fact as the vehicle of God's revelation. They ordained a canonical Scripture to enshrine this history and define the faith once and for all. Christianity today is held up as an historical religion—based on fact, not dreams. The fact that the Scripture refers often to visions, dreams and mystical revelations is an inconsistency that is disregarded; people came to think of visions as things of the past that simply introduced historical events and that is all—for example, the Nativity pageant, where the Angel Gabriel announces to the Virgin Mary that she is to conceive a child. That the angel appears to her *in the sixth month* is taken as a matter of fact and dismissed (*Luke 1:26*).

The term "Gnosticism" has been applied by scholars to those who turned inward to discover God's presence and the Risen Christ in their midst. Gnostics claimed to have knowledge of Jesus from their inward seeking that could not be contained or conferred by the church's formulas or liturgies. This valorization of the subjective side of experience—the inward look—is evident in many Gnostic writings. *The Gospel of Mary* relates Mary Magdalene's visit to the tomb on the first Easter; it sounds like *John 20*, except that when Mary reports to the disciples that in her vision she saw Jesus alive, Peter and Andrew do not believe her. Tearfully, Mary says to Peter:

> "My brother Peter, what do you think? Do you think that I thought this up myself in my heart? Do you think that I am lying about the Savior?" Levi answered and said to Peter, "Peter, you have always been hot-tempered. If the Savior found her worthy, who are you to reject her?"

Mary is vindicated, according to this account. Like Paul, she appealed to her "own heart" as a source of spiritual authority; Peter, on the other hand, rejects her story because it is subjective; he thus epitomizes the orthodox position.

Orthodoxy asserted that Jesus lived among us as incarnate deity, that he rose bodily from the tomb, was seen in the flesh by many witnesses, ascended bodily into heaven, and commissioned those witnesses to establish his church upon these foundations. Scholars have praised the Christian religion for asserting historical fact as its foundation, over against the tendency of the ancient world to rely upon visions and myths. But in the New Testament, "facts" are not what we take them to be; only the mind that turns inward upon itself can discover the Kingdom in which the "facts" of the gospel are true.

When a person experiences illumination his world is at first shattered. Paul, when he had his ascent-vision, was not sure if he was in his body or out of it. Solid matter takes on a subtle aspect, as if not quite real; suddenly a new reality intrudes; it does not displace the old—it is the truth of the old, a truth long obscured by the scales that cover the inner eye. The sense of being "out of the body" is often an aspect of illumination; the person seems to be both outside and inside his body simultaneously; the body seems more beautiful and powerful than he ever imagined; he believes he can do miracles with it. Some have said that when they are out of their bodies, their souls and bodies are seen to be truly fused. Dr. Bucke quotes Paul Tynor—a person whom he interviews—who said "In the light of this truth, soul and body are linked and glorified." Only in a transcendent vision does a person realize the truth about his body, that it is permeated by the spirit. The doctrine of the resurrection of the body, in this light, might best be interpreted as the visionary ascent of the mind to Paradise, where body and soul have been eternally joined and are one, and will be so forever.

Is this the secret teaching that Paul alludes to in *1 Corinthians 2:6*?

iii. The Secret Wisdom

The hero's journey brings him to the gates of Paradise where he discovers himself. We believe that Paul made this journey, and speaks of it in *2 Corinthians 12*; it may be that he alludes to it in this passage in the earlier text:

> "Yet among the mature we do impart wisdom, although it is not a wisdom of this age or of rulers of this age, who are doomed to pass away. But we impart a secret and hidden wisdom of God, which God decreed before the ages for our glorification." *1 Cor. 2:26*

To many scholars this text is an example of Jewish apocalyptic thought, implying that at some appointed end time God will reveal certain secrets to the elect. If this is what Paul means, then he makes no claim that he himself possesses this wisdom; he merely says that it will be imparted. But Paul says he imparts this wisdom to the mature, which necessarily means that he possesses it. And, as in the other text, he seems to base his authority upon having this wisdom. This wisdom is no human teaching, he says; it is something decreed by God from the beginning—and he, Paul, has it. (We can almost hear him say "And Apollos does not.") And we find a subjective note in 2:10-11, where Paul says that the Spirit searches everything, the depths of God, and "a man's thoughts." He is using an analogy, of course, intending to speak more of God's nature than his own. Yet he indicates that the spirit has entered his own thoughts, and thus imparted the spiritual truths in question.

There could be no end of speculation about Paul's vision and its implications. One could even entertain the thought that Paul was involved with the Eleusinian Mysteries—secret rites that involved mind-expansion, probably by drug induced out-of-body journeys; every spring and fall, the initiates greeted the midnight sun on the Rarian plain outside of Athens; Paul was in Athens just before he wrote the Corinthian epistle. We cannot know: but we do know that many Gnostics claimed Paul as one of their own. Valentinius, a famous Gnostic teacher from Egypt, claimed to have learned Paul's secret wisdom from one Theudas, who, according to Luke, was one of Paul's disciples. Other Gnostics claimed that Jesus gave a secret teaching to some of his disciples: indeed, according to Mark's *Gospel*, three times Jesus took aside three disciples to be with him and witness certain things in private, and Jesus spoke of the "secret of the kingdom of God" that should not be revealed to outsiders except as parables (4:10-11). Moreover, some Gnostics held that Jesus, long after his death and resurrection, continued to reveal himself by means of visions to many persons, and that they, the Gnostics, have been led deeper into the inner mysteries and they alone possess the key to these visions and mysteries.

The Gnostic Christians undid the gospel history; in place of the familiar history of Jesus on earth doing his deeds and instructing his disciples, then appearing to a relatively few followers after his death, the Gnostics began with visions of the dead and risen Jesus. (To some extent, the evangelists did the same—if, for example, they composed the Transfiguration in light of the Resurrection.) The scholar Elaine Pagels says, in her *Gnostic Gospels*, that the Gnostics simply reversed matters, beginning with their visions of the resurrected Christ and having little interest in biographical matters. Pagels cites the *Apocryphon of John*:

> ...immediately...the heavens were opened and the (whole) creation...under heaven shone and the world was shaken. I saw in the light a child...while I looked he became like an old man...he changed his form again becoming like a servant...I saw an image with multiple forms in the light.

John hears the image speak:

> "John, why do you doubt and why are you afraid? You are unfamiliar with this form, are you?...do not be afraid, I am the one who is with you always...I have come to teach you what is and what was and will come to be."

Another Gnostic text, *The Apocalypse of Peter*, tells of Peter's trance-vision—but it is unlike the one on the rooftop in Joppa; instead, we read:

> (The savior) said to me, "...put your hands upon your eyes...and say what you see!" But when I had done it, I did not see anything. I said, "No one sees (this way)." Again he told me, "Do it again." And there came into me fear with joy, for I saw a new light, greater than the light of day. Then it came down upon the savior...

Marcus, a student of Valentinus, tells how he discovered truth: a vision

> Descended upon him...in the form of a woman; and expounded to him its own nature and the origin of all things, which it had never revealed to anyone.

The Gnostics stated that each person sees the truth in a form appropriate to his capacity to understand it. To the relatively immature, Jesus appears as a child; to the mature, an old man, and so on. Another Gnostic, Theodorus, put it, "Each person recognizes the Lord in his own way, not all alike." Perhaps this is the lesson to be taken from the comparison of mystical states in different times and different cultures: that the Absolute, when perceived, takes on the aspect of the perceiver. The Greeks at Eleusis saw the goddess Persephone; the Gnostics saw Christ as a child, or a woman; they all entered the one divine sanctuary.

Underlying all these accounts of visions is the monomyth: the person hears a call or receives a vision that invites him or summons him to leave behind the world of ordinary day, to "shut his eyes," as it were, and journey inward to a new realm. The Gnostic spirituality is closer to the monomyth than orthodox incarnational Christology; the latter begins with God joining a human nature to himself at the conception of Jesus in the womb of the Virgin and celebrates God's actions through the historic Jesus; but Gnosticism looks into the human psyche and contemplates what is needed to transform it. What matters is not some intervention from outside man, or some legal fiction that imputes salvation to a person who fundamentally remains unchanged. What matters is the inner transformation that is summed up by the monomyth—a man makes a journey and returns to be like a god among his fellows.

Gnostics avoid literal interpretations of the tradition about Jesus; they look for the mystical application of a text to the human psyche. When they speak of the kingdom of God, for example, they refer not to a place or an event to take place in the world. The *Gospel of Thomas* reports

> ...rather the kingdom is inside you

(The text at *Luke 17:21*, "The kingdom of God is within you," seems to suggest an interior state of mind; but Luke can be deliberately ambiguous; on linguistic grounds, "within you" is correct, but in context, "among you" is the better reading.) Again, in *Thomas*, we read

> The kingdom of the father is spread out upon the earth, and men see it not.

Men do not see it because they are blinded to the truth.

What is the truth, according to Gnostics? While there is no one "doctrinal" position among Gnostics—they were not a church—we can say that generally the world for Gnostics was a waste-place, a *kenoma*. They longed to return—not to an original Paradise set at the beginning of time, but to an experience of "fullness," *Pleroma*, wherein God and humanity are one. Unlike Jews and orthodox Christians, Gnostics looked not for the beginning but for the bottom of life, the ultimate truth behind all life. They looked upon the God of the Jews as an imposter who has deceived men into believing that he created a good world and that the world is in good hands.

This false god has masked his deceit by redefining the *Pleroma* as the abyss, or chaos. Gnostics repudiate this deceit and strive for freedom to return to what lies behind the "creation-fall." This return involves a rebirth or resurrection. "Resurrection" means the *gnosis*— the word means *knowledge*—of the Resurrection body, the *Anthropos*. In *The Gospel of Thomas*, rebirth means sharing the solitude of Jesus, being a wayfarer at his side—making a mental migration. The *Treatise on Resurrection*, another Gnostic document, speaks enigmatically: resurrection is "the uncovering at any given time of the elements that have arisen." Basically, it involves a resurrection *before* death: *The Gospel of Philip* says that Christ "first arose then died." As for achieving this gnosis, some Gnostics may have devised certain "liturgies" such as "the bridal chamber," about which we know little, but it may have been a ceremonial passage to the *Pleroma.*

Often, when the Gnostics rhapsodize about the mysteries, they chant the trichotomy—the triads. All prime being consists of three aspects, according to a Gnostic group called Naassenes: these three aspects—the intelligible, the psychic, and the material—entered into Jesus and made him an instrument of revelation to the three types of humanity—the angelic, the psychic, and the material. They go on to say that three kinds of churches correspond to these three types of men: a "church" for the elect (Gnostics themselves), a church for their shallower brethren, the "called" ones ("Many are called but few are chosen"), and a "captive" church. (The "captive" church may correspond to Paul's statement in *Galatians* that the Jerusalem below is enslaved.) The three churches, therefore, consist of enlightened persons (and this is an invisible, hidden church—no church at all, really), Christians generally, and the rest of mankind. All the sacred numbers come into play among the Gnostic writings: "He who seeks me," says Christ, "will find me in children from seven years (seven days in other texts—ed.); for there in the fourteenth age, having been hidden, I shall be manifest." And, as the known Israel consisted of twelve tribes, the heavenly realm contained twelve gates, through which the Savior spoke to his twelve followers—four disciples for each of the three types of humans.

The New Testament is not devoid of Gnostic ideas—the orthodox to the contrary notwithstanding. Paul speaks of a "pleroma," in *Ephesians 3:17-19,* where he seems to make parody of Gnostic catch-phrases: for example, he says men should *know (gnosis)* the fourfold "breadth, length, height and depth," of Christ's love which fills men with the *fullness (pleroma)* of God. In passages such as this, we are not clear if we read Paul's hostility toward the Gnostic heretics or his affection for them. Paul, in his efforts to build up the new Israel, is in the difficult position of making mystical experience the basis for a corporate religious life; he may have heard from these heretics that the inner sense cannot be made into a church. Paul responds by saying that love is greater than knowledge, and all things are possible to those who love God. But beyond Paul's issues with the Gnostics, Luke and Mark have given us documents that seem deliberately ambivalent, as if they could be taken in a literal sense of a history and doctrine of time, from Genesis to the Eschaton; and also at times are capable of esoteric interpretation. A perfect example is Mark's "little apocalypse," (*Mark 13*), which seems on the surface to be a prediction of an end-time catastrophe, and may well have been intended as such for "Christians generally"—the second type. Yet Mark tells us that on Mt. Olivet three times Jesus warns his inner circle to "take heed," and presses upon them that they should "take heed, watch, and pray." This "prediction" of a darkened sun and a lightless moon, and the exhortations to "watch...watch...and watch and pray" find their fulfillment when Jesus returns to Olivet and then, in Gethsemene's dark night, exhorts the inner three to "watch and pray" so that, deprived of the light of ordinary day, the eye that spies on the inner world will be opened; and, at his third approach, he tells them to "Rise up," for the hour of their martyrly anastasis is at hand. All this happens outside the moonlit temple, for Jesus and his inner circle are outsiders to the institutional religion.

As we look back upon the Christian Church and its history, we may well conclude that the Gnostics were right; the experience of the inner light and the ascent to the fullness of life are not adaptable to the life of great institutions. The Gnostic travels a solitary path. He is a *knower*; not the disciple of another or an ecclesiastic. He is a seer who brings forth primal creations that were before the world began; who brings forth fruit from the tree that is planted in the center of the garden, which it is forbidden for the many to eat.

The experience of the light and its associated images arise in the minds of those today who practice these arts, and what they see in their visions is identical to what was seen by Valentinus and the Gnostics, and by those who drank from the cup at the Eleusinian mysteries, and many others. For there is only one human psyche, and it is universal. Those who have this vision have made the ascent to the Mount of Transfiguration; they have achieved the healing and the wholeness promised by Christ to those who follow him to that high place. They are homeward bound among the stars.

The ascent-journey is a discovery of the true Self that lies beyond the shallow ego. The journey begins with a psychic turning, departing from the familiar round of living and dying. The one who makes the journey becomes transformed—but the change is internal and not visible to others. Yet, he is constrained to make a gift to the world, a "pearl of great price," that few men will want.

Jews and Christians look for the kingdom to break into the world's history and right all its wrongs. No such kingdom has even broken in—even though from early times preachers have tried to rekindle the expectation. All these apocalyptic and millennial sermons distract from the real business of the soul—its inner transformation, and the realization of the eternally indwelling Christ. Few preachers speak of this. The night is long and the watchmen are few.

PREFACE TO CHAPTER THREE

The parable of the Good Samaritan is about law and grace, and the secret presence of Jesus among us.

I used to agonize over this parable and what people take it to mean. When I was in parish ministry and the Church lectionary required me to read it and preach about it (On the Thirteenth Sunday after Trinity) I was faced with a decision. I could avoid it and preach about something else. Or I could inflict my interpretation of it upon the unsuspecting congregation. I took the latter course only once: that was at Grace Church in New York City in August of 1980 during the course of the Sunday Eucharist. After the service, a fine gentleman, a member of the congregation, came up to me and complimented me on my "spellbinding" sermon. But he was the only one. (Happily, this gentleman became a personal friend and advisor about matters spiritual. He has passed on; may he rest in peace.)

My problems with the parable began in Memphis, Tennessee a few years before, when I was Assistant Minister of St. John's Church. At that time, another Episcopal Church in that city had the custom of inviting guest speakers to address a noontime congregation during Lent. I attended one of these events. The speaker was The Reverend Dr. Arthur McGill, a Canadian scholar—I remember little more about him. But I remember that he spoke about the parable of the Good Samaritan. I will never forget what he said.

CHAPTER THREE

"A Certain Man..."

i. "The Question"

The man with the curt black beard and dim eye has been standing near the synagogue door for an hour. He would never come out during the heat of the day, but this day is different. Word has gone around that Jesus and his band of followers are nearby. He waits patiently. At last he will be able to spring the trap and ensnare the detested prophet. He is a lawyer and he knows what to do.

For most of his life he has been the authority in this village. People come to him for advice, for he is trained in God's law. But as he peers inside the synagogue, and among the sun-baked, squat houses that surround it, it seems that the whole village has gathered to hear the words of the prophet. He will have a few words to say himself—to the prophet. He is well prepared. It is risky; people may think him rude and arrogant. And he will be attacking an acclaimed prophet whom some ignorantly have called "messiah." But he will take the risk. It is his duty to expose the man as a fraud. He strokes his beard–he thinks it makes him appear thoughtful—and rehearses his lines.

A simple question will do. He will ask this question of the prophet and tempt him to give an outlandish answer–as he is reputed to do. Then, armed with the prophet's words, he will go to the priests in Jerusalem. The priests know him, they will respect his reputation and learning. Three times each day he recites the *Shemoneh Esreh*, a prayer that God's kingdom will come. He has heard that the prophet says much about the kingdom. He will report everything to the priests. They will listen. They will be shocked and angered. They will act.

Suddenly from the hills come several men, strangers. In their midst is a tall one. The people rush to greet him crying, "He comes, he comes!" The lawyer cannot see, but he can hear. He cuts through the crowd and puts his question to the detested one:

"Master, what must I do to inherit eternal life?"

Jesus recognizes the type of man who stands before him: the man is a teacher, not a learner. These lawyers, he has said to his disciples many times, claim to be teachers of God's law; they make pronouncements in God's name and tell others what to do. If they ever ask questions, they are merely catechetical or rhetorical questions he puts to his students; not requests to be enlightened. That is why he chose to call his disciples not from their kind but from among the uneducated—men like Peter and James and John, men who are eager to learn. He looks steadily at the face of the lawyer who strokes his beard and squints at him.

"What is written in the law?" he asks of the lawyer. It is as if he had said, "Your question is routine, fit only for the children in your synagogue; all Israel knows the answer.

Challenged, the lawyer is compelled to answer his own question; he must not appear ignorant in the presence of his people. "You shall love the Lord your God with all your heart, and with all your soul, and with all your strength, and with all your mind; and your neighbor as yourself." Jesus then responds—in his best catechetical tone, as if he were addressing a child—*"You have answered right. Do this and you shall live."*

The man senses humiliation at the hands of this strange prophet from afar. Needing to justify himself, he explains that of course he knows the answer to the question; he merely brought it up so that he could query Jesus on a fine point. Who is this neighbor that one is supposed to love as oneself? It is a question much debated among teachers of the law. It is respectable, therefore, to debate it with the prophet. He will put the question to Jesus and wait for the answer: *"And who is my neighbor?"* he asks. Jesus answers:

> *A certain man was going down from Jerusalem to Jericho, and fell among robbers, who stripped him and beat him, and departed, leaving him half-dead. Now by chance a priest was going down that road; and when he saw him he passed by on the other side. So likewise a Levite, when he came to the place and saw him, passed by on the other side. But a Samaritan, as he journeyed, came to where he was; and when he saw him, he had compassion, and went to him, and bound up his wounds, pouring on oil and wine; then he set him on his own beast and brought him to an inn, and*

took care of him. And the next day he took out two denarii and gave them to the innkeeper saying, "Take care of him; and whatever more you spend, I will repay you when I come back." Which of these three, do you think, proved neighbor to the man who fell among the robbers?"

The parable is an outrage: it belittles the priests and Levites and makes a hero of an outcast Samaritan. Yet, it is nothing he can report as illegal to the authorities. The prophet simply speaks as prophets are wont to speak. He remembers hearing recently that this prophet challenged the nation's inheritance laws, having said, "Do not begin to say 'We have Abraham to our father,' for I tell you, God is able to raise up from these stones children to Abraham." Now he implies that God has raised up from the stones a new hero, the outcast. He would spit in the prophet's face, were it not unseemly before the crowd, who seem pleased by the prophet's words. He senses that the prophet and the crowd are staring at him. They expect an answer to the question: *"Which of the three, do you think, proved neighbor to the man who fell among robbers?"* The question is oddly formed. He knows he has been tricked, but how? He can only mumble an answer: *"The one who showed mercy upon him."* He is relieved when others claim the prophet's attention. His anger builds as he makes his way to his house. He strokes his beard and picks over the details of the parable. Yes, he was tricked, but how?

Jesus understands this lawyer. He knows that the man's dedication to the law is the strength of the nation. The law has held them together as a nation when their enemies swarmed over them and took away their pride and their worship. But it has also made the people narrow. Lawyers like this one protect the nation's pride but they destroy the nation's soul, indeed, their own souls. Their souls, which ought to be loving God and fellow man, whoever he may be, are instead directed toward petty details and observances. This lawyer will go to his home and sulk over his lost chance to humiliate him, and he will spend his days wondering why he had given such and such a definition of neighbor, and not some other, at the parable's end. The point is interesting, and the legalists will make much of it. He had truly answered the man's question. The man had not heard it.

In the evening, Jesus takes the inner three disciples aside and presses them for their thoughts. What did they think about the conversation with the lawyer? Were they listening? They seem puzzled. That is good; they have not settled for the obvious. But they should have been listening; they would then have understood what the lawyer had not. These three had just been with him on the Mount, where their eyes had seen what no man had seen since the week of creation, and where their ears had heard the Voice say "This is my Son...listen to him." At the foot of the Mount he had said to them, "Let these words sink into your ears." Then he had spoken about Israel's failure to listen to God's call—Capernaum will be sent down to Hades, he had said. Hardly ever had he used such harsh words. Again he mentioned listening: "He who hears you hears me," he had said. He then turned to the Father in prayer: he thanked God that He had hidden certain things from the wise of the earth. After he had thus prayed, he turned his face to the disciples and said, "Blessed are the eyes which see what you see, for many prophets and kings desired to see what you see and did not see it, and to hear what you hear, and did not hear it." And it was at that moment, Jesus reminds them, that they came over the top of the hill and encountered the lawyer who came up and said:

"Master, what must I do to inherit eternal life?"

The lawyer typifies all Israel, which has not listened.

ii. Left as Dead

Not listened to what? we might ask. Let us look again at the Lucan narrative to see what has been missed.

We shall put ourselves in the place of the lawyer and imagine one who has come to the brink of humiliation over his question about eternal life and is reduced to asking a mundane question like "Who is my neighbor." (The Greek word is "pleision," better rendered as "friend" or "fellow countryman.") He hears Jesus begin a parable that begins, "A certain man..." What is he to make of this? He listens as Jesus continues: "...went down from Jerusalem to Jericho, and he fell among robbers..." The lawyer has made this trip himself, often; but he cannot imagine that Jesus may be speaking *of him*—he has never fallen among robbers. "...who stripped him, and beat him, and departed, leaving him half dead." Now the man thinks he knows what Jesus is trying to say: a man has been attacked—he has heard of that happening to some friends—and soon a righteous man will come by and befriend him. Clearly, he says to himself, this is how the prophet will answer my question: the righteous man recognizes his neighbor in need. A simple parable.

And in the back of his mind he is prepared to identify with the righteous man. He, a student of the law and a custodian of the nation's righteousness, would have done exactly such a thing—the law required it. He extends himself to others, and preaches that others should do the same, as a sign of their righteousness. On another level, he calculates his gain: self-satisfaction, perhaps, or building a creditable relationship with God and others—staking a claim to a place in God's kingdom. For whatever reason, he claims virtue in the sight of the law, which is to say, in God's sight. This is his religion, his self-image. As he listens to Jesus' parable unfold, he anticipates that the third of three men will come and be the righteous hero. Three men? Yes, because so many parables were triadic in form—two wrongs followed by a right. He himself is to be the third man, the hero of the parable. It fits.

He listens as the prophet continues: *"By chance a priest was going down that road; and when he saw him, he passed by on the other side."*

We can picture the lawyer: his lips move, but he does not speak; he makes as if to tear his garments–a sign of horror. He is outraged. Jesus has denied righteousness to a priest and stated that the priest traveled the road by chance. No, the lawyer would want to say: priests are important, busy men, they do not go to or from Jerusalem by chance. Then, to make things worse, Jesus adds that a Levite passed by and likewise failed to do his duty. So, the lawyer would think, Jesus has not only insulted the priests, he has insulted their assistants as well. It is all he can do to hold his wrath.

Jesus finishes the parable: he tells of a Samaritan who came to that place, poured wine and oil into the victim's wounds, lifted him onto his beast, took him to an inn, cared for him during the night, and in the morning he told the innkeeper that he will return and pay all the victim's debts.

The lawyer is confounded. It is blasphemy, he believes, that Jesus ascribes righteousness to a loathsome heretic, one whose people worship at false shrines and make mockery of God's law. And the heretic goes beyond the law: he poured oil and wine—precious commodities in a desert—into the victim's wounds, stayed with him through the night, and promised to return to pay all the man's expenses. It is outlandish. Foolish, even. Why did the righteous man prove to be a Samaritan? Well, he reasons, it is a common teaching method to exaggerate; the prophet is skilled, he admits. But to what end?

Then he notices the twist. Jesus did not say, "Who is the neighbor who was shown love by a passing righteous man?" No:– he asked, "Which of the three was neighbor...": thus it was impossible to apply the expected response, that the neighbor is the victim whom righteous men are commanded to love. No: —The word "neighbor" was used to describe, not the wounded man, but the righteous hero—the Samaritan. The prophet put the question to him in such a way that he had to answer—like it or not—that the neighbor is one of the three travelers, not the wounded man by the side of the road. Why?

We may imagine the lawyer's head was spinning and that he went to his bed that night with the prayer that the perverse prophet himself will be set upon by thieves and left as dead.

iii. The Answer"

Had the lawyer not identified in his mind with the righteous hero, he might have recognized his true place in the parable. For he is there; he is both *outside* the parable and *inside* the parable. Outside, he stands in the presence of the true prophet and asks a question about eternal life. Inside, he is the man by the side of the road whose need for eternal life is immediate and urgent. Inside and outside, the question is the same:

"Master, what must I do to inherit eternal LIFE?"
(*ZOA*, in Greek)
Jesus states the problem thus:

"A certain man went down from Jerusalem to Jericho, and he fell among thieves...who left him half DEAD."

The lawyer, being a lawyer, got caught up in a legal definition of terms; and in so doing, he forgot his own question. When he hears Jesus tell the parable, therefore, he assumes the parable will address his interest in a definition of "neighbor." But it does not. It addresses the primal question, the question men have pondered since the fall of Adam.

The lawyer's question was conventional, routine. Jesus made it personal.

No doubt the man would have been displeased in the extreme had he realized the personal intent behind the prophet's words. For he was a legalist, a moralist; he thought about deeds and the law. He lost the moment when he could have gained his "inheritance." But of course what Jesus offers is not a matter of law or of inheritance; it is a matter of origin and destiny.

The lawyer's counterpart in the parable, however, the dying man, is the epitome of sincerity. The man has been stripped; what but sincerity is left to him? In desperate silence he asks the ultimate question, the question about LIFE. He had journeyed from Jerusalem toward Jericho—a true descent, for Jerusalem stands twenty five hundred feet about sea level, while Jericho, in the Jordan Valley five miles from the Dead Sea, is eight hundred feet below that level, in a strip of parched earth that is an abode of death. (The desert is one of three negative worlds in the Semitic mind: the desert, the dark, and death. The three are often equated: when the fourth evangelist wrote that "The Light shone in the darkness and the darkness comprehended it not," he must surely have alluded to the desert. It was beyond the reach of God's pity.) Truly, the man went down into the pit.

Paradoxically, the desert is also the realm of miracle and redemption. According to *Exodus* Moses led the Israelites out of Egypt's dark night to a place where after three days they worshiped God. They then made their escape from Pharaoh; they passed through the Red Sea waters and began their journey through the desert and came at length to Mt. Sinai and its fiery revelation; they came finally to the new land where their first conquest was Joshua's midday miracle at Jericho. The exodus journey is often on the minds of the New Testament authors: they depict Jesus as a new Moses and a new Joshua who leads his people on a new journey through the negative worlds. Jesus began his work in the desert, being baptized by that creature of the desert, John the Baptist, and when he came up from the waters, he began his journey that led him to the Mount of Transfiguration, where he encountered Moses. Luke's history is clear that Jesus' ministry passed through three stages: the desert baptism, the Transfiguration on the Mount, and the last journey to Jerusalem and his death. It was shortly after his descent from the Mount of Transfiguration that he met the lawyer and thereupon told his parable about Jerusalem and Jericho. As we read this text we see Jesus march through a mystical desert as real as the sand under Moses' feet, and speak in images taken from the desert mythology: the parable of the Samaritan plays on the images of desert, darkness and death. And in this context we are led to expect miracle.

But no miracle will come from the priest who by chance comes down that road. He passes by on the other side. Now, we cannot know in which direction the priest was going—to or from Jerusalem. (Christian lore about this parable has it that the priest was going to Jerusalem to lead a seminar on the subject of "Love of one's neighbor.") But what matters to Luke is that the man is there by chance and that he has no humanity. We may take it for certain that Luke shows his contempt for the Jewish hierarchy; the priest makes no spiritual journey; he simply happens to be there. (Students of Luke will recall that when he describes the duty of Zechariah the priest in 1:5-9, he points out that the priest's division was on duty and he had been chosen *by lot* to enter the temple and burn incense.) Those who make a spiritual journey do so not by chance but by choice.

(The briefest of footnotes: is it possible that the priest is a *pagan* priest? It seems unlikely, since he travels to—or from—Jerusalem; and we are aware of Luke's feelings about the Jewish priesthood. Yet, it is also true that Luke takes an interest in matters beyond the Jewish religion, and many among his readership may be Gentiles. Luke has used the word "lawyer," instead of scribe, and he speaks of "eternal life" instead of just life, thus giving the text a broad reference. Moreover, the priest travels alone: the Jewish priests assigned to temple worship would have made the trip in groups. If the priest is pagan, then the Levite following represents the Jewish religion quite by himself.)

Who is the Samaritan? We have assigned roles to the priest and the Levite; we should assign a role to the Samaritan. But we do not know who he is. We have hinted at the identity of the victim. Let us study the two as a linked pair. First, we note that neither is on the road by chance. It is said of the priest and likewise the Levite that they came that way by chance; but it is not said of the "certain man" and his rescuer. This is a destined rendezvous, for these two have been seeking each other since the beginning of time.

Let us take the dying man by the side of the road. With the voiceless cry of the sudden dead he calls out and the Samaritan—and the Samaritan only—hears him. His need is great—ETERNAL LIFE, for so it was defined by the lawyer's question. Who is it in Scripture who calls out thus? He is "a certain man," Luke calls him: *tis aner* in the Greek text; he is noted elsewhere in Scripture under different guises. Luke's friend, John, in his *Gospel*, calls him Lazarus, who is a man gone down into the same pit. Both men cry out for ETERNAL LIFE; both are Adam, who is the first of many things: the first to be smitten by an enemy, the first to be consigned to the pit of eternal death, the first—we may believe—to cry out for a savior.

Man sets out on a journey through the wilderness of this world seeking the way back to the Paradise that was his. Many religions have failed him. Then comes into the world a stranger, one whose origins are obscure and disputed—who was born in a manger, Luke says—and whose parentage is suspect; who rises above the law and takes man with him to an inn where he passes the dark of night. When Adam awakes in the morn, he will be in Paradise with his Christ.

Jesus journeys too. Luke wants us to understand this: twice, after Jesus has descended from the mount, Jesus sets his face toward Jerusalem. Jerusalem. Jerusalem is the spiritual center of the world; God established it a thousand years before he made the world. Jesus goes there to die and be glorified, to die and rise as the world's savior. On his way he preaches the kingdom, and accuses Israel of hypocrisy. Two men whom he encounters on his journey prove unworthy of the kingdom. He continues his journey down the road and searches for one who will typify those whose sincerity make them worthy. His journey takes him through Samaritan villages. He declares that the kingdom is present in his deeds, that Satan has been vanquished, that he is Lord of the Harvest. People do not listen; they do not understand. Finally he comes upon a third man, a man from whom all pretense has been stripped; this man has journeyed *from* Jerusalem, for he is Adam, expelled from Paradise by a primordial event that sent him spinning into darkness and void. The two meet in the mystical scene on the parabolic road. The new Adam, Lord of the Harvest, and third of three, gathers up the old Adam and takes him home.

The lawyer was there on the road, and not by chance; he had an intent. But it was malicious. He is a hypocrite typical of those whom Jesus has rebuked earlier on his journey. More: the man is a moralist; that too is fatal. If the preachments of the moralist constitute our religion, then we may indeed be a "good neighbor" unto others, but then life is but holding hands around the grave. We need to identify ourselves as needy ones; we may hold hands, but we need a redeemer to reach down and lift us up.

Outside the parable, the lawyer stands in the presence of the answer to his question about Eternal Life. The answer is, first, that he must recognize himself in the parable—recognize his humanity and his deepest needs. Then he will recognize the presence of Jesus in his life. He need only then to let the divine Samaritan do his wonders. But no, the lawyer does not listen; he does not perceive that Jesus has recreated in the parable the psychological situation that the two men share. But Jesus listens: he has listened to man's cries since the day of Adam. And he has never been far away.

Jesus, the Lord of Life, stood outside the parable when he spoke to the lawyer, and the lawyer failed to recognize him. But inside the parable he acted to rescue one who, recognizing him, called out to him. Thus it will be when he comes to Bethany; he will come to those who know him. Bethany stands on the road that leads from Jerusalem to Jericho. Luke alludes to it as "a certain village." Only two miles outside the holy city, on the southeast slope of Mt. Olivet, it is today called El-Azirieh by the Arabs, after Lazarus who lived there with his sisters Mary and Martha. Anyone making the journey between Jericho and Jerusalem must pass through it. Luke is the first to tell us that Jesus came that way. Immediately following his encounter with the lawyer, Jesus comes to the "certain village" and enters into the house of Mary and Martha.

Suddenly we have entered the spiritual world of John's Gospel. The fourth evangelist, in his tenth chapter, has been relating words of Jesus: that he is the good shepherd, the door of the sheep—all who came before him are thieves and robbers. The sheep hear his voice, he says, and he knows them; he will give them eternal life and they will not perish. Having made these declarations, he pauses a moment in the desert where John first baptized, then goes directly to the village of Mary and Martha, where "a certain man" is ill. It is Lazarus. Many Scripture commentators have remarked how strange it is that the four characters here seem to know each other, though they have never met. We must understand that this is no ordinary story; it is a rendering of origin and destiny. What Jesus has done inside his parable as good Samaritan, he now will do in Bethany as good shepherd, who confers eternal life upon those sheep who hear his voice.

That John tells Luke's story and finishes it is hardly to be doubted when we note the parallels:

> Luke 10. The failure of Israel; its hypocrites—priests and Levites who fail to love the "certain man" attacked by thieves, and who fail to perceive that the Lord's healings are from God.

John 10   Strangers whom the sheep do not follow; thieves and robbers; Jesus states that he does the works of the Father.

Luke 10:29   "A certain man" went down...was left half dead. (*anthropos tis.*)

John 11:1 "A certain man was ill," and (11:14) dead. (*tis.*)

Luke 10:38   Now he entered a village...(*komas tina*, certain village)

John 11:1...the village of Mary and Martha (*komas*, village)

Luke 10:39   Mary sat at the Lord's feet...

Luke 10:25-37   The lawyer and the "certain man" have need of Life; Adam and his children.   The lawyer's ignorance is unto death. The Samaritan, who risks his own life to bind up the dying man.

John 10:1-11:44 A "certain man," Lazarus, in dire need, is granted Life. His illness was not unto death. Martha utters words of pure faith. The shepherd, in danger from those who would kill him; but he will lay down his life for the sheep.

We may believe that when we read the Lazarus episode in John, we are probing the evangelist's mind on the Good Samaritan parable. Other parallels come to light: Luke relates that Jesus, after he visited Mary and Martha, told parables about giving to those who have not (11:ff); these parables are transfigured in the parable of Dives and Lazarus (16:19-31), which also tells of giving to those who have not—Lazarus being the beggar who stands in need. Luke ends this parable by speaking of one who comes back from the dead. Lazarus is a name mentioned only in this parable and in John's story of the man come back from the dead. In Luke, he is a poor man; in John, his head is bandaged—a sign of poverty.

John, in his subtle way, has introduced the sacred number three into the Lazarus narrative. In the New Testament, this number is used to signify God's presence and the final destiny of pilgrims who seek him along life's road. As we have indicated, the wilderness tradition included this number: (*Exodus 8:27*), wherein the children of Israel gained a three day headstart over pharaoh when they began their journey to the promised land. In the third month, they came upon the Sinai desert (*Exodus 19:1-16*) and on the third day they heard the thunderings and saw the lightening flashes from the mount, as the Lord came upon it amidst the fire. In this way, God inaugurated the salvation-history that brings us to the pages of Luke and John as they relate Jesus' threefold saving work among the people of their day. Where do we find it? John says that Jesus delayed two days after hearing word about Lazarus, then he set forth with the disciples to go to Bethany. (11:6). It is the third day, therefore, when he comes to the tomb and hears that Lazarus has been dead four days. Lazarus is dead indeed (Jews believed that a man's spirit hovered about his corpse three days, then departed), and Jesus comes to him bearing the word that Lazarus would utter were he able—ZOA, LIFE. "I am the resurrection and the LIFE," he says to Lazarus' sister. Three times he uses the word. This is no parable: the word ZOA is on the lips of Jesus himself, not on the lips of the hypocrite who in Luke first used the word, and who now is exposed as the true outsider, for Jesus is with men and women of purity and faith. Martha's response is that of an untrained layperson and a woman, to whom Jesus does not hesitate to speak, and from whom such a response would be unlikely; but on this third day she utters a confession of Easter praise—"Yes, Lord, I believe..."

The number three is often used by the evangelists to mark stages in a person's progress toward the Divine Person. In Luke, we read the parable of the man who planted a vineyard (20:9-18) and let it out to tenants. He sends two messengers to require the payment of fruit, then finally he sends his "beloved son." The Son is clearly a Christ-figure. Thus we compare:

Parable of 20:9	Parable of 10:30
(1) first messenger,	(1) priest,
(2) second messenger,	(2) levitical priest,
(3) the Son;	(3) the Samaritan.

We might ponder also the parable at 20:27-38, together with the explanation that serves as context; here three men out of seven must perform a task on behalf of a deceased brother; it is not the same pattern, but it pertains to the God unto whom all live (*zoa*) and the sons of the resurrection. But it is in the beloved prodigal son parable that Luke's mind works on many levels as he takes us to the heart of mystery. "A certain man" has two sons...(15:11-32). The first is a "spendthrift," who left home for a far country, but fell upon bad days and fed among the swine. The older brother stayed home. When the first son returns home, this son complains but the father rejoices: "This my son was dead and is alive again," he exclaims. There is a fourth character who hovers about this parable and enters into it where he hides as a mythic third son. Neither prodigal nor carping, he is the pattern son, who himself left home and security with his Father and went to a far country to live with those who feed with swine. He truly is the Son who was dead and is alive again.

iv. An Unusual Interpretation

When Dr. McGill had finished speaking, there was a round of applause. The Doctor announced that he would be available for questions and answers. No one spoke at first. The doctor primed the pump by acknowledging that his interpretation of the parable is unusual, that most people take it as a simple lesson that we should be kind to those in trouble. He went on like this until a man rose and addressed the Doctor: "I still don't understand," the man said, "Who is *my* neighbor?" The audience seemed stunned. Here was a layman addressing the learned doctor—the reverse of the situation that called forth the parable—and asking the same question. The question was sincerely asked. And graciously answered:

"Do you mean, inside the parable, or outside of it," the doctor answered. He smiled, lifted a glass of water to his lips, and started in again. His motions enabled us all to laugh; we had already been given permission to do that by the fine humor sprinkled about the course of his talk.

"Luke wants to draw us inside the parable and meet Jesus there," he began. "But no one will recognize Jesus if he wants to be the hero himself. It has to do with identifying, you see. The lawyer wanted to be the hero, so he failed to see himself as part of the suffering and dying human race that cries out for the Savior. As a moralist, he thought the law was all he needed, the answer to all questions. And, as a moralist, he was an egotist. He asks "What must I do, *ego poesas, ego poesas*, in the Greek; or, in Latin, *ego faciendo*. He wanted to be center-stage, a show-off. But Jesus blocked him when he said 'Which of the three, do you think, was neighbor to him who fell among the thieves?' The lawyer must have felt it like a body slam. He had wanted the neighbor to be the dying man, so that he could identify with the hero who obeys the law to help his fellow man. Not possible. The hero turns out to be a half-breed; how could the lawyer identify with *that*? The wording of Jesus' question confirms that the lawyer cannot be the hero. The Samaritan is the neighbor. The lawyer, realizing this, is so upset that he cannot utter the word *Samaritan*; he can only answer Jesus' question by saying, 'He who showed mercy...' "

One of the clergy in the audience stood and commented: "Dr. McGill, you are saying that moralists like the lawyer really demand that Jesus treat them exactly as they think they are, as if to say, 'Jesus, approve of me, I am a righteous hero.' "

"Yes, that is exactly so," the doctor agreed. "They try to earn their place in the kingdom of God's love. And that's another thing about moralists—they do not love. They judge people so harshly that they render people unlovable in their sight. No wonder they can't love. But the summary of the law quoted by the lawyer really favors Jesus more than Moses, because it speaks of love. Jesus stressed love. Who is it in the parable who loves?" Everyone agreed that the Samaritan loved, that he acted out of love.

"The lawyer typifies *our* problem—we have all been raised to believe in law as a religion and religion as law. We see this in the lawyer. In him the legalistic striving for Eternal Life is a narrow self-preservation and prideful self-exaltation. We see this writ large in many politicians and preachers: they flatter themselves...and others; they confirm for people that their virtues and conduct are ever so important and that they will surely earn a place in God's kingdom. When the moralist addresses Jesus—or thinks of him—he says this: "Master, I keep the righteous law. If there is any little thing I lack, just let me know and I'll correct it for sure so you can reward me." Luke gives an example where a ruler expresses interest in Eternal Life but he hears from Jesus the unexpected words that no one is good but God alone. That's at 18:18, I think."

But the first man rose slowly to his feet again. The doctor smiled at him and said, "You are wondering who is your neighbor *outside* the parable, I'll bet." Indeed he was.

"Well," said the doctor, "let me put it this way. Who is the most lovable person in the world, inside or outside the parable?" The man didn't hesitate: "Why, our Lord, of course." The doctor said, "Yes. Jesus in the parable is the loving hero, and he is that in our lives as well. He is easy for us to love. Therefore, we can fulfill the law to love our neighbor—he is our neighbor."

Several of the clergy looked at each other; one of them frowned, another stroked his chin. One of them got up and put his question to the doctor: "But what about our fellow man. We are commanded to love our neighbor as ourselves. Do you mean to say that we are simply commanded to love Jesus?"

"The parable speaks first of life," the doctor said. "We can't forget that. When a person has been blessed by the gift of eternal life, and knows this in his heart, he can begin to love. First, life; then, love. Otherwise, we are dead—to use Scriptural terms—and dead people don't love."

He turned to the blackboard and put up a few words and arrows. "Look here," he said, pointing to a round face and a few arrows. "The moralist looks up and he looks down at the same time. He looks up to God in prayer." He pointed to an arrow that pointed up. "He looks up to God, but he listens only to the voice of Moses. He does not get through to God. Then, when he looks down..."—he pointed to the downward facing arrow— "... as he often does, he looks down upon those less righteous than himself."

The doctor was in trouble. Many of the same clergy made remarks beginning with "Yes, but..." Finally the doctor appealed to the Apostle Paul. "Paul says this all the time, that the works of the law cannot save us. Law is only our schoolmaster to teach us of Christ. After we have been transformed inwardly by the Samaritan, then we have the power to love others. By love, I mean unconditional love, *agape*, such as the Samaritan had for the victim." He went on at length about Paul and *agape*, but the clergy voiced objections. It came as a relief when another clergyman asked a different question: "How do you find Adam in the parable," he asked.

"The victim is not just any man, he is 'a certain man'—that is Luke's way of underscoring him, spotlighting him so we will look closely. Some of the early Church fathers saw Adam as the dying man, and Christ as the Samaritan; the inn was the church, the two denarii the two sacraments of baptism and the Eucharist; the Samaritan's promise spoke of the Lord's second coming to earth. Well, I'm not so sure about how much church is in the parable. But I'm sure about the Samaritan as Christ, and the 'certain man' as Adam. In *Genesis*, Adam was attacked by our common enemy— Satan—and stripped of his inheritance, Eternal Life. And remember, Luke, in his genealogy of the Christ—and only Luke does this—takes Christ's roots right back to Adam. So the line that governs inheritance runs from Adam to Christ."

A new questioner rises: "Can you explain more about how Adam and the Samaritan are linked?"

"Well," the doctor went on, "as I said, the genealogy is outlined by Luke so that what Adam lost, his inherent right to Eternal Life, must be restored by someone in the line to inherit—the Christ. It's not a legal matter, it is suggestive, allusive. That's how Luke's mind works. He is not a legalist. Also, Jesus is called 'the new Adam' in the New Testament."

A young man stood up—he later identified himself as a divinity student. "I've read in Irenaeus—he's one of the fathers you mentioned, who understood that the Samaritan is Christ, that Christ is the physician who heals. The parable is about healing."

The doctor went to the podium and turned through pages of notes. "Yes," he said, "I had meant to get to that point. Here it is...Man by original sin became *spoliatus gratuitis, vulneratus in naturalibus*— pardon the Latin—which means stripped of his gifts and wounded in his nature. And Luke is called the physician among the evangelists. That's a good perspective."

Several were standing or showing their hands; questions were flying from all quarters. "The robbers could be anyone or group that abuses what's best in us, dictators, predators...and the like, would you agree?"

He agreed readily. "Yes, but to say this is to step outside the parable. Inside the parable, it was the original enemy—Satan is probably intended—and then the uncaring religions. And in the parable, notice the oppositions: the robbers take life, the Samaritan restores it. The robbers take money; the Samaritan gives it. Yet, they are similar in that they have no fixed place on the road. The priest and the Levite are fixtures on the road—they belong there. Others must be from above or below it. The Samaritan enters from above; the robbers from below. By the way, Bishop Sheen told a joke on one of his TV programs recently: he said that the reason the priests kept on going was they perceived the man had already been robbed."

He had united his audience with his humor; and regained his momentum.

But soon another clergyman objected that the priest and Levite in the parable were overly scolded by the doctor; all clergymen would not be like that. The doctor responded: "I did not say that the priests were evil; I said that they would not take risk; they were too conservative—they stayed on the road. They are not of the kingdom." His words dropped like a stone in the midst of the clergy who had previously questioned him. Eventually the doctor had to defend his words about the role of law in religion. "Those who look to the law for their communion with God will not find Him. They will have neither intimacy nor ecstasy."

The clergyman spoke up again. "But, Dr. McGill, what about *Romans 13,* where we are taught to obey laws and rulers. We live in a Christian nation..." Soon many voices were heard in support of this position. But the doctor was not about to be overwhelmed: "Society of course must have its laws," he said, "but the parable speaks of spirituality—matters of the spirit. A religion based on law cannot redeem. The wounded man in the parable was rescued not by the lawyer but by the Samaritan."

A scholarly looking gentleman who had been sitting in the back got up; he identified himself as a professor of religious studies at Southwestern University in Memphis. "Dr. McGill, will you please go over what you said about the "three" symbol in the Lazarus story?" he asked.

The doctor seemed to appreciate this question more than some of the others. "Yes, the number is sometimes obvious, sometimes hidden. First, the scholar Rudolph Bultmann considers that the Lazarus story is told in three stages. I agree with him. Then, another scholar, Alfred Loisy, looks at John's Gospel as centered on the number seven, which is a four and a three: he says that Lazarus died at the moment Jesus announced his death; Jesus waits two days after receiving the message—three days there; he journeys four days to reach Lazarus on a symbolic seventh day. Loisy, by the way, lost his teaching office for finding too much symbolism in John's Gospel. That was back in 1892. But most scholars since that time have accepted the fact of symbolism, not just in John, but throughout the New Testament."

At that more hands shot up. One woman took aim at the doctor: "Doctor McGill, do you believe the Bible is the Word of God?"

"No," he said. "I believe God plants his words like seeds directly into the hearts of people. Not books, but people. Now, tonight we have been speaking about a lawyer's question about Life. Let me quote an authority on the subject—Jesus, himself. He rebuked some people once when he said, "You search the scriptures...but you refuse to come to me for Life."

At that, he moved toward the steps that led from the platform to signal that the evening was over. But one more voice sounded through the hall: "What did Jesus mean when he said 'Go and do thou likewise' to the lawyer?"

Speaking from the edge of the platform, he answered. "I have in the past heard the voice of Moses in that command. But I was wrong. Not Moses, not another law—God forbid—but an utterance of Christ. The words were addressed to the lawyer, but I'm sure they were wasted on him; they fly over his head and enter the ears of Christians of the early communities, people who were called to discipleship, to martyrdom even. They were called to be Christ-like to one another, to bind one another's wounds, provide comfort and refuge, and share dark hours, as they awaited the Lord's coming. Many Christians in those days lived in communes, they shared their lives and hopes. Luke considered them perfectly capable of being Christ-like because they had been transfigured by His secret presence in their midst."

CHAPTER FOUR

The Mark of the Beast

Carter J. Gregory

The angel fastening the gates of hell

186

i. *"The Devil is Nobody's Fool"*

Father James LeBar is an exorcist. He does his work as a priest of the Catholic Church in the Archdiocese of New York, where he is well known and honored for his work. I met Father LeBar at a conference in 1990, when he spoke about Satanism, possession, and evil doings around the world. He kindly gave me a copy of his book, Cults, Sects, and the New Age, which has aided me in preparing the manuscript for this chapter. Since I work at a hospital close to his parish assignment in Hyde Park, New York, I am able to meet with him for lunch at a local diner where we talk about many things, but especially I look forward to hearing about his latest encounter with the Evil One. I have seen videos he has taken of some of these encounters. they could never have been staged, not even by Steve Spielberg.

A few years ago Fr. LeBar was interviewed by Tom Gerald for 20/20, a TV program that fancies the lurid and exotic. (He justifies appearing on shows like this: it get out the word that he is available to help people.) Some harrowing film footage was shown during that interview (not LeBar's—the work of another priest who was his mentor.) But LeBar has videos of some of his own exorcisms, and these set me on edge. I should explain that he makes these videos not for show, but for a more sensible reason: "One never knows what issues might arise in the wake of such an intervention in a person's life," he points out. That remark is a reminder to me that an exorcism is a violent real-life drama that does not always go according to script.

LeBar is not one to repeat himself; when he says something that captures my interest I take instant note of it. After lunch at the diner one day, while rummaging for his car keys, he muttered, "The Devil is nobody's fool." When he found the keys in a deep pocket, his mind turned to something else. But I sensed mystery. "What's the Devil got to do with your car keys?" I asked. "Oh, one of his tricks," he said. He explained: he had booked a flight to Milwaukee where he was needed by the parents of a possessed child. When he was ready to leave for the airport, he couldn't find his car keys. He searched the rectory from the porch to the altar. No keys. But he was prepared for this sort of thing; a fellow priest was standing by to drive him to the

187

airport. There, his flight was delayed due to mechanical trouble. A day late, he arrived in Milwaukee to learn that the Devil had left the child, who appeared normal. "Well," he said, "I see I'm not needed. I'll go home." He took a room at a nearby motel. The next day the call came. He pushed through the back door of the house and into the bedroom where he found the boy four feet off the floor and cursing in church Latin. "**So you tried to fool me**," the Devil said. LeBar said "Yes,—and now you must leave." He pulled out his missal and recited the prayers that invoke God's power over evil. Before long, the Devil left, screaming that he was "nobody's fool," and that LeBar hadn't heard the last of him. When LeBar returned to his rectory, he found the car keys on top of his bureau, exactly where he always kept them. This time they were visible.

"You outwitted him," I said.

"No—it's been a draw for a few thousand years." He paused as the table server took our order— I knew he didn't want to be overheard; he cradled his coffee cup in two large hands and stared directly at me. I studied his square-jawed resolve, but I also noted his wary gaze. Finally he explained: "It all began when the father of lies outwitted Adam." He took on a deep timbre when he spoke of his enemy; I almost felt a chill—his eyes, usually warm and deep, turned stone cold and each word was packed in ice.

"The evil one baits and traps. When he tricked Adam, he was trying to hurt God. When he enters a person today, he tries to hurt God again, this time by seducing God's priest."

"You mean," I said, "that the exorcist—you—are the intended victim? The first victim is bait—when you come, the Devil springs the trap?"

"That is exactly what I mean."

I never asked why he did this work. But this time he came close when he said, "The Devil loves nothing more than to destroy God's Church, and he goes after priests because they are the ministers of Christ. The first Christian exorcist was Jesus himself. A priest must do the work he began."

He pulled his chair closer to the table and scanned the room. "Many priests," he whispered, "no longer believe the Devil exists. This is sad."

His eyes held mine.

In the ensuing pause, I pondered my response.

"I do not believe in a literal Devil. Evil exists, certainly, but evil is...."

"If Goodness is personal," he added, "so is Evil."

"You mean, God and the Devil?"

He cut into his open roast beef sandwich, leaving a silence between us.

I prompted him: "I'm a liberal Episcopalian, you know; we tend to be a bit skeptical at times..."

"No you aren't." he said.

"Not what?"

"Skeptical."

I was puzzled.

He put down his knife and stared at me. "A skeptic," he said, "is someone who has studied a difficult matter long and hard, but still cannot accept some position or doctrine about it." He reached for his coffee, and broke out in broad smile. "You, on the other hand..."

"...are merely ignorant." I finished the sentence for him.

From that moment on he and I had an understanding: he would do exorcisms, and I would study the subject—at a distance. He told me many stories about exorcisms and exorcists—his stories and those of other priests, such as Father Gabriel Amorth of Rome—and he gave me some books. Most of the books I found pedantic or doctrinaire. But one day at the diner he handed me a new book by a journalist, Tom Allen. He told me it was a "blow by blow" account of an exorcism in St. Louis in 1949 that served as material for the movie "The Exorcist." I thumbed through it, then read a few pages.

"Is this all true?" I asked.

"Very much so, down to the last detail." He told how one of the priests, Father Raymond Bishop, had kept a secret diary that had been forgotten for years, but finally discovered during a renovation of the hospital in which the exorcism took place. Allen heard about it, got hold of the diary, interviewed some of the priests who were still alive, and wrote the book. I took it home to read.

A few days later I called him. "We have to talk," I said. We arranged to meet at the diner. I got there first and began to mark pages in the book that I wanted to talk about. Suddenly I heard the table servers call out, "There he is!" I looked up. LeBar, a broad-boned six footer in clerical black, is easy to spot—the women intercepted him as he strode toward my table. "We saw your picture in the paper," one of them said, as she held up a copy of the New York Daily News— "We didn't know you did all of that."

Finally I got hold of the paper. "Exorcist drives out devils," said the header. The article described his work, adding some things I hadn't known—LeBar served as consultant to some popular movies about devil possession.

At lunch—we got superb table service—I asked him why, according to Allen, when the chief exorcist, Father William S. Bowdern, went to pray for the victim, he had two others with him— three priests. He had the answer: "A medieval rubric specifies that an exorcism must, if possible, be done by three priests. That's in case the chief exorcist faints...or drops dead."

That made practical sense.

"The urinating and defecating...such velocity, such capacity..." — I wanted to say that Allen exaggerated, but chose my words more carefully—"have you seen anything like that?"

"I'm afraid so. And vomiting. It's called projectile vomiting or voiding; the Devil aims at the priest through the victim's stomach, bladder and bowels. He never misses."

"Viewed psychologically," I said—trying not to sound clinical— "the Devil in that 1949 exorcism behaved childishly. Children void on furniture, rugs, in public places, to embarrass their parents..."

He raised an eyebrow and gave me a corrective stare. "The Devil is much too old to be a child," he said.

I closed Allen's book and got onto another subject. "In Mark's Gospel, Satan stalks Jesus from start to finish. Do you believe Satan stalks you?"

"Of course. He picks his victims, looks for a weakness, then attacks."

The notion that Satan stalks his victims had a perverse tone to it— Satan is a psychopath, it seemed, a symbol of all predator psychotics and antisocials that humanity has unhappily bred since the days of Cain. That evening a text from my evening prayer office struck me with uncanny force:

> The Devil, like a roaring lion, goeth about seeking whom he may devour.

The text is from Peter's *First Epistle*. What could have inspired the great saint to depict the Devil as a lion stalking its prey? I opened my bible to the two epistles. In the second epistle, the name Noah caught my eye. Noah's ark was full of animals, to be sure—but what of it? The saint envisions apocalyptic fury as the world comes to its end—and he speaks to us about animals. Curious. He goes on to mention that seven persons other than Noah were saved from the flood waters—numbers were on my mind; I was contemplating the numerology in Mark's *Gospel*. The saint speaks of "irrational animals," Balaam's ass, dog's vomit and sow's mire. He even alludes to exorcism: wicked doers are like "waterless springs and mists driven by a storm," who entice others into their folly, men whose "last state will be worse than the first." *Their last state...?* The words resonated: finally I found what I was looking for: in Luke's *Gospel*, I read, "When the unclean spirit has passed out of a man, he passes through waterless places seeking rest; and finding none he says 'I will return to my house from which I came.' And when he comes he finds it swept and put in order. Then he goes and brings seven other spirits more evil than himself, and they enter and dwell there; and the last state of that man becomes worse than the first."

The saint contemplates the second coming of Christ, having said that by the word of God the heavens existed long ago, and an earth formed out of water and by means of water, through which the world that then existed was deluged with water and perished. The text in *Luke* (*11:14ff.*) follows upon a confrontation between Jesus his enemies concerning his work as an exorcist; the parallel in *Matthew* (*12:38ff.*) follows hard upon a reference to Jonah, who was devoured by a sea monster and spent three days in its dark belly. I had a madhouse of themes, numbers, and images: Christ coming again, water, Noah, Jonah, the sacred numbers three and seven, wicked men and violence, animals seeking their prey, animals and their mire, demons, and exorcisms.

And it was this saint who, on the rooftop in Joppa, saw a vision of animals and heard the voice say, "Rise, Peter, kill and eat." Peter was stunned: all his life he had not eaten unclean animals.

The confrontation between Jesus and his enemies is called "The Beelzebub controversy"— Beelzebub is one of many names for the Devil; it means "lord of flies," and when Luke uses that name, he has alluded to a popular notion among the people that in the last days

Satan will be bound. (My mind's eye sees flies setting on carrion, and the stink of it.) *The Book of Tobit* adds to the lore: when a demon or devil is expelled from its victim, an angel will appear and carry the demon back to the desert where he came from and bind him so that he can never return. The desert is the "waterless place," a place where there can be no life. The little known *Book of Jude* echos Peter's words with a forthright denunciation of evil doers: he compares their sins to the instincts of "irrational animals" and he reminds his readers of the Archangel Michael, alluding to a destined battle between the devil and the angel in some wilderness that he does not name.

At the time I was writing the first chapter of the manuscript that eventually materialized into this book. The reader will understand my interest in these themes—particularly the sacred numbers. My thoughts about the animals and water and numbers had coalesced into a theme for the fourth chapter of my book. I brought my thoughts before the watchful intelligence of Jim LeBar. He had read a draft of the first chapter and seemed politely adrift at the associations I made in that chapter. But he did comment on Peter's simile that joined the devil and a roaring lion:

"Peter's epistle is an early baptismal homily," he said. "Peter reminds the converts that Satan will be on the prowl for them because they are about to renounce him. Of course, the image of the lion is apt: didn't Nero toss Christians to the lions in the arena?"

He gave me that wide grin. "You must forgive me," he said, as he finished his coffee. "I enjoyed reading your manuscript. Some of your ideas are interesting. But I'm a skeptic."

ii. The Cavernous Mystery

Twenty million years ago a lush forest sprawled across the African continent from west to east. On the forest floor reptiles, rodents, scorpions, lemurs and tiny animals lived amidst thick vegetation, while above was a leafy upper world inhabited by screeching birds and small ape-like creatures who felt safer in the treetops. No distant sky could be seen through the density of the trunks and vines that made of this forest a perfect enclosure: creatures within could not get out, for they would not survive without the food and shelter the forest provided; and creatures from without—if there were any—would not intrude. In this primaeval setting our ancestors were not likely to evolve, for there were no forces that challenged them to change and adapt. At least, no forces within the forest itself. But there were invisible forces beneath the forest floor that had the power to break in upon the peace and change these creatures forever.

The continental rock under Africa rested on moveable platelets. In time, these platelets pushed up the land above. They erupted and formed huge "blisters" or "domes" that today are called the Ethiopic dome and the Kenyan Dome, each about 6000 feet high. After eight million years of upward thrust, the rock between the two domes gave way, creating the "great rift," as it is called. Now, moist air that used to drift in from the west met a spout of upward rushing air from the valley below; the vectors from this collision sucked the moisture up and away. East Africa, deprived of humid winds, became a hot, parched plain–a "savannah."

During this period—called the Miocene—a chimp sized creature who lived in the treetops and ate fruit would occasionally risk coming to the forest floor to eat caterpillars and insects. But not often, we imagine; for he had enemies on the ground, creatures larger and faster than he, who demanded more than insects. When the torrid heat moved in, however, trees around the fringe of the forest withered and the forest thinned out; the fruit-eating, bug-snapping tree dweller faced a crisis. He no longer enjoyed the safety of the treetops; the forest was scorched, or there was no forest at all. He was driven down onto the scrub land. The issue for him was how to survive without trees and branches, even without ground cover. He was a fruit eater, but there was no fruit. His teeth were puny. His four hands were better at gripping than walking; running was impossible. And what was he to drink? The few water holes were deathtraps—for that is where the man-eaters came to drink.

But these preconsulids, as we call them, did survive, and over millions of years they split into several species. Some learned to swing from skimpy branches in patches of forest that endured the scorching blast of heat: these may have been the largest species—Proconsul Major. Other species, like Micropithecus Clarki, weighed no more than ten pounds. It was probably a mid-sized species, however, that evolved into our remote ancestors. It is clear that our human beginnings go back to the windswept Miocene forest that dried up and left us to hide, as best we could, in the short and tall grasses that spread out between clumps of barren trees.

According to one theory, some of these preconsulids may have survived by migrating eastward as far as the Indian Ocean, where they waded out just far enough to escape the teeth of their pursuing enemies. If so, of necessity they had to learn to stand erect—how else could they keep their chins above water? And they shed their furry coats—a nuisance in the water—and became as naked as Adam in the garden. It must have been an aquatic paradise; seafood was abundant, mainly shrimp and crabs. When the enemy who pursued them to the water's edge withdrew into the grass, they could come out of the water, eat insects and risk sleeping on the sandy beach. This water-baptism, therefore, was their salvation–and ours.

Recent fossil discoveries, however, pinpoint Ethiopia's forests as our first home, for there, about 5.8 million years ago, lived a creature whom paleontologists call Ardipithecus ramidus kadabba. He was about the size of a modern chimpanzee, about four feet tall, and walked upright. Then, another discovery: 1500 miles to the west, the skull of another creature, Sahelanthropus tchadensis, surfaced from the dusty plain in Chad to tell us that he and his fellows roamed the savannah 6 or 7 million years ago. During these and subsequent years these preconsulids, or others like them, eluded the enemy well enough to evolve from a single species in a genus, from frightened creatures scampering away through the grass, to our world-dominant human race today.

We have been vague about our enemy, saying only that he lived on the ground, was bigger and faster than our ancestors, had teeth and ate us. We can do better. His name today is Panthera tigris. He consumes ten pounds of meat every day. We know this from observing him in his native habitat in eastern Siberia where he roams free. Peter Mathhiessen, author of *Tigers in the Snow*, tells us that when the tiger attacks humans, as he is wont to do, search parties rarely find more than scraps. And his Miocene ancestors (Dinofelis, for example, a big cat among big cats, weighed up to 600 pounds and moved like lightening) required more than ten pounds of victim. They were the hunters and we the hunted. Proconsul preferred the treetops and vines for good reason, therefore, there would have been snakes in the vines, but he took that risk rather than run across Dinofelis. He stayed in the treetops until the baked heart of Africa drove him out of the trees and onto the bare ground.

The familiar "hunting hypothesis" has obscured this prehistory. According to this hypothesis, when our ancestors emerged from the forest onto the savannah they were carnivorous. And there were many kinds of edible ungulates. Our ancestors learned to hunt, therefore, and hunting became the dominant activity (for males). Men fashioned weapons and went out in packs to make the kill, while women remained behind to nurse the children. Our brains grew in size, as the making and using of weapons tightened the eye to hand neural link. We learned to stand erect so that we could see over the tall grass and spot the game at a distance. In this way we laid down the fundamentals of our culture. The "hunting hypothesis" has also inspired thinking about the origins of religion: we felt guilt over the act of killing and eating those with whom we shared the grasslands and we devised religious rites to enable us to go about the great hunt without the constraints of our guilt. The animals we ate were willing victims, we believed, in covenant with us; they gave their lives for us; in return we prayed for them to be reborn.

Now, there was a great hunt—this is not to be denied. The question is, what happened? How did we get from fruit to meat? Were we predetermined to be carnivorous once we came down from the trees, and prone to the violence that is a component of the killing? If anything was bred into us during all those years in the forest, it ought to have been bananas. What happened during this "prehistory?"

A hideous truth has come to light. We were prey. Many scenes come to mind. As we scavaged for food we come upon a kill site; a leopard or sabre-tooth has left some remains from his recent kill. This would dispose us to eating meat— but if the beast returned suddenly, *we were meat.* Another scene: we are marching along in the tall grass, but hindered by our older or sick hominid fellows; they slow us down and we have the added burden of having to share food with them. They fall behind and disappear forever. Our burden is eased. In time, we learn to drop them off; they will fill the belly of the beast for an evening; the band will live to see the rising of one more sun. This is what has been missing from the "hunting hypothesis"—the splintered bones, the bloodletting, the gouged entrails, the night terrors. Some scientists today are beginning to believe that we became big-brained and learned to walk erect so that we could escape the predator beast.

Each hominid must have known his end. How could he not? He had seen it happen many times to his mates: the old, the sick, the wounded, the unlucky, who fell behind on the trail or got picked off. Or the band would designate a victim, a sacrificial offering. This is what each hominid understood to be his own destiny: meat in the jaws of the monster cat. Elias Canetti describes the orifice through which the hominid's fate will thrust him:

> The narrow gorge through which everything has to pass is...the ultimate terror. Man's imagination has been occupied by the several stages of incorporation. The gaping jaws of the large beasts which threatened him have pursued him even into his dreams and myths.
>
> Crowds and Power, 1962

Hunting? Small stuff only. Otherwise, they would march into the jaws of every hominid's nightmare.

Are we their meal of choice? Not quite, but Sy Montgomery, author of *The Man-eating Tigers of the Sundarbans*, makes it appear so. She describes the predatory acts of tigers in the mangrove forest of India and Bangladesh where the beasts ambush humans near their thatched huts; the beasts even swim out silently to snatch fishermen from their boats, she says, and over three hundred persons are snatched away each year by those jaws. Her critics wonder if the numbers are exaggerated: the worshipful awe of the people who have witnessed the beast snatch an infant in its jaws and make off with it, may give rise to grand gestures of the tongue—but the man-eater's aggressive interest in human flesh is not to be denied. In 1991, lions of the Gir Forest of Western India pounced on forty unlucky victims and drove the villagers indoors at sunset—and by day, people move about only in armed groups. When the British in India started reporting their losses from tiger attacks in 1880 they documented that over three hundred thousand of their numbers had been consumed in over a century. In Africa, when the Ugandan railway was being constructed in 1875, lions mauled and killed twenty eight native workmen and over a hundred others who camped near the work sites; surviving workers had to sleep atop towers or in beds lashed to trees.

If we looked at the same savannah today, what might we find? Alison Richard, in *Primates in Nature*, describes how chimpanzees and baboons have to band together to thwart the big cats, who are apt to pounce on them at any time. Among the chimps, if a member falls behind, he may be picked off by a cat in an hour or two and devoured before its heart stops beating. Baboons, who lose as much as twenty-five percent of their members annually to the cats, are sharp-toothed street fighters, Richard notes, and can inflict pain upon any attacker; yet the cat will pass over far less formidable foes to chase down a baboon or a pack of them. The cat, it seems, does discriminate in matters of diet.

Barbara Ehrenreich, an essayist and amateur student of our "prehistory," comments on some of the recent instances of animal predation cited, and adds the thought that the savannah during Paleolithic times would have been even more heavily infested with the large cats than it is today. She expresses the opinion that we need not have been the favorite meal of these predators in order to end up in its jaws, for we were constantly crossing their paths. She refers to the kill-sites, and says that we were drawn to these sites of necessity, for we needed food. The big cats today will fight any poachers they discover at their kill-sites—wild dogs or hyenas, for example—and it would have been easy for the Paleolithic cat to snap up the hominid as well. In her *Blood Rites*, she offers the theory that our culture derives from our ancient need to band together to resist predation, and she states that many anthropologists are being attracted to this theory. "Strength in numbers" was the key to survival on the savannah—

many eyes and ears instead of a few, especially in the deep night when the beast was abroad and in need of his evening meal.

During an interview with Rob Killheffer on Prime Time, in 1977, Barbara spoke of the euphoria that some people experience when they band together to defend against an outside enemy. This emotion has deep roots, she said, and we owe it to the beast—to our need to overcome our fears and do battle with a force greater than ourselves. In these words, Barbara sums up a new hypothesis: the origin of our passions for war, for human sacrifices at bloody altars, and for religion itself, is here, in this primitive banding together for the common good.

We may extend her hypothesis and assert the following: Banded together for merciful moments of comfort in the dark, hyper-alert for the phobic-object who was hard to see but easier to hear, the hominids developed sensitive hearing. They were alert to every rustle in the brush, every snap of a twig. They developed a way to speak, to call out, to warn those who strayed too far into the tall grass, to call for help. Babies learned to cry from the moment they are born, so that the mother will not forget and lose them in the dark. Beyond all these natural endowments, they became–to use our term–psychic. Somehow they always or almost always knew when the beast was abroad. How else could the bulk of them have survived long enough to become us?

These ancestors of ours could peer into the night, but see nothing. Like us, they were not good at seeing in the dark. They had little visual contact with the enemy, a night stalker. If the beast did charge by day, little time was left to the victim to see the enemy and describe him to others in the band. But they could all hear him charge through the brush. The enemy, therefore, was a nocturnal presence to the ears. Today, in mental hospitals, schizophrenics usually have *audible* hallucinations, as opposed to visual; it is hearing sensitivity that characterizes this patient; he hears sounds from nowhere—voices detached from bodies, voices of devils who torment him and turn his days into nights. Malachi Martin, author of *Hostage to the Devil*, describes several cases of "demonic possession" in which the early symptoms suggest psychosis; the victims experience isolation, vague fears and forebodings, and they hear voices; they seem less aware of immediate surroundings but more aware of something neither they nor we can see.

The difficulty of detecting the beast hidden in the grass and in the dark could have spelled the end of the species. But nature saw fit to intervene. Much scientific attention lately has been focused on the amygdala, an inner brain structure, part of our limbic system, that detects and deciphers the emotions of others—especially fear and anger—and fires messages to the cerebral cortex and sympathetic nervous system so that we can sense our enemies and their intentions. A hominid foraging some distance from the band, by this means, would be instantly alerted when another hominid signals his fear of the beast whom he hears moving through the deep grass. Fear teaches us what to avoid; anger arouses us for battle. The amygdala gave us a thrust into our evolutionary future; we survived in a setting where we were outmatched if not outnumbered. It behooved the individual hominid to be attuned to the band and its sensitive leaders. In this way, we and they live to see the rising of the new sun.

The role of the shaman and other psychic sentries in early coeval bands was to locate potential danger—to track the beast with their ears–and sound an alarm so that the members would know to run, hide, or fight, according to the sentry's call. In the Old Testament we read of psychic prophets who warned the nation of danger to the north, or south...or within. The psychic Elisha tapped into the plans of the hostile Syrian king and urged his fellow Israelites to unite against their common foe. If the danger was internal, the prophet issued strong words to the offenders. The warning call often serves to forge a commonality among threatened peoples, or restore it, even in our own day. Barbara Ehrenreich points out that in the Kalahari desert, the! Kung people, who for centuries have been menaced by wild animals, pitch their campsites close together in tight configurations; but the Aborigines, who face no enemy, space their sites at random, even fifty yards apart. Our hominid ancestors would have posted sentries to warn their sleeping fellows of danger in the grass, and to keep the members banded together for the salvation of all. These sentries must have relied on psychic powers, as they listened through the watches of the night.

The night was long—perhaps three million years long. During this reign of terror the hominids developed a sense of religious awe, what the Germans call "the holy shiver." The German theologian

Rudolph Otto speaks of holiness, a numenous concept compounded of fear and awe, and which is a staple of our religious doctrines and rites. Otto was not speaking of our "prehistory," but his description might well apply to the hominids as they contemplated the monster who ate their flesh and drank their blood. The beast was giver and taker of life; he gave life by leaving ungulate meat at his kill sites, and he took it by returning to devour the surprised hominid at his meal. The kill-site was the world's first altar; it is where we learned to worship a "higher power," a deity that dispenses no mercy.

The visage of the beast takes on many guises as he appears in later cultures, but he is always the same. The Sumerian god Marduk, for example, made abject votaries of all who knew him, so terrifying was his dragon-like countenance (and his mother Tiamat was no relief: the two of them were attended by swarms of demons). The beast was present when humans practiced rites of child sacrifice, for he is the god who requires the child's blood. And even today, the Indians of the tiger-infested Sundarbans worship the pre-Vedic tiger-god Daksin Ray who, according to their lore, once demanded humans to be sacrificed to him amidst orgiastic rites of revelry and religious ecstasy.

The pantheon of the Pleistocene consisted of many demonic beings, who are worshiped even today in many cultures and religions with great fear and fervor. By whatever names they are called and worshiped, however, they have one thing in common—they are always hungry.

iii. "From the Ambushes of the Evil Spirit...Deliver us
(Rituale Romanum)

M. Scott Peck, in his *People of the Lie*, speaks of his personal struggle to comprehend evil. He describes an exorcism he attended and remarks that

> An expression appeared on the patient's face that can only be described as satanic. It was an incredibly contemptuous grin of utter hostile malevolence...in another patient, the demonic revealed itself with a still more ghastly expression...he suddenly resembled a whirling snake of great strength, viciously attempting to bite team members...the eyes were hooded with lazy reptilian torpor–except when the reptile darted out in attack, at which moment the eyes would open wide with blazing hatred...what upset me most was the extraordinary sense of a fifty million year old heaviness I received from this serpentine being.

(Author's note: Dr. Peck is not alone when he feels the presence of evil and the weight of it. I too have felt it in hospitals where people despair and give up on life. It is not fifty million years old, quite— sixteen to twenty million, if we look no further than hominid evolution. But if we look back past the hills and the icecaps and the forest, we come to deep waters. The water is our womb, our first home. But we were "bottom feeders," small aquatic organisms that served as food for larger forms—predator sharks and their kin. To be consumed is our heritage from earliest times: we eat and we are eaten; we come to the banquet, we are the banquet. So then, Dr. Peck contemplates evil. So do we all. With our big brains we philosophize and we try to explain it. We fail. Nor could our hominid ancestors have explained it; they had no capacity for abstract thinking, their brains were too small and their lives too short. But we may believe that for them evil meant one thing only—being eaten alive.)

The terrors of dark nights past when our race was in its infancy are rehearsed again today in the phenomenon called demonic possession. The image of the beast is stamped on the victim's flesh and psyche. Malachi Martin, a priest and a student of the subject, interviewed a woman who remembered details of her ordeal: "It was like being fucked by a big-bellied spider," she reported. Believing she was being attacked by a beast, she became a beast herself. The men who restrained her said she was "like a wild animal, a tiger...a hyena...a sow fighting the hands in a slaughterhouse." Martin interviewed the exorcist, who recalled that "the sides of her mouth were pulled back, bearing teeth, gums, tongue, and she emitted long howling wails..." The demon then leapt from the woman to the exorcist, who said it was as if his skin was racked by claws. Another of Martin's cases involved a man who walked into a chapel where he saw an image of Jonah in the mouth of a whale; the man fell to the ground in a seizure, and before long manifested all the signs of being possessed by the Devil.

Walter Burkert, the Swiss "biohistorian," in his *Creation of the Sacred: Tracks of Biology in Early Religions*, states that hell is often pictured as a "huge devouring animal with yawning jaws." His observation is apt, for in popular culture, Satan or the Devil is often pictured as a horned beast with a long tail, cloven hoofs—and often reptilian connotations. Moreover, we associate him with fire and smoke; we suspect someone is cooking—it is his dinner, and one of us is at the end of his pitchfork.

The Devil and the beast, Satan and the serpent, are one and the same. Some unfortunate ones among us, left behind in life's trail, stumble and fall prey to the beast who rises from our ancestral memory and masquerades in our imaginations as a devil. The exorcist comes and we rehearse the somber legend of millennia past. A credible theory: but how does it explain why the victim acts like the beast and even takes on the face of the beast?

A rebellion took place on the Miocene grassland. Our ancestor needed to look up and over the tall grasses for sight of the enemy. To do this he had to take on a new posture. It took millennia, but he learned to walk erect. And his head grew larger, his hands stronger. In moments of danger, he could shriek a warning to his fellows. Heroic stone throwers confronted the enemy, risking their lives for the sake of the others. Eventually packs of stone throwers learned to attack the enemy from all sides and confuse him while the others escaped into the brush. Then he learned to fashion weapons.

Eventually nature came to his aid: he developed quick responses when he engaged in battle—the "fight or flight" reflex. The adrenal gland spikes the blood sugar as it pumps juices into the system, he sucks in more oxygen, his blood prepares to clot when he gets gouged: he now has great strength when he takes on the supernatural foe. And the endorphins, our natural analgesic drugs, inspire him. Barbara Ehrenreich, who is a lighthouse on this subject, quotes a Greek myth concerning Queen Ino of Boeotia, who was attacked by a lynx; her distraught husband comes upon her blood-stained tunic and believes she is dead; but in reality "a sudden Bacchic frenzy had come upon her" at the moment of attack and she "had strangled the lynx, flayed it with her teeth and nails, and gone off, dressed only in the pelt, for a prolonged revel on Mount Parnassus." (*Blood Rites, p. 80*) The rebellion became a revolution: the beast will be deposed from his lordly status, and our ancestor takes on an ecstatic element as he becomes more and more like the beast—aggressive and predatory.

In 1928 the family of an Iowan farm girl named "Mary" became alarmed when she began to curse and stammer—behavior out of character for this docile person. The family doctor was baffled. A priest was summoned, Father Steiger, from a local parish; he came and instantly determined that she was possessed by the Devil. It was not her behavior alone that convinced him: her body had swollen to twice its size—almost overnight; her eyes bulged as if they would spring from their sockets, her lips were like purses, thick and wrinkled. Steiger brought in an exorcist, Father Reisinger. When Reisinger began the rite, a stream of vomit issued from Mary's mouth that filled a bucket in minutes. Streams of urine filled another bucket. She then floated to the ceiling and remained there until several men finally pulled her down.

Ancestral memory has taken Mary far from the farm in Iowa. She is old and sick; she has fallen behind the others who keep to the trail and will not turn back. She is alone. She knows what will happen. Instinctively she lifts her eyes to the heavens. But the ancient treetops are gone. (Tonight her memory is a million years old.) The infinite black sky and innumerable stars above offer no comfort or refuge. There is a cliff over there, she could jump off it—but

---

> *her limbs no longer obey. She can only lie still in the grassy plain and await the end. Her stomach pumps gastrin to speed up her metabolism; her heart races sending energy to her muscles; her bladder and bowels move and empty; her blood takes on metabolites so it will clot quickly when she starts to bleed. She hears a noise. Her body swells, her eyes protrude, she smells her own stench. Small sounds of the night everywhere...but there! Suddenly from behind something parts the grass...*

Conrad Lorenz, who has made field studies of numerous animals, has written in his *On Aggression*, that the chimp has a fancy way of protecting himself from an enemy. The chimp sticks out his chin, stiffens his body, and raises his elbows; his hair stands on end. The famous biologist states that all of these motions make the chimp look larger and more fierce than he really is. The chimp will even rotate his arms awkwardly, so as to expose his hairy side—in case the enemy has no taste for hair. It is all bluff, of course; but like the cat that arches its back, the effect can be convincing. (Lorenz mentions the physiological parallels between "religious awe" and the ability of some animals to make their hair or fur stand on end. Have we modern animals shed the fur but not the shiver? he wonders.)

All animals, birds, and even fish have ways to protect themselves from the predator. Mimicry and deception are commonly observed among animals that are threatened. Mary's weapons on the grassy plain were deception and repulsion—she made herself larger and repulsive, even inedible. In time, her fellows would learn imitation. When they took up weapons of sharpened sticks and pointed stones, for example, they were imitating the predator's teeth.

Again, Barbara Ehrenreich, in *Blood Rites*, serves us well when she writes of "fearful symmetries." She has no interest in demonic possession or exorcisms, of course; rather, she is concerned with war and our passion for it. She contends that a group at war will mimic the enemy, and—no matter what the issue of difference between them—become not less like him but more so. A quote from Martin VanCrevold underscores her point:

...given time, the fighting itself will cause the two sides to become more like each other, even to the point where opposites converge, merge, and change places...the principal reason behind this phenomenon is that war represents perhaps the most imitative activity known to man.

Mary, the Iowan farm girl, reverted to the status of prey. She passed through a psychological fissure and came out upon the Miocene grassland where an old enemy parted the grass and took her. Of course, she lived in Iowa in 1928; but the grassland lived there too, in her humanity. The exorcist came and invoked the ancient scene involving an attacking beast and us as its victim. The scene has a supernatural aspect because the attacking beast is an invisible "higher power" in relation to us as powerless victims. We disappear into the jaws of a cavernous mystery. Thus Mary fought against the beast by becoming like the beast; she was both prey and predator. Unconscious reflexes took over, the same ones that the hominids used to ward off the big cat. She shucked off her conscious self so that these reflexes could work without the need to calculate; she became a hominid under siege and did what a hominid or animal would do: he imitates the ferocity of the big cat by his posture of defiance and bravado; he grunts and growls; or he may imitate a snake–the cat's natural enemy. He may become several beings at once, a pack of imitators who surround the cat on all sides and scare it off (as in the "legion" exorcism), to magnify his imputed prowess. He becomes a supernatural being himself attacking the one who attacks him; the two are equal in divinity.

What precipitated this crisis in the life of an Iowan farm girl? In psychiatry, there is a theory called Antecedent Conflict, which states that childhood conflict and trauma are often the basis for mental disturbances in the life of an adult. Another theory, the Attention Hypothesis, explains a puzzling aspect of adult phobias: the phobic patient has the hyperacute ability to "find" his phobic object—the thing that scares him. It seems "uncanny"—that is what Dr. Henry P. Laughlin calls it (*The Neuroses, p. 586*).

Dr. Laughlin relates the story of "Hans," who was afraid of horses; wherever Hans went, he was reminded of horses; he saw them everywhere. Laughlin calls this "the phobic dilemma"—the patient searches for the very thing he fears. Should he not strive to avoid it and forget it? The doctor gives no answer. But the answer may lie far back in Hans' ancestral memory: his hominid ancestor sought out the predatory beast in order to locate it, assess the danger, and warn his fellows of the enemy in the deep Miocene night. The Antecedent Conflict is the life-death struggle for survival in the African grasslands. We might, therefore, state an hypothesis of our own: Mary was victimized by a human predator—real or imagined—and she developed a twenty million year old phobia.

(In psychoanalytic theory, children at play or in their dreams may identify with animals as a ruse to escape the unwanted attention of an aggressive adult. It is also known that a victim may identify with a powerful human aggressor, such as kidnapper or abuser; if the aggressor is perceived as supernatural, the victim acquires this status as well.)

Mary became a psychic sentry, one who scans the ancient grassland for the approach of the enemy. Her eyes bulge, her ears bend to the touch of her cupped hands. She sees nothing, but her hearing is acute; it discriminates among the small sounds of the night––snapping twigs, grass rustling in the wind...

The enemy in the night can frighten a child out of his wits—literally, perhaps. H. Strozier has studied the effects of childhood abuse among the religious fundamentalists, and he finds (*Apocalypse: The Psychology of Fundamentalism in America*) that victims may "leave their bodies" and have various dissociative reactions. Their religion purports to give them solace by preaching the apocalypse and the rising of bodies into the sky during the "rapture" (a hominid's nostalgic longing for the sheltering treetops?)—but they anticipate an end even more violent than their abused beginnings.

Other things can precipitate a crisis reaction. Malachi Martin reports that people who experiment with the occult may develop sharpened psychic powers, which in turn may lead to diabolical infestation (*Hostage to the Devil*). Fr. James LeBar, in his book, *Cults, Sects, and the New Age*, deplores cultic practices that induce altered states of mind and make a person susceptible to Satan's advances. The famous 1949 exorcism in St. Louis, the subject of the film *The Exorcist*, may have been triggered when a young boy became obsessed with a Ouija board game. Still other persons are born with psychic abilities—for better or worse; they have no need for training in the black arts. As for Mary, we know little about her life on the farm—although there is anecdotal evidence that she was abused by her father. But for certain she is human and the collective unconscious exists in her; her enemy is the common enemy of our ancestors, the beast itself and the beast in all of us. She does not distinguish between human and non-human foe; she *cannot* distinguish, for the primitive apparatus that watches for predators in the night knows no "golden barrier" between man and animal. Mary cries out with the psalmist:

> Strong bulls of Bashan have beset me round, they gaped upon me with their mouths as a ravening and roaring lion. I am poured out like water, all my bones are out of joint; my heart is like wax; it is melted in the midst of my bowels. My strength is dried up like a potsherd; and my tongue cleaveth to the roof of my mouth; and thou has brought me to the dust of death. For dogs have compassed me; the assembly of the wicked have inclosed me...save me from the lion's mouth. Psalm 22

The exorcist comes to Mary's house to find her and the enemy locked in embrace. His task is to separate the two; to save the one and banish the other. It will not be easy. For millions of years the beast has stalked us: first in the grasslands, now in our memories and metaphors. He is our incubus; at times he is us. Mary has entered the gaping orifice: her heart pounds, her bladder contracts, her bowels move; the breath is crushed from her lungs, her spirit is sucked up by the god who consumes her. At the same time Mary the Iowan farm girl enters the beast, the beast enters her and finds utterance through her body and her tongue. The exorcist who would separate these two must be a powerful and holy man: he must come upon the scene as a third force, a Samaritan, who answers the questions about LIFE.

The Samaritan comes from afar; he is an "outsider" who has powers greater than those known to the victim's fellows. The archetype of the Samaritan is the psychic sentry, the shaman, to whom a wounded hominid would call for help. The psychic is a leader, he has the power to summon the others, who, when gathered, perform wonderful saving rites; they sing, dance, and march to quicken their spirits and discourage the enemy; they surround him and make noises to confuse him and chase him from his prey. The psychic's powers seem to come from an "outside" source; but in reality he taps into the secret sources of power that reside within the group's communal will to live. Yet, the psychic sentry is set apart; the group confers its powers upon him so they may sleep during the long, dark night. He must not sleep during his watch.

He stands apart—but he represents many. The exorcist has the power to summon an army of saints and martyrs to aid the possessed victim: the quickening rhythm of the oft-repeated litany suggests the pounding of many feet rushing through the grassland as they come to aid a fallen fellow.

But what if the fallen hominid was one of the weak ones, like Mary, whom the group abandoned or designated a sacrificial lamb? The exorcist may pray for the army of saints to come and pick her up, but his prayers may not suffice—or the saints may not come. What then? The exorcist may offer himself to the beast. His mentors warn him about this, but he carries with him this mantle, that he will suffer on behalf of others. An early form of Christian atonement theology granted that Satan had a claim upon humanity, but Christ on the cross "paid off" the claim and set us free. The exorcist is a priest of Christ; he must do what his Master has done.

The belief that we owe something to the beast and that we have to "purchase" our freedom is plainly stated in one of the exorcism prayers The exorcist prays to Michael the Archangel, "Come to the assistance of mankind, whom God has created in His own image and likeness, and whom he has purchased at great price from Satan's tyranny."

When the exorcist comes, Michael the Archangel is not far behind. But there will be no purchase, no legal fictions. Michael, like the Samaritan, is not an agent but a symbol. He is the symbol of a person's innermost and sacred Self, the apogee of a person's individuation; and he is a symbol of the powers of the communal spirit of the race—the Unconscious. The powers latent in the Unconscious, that delivered mankind through the long Miocene nights, prevail again in the Life of this victim—he is saved. The Michael symbol reveals the reality of the text that says God made man in His own image—that there is divinity in humanity, and therefore immortality.

Because the reality of the communal Unconscious makes known its powers in the shape of images, symbols, signs, and stories, we access this reality with our inner vision that makes the journey to that communal center. The third eye beholds the face of the Archangel. He, in our culture, is a Christ presence, perhaps the greatest of the symbols and stories.

If the exorcist, however, is a predator at heart, he is the thief who robs the traveler and leaves him by the side of the road to die.

But if the exorcist is pure in heart, Michael comes and, like the shaman of old, gives a sign—an "all clear," so his fellows may sleep in peace during the long watch of the night.

iv. The Trap

A woman, whom Pastor Schulze barely knew, grabbed him by the sleeve of his vestment after the Sunday morning service and in hushed tones demanded to speak to him in confidence. He was taken aback, she seemed so urgent. Now he recognized her: she was an infrequent worshiper at his church. What was her name?—Oh, yes, Klara Hipp. But why would she suddenly show up like this—pale and drawn? He led her to the office and sat down behind his desk. The woman was plainly nervous. He put on his patient face and waited for her to speak. After a hesitant moment she explained that her son had taken to strange behaviors. Normally a quiet thirteen year old, he was disrupting the entire household by playing pranks: last night he barricaded himself inside his bedroom and grunted and snorted like some farm animal. And he made a noise like rainwater falling on a tin roof. And the smells in there—like an outhouse. They— she and her husband Frederick—couldn't get in to find out what he was doing, and he wouldn't come out. This morning when he woke up and let them in, they found no sign of animals or water. The pranks started Thanksgiving, she added, when after a late dinner he refused to go to bed; he just sat there in a heavy chair that tipped over and spilled him on the floor. She accused him of making a scene in front of the relatives, but he cried and said he didn't make it happen. She asked Pastor Schulze to come to the house, talk to the boy, and set him straight. Schulze frowned: he lacked the skill to handle adolescents. But he knew the duties of his calling. Yes, he said he would speak to the boy. The prospect of it bothered him all afternoon; but he braced himself and drove to the Hipp's residence just after dark.

Far from wanting to talk about the boy's pranks, he would instead talk about getting the boy to attend confirmation class. He arrived at the Hipp's suburban home at seven, and immediately felt tension in the air: Klara's face was hard-set and Fred was sullen. They must have argued. Fred was a Catholic, he remembered: would there be a religious issue here? He hoped not; he hated religious issues. Klara took him to the living room and pointed to the floor. He saw shards, broken pottery. It just happened when he rang the bell, Klara said; it flew off the mantle...her beautiful Bristol vase. And Ritchie was upstairs when it happened, Fred said. Klara shook her head: No, he wasn't, she said. Where is Ritchie now? Schulze asked. Klara shrugged.

Klara invited him to sit at the dining room table where she served coffee and dessert. The problem actually began before Thanksgiving, she explained. Fred's sister, Ilse, came from St. Louis to visit her brother in September and gave Ritchie a Ouija board. Ritchie and Ilse played at it for hours, she said, as she opened a drawer in the hutch and produced the object. He stared at it: the alphabet was inscribed on it, the numbers 0 through 9, and, in Klara's shaking hand, a wooden piece with rollers—Klara called it a planchette; the thing skimmed across the board when the player put his hands on it, and it answered his questions. No harm in it, Fred said. Klara interrupted: no harm, she said, until Ilse suddenly died. Ritchie took to himself after that, and played with the board endless hours—and that's when the pranks began.

Schulze was relieved the boy didn't come down...or from wherever he was hiding. He wasn't clear how he wanted to approach the boy, especially with the parents listening in. At a loss for words, he suggested to Klara and Fred that he knew a doctor—a certain kind of doctor, and a member of the church—who helped people with their troubles. Immediately he realized his blunder. Klara flared at him: the Hipps wanted no part of a psychiatrist, she said; their boy wasn't crazy...how could he even think that?

Flustered, Schulze made another suggestion. He and Mrs. Schulze would be delighted if Ritchie spent a day or two at the parsonage. They had a new pup in the house that would take to Ritchie right away; maybe Ritchie could help train Max, he added, with a smile; Max isn't quite housebroken—he's still trying to stake out territory for himself. There—he had lightened things up a bit. And the parsonage had a new radio console so Ritchie could listen to his favorite programs. And, most important–he wagged his finger—Ritchie could study the catechism, attend church on Sunday, and learn not to play pranks on his parents. This, he said, should solve everything. They agreed.

On his way home something occurred to him. When visiting homes, it was his custom to say a prayer and leave with a blessing. This time he forgot.

At the parsonage, Schulze checked his desk calendar: the boy could stay for a long weekend—that would be from Thursday, February 17 through the 20th —time enough for instructions and the Sunday service. At seven Klara dropped her son off. Schulze took him straight to the spare guest room, just off the pastor's study and the master bedroom. Max the beagle had been asleep on the bed but he yelped and dashed out. Schulze caught his wife's eye: if Max didn't like Ritchie, he whispered, they had an entertainment problem; they would have to fall back on board games—like Parcheesi. At dinner the conversation was sluggish and forced. Ritchie had little to say. But Mrs. Schulze did: she looked at the boy pointedly: at the parsonage, she said, everybody went to bed early because the pastor needed his sleep. Schulze nodded. There would be no nonsense at the parsonage.

Shortly after nine, Schulze took the boy to the bedroom, taught him a bedtime prayer, and turned out the light. He went to the kitchen to warm some milk and settled into his lounge chair. In the morning he would call Klara Hipp and tell her that Ritchie had behaved perfectly—no pranks. But his mind turned to the Ouija board—he reached for a volume of the encyclopedia and found only a few words on the subject. What about Martin Luther?— the great founder had written about tempting spirits. That book would be in the bookcase down the hall by the spare room. But it was gone. And some other books were missing, too. He searched in his study; not there. Puzzled, he went back to the lounge chair. Mrs. Schulze was dusting near the bookcase before she went to bed; she may know what happened to the book.

But he found no peace; he fretted over the missing books. Where were they? Again, he went down the darkened hallway. No books. With a shrug he turned toward the spare room; he would look in on his guest, then go to bed himself. He opened the door and slipped in...it was dark, but if he got to the window and adjusted the blinds...slatted moonlight streaked into the room...a tiny flutter of air...the faint odor of urine—Max! ...the dog had been in the room, he must have pissed on the rug. In a far corner, several books were scattered about in tatters. He picked up one—it was Luther's text.

Max scattered the books? Max made this mess? He heard a faint noise behind him...it was cold, was the boy shivering? Light from the window fell on the frail figure in the bed. Suddenly the eyes opened and fixed on him; the mouth twitched and a wide grin split the face in two. The boy mocked him? The boy needs a stern speaking to. He moved toward the bed, stared straight into the eyes...the eyes!...he was standing, the boy lying in bed, yet their eyes were on a level...how? The mattress was moving...he fell back. It was rising from the floor, separated from the frame. It rose to the ceiling, where it hovered, its white sheets hanging over the sides like limp sails. The eyes stared down at him. He gaped at the sight, then slumped to the floor.

... a thumping on the door...would that be Mrs. Schulze?...he hoped to God...his head was still light, how long had he been out?...he staggered to his feet, shivering. The air was foul—he couldn't breathe. Where was the boy? Something blocked the door, he couldn't get out. He found the light switch. The bed was back on the floor, but against the door. The boy was not in it. There he was—crouched in the corner, naked, spouting urine and dropping feces.

Cupping his nostrils with his hands—he didn't want to suck air–he moved towards the window to throw it open...no, he'd have to step in excrement. Open the door?...yes; he tugged at the bedposts and shoved it to the side. Finally he was free—he dashed out, knelt before the toilet, and heaved.

In the morning they bathed him, dressed him, and took him home.

What could he have done? He asked of Mrs. Schulze later in the day, as he tried to describe to her the smirk on the boy's face, the mattress as it soared to the ceiling—on its own! On its own!— it was supernatural, he insisted, even the stench. He knew better than to fool with the supernatural. Yet, he went on, he owed Klara Hipp; she was a member of his congregation. But what? Mrs. Schulze had no answer. He picked up the shredded pages of books. Luther's text was mangled and stained—impossible to read; besides, his hands were shaking. On unsteady feet he limped to the church office where he had other texts. The reformer, he remembered, believed that a person could be possessed by a demon or by the Devil himself. His knees buckled under him and he collapsed into a chair. Yes, evil spirits—but what could he do? The Catholics, he knew, had a rite called exorcism, in which a priest drives out the demons. But Luther's reformation drove out...not the demons, but the exorcists.

He picked up the phone and dialed a young priest he had met while making hospital rounds, Father Albert Hughes, a pleasant

Irishman, new at St. James' Church in the city. He had an excuse to call, for Fred Hipp was a Catholic; didn't they take care of their own? Even so, he knew his request was outlandish. He would invite the priest to the parsonage for coffee. Then he would lay out the matter.

Hughes arrived at the parsonage Sunday evening. He listened politely to Schulze's story, but saw no reason to intervene in the Hipp family's business. The boy should see a doctor and that was that. But Schulze pressed him: what about the spiritual side? he asked. Hughes advised holy water; he would drop off a vial the next day, along with some printed prayers, and Schulze could bless the house and its occupants.

Schulze had the answer to that: yes, holy water sounds like the right thing, but only a priest can give a valid blessing. There—he trapped him; Hughes would have to go to the house; he would see for himself. Schulze reached for the phone; he wanted to confirm it for that very evening. He spoke to Klara and explained that he would bring a priest with him. Funny— he heard in the background, as Klara spoke, a loud news broadcast on the radio...or was it? In a foreign language? He passed the phone to Hughes. Yes, the priest agreed: somebody in that house spoke Latin, he was sure of it. He agreed to go—if for no other reason, he said, he'd like to meet someone who spoke ancient church Latin.

After dinner, Schulze picked up his priest friend and drove to the Hipp's home. Fred answered their ring instantly, and led them into the foyer where they began to remove their hats and coats. Schulze glanced about: the living room to his left was poorly lit by a small table lamp; ahead was a staircase—a dim light at the top revealed nothing but a tear and a stain in the carpet that stretched to the landing. Would Hughes understand the need for dim light? Klara hurried down the stairs and reached for their hats. Suddenly a deep male voice issued from behind her:

O sacerdos Christi, tu scis me esse diabolum.
Cur me derogas?

Hughes was slammed against the door that Fred had just closed behind him. He slid to the floor, doubled over; his lungs sucked air and his stomach heaved. Klara screamed.

They picked him up, unconscious, and carried him to the sofa, where Klara held smelling salts under his nostrils and brought him back.. Schulze noted that Klara had salts handy—more had been going on in this house than she let on to. When Hughes was revived, Schulze motioned with his hand to follow him into the kitchen where they could talk...the priest got up slowly, his hands to his ears, his eyes darting from side to side; he was no longer the jolly Irishman that Schulze brought to the house.

Schulze told him about the voice he and the others heard—did Hughes hear it too? What did it mean? Hughes rubbed his eyes and blinked: yes it was coming back to him—he heard a deep voice in his head, like a nightmare several times repeated: it sounded between his ears and kept repeating. His hands still to his ears, his elbows resting on the kitchen table, he mumbled, "O sacerdos Christi"—that's me, he said.

He explained that the voice had addressed him as Christ's priest and identified himself as the Devil—diabolum. Schulze felt his spine quiver—he had recognized that one word—diabolum, diabolical. What he and the others heard, Hughes had heard while he was out. What about the rest of it? Hughes managed to steady his eyes and hands; he stared directly at Schulze; the Devil demanded to know why a priest had come to disturb him. Hughes rolled his eyes and clasped his hands as if in prayer: he, of all people, he said, was least likely to disturb the Devil—he even ignored him during his homilies. Why him?...why now?...why?

Schulze drove the priest back to the St. James later that evening; they agreed to discuss the Hipp family predicament later in the week, after the priest had contacted his ecclesiastical authority for guidance. Schulze realized that his friend was taking the matter as an affront to him personally. He himself had not reacted that way when the boy was at the parsonage. It was his own idea to invite the boy to the parsonage; the evil spirit had not stalked him. It seemed that the spirit didn't want to stay in the house—the massive defecation led to a hasty eviction. But with Hughes, it was different—the Demon spoke.

But was the Demon stalking Hughes? The thought came to him later in the week, when he came upon some texts about demonic possession. The people who first have trouble with the Demon's infestation, he read, are merely bait; they call for the priest to come and help. The priest comes, and he is trapped.

He waited to hear from Hughes, but the call never came. But on Sunday Klara came up to him: Ritchie had been hospitalized, she told him, at Fr. Hughes' insistence. The priest had done some prayer service called an exorcism. And—Klara glanced from side to side—things went badly. Ritchie ripped Father Hughes' arm from wrist to shoulder with a coiled bedspring; he needed over a hundred stitches. And, she whispered, she had persuaded her husband to have nothing more to do with Catholic priests; they made things worse.

One more thing. Scratches and blisters had appeared on Ritchie's chest and thighs. They spelled out a message: she and Fred were to take Ritchie away to St. Louis in three days—or stay there three weeks—she wasn't sure, to stay with Fred's brother. They were packed up and would leave from Union station on Saturday, March 5, for St. Louis.

v. The Sign

Fr. William J. Bowdern, S.J. rose and with an eye to the clock he donned the black trousers and clerical shirt that he had set out the night before, wrapped himself in a double-breasted cassock, and sped down the rectory stairs to the study where he would spend a few quiet minutes before his mass, enjoy his first cigarette of the day, and sort out the messages from last night that his housekeeper, Michael, had laid on his desk. The night had been long and he felt the weight of it: the final prayers of a novena at the church, then several more hours with a dying parishioner and the last rites. Now he must deal with the messages that were neatly laid out. Thank God for Michael, who respected his need for order. Atop the pile was a note: Urgent: a call came in late tonight that should be returned right away—from Fr. Raymond Bishop. Michael was a good judge of what was urgent. Flicking cigarette ash from his black cassock, he picked up the phone. He hadn't heard from Ray in a while—could he be sick? Ray was a fellow Jesuit and a good friend—one who never complained about the ashes that fell from his smokes or the nicotine that the Bishop said fouled his breath. Funny how only bishops were critical of his smoking; the lay people at Xavier parish put up with him well enough.

Ray's voice was harsh and raspy. What he had to say didn't sound well, either. Ray had been up late himself the last few evenings, but for a reason that didn't sound like fit business for a Jesuit who happened also to be a department head at St. Louis University. You don't get to Ray's station in life if you hallucinate. Why, then was Ray talking about his visit to a haunted house?

He insisted his friend come over for lunch and explain himself: even if Ray were not well, he could easily drop by; he lived at Verhagen Hall, the Jesuit's quarters, just beyond the church—an easy walk. Michael, a superb cook, would prepare a five cheese macaroni and broccoli rabini, which happened to be Ray's favorite dish. At noon Michael led Ray into the study. Bowdern was startled; he had never seen Ray so haggard and drawn. He cautioned Ray to keep his voice muted: Michael had been at Xavier for years and was loyal, but some things were not suitable for his ears. They spoke softly as they

217

ate. Ray said that a young student at the University, Eleanor Hipp, had come to him with a problem. A fine student, Ray said—he knew her in classes, and he took her seriously. Her cousin and his parents had come to visit because their house in Maryland was haunted. And strange things were beginning to happen at their house, now that Ritchie—the nephew—had moved in: noises, like tappings and thumpings, the tramping of feet, the bed rising off the floor. He had gone to Fr. Kenny—Bowdern remembered Kenny, the retired sage of the campus, who had heard everyone's confession and knew more about sin than the Devil himself—and Kenny said it sounded like demonic possession. Bowdern looked askance at his friend; he hoped that the two had not taken this poppycock to Reinert—if the University president heard of it, reputations were at stake.

But Ray and Kenny had done exactly that. Bowdern pulled back from the table: he wiped his glasses, lit a cigarette and crossed his legs—a signal that he was taking all this casually. Ray went on: he had been to Eleanor's house and seen for himself: the boy's behavior was beyond perversity. When he put it to Reinert, the president shared their suspicions, but wanted to protect the school from ridicule. Bowdern threw up his hands: yes, protect the school from ridicule—nobody talks about demonic possession in the twentieth century, least of all a respectable institution like the University. Ray turned a wane smile toward him, as if to say he would ignore the outburst, and went on to present a dilemma posed by Reinert: true, the school wanted no embarrassment; but Jesuits had never backed away from a moral demand. Bowdern frowned. The matter was looming as serious. But why was Ray here telling him all this? He was the Pastor of the college church: a Jesuit, but detached and deployed as pastor of St. Francis Xavier Church. He would not get involved, if that was Ray's mission. Surely the boy was mentally ill. Take him to the Alexian Brothers hospital down the river; they knew how to care for impossible cases.

But he could see that Ray would not be put off. He stared as his friend opened a large leather-bound notebook. Ray was a meticulous note taker, he knew; his notes had the weight of scripture. He rested his chin on two hands joined as in prayer and narrowed his eyes at his friend. What exactly did Ray see?

Bishop's notes told the story: how he brought holy water and a relic to the house and explained to the boy's parents that the relic was a piece of clothing from St. Mary Margaret Alacocque, who saw Jesus and founded the devotion to the Sacred Heart. Then he told how he went about the house sprinkling the water and explained that the water had been blessed in the name of Ignatius Loyola, who in the seventeenth century founded the order that he belonged to, and who once came upon a deeply troubled person whom he helped by reciting certain prayers called exorcism. He then went to the boy's room just before Ritchie was to go to sleep and pinned the relic in its pouch to the boy's pillow. All seemed well, he added, until he returned to the parlor, picked up his hat and coat, and glanced at Eleanor, who had driven him to the house and would drive him home. But Eleanor looked at the clock on the mantle and then with a sidewise nod of her head indicated that he should stay. Before long they heard a loud yelp from the bedroom above, where Ritchie was supposed to be asleep. The noise could not have come from Ritchie, he said; neither could it have come from anyone else. It wasn't human.

Bowdern uncrossed his legs, set his jaw and leaned toward his friend as if he were bucking a windstorm. Never before had he questioned his friend's sanity—but this? He reached for the note book—he knew that Ray was a compulsive note taker, detailed, meticulous. He read the rest of the story for himself.

Bishop described how Fred and Werner charged up the stairs in response to the noise, with Klara and Eleanor close behind. They stopped at the landing, however, and looked down at Bishop—they wanted him to come up. He passed by them into the poorly lit bedroom. There he saw Ritchie. The boy was sitting up in bed, and the bed was slowly rising from the floor. The boy's eyes were fixed on him. He reached for the vial of holy water and sprinkled the water around the four corners of the room, on the four corners of the bed, and finally on Ritchie himself. The boy screamed. The bed crashed to the floor. Klara rushed past him and put her arms around her son. Bishop stood back, but he could see the boy's face over his mother's shoulders. The eyes were still on him, his face an ugly mask. The vial slipped from his fingers and fell to the floor.

The written word lent veracity to his friend's story, as if it were scripture. The bed had indeed levitated, the boy's face changed into something vile, and holy water tormented him. Now for the real question: Why had Bishop come to him with this story?

He lit another cigarette, crossed his legs again, and listened. Bishop, Kenny and Reinert had gone to Archbishop Ritter, who had taken the matter into consideration and would soon render a decision. The University would have nothing to do with it, officially—that was clear to Ritter and Reinert. But Ritter determined that Father Bill Bowdern should visit the boy, say some prayers for the family, and report back. He was the man for the job Ritter said, because he was a Jesuit, yet detached from the academic institution by virtue of being the pastor of the University Church. And he had a reputation for ministering generally to all who came to him, Catholics and non-Catholics alike—he could go in there without arousing comment. Bowdern smiled as his friend rehearsed what Ritter had said: that he was a tireless worker, a former military chaplain who volunteered for duty in Burma and China, and had a boxer's sturdy frame. Ritter didn't know that Bishop and he knew each other well. But his friend did not return the smile. Ritter considered Bowdern a loner, Bishop said, a pastor who had trouble holding on to assistant priests because he left them little to do and they became bored. This time, Ritter insisted, Bowdern was not to attempt anything alone—that was an order.

Bishop got up to leave. The Archbishop would call in a day or two, he added, probably to advise him to quit smoking—a chronic concern of his—and to tell him about two previous attempts to rid the boy of the Demon, both of which failed. Bishop spared him the details, except to say that a priest's arm was slashed. Bowdern got the point: he had better take this seriously. He asked Bishop to recruit another helper and plan to visit the Hipp home later in the week; he would need time to prepare himself while his friend would do a diplomat's work with the parents, who—to say the least—were leery of priestcraft. He lit another cigarette as he escorted Bishop to the door. He was obligated to obey his superior's orders, but when it came to smoking, the Archbishop's authority had its limits.

Friday, March 11, Bill Bowdern and his two helpers stepped onto the porch of the Werner Hipp home. He let Ray Bishop ring the bell, and he motioned to Walter Halloran to stand near the door while he slipped back quickly to flip cigarette ash onto the lawn. He looked carefully at Halloran, a tall scholarly looking youth with angular, fragile features. This was Ritter's choice for strong armed helper? Of course, Halloran could drive, and that was important. But how well was this young man prepared for what was inside? Had Bishop warned him? Too late: the door opened, and he saw the face of Eleanor Hipp for the first time; he sensed strength in her, more than in Halloran even. How much strength remained to be seen. He held back as his two helpers passed through the door. He would have one last draw from his cigarette, then follow his two helpers inside, just as if he were the celebrant at a solemn procession, preceded by deacon and sub-deacon. Except that this was not the altar at St. Francis Xavier, and God might not be here.

In the dimly lit parlor Ray introduced him to Eleanor and Fred, then to Werner and Anna Hipp. Klara nodded politely, but held back. He felt a chill from the woman. Never mind, he had met difficult people before; he could win her over in due course. He announced that he wanted to see Ritchie right away. Bishop, however, shook his head: the Hipps would want to see the relics, he explained. Ray had overstepped his bounds, but he was right. Klara was a Lutheran and would know nothing about Catholic practices, and even the others might need some preparation. Very well, then, he would show them the three precious objects he kept inside his small carrying case.

He reminded them that Fr. Bishop had pinned a relic to Ritchie's pillow. The relic was a shred of clothing from Mary Margaret Alacoque, he explained, a seventeenth century French woman who saw Jesus in a vision, who placed her heart inside his and he returned it to her, ablaze with divine love. Catholics venerate her vision in a devotion called the Sacred Heart. He then told them of the Jesuit martyrs who were killed by Indians in French America in the same century. From his black carrying case he took a small pouch and showed them the artifact taken from one of these martyrs. Many people took courage from these relics in times of crisis. He glanced about to see if his words were having an effect.

Bishop seemed pleased, as did Eleanor, who was beaming in approval. Klara was mute. He was feeling cramped by this woman. Reaching into his case, he brought forth the second object. A small crucifix, it had a hollow center; he placed it on the table and told them

221

that it was a "first class" relic—not a shred of garment but something from the body of the saint. The saint was Peter Canisius, who founded Jesuit schools in the sixteenth century and recently had been declared a "Doctor of the Church" by the Pope. But what did Klara care about the Pope? He reached again into the case: he showed her a velvet lined glass and gold reliquary. It held his prized relic, he told her—a bone from the right arm of St. Francis Xavier. Looking directly at Klara's hardened face, he told her that he particularly admired this great saint who went to the East Indies and Japan as a missionary—like the Apostle Paul; surely she heard of Paul!—where he braved many dangers and converted thousands to Christ. In fact, Xavier, a warrior for Christ, is the patron saint of the parish church where he, Father Bowdern, serves as pastor. Klara did not respond.

The room seemed suddenly cold. He heard a noise from upstairs. Ritchie! Quickly he put the objects back into the case and reached for his vestment carrier, which Halloran had brought in. Putting on his surplice and stole, he uttered a prayer and quoted St. Paul—he had Klara in mind—that they should put on the whole armor of God, especially, he added, the shield of faith, which shall protect Christians from the fiery darts of the evil one. At that he turned toward the stairs. He was ready for Ritchie.

Ritchie was dazed but awake, propped up in bed, staring at his visitors. Bowdern softly called his name; the boy stirred. Bowdern raised the reliquary high over his head and traced the sign of the cross with it, invoking the three persons of Godhead upon the victim that stared at him from the bed. Behind him, he heard the hushed tones of Eleanor speaking to Bishop: the relic of St. Mary Margaret, she whispered, was on the floor over in the far corner.

Suddenly Ritchie's left arm shot up—something was there, on his outer forearm. *What is the boy trying to show me?* The only light in the room was from the hall light; he looked about in the dimness for a lamp. Someone behind him switched on an overhead light. He fixed his eyes on a rash that had emerged on Ritchie's arm: two red lines crossing each other...an X? He moved closer. *No, a cross, a crude crucifix.* Bowdern was stunned but regained his composure: he began to read the novena prayer of St. Francis Xavier and a second time he raised the reliquary containing the fragment of the saint's body and pronounced a threefold blessing. It occurred to him, as he did so, that he had blessed a bleeding forearm with the forearm of a deceased martyr.

The boy fell back upon his pillow, his eyes shut. Bowdern picked up the St. Mary Margaret relic and brought it to the side of the bed. When he was sure the boy was asleep, he pinned the pouch to the pillow, and then the reliquary itself to the pillow's underside. Double protection, he thought. He signaled Bishop to turn out the light; he wanted the boy to stay asleep. Quietly he led the way downstairs to the parlor where he spoke to Frederick and Klara about the need for patience and faith. He was undecided what was going on with the boy—the rash was strange, but only a rash; the bed did not move, no tramping feet were heard—but certainly he could come back in a few days and pray. Eleanor handed him his hat and coat, and he prepared to leave. Suddenly his head spun around at the sound of a loud crash from above.

Bishop was up the stairs first, followed closely by the Hipps. When Bowdern entered the room it was still dark, but the boy was not asleep—he sensed the boy's eyes upon him. Suddenly, the boy spoke: he asked that the light be turned on. He rubbed his eyes, and explained that he dozed off, but was awakened by the bottle of holy water—it flew across the room, he said, by itself; he didn't touch it. Bowdern remembered that the bottle—Bishop must have left it there a few nights ago–was on a night stand about two feet from the bed when he and the others left the room. The bottle now—he studied it––was in a corner on the floor, unbroken. Just where the relic had been.

Under the bright light Ritchie appeared numb, his gaze torpid. But he was awake. Bowdern took a personal approach: he introduced himself and his two companions, and told Ritchie that they had come from a local church—a Catholic church—to visit him and his family, and perhaps teach them some prayers. One prayer, he said, he was sure they knew already—the Our Father. Ritchie seemed to drift off into sleep. Bowdern recited the Our Father along with the Hail Mary and asked if the boy had heard it. Ritchie opened his eyes: yes, he heard it—what did the prayers mean? He asked. Bowdern was elated: The boy cannot be fully possessed, he concluded: he heard the prayers; he has his faculties—and the Demon couldn't stop him.

Pulling up a chair, he began to tell Ritchie the story of the rosary. Mary is the mother of Jesus, he said, and the rosary is a way we ask her to help us when we are in trouble. The word "trouble" seemed to mean nothing to the boy—he may know nothing of the quaking bed, the noises, the flying relics. Is this possible? He went on to tell Ritchie about the three shepherd children of Portugal: Lucia, Jacinta and Francisco, about Ritchie's age, who one day saw a beautiful lady. She called herself the Lady of the Rosary and she taught the children to trust her. Then she showed them one of God's greatest miracles: the sun whirled like a giant silver ball, flaring off colors of every kind. This happened three times before a great crowd of people, about seventy thousand, who came to see the miracle at Fatima. The Lady told the children that this miracle would help people believe in God and His son Jesus and they should pray the rosary often. Bowdern showed Ritchie how he prayed using the rosary beads. As the Lady taught the children, he would teach Ritchie. Ritchie smiled. *His smile...perfect innocence...the demon has not conquered.*

At midnight Ritchie fell into a natural sleep, so it seemed to Bowdern. He motioned to his companions to collect their belongings, it was time to go. The men were silent as Halloran drove them through the night. At the rectory, he plunged into his bed and slept deeply until the break of dawn. In the morning, his dreams danced mischievously on the cusp of his memory. One of them bore the weight of the ages, it seemed, yet it was his own youth: he stood for the first time before the huge oak doors of the Jesuit seminary and he feared to enter; awe and dread overcame him as he contemplated his new life—dedication, excellence, celibacy; he stood still and watched the others enter to begin their studies. Finally he took hold of himself by some inward motion and passed through the doors. That was how he did things—by himself.

He had a good spirit within, he knew that; he meant well, he worked hard. But today he was low; the dreams—the one he remembered, and one other that faded—were oppressive. At the early mass he struggled to find his spiritual source but it eluded him. Nor did he take much interest in the perfect four minute eggs that Michael prepared for him. He hated to disappoint Michael, but the eggs would not stay down if he ate them. Suddenly Michael summoned him to the phone in the study. It was Bishop, his voice scraping terribly. Eleanor just called him...after they left last night, the family heard thumping noises from Ritchie's room...they couldn't push the door open, something inside was lodged against it. Finally, Eleanor said, they cracked the door and got in. The bed was blocking their way, and Ritchie was crumpled on the floor, screaming for help. They got in, somehow...Klara rushed to pick up Ritchie, but a stool from the dressing table flew over her head; it crashed against the wall, and splintered. Finally she picked him up and ran downstairs with him. Bishop seemed to hesitate...more bad news?

Dear God! —he was dreaming when he should have been on watch. The disciples were dreaming when Jesus sweat blood in Gethsemene—he was no better. With his bulk, he could have broken down that door for Klara. He asked Bishop to wait while he reached for a cigarette. The other dream...what was it? He remembered only the weight of it. And the age of it. It was a million years old. Now, what more went on last night?

Remember Aunt Ilse? Bishop asked. No, he had not said much about Ilse. She was a spiritualist of sorts, Bishop explained; who believed in consulting spirits of the dead, and the trouble began last fall when she gave Ritchie a Ouija board. Klara hadn't liked the idea. But Ilse was dead now, and Klara was trying to get through to her. She called the family down to the parlor for a seance, but they refused. So she did it by herself. She carried Ritchie back up to the bedroom and did a private seance by his bedside. Eleanor heard it from her room down the hall. Klara accused Ilse of hiding money before she died, and she kept repeating something about 3 am. It was odd, Eleanor said: Ilse died at 3 am, and that's when the thumping began—at 3 am.

Who tricked him? Not the boy, the Demon. For it is the evil one who deceives priests, not innocent boys. The Demon feigned his sleep; it was unnatural. It is the Mysterium Iniquitatis, the mystery of evil, that confronted him in the boy's bedroom. The depths of theological learning were beyond him, but not the basics: Goodness, he knew, resides in the bosom of God; evil in...does the Devil have a bosom? An ugly thought. Now he had his answer for Ritter: Yes, the boy could be possessed by a Demon and, yes, His Eminence should appoint an exorcist to drive out this evil.

Ritter was adamant: Bowdern himself was the man for the job. Bowdern, on the phone in his study, smoking furiously, declined the honor. Thus it was settled, said Ritter: Bowdern will accept his godly counsel to prepare himself spiritually and begin the exorcism at his immediate convenience. At the same time, Ritter cautioned, he was not to rush into this like a fool. And he was to quit smoking.

No one needed counsel him to search through the University library for practical helps. Practical was the word, for he was a practical man. Like the apostle Peter, who acted forcefully and with good intent. Some called Peter brash, but Peter never held back when a job was to be done. As he made his way through the card catalogue, a thought struck him: the apostle would have broken down that bedroom door last night. That is what he should have done, and would have, had he not been dreaming about his personal doors. Well, no more dreaming. The time had come to act.

The librarian gave him a book by the Jesuit Martin DelRio which chronicled some pranks that demons play on their victims; but the book contained little more than prayerful exhortations. He needed more. The word Loudun rose in his memory: in his notebook, from a seminar on evil...yes, an entire convent in France, in the sixteenth century—it was taken over by a pack of demons. The librarian helped him find something on it. Many exorcists were called in to save the convent; one in particular, Jean Joseph Surin, himself became possessed. The priest had attempted to save the prioress, sister Jeanne des Agnes, by praying that the Demon would leave the woman and enter him instead. And that is what happened. Bowdern was shocked to read that in the opinion of some theologians the Demon was the instigator of the priest's prayers. The Demon tricked him into praying for the Prioress's deliverance at the cost of his sanity. The Prioress was merely bait.

He put the book down and stared at the high vaulted ceiling as thoughts swarmed through his head. The Loudun exorcism was centuries ago and in a different part of the world: a superstitious time. Who could say what really happened at that convent? DelRio's book was even older—1599. Something modern would be better. Again the librarian had the answer: a pamphlet about an exorcism in 1928. An Iowan farm girl names Mary had to be taken to a convent where an exorcist, Father Theophilus Riesinger strapped her to a bed and attempted to drive out demons that had tormented her for years. Things went badly. Mary burst out of her straps and levitated to the ceiling. When the priest's helpers finally pulled her down she began to swell up, her eyes turned red "like glowing embers," and she yelped "like a pack of wild beasts." One of the demons cried out that he was Mary's dead father, angry that he had never been able to force his incestuous will upon her. As for the exorcist, he went about looking like a "corpse," and another priest, Father Steiger, was blinded as he was driving his car and almost killed; when he struggled free of the wreckage and staggered into the convent, the demons gloated over his near death.

Such evil! As a priest, he should know about evil. Yet, it was mysterious: why would the father attack his daughter; why would the demon then attack the daughter?—why not the father? How did Mary escape all those years?...if indeed she did escape. In her dreams, the poor woman must have imagined herself rising to the ceiling where the man could not follow. Her yelping...that too would scare him off. But the man was dead when she yelped and rose to the ceiling. How did he die? Was it wise for Reisinger to strap Mary to the bed, if a bed was the scene of her trauma? So many questions. So then, should Mary have been treated by a psychiatrist? But what psychiatrist could explain the things that took place in the Iowan convent? No:—Mary needed a priest. So does Ritchie.

So far his readings were useless. He was going against a faceless enemy who hated God and all his works, including him, Bill Bowdern. No book learning would save him. He was a David up against a Goliath—without even a stone to throw. Was there no one he could turn to? Bishop had set up another visit to the Hipp's home Wednesday night; he checked his calendar—the 16th. Soon it would be holy week with its many demands. Yet, that was fitting: the sacred season might give him sustenance. Jesus' death on the cross would be the subject of his meditations. It struck him as never before that as a priest, he was called to follow Jesus his Master where he had gone.

Wednesday he invited Ray Bishop for a light supper. They ate in silence until he asked Bishop about Ilse: had she ever lived in the Hipp's house? No, Bishop answered, she never did. Then they talked about the Demon's tricks. How could they defend against the sly one and his deceits? They knew so little. When they finished eating, Bowdern got up and paced the floor in his study, trailing clouds of smoke. Something eluded him, something from a few years back. He slammed his fist into his palm—he had it! He grabbed the phone and demanded of the information operator that she give him a number in New York. In minutes he was speaking to Father Herman Heidi, the Catholic chaplain at Hunter College. Heidi, he remembered, knew a thing or two about demons.

A few years ago a worried parishioner came to him with a story about her nephew, a boy of ten who lived in New York City with his parents and sister. The boy suddenly turned sullen—was afraid to attend mass, used ugly language; he used to love the priests at his parochial school, she said, but now he wouldn't speak to them. The parents took him to a child psychiatrist who was baffled. The sister, however, who attended Hunter College, spoke to the Chaplain, who met with the boy, the parents, and then the psychiatrist. Bowdern hadn't known how he could help, but he did put a call into Heidi. Something Heidi said stuck in his mind: he ruled out demonic possession. A strange remark. Who said anything about the Devil?

Pleased that Heidi would remember him, Bowdern began by asking how the earlier matter had been resolved. Heidi avoided the subject and hastily asked why he was calling. Bowdern forged ahead with his questions, however, and Heidi warmed to the subject of Ritchie. When the boy asked what the prayers meant, Heidi explained, that was a trick—the Demon distracted him from the prayers and thus put an end to the power of the exorcism. And remember, he added, the prayers are most effective in Latin; use English only sparingly. Most important, you must demand to know the sign of his departure; the Demon will not leave without a sign. And his name—get his name if you can.

Names are important, Heidi explained: the Devil gives his name to witches, he said, when they make a compact with him, and the Devil will sometimes show himself to them as some beast. Heidi didn't give much credence to witches but the tradition was strong. Jesus knew the name of the Gergasene demoniac, and thus drove him into swine, then into the sea. Even in Macbeth, Heidi added, the witches in compact with the Devil know his names and know him under the signs of certain beasts: Graymalkin is the Devil known to the first witch, and he is a brindled cat; Paddock is an urchin or hedgehog; and the third—the leader of the pack—is Harpier, a large owl. These three Devils put all that evil into play—treachery, stealth, murder. Bowdern heard his fellow priest shudder as if the deed was done at Hunter College under his nose.

Remember, Heidi warned, the victim is bait, the priest is the prize. What is holy, and what is hidden among the holy, is his object; he is on the scent for secret sins in holy places. In fact, Heidi added, among the three signs the *Rituale* ascribes to possession, is the power to discern and uncover hidden things–secrets–in the past of the priest whom he has lured into his trap. The priest is close to God, so the Devil will attack us by every means, to corrupt us and expose us. That is the lesson of some medieval art that depicts the Devil with long hair and a woman's breasts, a female figure like Eve's. Far from being a bias against women—that women are seducers of men—it means that the Devil has the power to enter our very flesh and bones and tempt us from within.

Use all the powers our faith gives you, he urged. He told the story of a priest in Alsatia who, in 1869, together with another priest and a nun, were in a coach rushing to the home of a victim. The Devil pursued them and was about to overturn the coach and kill the three of them, but miraculously, the coachman brought forth a medal of St. Benedict that he had just been given. The medal saved them. You must fortify yourself with the images of faith.

Finally Heidi told him how Pope Leo XIII was inspired to compose the Michael prayer that every priest recited at the end of mass. One day the great Pope was at mass and happened to look up: over the altar a hoard of demons was swarming about–in the chapel!––ready to attack Rome and Holy Church. He hastened to his private study and fell to his knees. When he rose he bent over his desk and labored to produce the prayer to Michael, the warrior Archangel, the head of God's armies:

> St. Michael the Archangel, defend us in battle, be our protector against the wickedness and snares of the Devil; may God rebuke him, we humbly pray; and do thou, O Prince of the heavenly host, by the power of God, thrust into hell Satan and all the evil spirits who wander through the world for the ruin of souls. Amen.

Heidi was a help—something practical. Even though he said the prayer every day, he had not thought to use it as a weapon against the

Demon. And why not teach the prayer to Ritchie?—make him a partner in the battle. Heidi approved.

It was time to go. First, he and Bishop would slip into the back of Xavier church to pray. Several Jesuits were there also to recite the last prayer office of the day. They came often, and he knew why: the immense dark of Xavier's lofty interior drew them—a night sky with no stars save for a red lamp that burned before the tabernacle. That one light, to him, was the sole source of salvation—the savior, the light of the world. He and Bishop added their voices to the chants, then they listened as a lector read a passage from Peter's First Epistle: "Sobrii estate, et vigilate: quia adversarius vester diabolus tamquam leo rugiens circuit, quaerens quem devoret." The reader was a young man in his twenties, a "scholastic," he guessed, as novices were called. They were all young. What do they know? They read of the Devil, a roaring lion who goes about seeking whom it may devour. They are sheltered in their cloister; he, Bill Bowdern, will go up against their roaring lion.

As Halloran drove them down Lindell Boulevard to the Hipp's, his thoughts turned to Klara. She was a fine woman in her own way and she meant well, but she lacked the clarity of true religious faith. He would speak to her immediately: the seances had to stop. At the house he kept his emotions in check as he explained that the bible forbade such superstitious doings. Far from respecting him and his words, however, she remained silent. He felt her suspicious eye fall upon him as he kissed his stole and placed it over his surplice.

He said a brief prayer and turned toward the stairs. Bishop and Halloran, who had hardly removed their hats and coats, followed him into Ritchie's room and flanked him, slightly behind; their job was to make the responses to his prayers.

PRAECIPIO TIBI...he thundered, confident that his words— God's words—would compel the Demon to yield up its name and the hour of its departure. At the sound of his words, Ritchie, who had been lying still, screamed and clutched at his throat. Instantly Klara swept into the room and stationed herself between him and the bed. She glared at him, then looked down at her son. He saw the horror on her face. He strained to look past her to see what she saw but he didn't. Now he saw it, something red—a welt on his throat, rising up fast and ugly. Klara pulled open the pajama top to expose another welt on his stomach...and another. Three in all, as if painted by an invisible artist. Red streaks joined the welts. Suddenly, on the chest, four marks. He read the Demon's message: **HELL**.

PRAECIPIO TIBI, he repeated, at the top of his lungs. Thanks to Heidi, he knew better than to lose concentration. But Klara had more to show him. She pulled down Ritchie's pajama bottoms and turned her inflamed eyes upon him: in one moment he felt the full weight of her emotion: she detested him. Then she looked down at her son. Her hands flew to her face. Whatever she saw was unfit for a mother to behold. He took her gently by the shoulders and moved her aside. On the left thigh a large welt presented a new image: a horned head smirked at him. He wanted to say to Klara, *I do not cause these things to happen, they do not come from me*. He did not: his job was to pray. But the smirk and the glare from Klara's eyes were hammer blows aimed at his spirit.

Lifting the water vial with his right arm, he cut the air with swift moves, carving the sign of the cross and spraying water over the boy on the bed. The Demon had proved adverse to holy water, he knew. But Ritchie closed his eyes as if he too were at prayer. Bowdern reached down and slapped the boy on the face. Klara will be enraged, but the *Rituale* urged it; the trickster Demon puts the victim into an unnatural sleep so he cannot hear the words of Christ's priest or accept the Holy Water as a catechumen. He slapped him again, ignoring Klara's scream. Ritchie woke up; his eyes rolled upward in their sockets and he hissed at him. He repeated the command PRAECIPIO TIBI...The mattress began to quiver. Klara screamed again and tugged at his surplice to pull him away.

O HOLY LORD, he prayed, SNATCH FROM RUINATION AND FROM THE NOONDAY DEMON A HUMAN BEING, CREATED IN THINE IMAGE AND LIKENESS...AND STRIKE TERROR INTO THE BEAST THAT LAYS WASTE THY VINEYARD. The mattress heaved. Klara forced her way past him and tried to pull her son from the bed. But Ritchie was kicking and flailing; she fell back. Bowdern sprayed the bed with more holy water. The kicking stopped and again Ritchie shut his eyes. But a new eruption, low on his stomach, near the pubic hairs, spelled out a message: three letters, he could make out two. **GO**, it said.

Bowdern gasped at the sight. The Demon had etched its will on the boy's rickety frame. *The Demon commands me to go?* Another mark burst through the skin. On the upper right thigh, an **X**. Unmistakable—an **X**. *A command? No:—an answer. Go X: The hour of its departure*! He glanced at his watch: almost ten. Scripture told of the Gergesene demoniac that had yielded its name—Legion— to Jesus when the Lord demanded it. This Demon hides its name but tells when it will go. He was sure of it: The Demon will go at ten. *It is ready to go, I will help it with my prayers.* Picking up his book, he fired prayers like daggers at the heart of the beast that had wracked the small body on the bed.

Klara brought a wash cloth and began to wipe her son's face. Ritchie—*or the Demon...which is it?*—snatched the cloth with its teeth and tossed it aside with a violent shake of the head. Then it spat in Klara's face and urinated. She was drenched in her son's effluvia. Bowdern pitied her: *she is a good mother, after all,* he thought. He could hear her in a corner, weeping.

Again Ritchie closed his eyes and appeared to sleep. Bowdern heard the door behind him open and close. Klara must have left. He wished he could tell her that the end is near. The room fell quiet save for Bowdern's raspy voice as he appealed to the glorious Archangel Michael: PRINCEPS GLORIOISSIME CAELESTIS MILITAE...If the Demon were still present, the Archangel would rout him: Michael, who fights the rulers of the world's darkness on behalf of the people whom God has made and purchased at great price from Satan's tyranny, the ancient serpent, and who will cast Satan into the abyss. This exorcism was not about Ritchie alone; it was about the terror that Satan laid upon the whole world. PRINCEPS GLORIOISSIME...he shouted. Ritchie opened his eyes.

Bowdern felt a stir beside him. It was Halloran, who had reached for a handkerchief and stepped close to mop the boy's face, which was soaked in sweat and his eyes seemed to plead for relief. He shook his head and tried to nudge Halloran to back off. This was the wrong time. But the priest had reached in...too late. Ritchie's leg shot out and caught the priest in his groin. He heard a groan, as the priest crumpled on the floor and retched. From the body on the bed came a new odor, something he had not smelled since he was a boy and came upon entrails in back of a butcher's shop near his home in St. Charles. He felt alone in the midst of decay and dead earth.

But he was not alone...not with the relic of St. Francis Xavier, which he lifted high over Ritchie's head as he traced the sign of the cross in the air. Xavier had once aided such a victim, and the saint would do so again. He felt the blood of Xavier's companion, the warrior Ignatius, coursing through his veins. Once more he splashed the bed and the room with holy water. The Demon will perish in this water, he believed, for it is the baptismal water that priests pour over the heads of pure catechumens at the beginning of their Christian journeys. Angels and clouds of holy witnesses stand by when these waters are invoked. He uttered the second command, EXORCIZO TE...Ritchie tensed and twisted his head toward him. Suddenly a stream of spittle issued from his mouth as from a firehouse. Bowdern was stunned. *The Demon reads my thoughts! It baptizes me with filth from his mouth.*

What time is it? He could not read his watch, his glasses were clouded with spittle. EXORCISO TE...he repeated, IMMUNDISSIME SPIRITUS, OMNIS INCURSIO ADVERSARII, OMNI PHANTASMA, OMNIS LEGIO...The Latin imperative stung as it passed his lips; so sharp and final: Take your hordes of phantasms and diabolical legions and be gone! Be cut off! Ritchie rolled over and screamed obscenities. Klara had left the room; she could not hear her son speak such words...or could she? Ritchie writhed as if in pain. *Who feels the pain? Who curses? The boy or the Demon? The Demon, surely.* He could not bear the thought that he caused pain to the boy.

Ritchie rose to a squat, broke wind, and defecated. Bowdern could scarcely breathe. He covered his nose with the tip of his stole––no help. *If only I could stop and open a window.* No:––he must pray. EXORCIZO TE...Through his caked glasses he saw Ritchie's face close to his. The bed was shaking and rising. Ritchie, from atop his rocking perch, stood and splattered him with a stream of urine. The urine was cold.

ADJURO TE...He began the last of the three commands. The Latin put brave words on his tongue: he had dared to call the Demon an ancient serpent and to require it to tremble in his presence. But he himself trembled in the cold of this forsaken world, alone with a frail boy and the Prince of Reptiles. Again he knifed the air with the relic, placing the divine signature directly over the exposed belly. The red streaks rose up again: **HELL**, the Demon said, and urine from the tiny spout below rained down upon him. The Demon had blasphemed with every orifice that God gave a human being created in His likeness.

"...be in dread of the image of God," he read, "...make no delay in leaving this person, for it has pleased Christ to take his dwelling in man." He stared at Ritchie, all the more grotesque through the distortions of his clouded lenses. This is the Imago Dei? What he saw before him was a shell, a stump, of the likeness—a child of God robbed of his humanity. Human nature under siege. He too was under siege, as the Demon pumped more yellow stream from his victim's now swollen member. Heidi had warned him that the Demon would strip away his humanity, reduce him to type. Again he felt alone; he was the last soldier standing.

Heidi's words came back to him: "Michael is head of God's armies." Yes, and the bible says Michael will bind the Demon in a pit: ST. MICHAEL...DEFEND US IN BATTLE, BE OUR PROTECTOR AGAINST THE WICKEDNESS AND THE SNARES OF THE DEVIL...INTERCEDE FOR US TO THE GOD OF PEACE THAT HE WOULD CRUSH SATAN UNDER OUR FEET. LAY HOLD OF THE DRAGON, THE ANCIENT SERPENT SATAN AND CAST HIM BOUND INTO THE ABYSS, SO THAT HE MAY NO LONGER SEDUCE MANKIND. He needed Michael to be at his side. *But*, he wondered, *does Michael hear me? Does the Demon hear me?*

Ritchie collapsed upon the bed, rolled his eyes, and arched his back. His lips parted and trembled. Short snatches of words, syllables only, rippled from his mouth. Bowdern could make nothing of it. *Latin? The boy knows no Latin. Does he imitate me? Mock me?* The *Rituale* warned that the Demon's victim might speak in unknown tongues—a sign of possession. Or was it a sign of the Demon's talent for imitation?—repeating in gnarled form what he had just heard from the *Rituale*. Or had the Demon been at it from the days of Constantine? The body on the bed shuddered, fell back, turned toward him and exposed its stomach: the rash flared, visible through the caked glass: **HELL**, it said.

The Demon was trying to speak to him? Or was it Ritchie? If the Demon, it was a trick—Heidi had warned him: his job was not to talk, it was to pray. DOMINUS! DEUS! He cried out to the Lord God, as he began another prayer. The body on the bed yelped, twisted around, and pounded the headboard with its fists. DOMINUS! DEUS! he repeated. The body moved its bowels again, arched its back, and unleashed another stream of syllables. *Latin? Yes, it tries to repeat the prayer that began Dominus, Deus.* But the words were malformed, twisted—a mockery.

As he reached for the holy water, the boy flopped back upon the bed and began to hum a simple tune. He peered at the boy through his glasses. The boy's eyes were open; he gazed steadily at him. *What is he up to now?* The boy lifted himself upon one elbow and brought his head close to him. His eyes turned warm and fluttered. In sweet, delicate tones he told him about a dream he had just had, in which he saw a big, red Devil, covered with slime and very powerful; the Devil stopped him from passing through iron gates that covered a deep pit that was very hot. The Devil was strong, but not so strong as before.

He wanted to believe, but he did not. ADJURO TE...he commanded. The eyes rolled up in their sockets, the tongue protruded quivering on a stream of foam, and the silence was split by a scream that brought Bowdern's stole to his ears. BE IN DREAD OF THE IMAGE OF GOD...he charged. But his prayers brought no respite. The chest heaved and bile poured out...QUAKE BEFORE HIS ARM, FOR IT IS HE WHO SILENCED THE GROANS OF HELL. The voice from the bed dropped in pitch: deep and guttural, it bellowed, while the hand reached for the spout and pitched liquid stench at him. ADJURO TE...he repeated, forcing the words out between shallow gulps of air...FOR THE LORD CAST THEE FROM A HERD OF SWINE...HE WHO COMMANDS YOU IS RULER OF THE LIVING AND THE DEAD, WHO SHALL COME TO JUDGE THE WORLD BY FIRE. With the strength left in him, he demanded the profligate dragon, in the name of the spotless Lamb who walked upon the asp and the basilisk and trod underfoot the lion and the dragon, to let go of its victim. The prayer reeked of desert soil, as he imagined the land where the Lord set his feet and was succored by angels.

Images of carrion and fetid flesh from some waterless place unknown to man and forgotten by God rose up to afflict him—a ghenna of the spirit, where even Christ felt abandoned. *My God why hast thou forsaken me?* Water, he needed water. No, not the vial, the prayer. He thumbed back to the second prayer: EXORCIZO TE...he repeated. The prayer was a threat and a curse: God will drown the unclean spirit as He drowned Pharaoh's army that pursued the children through the Sinai to the sea. He, Bowdern, was a new Moses who would lead this child from the desert of death through holy waters to safety. He prayed on in Latin and heard the words in English: I CAST THEE OUT, UNCLEAN SPIRIT, IN THE NAME OF JESUS CHRIST WHO AFTER JOHN BAPTIZED HIM WAS LED INTO THE DESERT AND VANQUISHED THEE IN THY CITADEL. He emptied the vial upon the body that glared at him from the bed.

I could have baptized him with that water. Baptism is an exorcism—I read that somewhere. I know my theology!

DISCEDE ERGO NUNC...he shouted. Holding the *Rituale* with his left hand, a finger marking the place, he took the Xavier relic and cut the air with a savage motion—the sign of the cross, the fiery sign that Constantine saw in the sky, that told him he would conquer. The power of the cross,...it was his—he would conquer. *Such thoughts—I am delirious.* In God's Name he commanded the Demon to depart: NUNC—now! Ritchie stopped his heaving and spouting. All was calm.

With bent knee he prayed silently by the side of the bed. The boy was not asleep; his eyes were open—like slits. Something was wrong. Ritchie's lips began to move, slowly...the strange Latin again? No:—a singsong rhythm, the words—some of them—in English. What? Suddenly Ritchie sat up and began to sing louder, his arms swaying: **Way down upon the Sewanee River, far, far away**, he sang, in a shrill, piercing voice. Then **Ole man river, dat ole man river, he mus' know sumpin.'** His legs beat time in the air. Bowdern leapt to his feet and resumed the prayers. His voice was weak, he could not compete with the boy—or the Demon.

KYRIE ELEISON, CHRISTE ELEISON, KYRIE ELEISON, he exclaimed. Mercy, he was tired. How much longer? The banality of the boy's singing depressed him. He felt the need to relieve himself.

All those words about water, streams of water...he was only human. Lord! Ritchie turned toward him and issued another stream of urine as if from a firehose. Bowdern was saturated, his nose stung with the odor. Suddenly he understood. *This is the Demon's sign to me—he has baptized me in urine. A sign for a sign. Dirty water for purging water. And the songs—ignorant waters, river beds full of flowing waters that cannot save. A parody of the sacrament. The Demon has blasphemed.*

The sting of rebuke—everything was aimed at him, the filth, the curses. *No, I am God's theandric minister; if it rebukes me, it rebukes God and thus it blasphemes. But it aims its fifth at me.* Ritchie leered and grasped his swollen organ; he pumped another stream, all the while swaying and singing his ditties. *The Demon has summoned the Minister of Christ so that it can humiliate me, trample me under its feet.* Yes, he was the object of the venom. He came as Samaritan to rescue a fallen member of his race, but the enemy has thrown him and the other victim into a pit of mire and dung.

He tried to pray but his voice sank to a whisper; he could no longer hear his voice resonate in the cavity of his head...From the bed came a low hiss of breath. The boy had assumed a crouching position, as if the Demon wanted to pounce on its priestly victim. But the boy defecated again. Dare he open the window? The noise would rattle the neighborhood—Klara would berate him. Never mind Klara and the neighbors: He motioned to Bishop to lift the shade and throw open the window. A pale sun peered into the room. They sucked the fresh dawn into their lungs. *What time is it?* Someone passed him a towel. At last he could look at his watch, for the boy had fallen back upon the pillow and closed his eyes. It was 7:30.

Klara stirred. She must have been asleep during the night. No:— she would have been standing behind him at the door, looking, waiting. Now she wanted to bathe her son. Of course. He stepped back. There were the others: Bishop, Halloran, Eleanor, Werner, Frederick. They had been faithful through the night. They looked at him with a question in their eyes—is the Demon gone? They wanted to know. He had no answer.

It was the end of a day; it was the beginning of a day. He must ready himself for the early mass at Xavier—the altar boys were vested—then get on with his pastoral rounds, beginning at the local hospitals where many ailing parishioners needed him, then on to several afternoon appointments with distressed persons, even a young couple who need pre-marital counseling, then, in the early evening, a wake. He had a reputation when it came to wakes: he hadn't missed one in his three years at Xavier. He would do all these things, but the day would drain him: he had just finished a nine day novena at the church when this exorcism came up—prayer services each day at noon, at three, at six, and at nine. And Holy Week was almost upon him. In the clean and pure world of the liturgy, he prayed for his private intention: for Ritchie, that the X was the Roman numeral "ten," that the demon would depart in a few hours. Certainly, the Demon had obeyed the Lord's command and revealed that it would GO at X. That would mean ten this morning—in a few hours.

After the morning mass he took a light breakfast into his study and stacked four records on the turntable spindle. His prayers having been said, music would refresh another aspect of his soul. He dropped the stylus on side 1 of the *Fifth Symphony*—allegro con brio. Four notes sounded from a voice that existed in no nature known to him. A dumb, brutish utterance. A pause. Four notes repeated, their pulse a vain and godless menace. In the movement that passed for a scherzo, an enemy lurked in the shadows, but he strutted forth to a march-like phrase on glinted horns that echoed the four dumb notes. Then a jerky motion in the basses, stated once, repeated, came across as mocking laughter from some fiend whose face is hidden, but his mockery is heard from some hollow beneath the earth. Still, this enemy could only repeat his dumb phrases; he never came to a resolution. The Demon that inhabited Ritchie could only repeat dumb phrases. Could the Demon who possessed Beethoven also possess Ritchie? If so, he knew the answer: he cupped his hands behind his ears to augment the swelling tones as three trombones, their majesty held back for this moment, blazed; drums and brass thundered; and the full throated orchestra exulted in C Major— a mighty shout from the heavens that ridded the world once and for all of its terrors.

But the answer is not in music, it is in prayer. He put the records back into the album cover and thumbed through the *Rituale* and his notes from the library. This compendium of wisdom and prayer evolved from struggles with a dumb spirit. Dumb but stubborn: one night of prayer would not drive him back to his hollow under the earth. How long had the Loudun exorcism taken? Many days, weeks. Those red ripples on Ritchie's skin: did the X mean ten? Did GO mean depart? What was the third letter?—how ironic if it were D: GOD. What would GOD X mean? He had not stared at the mark—it was too close to the boy's pubic area. Some literature said the Demon would depart through a bodily orifice. The penis?

It was after ten and Bishop had not called. He picked up the phone and called his friend at the house. The boy was asleep, nothing had happened. No sign, nothing dramatic? The Demon's departure should be noted by a sign. The Demon had only given those two letters and the X. And HELL! He forgot HELL! *Dear God, could it mean: eXorcist, GO TO HELL?*

It was St. Patrick's day—the great saint reputedly drove the snakes out of Ireland. Well, Patrick knew nothing about this kind of snake, the one that inhabited Ritchie. He typed out the Michael prayer on a card to give to Ritchie; he had forgotten to do that—how could he? He would be returning this evening to the house—just in case—and he would teach it to Ritchie: should he give it in English or Latin? English, surely. Ritchie could help himself with his own prayers. It would help even more if he were truly baptized—not just sprinkled by symbolic water. But first, he would see what the evening would bring. Prayers of thanksgiving, if God were merciful.

Halloran arrived promptly at nine and picked him up, along with Bishop. At the house he studied Eleanor's face for signs of the household disposition; he liked this young woman, she was transparent. The boy had a quiet day, she told him, although he seemed a little cranky after supper. Klara was upstairs with him now, getting him settled for bed. He heard her voice above, through closed doors—she was giving orders to Werner and Frederick. A door opened: he heard her say that when the priests arrived they would make things worse. Eleanor flushed. Obviously Klara intended him to hear it. Then she called to Werner, No Relics. He was supposed to hear that, too.

Was it not enough that he had to bear the assaults of the Demon, that he had also to bear the insolent tongue of this woman? Never mind, he was here to pray. If prayer was needed, for the boy had spent a quiet day. Did the Demon leave this morning? Not without a sign, the *Rituale* said that a sign must be given. But was not the X itself a sign? From the room above came a curdling howl that resonated throughout the house and inside his tired brain.

He dashed up the stairs. There, pinned to the bed by the full weight of Werner and Frederick, was the howling Ritchie. But a leg sprung free and clipped Werner in the groin, who spun around, staggered to a corner, and collapsed on the floor. Halloran and Bishop moved in quickly to take his place. He knew to begin the prayers: in his mightiest tone, as if he were presiding at a cathedral altar, he again demanded that the Demon reveal its name and the time of its departure: PRAECIPIO TIBI...The body on the bed wrestled an arm free from the weight that bore it down, ripped open its pajama bottoms, and released a yellow stream that soaked the fresh mattress in a briny sea of urine. *If this pestilent creature thinks it has claimed the bed as its own, it has befouled its own lair.* The body jerked to one side to expose its vessel and sprayed icy torrents at him, its accuracy the equal of last night but its force must greater. *It tries to drive me away from its lair. No:*—he shuddered—*it claims me as one of its own, it has baptized me and staked me to an altar in hell.*

PRAECIPIO TIBI...he repeated, his own chest heaving in rhythm with the boy's. Again, the air was foul; the boy had emitted gas and defecated. *Our Father Who Art in Heaven*...he led them in the familiar prayer and was pleased to hear voices from the women in the corner. Then the PRAECIPIO TIBI...again and holy water; Ritchie groaned and arched his body when he heard the word *Deus* or *Dominus.* The singing broke out again: WAY DOWN UPON THE SEWANEE RIVER...off key and shrill.

Finally it all stopped. After a moment Bowdern took off his glasses, and Eleanor gave him a cloth to wipe them clean. The boy had gone limp in the arms of the men who had been holding him and who now stepped back, exhausted. Klara and Eleanor rushed in immediately to clean up. Bishop took Ritchie's pulse, and nodded to Bowdern that it was normal. And no signs carved in the flesh. *No sign, no name!*—*the Demon has not gone, not yet. The X did not mean ten hours*—*I was wrong. But ten days? Can I survive ten days?*

He sat down in a chair that Eleanor brought for him—that blessed girl, he must thank her. He had a chance to think: *How many days? This is the 17th. I first saw the boy on the 11th. Ten days*—*to the 20th or 21st. But the X appeared on the 16th, when I did the first exorcism! Dear God, let it not be the 26th.*

No, it was the 18th —after midnight. His second night of terrors. No doubt tomorrow there would be a third and a fourth and a fifth— unless God granted a third day miracle. He would pray.

Five hours of sleep—not much, and fitful at that. Something heavy pressed down on him when he awoke, a spiritual affliction; he knew nothing like it. He ignored Michael's call to breakfast and went straight to the altar. On bent knees he turned to Deus, or Dominus— his friend, the Demon's foe—and in prayer he contemplated the two evenings he had confronted the Demon. The singsong routine—the Demon has limited repertoire; he only imitates and repeats; he is dumb. And he comes out only at night—why? But the heaviness he felt—was the Demon stalking Ritchie by night and him by day?

After lunch—a lunch he picked at but did not consume—he closed the study door behind him and reached for the phone. Heidi, he needed Heidi. Some disturbing thoughts had come to him. He dialed the number at Hunter College. A secretary answered: it was Friday, she said—the Newman Club would be meeting at the Bronx campus and Father would be there. Unfortunate. He would call again in the evening. But no, he will be at the boy's house; the call would have to wait.

It will be his third exorcism, he thought, aware of a deep chill that gripped him and stifled his spirit. What could he do that he had not already done? Was he doomed to simple repetitions like the Demon himself—the two of them locked in a round of prayers and curses, holy water and spittle, Praecipio Tibi and Sewanee River—forever trapped in a night-house with the beast against whom his body and soul must be measured? He was tired: having made his hospital calls, he returned to the rectory and rested in the shaded dark of his bedroom. He intended to nap briefly: but when he awoke it was later than he thought: he had dreamed of infested waters, underground currents, reptile haunted rocks in a wilderness. Halloran and Bishop would be here soon—it was almost seven. Would there be a third day miracle?

At the house Eleanor reported that Ritchie spent a quiet day reading and playing monopoly, except for a brief "spell" after lunch, but he took a nap and felt better when he awoke. Bowdern reached into his deep vest pocket for his pyx: this time, he would have the fortification of the Blessed Sacrament. It was one thing he could do that he had not already done—bless the boy with the Sacrament. Pity he could not place its sacred contents into the boy's mouth. If only the boy were a Catholic. He waited patiently as Klara assisted Ritchie to bed. Klara!—what would she do if she knew his thoughts? It was almost eight; the three priests gathered again in the dimly lit bedroom and began to pray.

With the *Rituale* in one hand and the vial in the other, he began the Litany of Saints. The long list of Apostles and Martyrs fell like footsteps—Cornelli, Cypriani, Laurentii, Christolgi...what would these names mean to Ritchie? To Klara? The Latin names ran into each other on his hasty tongue: he sensed Klara's impatience. But he was calling upon the prayers of the living and the dead who served God in their day, who had fought the good fight, and whose help he needed. Suddenly he felt a motion under his feet. The bed—it was moving. It scraped a few inches across the floor until it nudged his kneecaps. It rose a few inches in a rocking motion, then fell back. He opened the vial and doused the bed with water. Ritchie squealed and clawed the air; his eyes blazed at him with glassy hatred. The names of the saints had no salutary effect. But he prayed on. Ritchie lunged at him—the first physical assault—but the men moved in to hold him down. The men toiled as the twisted body beneath them flailed arms and legs in rhythm with the Latin words as he prayed on through the night.

Armies marched to battle like this:—arms and legs in sway to the beat of a drum; he had seen men in Burma march off to some distant battle, some lawless place of death: dumb, mindless—it seemed—of their fate. As a chaplain, he was called to pray with every breath he took. What else could he do? Here, too, he could but pray in step with the boy's mysterious march. *Where is the boy going?* The boy gathered strength with every step. *Lord, the Demon gets stronger; I get weaker.*

He was getting weaker, but he was still a priest, Heidi would say to him. And what does a priest do? He prays. But this Demon does not heed the call of prayer. What else does a priest do? He administers saving waters. Many times already he had flooded the boy and the bed and the room, but always these saving waters made the boy scream, and turn, and twist in fury or pain. *But he has not gone under the waters of Holy Baptism.* At that moment the debate was over and the matter settled: Klara will object, but he will instruct the boy in the faith, baptize him, and give him holy communion. Ritchie will be a new born saint and march to the beat of God's drum.

Ritchie twisted free of grasping hands, thrust his upper body toward Bowdern, and spat. The boy was infallible in his accuracy. Eyes open or closed, the boy never missed. Again, the point was not lost on him—the Demon knew his thoughts, and returned water for water.

He reached for another vial and emptied it over the boy's head. *There, I have answered the Demon; he defies me, I defy him. One of us will perish in the waters.* The apostle Peter almost perished in the waters of Galilee, when he leapt into it at the sight of the Lord on the waves; but he was raised up at the touch of the Lord's hand. That was Peter's figurative baptism. Then, and only then, were the wind and waves calmed. He remembered this point from a seminary lecture: everyone has to go under the waters—or be swept away.

He peered, through his bespattered glasses, at the distorted face that used to belong to Ritchie. It was the Demon. If he poured waters over that head, whom did he baptize—the boy or the Demon? Yes, there was something mystical about the waters. Peter's faith grew during that dark night that the evangelist called the fourth watch of the night, the dark before the dawn. Theologians spoke of the mystery, but he was no theologian. He only poured the water. God did the rest.

Suddenly, Ritchie cried out in his natural voice that his arms were sore, the men were hurting him. He turned pleading eyes upon his father and the priests. Bowdern knew what to expect, but he had no time to warn the men. They would let up, he knew that; and the boy would spring free and do...God knows what. In a flash Ritchie was up. His fists and knees sent the men sprawling to the floor.

His glasses were caked with spittle, he could not see. He feared the boy would turn upon him next, for he heard the gnashing of teeth, but he could only raise his hand—not in blessing, but to stiff-arm the boy if he attacked. The next noise he heard, however, was the scuffing of feet beside him–thank God, it must be Halloran and Bishop, who scrambled to their feet; then he heard Ritchie howl as he was forced back upon the bed. His two friends were winded, they were panting; but they held until Werner and Frederick joined in, and Ritchie was pinned down finally. *Yes, the Demon gets stronger. No skinny adolescent could toss two, three, four grown men about like that. And I grow weaker.*

He droned on: HOLY MARY MOTHER OF GOD PRAY FOR US NOW AND AT THE HOUR OF OUR DEATH...Ritchie had been subdued for some time now: at least he was quiet. He took a moment to hand his glasses to Eleanor who wiped them clean; he missed not a beat of the prayers. Ritchie's eyes closed and he appeared to sleep: the four men sat down to catch their breath. Slowly Ritchie's feet began to twitch: then, bent at the knees, his legs etched circles in the air, as if he were pedaling an imaginary bicycle. *The Demon mocks me again, causing the boy's feet to tremble and flee, pretending to be afraid of my prayers.* Ritchie pedaled faster; then, before the men could grasp him, he sprang to his feet, faced him, and made a profound bow. Three times he made the obeisance as the prayers **Our Lady of Fatima pray for us**, and **Holy Mary mother of God pray for us now and at the hour of our death** broke from his lips and fell upon Bowdern's ears like caustic. *The Demon steals my prayers and befouls them, then puts them on the lips of this innocent boy. Blasphemy!*

He had been upstaged by the Demon's flair for theater. Should he repeat the prayers? Engage it in a shouting match? Who was blaspheming: Ritchie or the Demon? This masked ball of transformations—echos of marching, the music hall, and the church—made his head spin. Suddenly Ritchie threw off his pajama top and stretched out his arms, making a cross of himself; then slowly lifted his arms over his head. *My God, he mimics Christ, who sacrificed himself upon the cross and offered himself to the Father above.* Ritchie then clamped his hands over his stomach and opened his mouth wide as if to vomit. *What is it—the Demon—doing now?* Ritchie spun around to face the window, still bent at the waist, and raised one hand toward the window: **Open the window**, he—Ritchie?—demanded. Bowdern nodded to Halloran, who moved quickly and flung it open.

Ritchie's mouth was open: the window was open. *Is he trying to rid himself like this...Demons leave through open mouths and windows?* Ritchie pivoted and stared directly at him. The cold night air swept in. Ritchie shuddered and reached for his pajama top, his eyes fixed on him. **He's gone**, said the boy, in his pure, natural voice. Klara and Frederick rushed to the bed and embraced their son. **He's gone**, the boy repeated, peering over his mother's shoulder and smiling sweetly at him.

A third day miracle? He wanted to believe, but he did not. The Demon could use the boy's natural voice as well as he could use any part of him—his bowels, his breath, his bladder. As for the prayers—true, they were not in the singsong style as before, but the Demon imitates. Eleanor and the priests glanced his way; they wanted something—a prayer of thanksgiving? They believed: he did not. But the family gathered about the bed expected it: he improvised a prayer, glancing as he did toward Klara: tears of joy streamed from her eyes. How will she feel when the Demon returns?

Klara washed her son with sponges and put his pajamas back on. All the while the boy smiled at Bowdern. Relentlessly, it seemed. It made him uncomfortable. Why not smile at his mother? He turned and went downstairs to wait for the others to finish mopping up. Later, Ritchie—the most wide awake of all, despite the lateness of the hour—came down in a clean bathrobe and chatted away about his visitor. A dark, cowled figure had come to him upon a heavy cloud, but it walked away, growing smaller and smaller, until it was gone. When the three men rose to leave, Ritchie, with a broad smile, walked them to the door and wished them a good evening.

He kept his doubts to himself during the drive home, while Bishop and Halloran waxed ecstatic. Klara bathed her son with sponges, he noted; but the boy needed another kind of washing, and that was his job to do. And the boy's bathrobe—he needed rather a glistening white garment, fit for the font where he could drown the foul one in the waters of purity. He glanced at his watch: it was 1:30 am. Tomorrow he would call Heidi. Tonight he would rest.

The night was long and, Lord, he needed rest...*It was too theatrical, the open mouth, the open window, the prayers*...doubts robbed him of sleep. He needed music. In the study he reached for a heavy album—the Ninth. The cover art caught his eye: a human silhouette imprisoned inside a cube. *Ritchie trapped inside his small room, no way out.* He set the records on the spindle, turned down the lights. Quivering strings gave rise to a world that came from a single thought—inane, without life, without humanity. The scherzo: demons of hell come forth—a defiant dance, beat to a drum that repeats its simple phrase: *Yes, the demons are dumb.* The adagio—a prayer of peace. Violence again: No humanity—until the din was gone and then at last a voice was heard: "No more these tones of sadness; brethren. Sing a song of joy and seek our loving father in the starry sky above." Never before had he understood this music: the tenor spoke directly to him to assure him of his humanity, that the evil one had not robbed him, that all was not lost.

At 3:15 the call came. Still in his clerical collar and cassock, he woke up his two friends and soon they were speeding though the night. The Hipp residence was lit like a beacon on the dark street. The three men filed into the house. Eleanor had not exaggerated: Ritchie had "broken out" again, as she put it...The boy was crouched upon his bed ready to pounce. The men wrestled him to the bed and pinned him down. PRAECIPIO TIBI...he began, with all the breath he had left in him. As before, he commanded the Demon to give a sign of its departure. Ritchie defecated and hosed his captors with urine.

Toward dawn, Ritchie slandered the Holy Mother, all the saints, and the three priests in particular—by name. How did he know their first names? And the names of their mothers! *I do not know the Demon's name, but he knows mine—and my mother's—and the names of the others' mothers! What more can he know about me? About us? Soon it will be light and a new day, and the Demon will depart. Through the window?* The window was shut. *Open it? How foolish!* He knew that the Demon would not depart until the prayers forced a sign from it. An open window was no sign.

At the rectory the early morning sun was already streaming into his bedroom, lighting up the corners and exposing the bed he had not slept in. Usually the sun called him to rise and pray, but today it reminded him of frustrated hopes and prayers. He stared at the bed. Wearily, he pulled the blinds and sat on it for several minutes, still fully vested, smoking cigarettes. Finally he removed his vestments and put them in the hamper. Michael, who always did the laundry on Saturdays, would be shocked at the stains and odor he would find on them. Michael put up with a lot. He would apologize to Michael after breakfast—and he would please him by eating it.

Still staring at his bed, he thought of Ritchie in the Hipp's bedroom. That place had become a calvary, a place of stench and death, where the Demon mimicked him—arms stretched toward heaven, as if the Demon were the true priest. In that room Satan was the priest, not Bill Bowdern—the bed the altar, Ritchie the bait, and Bill Bowdern the victim. Satan had stalked him, as he had stalked his Lord, and brought him to that place to die.

At the mass, his gaze wandered toward the high vault above the altar: the pack of demons that the great pope saw in Rome...could they be here now, at Xavier? If so, the Lord of flies would hear him call upon the Lord of hosts to send the legions of angels and archangels to protect him and the faithful—the Lord of flies would find no carrion here among the sanctified faithful, who were baptized, cleansed in the blood of the Lamb. As the altar boy approached him with the lavabo he thought again of the baptismal waters. Ritchie was going to be baptized. His mind was set on it.

When he picked up the phone later in the day to call Heidi, he could hear Michael in the kitchen, fretting and mumbling as he always did when he feared the meal would not be eaten, in which case Michael would display his disapproval by leaving the meal on the table until the next morning. But Michael would have to go on fretting—the call to Heidi was important. How did Heidi come to know so much about demons? What lay behind his remarks about the sins of priests? Should he baptize Ritchie and make him a Catholic? Why does the Demon attack only at night? A new thought struck him. He slammed down the phone and reached for his bible.

It was the text in *Luke 9* that disrupted his thoughts: Jesus gives power to his disciples to cast out devils, but in their first test they fail. A man comes to Jesus saying that a spirit seized his son and he called upon the disciples to drive it out but they did nothing. Jesus heals the boy himself. What happened to the power Jesus gave to his disciples?

If Heidi had answers, he would wangle them out of him—who else could he turn to? The call was answered by Heidi himself, who seemed remote; perhaps it was best to lead him gently into the deeper issues, for which the Scripture text would suffice. Yes, Heidi said, he had pondered the text himself and so had the artist Raphael, whose last painting, The Transfiguration, hangs in the Vatican museum where it has baffled the critics. The odd thing, Heidi said, is that Raphael flung together two scenes—the shining transfiguration of the Lord on the Mount and the commotion below, where the disciples fail to heal the stricken boy. No connection—say the critics. But read Luke! The whole chapter is about the Kingdom, he exclaimed: the death of the son, his third day resurrection and his eighth day exaltation. On the Mount, a voice is heard: "This is my son, listen to him." Well, said Heidi, someone heard the Son and came to him; a man whose son—his only son—was seized by a spirit that convulsed him. Bowdern was stunned: yes, the two scenes are connected; he had never seen the painting, but in his mind's eye the father asks the transfigured Lord—an only son of his Father—to grant his request— the man himself being the father of an only son. The point? Ah, said Heidi—in Luke all the healings are premonitions of the resurrected life in heaven with the Father. The father saw the resurrected life in the presence of the transfigured Jesus, and the gathering at the foot of the Mount has to do with the death of an only son—will he be able to stand up or not? Jesus is the answer to that question once and for all— -the boy stands. But, protested Bowdern, the disciples failed. Of course they failed, Heidi responded: because—look at them—they clamor among themselves; who is the greatest? they ask. They reverted to their own powers, and failed to let Christ work through them. The artist shows this: in the picture—I have studied it—the boy is rising. Yes, rising! Look! Look! The possessed, when they are stricken they will fall and foam at the mouth; when they recover they stand. The boy stands! My friend the psychiatrist tells me the boy is coming out of a seizure, not entering into it. And the boy looks up: Who will he see? The transfigured Lord overhead. The disciples, when they failed, listened to demonic voices of power; but look at verse 44, "Let these words sink into your ears." If they had listened to the only Son of the Father, they would have raised the boy through the Son's power. So the artist tells us—and he is right.

Heidi's oratory resonated with conviction. Yes, it made sense; and it chilled him to the bone. The disciples failed because they did not listen to the Lord's demand for sacrifice, that they should face their own death. If the exorcist is not prepared to face his own death, he will fail Ritchie, the only son of his father. To which Heidi's answer was: We are all sons of the Father, even when evil swallows us up.

How did Heidi know so much about evil? Through friends of G. K. Chesterton, Heidi responded. Bowdern had thrilled to the English author's Father Brown mystery stories about a dumpling shaped dullard—so the world thought—whose spiritual powers rooted out the Devil in the course of his many evil works. Chesterton, said Heidi, learned about satanic practices when he met Monsignor John O'Connor, who had stumbled across "certain horrors" that took place upon the high moors of the West Riding. What it came down to was this: the darkest hours of the night appeal to the Satanists because, they believe, the creature they have seized is in a sensitive state and fit for their purposes. They torture it to make its glands pump juices into the blood, making the blood highly potent. They kill it, offer it to Satan, and drink its blood, which quickens the psyche and enables it to leap out of the body. Bowdern, taking what he could from Heidi's words, reasoned that Satan seeks his victims at night when they are most susceptible to him, and he tortures them to inflame their blood.

The Demon was seeking him at night, Bowdern believed; calling him, tormenting his brain, sapping him of strength. Heidi, as if listening to Bowdern's thoughts, added: the priest who approaches the Demon and his victim must be pure as the Beatitudes themselves, because, he repeated, the priest is himself the victim. And the Demon will tempt him: it's passion is to uncover priestly sins. At night, he added, men are moved to sin—all men, even priests. Something at the heart of priesthood is hidden—a ghastly secret.

Jesus himself was tempted, Heidi added, expanding his homily: when he came up from the waters of his baptism, the Devil rushed in to test him. Water and darkness, Heidi brooded, are twin realities for the spirit, for good or for evil. A friend of his at the Jewish Theological Seminary lectured recently about the ancient water-test, a mythic testing of a man's spirit. An initiate who would enter a certain society strives to achieve heaven under the image of a palace. The guardians of the sixth palace test him by releasing an ocean of water upon the initiate as he strives to ascend to the...Heidi seemed to fumble for his notes...yes, hekhal, palace. But there is really no water at all, it is an illusion; if the initiate believes the water is real, he perishes in it.

Bowdern gripped the phone with a tense fist as he reached with his other hand for a pack of cigarettes. How would he open it and light a cigarette without the use of both hands? Better he forfeit the smoke and listen to Heidi, who was approaching the subject of water and, no doubt, the need to baptize Ritchie. Heidi told him to read Matthew's account of Peter's plunge into the dark waters of the Galilean Sea to join Jesus. It was the fourth watch of the night, Heidi related, and Jesus' disciples are in a boat attempting to cross over to the other side, as Jesus had bade them. But the wind is against them and they struggle. Suddenly, in the dark, they see Jesus walking over the waves toward them. They take him for a ghost. Peter however jumps into the water as Jesus calls and begins to walk toward the voice that called him. But when Peter feels the slap of the wind against his face he begins to sink. Jesus holds out his arm to him, lifts him up, and says "...why did you doubt?" There, exclaimed Heidi, what do you make of that?

Bowdern was mystified; he was no theologian, he was over his head. Heidi went on: The early Christians immersed an initiate three times in water; sometimes they held him down almost to the moment of death. When a man goes under water, he goes back to his roots, so to speak; he meets up with his most ancient fears: our first enemies are there—remember St. John's vision of the great beast that rose up from the sea and made war against the children of Eve. The baptizand conquers these fears; when he is lifted up from the dark waters by the hand of the priest he sees light and he is reborn, saved from the ancient foe.

When he hung up with Heidi he knelt alone in the cavernous nave of Xavier church, made the sign of the cross, and meditated upon his words. It is the lot of disciples that they must be tested, and his time had come. He prayed for strength to endure in the windswept sea of evils that Jesus had called him to. Yes: it is not the Demon but Jesus who calls him, and whose hand will reach out to save him. He prayed until the pale evening light was gone and the church was dark except for the red lamp at the tabernacle by the altar.

When he returned to his study, he had a plan. Klara, of course, would object to Ritchie's baptism at the hands of a priest; the boy had already been baptized in the Lutheran church, she would argue. Therefore he would have to be as crafty as the Demon himself. He picked up the phone and called Brother Rector Cornelius at the Alexian hospital outside the city. The Order had been rescuing desperate people since the Black Death swept Europe in the 14th century, when they nursed the feeble and dying, and those whom they could not save they blessed and buried. Brother Rector he met a few years ago, when he went to their hospital to visit one of his parishioners who was mentally ill, and he was impressed—they took on people nobody else wanted. He explained matters to the Brother on the phone: Ritchie, Klara—everything. The Brother didn't hesitate: he told Bowdern that they had a "secure room" at the end of a 120 foot wing on the fifth floor, ready when needed.

Klara would not tolerate many more visits to the house, he knew, so he would have to act fast. Saturday night, when he finished his ordeal with Ritchie, he took her aside and told her she needed some rest. She would feel better, he said, and so might Ritchie, if he were out of the house for a day or two; and he added the thought that the prayers would work better somewhere else. He knew a place. She said she would not object to just one night.

By Monday, he needed a rest himself, and he read the same need in the puffy eyes of his helpers. The family was suffering too; they had heard the groans of hell for many days, they were shaken and worn. His issue was acute: he hoped that the X on Ritchie's body meant the Demon would depart on the tenth day. That meant the tenth night of prayers: he wanted that day to have Ritchie in a special place: at the Alexian chapel, or at Xavier by the font. That would be March 25, the Feast of the Annunciation—when an angel's voice told of God's new Kingdom.

In the first dark of the evening, Monday the 21st, Halloran drove Bowdern and Ritchie to the Alexian Brothers hospital outside St. Louis, where Brother Rector Cornelius and Brother Bruno greeted them. The room near the chapel was prepared: the bed had straps, and several of the stronger brothers were standing by if needed. They brought in a divan and some chairs, so that Ritchie could have company, and they took time to talk to him. Bowdern introduced him to Father Widman, the hospital chaplain, and reminded him why he was here: he was here, Bowdern said, just for a day, to get to know more about God and Jesus. Widman met with Ritchie for an hour of instruction. Shortly after nine Ritchie fell asleep and put in a quiet night as Bowdern and the others kept watch.

After breakfast Tuesday morning, Halloran drove him to the hospital where he found Ritchie in good spirits as he chatted with Father Widman and the others. The plan appeared to be shaping up. He was particularly pleased that the Demon had not interfered. Holiness was a shield, and this point would be brought to Klara's attention. Perhaps now she will be more approachable. But when Klara came to pick up her son later in the afternoon, she made short shrift of him. Before he could speak, she had Ritchie in the elevator and out the door.

That evening he heard from Bishop that Ritchie's bed was shaking. They must go back. That woman! She always called Bishop—why not call him at the rectory? Never mind—he knew why. He threw a woolen cape over his cassock and stood by Xavier's broad steps to wait for Bishop with the parish car. Braced against the wind that coursed down Lindell Boulevard, he lit a Camel and contemplated the need to bring Ritchie to the Xavier font. The font is where good spirits gather, he believed; it is safe—thus it is called a sanctuary. "Spirit" means wind, he remembered: the Holy Spirit was a rushing wind at Pentecost. The holy wind sweeps clean. As he got into the car, he realized he was turning his back on Xavier. He must right the course, bring Ritchie to the font.

At the house, Eleanor escorted him to Ritchie's room where he began the prayers immediately: PRAECIPIO TIBI...He issued another ultimatum, informing the Demon that God orders it to depart, He who once ordered the wind and the sea and the storm to obey. In minutes the bed quit its rocking motion and peace settled over the boy, who smiled and spoke sweetly to him. Had the prayers calmed the bed and the boy as they had calmed the sea? Or was it a trick? Heidi would say pray on, but his intuition told him something new was happening. Putting down the *Rituale*, he turned to look for Klara. She stood there in the hall, a gaunt presence, cold fire in her eyes.

They spoke in the kitchen. He reminded her that Ritchie did well at the Alexian hospital: if only Ritchie could have stayed there another day or two... But Klara was silent, unheeding. Pressing on, he spoke about baptism; Ritchie had been baptized as a Lutheran, of course, and he respected that; but as a baptized Catholic, he said, Ritchie could come to the beautiful Xavier sanctuary, receive holy communion, and be surrounded by all God's saints. She snapped at him: her son had already been baptized, thank you, and they had a Pastor at home, Reverend Schulze, who would give Ritchie communion. It was hopeless. But Eleanor and Frederick and the others would talk to her later. God willing, they will bring her to the light.

A room on the third floor of the rectory was empty; he asked Michael to get it ready for the guest, and to serve meals that might be appealing to a boy's taste. Wednesday afternoon, as he returned from making home communions, he found an urgent note Michael placed on his desk. It was from Bishop: Ritchie would be there tonight, along with his father. A problem: Bishop might be unavailable for a few days; Bowdern should call over to Verhagen for Fr. William A. VanRoo, whom the chancery office described as a brilliant young scholar. That, Bowdern noted, was a quality irrelevant to his purposes; he needed a man for the strong arm squad; but brilliant or not, VanRoo would have to do. Just after supper he heard the rectory bell ring and Michael's voice calling him: Ritchie and Frederick stepped into his study, and moments later, VanRoo and Halloran rang. The plan was in motion.

They would begin the evening with a prayer in the church, he decided; and it would be good for Ritchie to see the font. He asked Michael to lead the guests to the church and turn on the lights while he had a brief word with VanRoo. The young priest, he learned, believed his work was to instruct a candidate for baptism—he had no notion of what was going on. Well if he is lucky, he will remain ignorant, for there was no time to tell him now—he couldn't leave the boy alone in the church with only Michael. The interior was ablaze with light; Michael had turned on the spotlights over the font in the rear of the nave, and removed the canopy top. Bowdern saw his chance to instruct: the font is the womb of Mother Church, he began; Christians are born here as they shed their sins.

At nine-thirty Bowdern led the boy to his room. Halloran and VanRoo followed, along with Frederick. Continuing his instruction, Bowdern told Ritchie about the four great prayers—the Acts of Faith, Hope, Love, and Contrition—and asked Ritchie to memorize the prayer that he would detest his sins and avoid every occasion of sin. The three priests circled the bed and joined Ritchie in reciting the prayers that would prepare him for his new life as a Catholic, free from Satan and sin. Suddenly Ritchie erupted, arms and legs flailing,

253

his eyes tightly shut. Obscenities poured from his mouth. Halloran pressed down upon him with his full weight and called to VanRoo to help. Bowdern began, PRAECIPIO TIBI...VanRoo, stunned, did nothing. Then Ritchie stopped his kicking, and in the sweetest of tones said that Halloran was hurting him, would he please let go of his arms? Halloran knew better, but VanRoo, who outranked Halloran, did not. Bowdern shot a look at VanRoo to warn him off, but he was too late. VanRoo ordered Halloran to let up, and Halloran loosed his clamp hold on Ritchie's arms. In a flash the boy bounded to an erect position and slammed his fist into Halloran's nose. Then he went for VanRoo: blood spurted from his nose over his shirt front and onto the floor.

Frederick rushed in to lend weight to the effort. After several minutes, the three men subdued Ritchie's most violent movements, but they could not curtail his mouth and bladder: he screamed that his penis was on fire and tore at his pajama bottoms to expose the penis, which he aimed at the men who were holding him down. In moments they were drenched in urine. Bowdern's first fear was that the shrill voice would carry to Verhagen Hall just off the rear window—he would have a lot of explaining to do. Then he worried about VanRoo, who seemed to be in shock. But the priest held on to Ritchie's left foot, although he was dripping blood into pools of urine.

After an hour Ritchie whimpered and drifted off to sleep. The men rose up slowly from the bed and staggered off, Halloran to the bathroom, VanRoo to a chair in the hall where Eleanor mopped his face with a damp towel, and Frederick...out of sight...Bowdern couldn't see him...to use the downstairs bathroom maybe. Bowdern kept on praying: ADJURO TE...he uttered. Ritchie opened an eye—it was bloodshot and rolling in its socket. Bowdern expected trouble: too late to call the men back...Ritchie leapt from the bed, squatted in the center of the room and defecated to the sound of wind and thunder.

ECCE CRUCEM DOMINI, FUGITE, PARTES ADVERSDAE...Bowdern prayed, as he held up a crucifix. He would make the response himself. VINCIT LEO DE TRIBU JUDA, RADIX DAVID. The words of the prayer were fitting: Calvary must have had this odor: stinking rotting flesh and excrement—anyone would flee from such filth. Yet, demons congregated there—

something about filth...and David, the lion of Judah, impaled upon the cross, will win out because he is pure and righteous, a perfect sacrifice. Ritchie, squatting over his own dung, broke out into melody: The Old Rugged Cross, a beloved Protestant hymn—Ritchie's riposte to his meditation upon the cross. Calvary—the sewage of the spirit. It's stench lodged in his nostrils and seized his sinuses. There is no salvation here—God has turned away. In the corner of his eyes he saw VanRoo grasping his stomach, one hand over his mouth. Dare he crack open a window? No: the Jesuits at Verhagen would be roused from their cells. But if he dimmed the light, he might...Ritchie beckoned with a finger and in a sultry voice called to him: **You like to stay with me, well, I like it too**. He recoiled at the suggestive words that issued from the naked boy in the bed. *Has he sensed I would dim the lights and...what?* EXOCIZO TE...he prayed, in faint, gasping tones. The sultry voice turned harsh: **Cut out the damned Latin and get away from me you goddam bastards**. He kept on praying. Someone behind him retched—probably VanRoo.

Ritchie pointed to his penis and chanted: the words were gibberish, but Bowdern could make out: pecker, a willy dilly, round firm pecker, with a red top and a hole in the middle. Then Ritchie pointed to Bowdern and, his hand to his mouth as if in horror, Oh you have a big fat penis! He jumped back into the bed and arching his back stroked his penis as if masturbating. He accompanied his gestures with songs—Bowdern could not make out the words or the tunes—then he cried out that he was in hell surrounded by bad men who were doing terrible things. He grabbed a sodden towel and covered his loins with it. Halloran and VanRoo rushed back into the room. Ritchie tossed aside the towel, grabbed his penis again, and accused the two clerics of having big fat penises and stroking them up and down, just like he was doing. VanRoo turned scarlet.

Finally Ritchie turned over, asked for his pillow, and fell into a deep slumber. Bowdern recognized true sleep; he knew the evening was over. The plan had not worked; Ritchie was more vitriolic than ever. He took off his glasses, wiped them clean, and looked at his watch: it was two-thirty Thursday morning, March 24, the feast of St. Gabriel the Archangel. But only nine days, by his reckoning, from the beginning of the prayers. Friday would be the 25th, the Feast of the Annunciation, the tenth day—unless the count begins on the 17th.

No—begin the count on the 16th; he will baptize Ritchie on the great Feast and the Demon will flee.

VanRoo had a broken nose, Halloran was exhausted, and Frederick was repulsed by his son's sexual exhibitions. And he was exhausted himself. He would go on doing the prayers himself, of course, because he was the Samaritan: in the parable, the Samaritan had no helpers but the ass; he did it all himself. But he needed strong arms to keep the boy on his bed. Who? Bishop would be back in a day, but still he needed a new man. Who? He promised Ritter that he would keep this quiet, involve few people; at the same time Ritter demanded he use helpers. A dilemma. He could risk recruiting one new priest from Verhagen, but he needed a third man. Michael can be trusted to keep his mouth shut and he has strong arms. He would speak to Michael.

In the evening, however, he was elated that Halloran, ignoring his pain, returned; well, he would go at it with four men—all to the good if Halloran can't hold up, and if the Demon has saved his worst for the end. Ritchie erupted the moment they entered his room: he ripped off his pajamas and sent a stream of urine directly at Michael. Bowdern began the prayers: PRAECIPIO TIBI...Ritchie swivelled his head and glared at the new priest, who had gone to the other side of the bed; he snapped and barked at him, then called him a big fat ass, an ox. Odd:—Has the Demon again read his mind and played with his thoughts? Last night when he prayed EXORCIZO TE...Ritchie said, **Cut out the Latin**. Exorcizo—it means cut out, doesn't it? And when he meditated about the Samaritan's helper, the ass, the Demon must have listened in and then flung those words at the new assistant priest whom it just called an ass. The Demon broke in upon his thoughts as it aimed more darts against his household assistant: **Michael, pikl, likel, sikel**. The Demon shrieked. Again, a play on words, a childish taunt. **You look so dirty, Michael**, the Demon hissed. *How does the Demon know my housekeeper's name?* By midnight, Ritchie's sexual taunting had become overt: **Kiss my pecker**, he said, and **Use my stick**. *In this way he honors the Feast. Blasphemy!*

On the 25th he celebrated the Annunciation Mass with a renewed spirit; it was the tenth day of the ordeal; and the X, although in itself ambiguous, most likely referred to this day, and he interpreted the Demon's scatology as a feeble effort to get in a last word. Moreover, the boy's strength seemed to be on the wane; it was still prodigious, but the men had been able to stop him from leaping out of the bed. The baptism, however, presented a problem: Ritchie was old enough so that his rational consent was required. But Ritchie's rationality, hence his free will—even during the day—was in doubt. Of course, if the Demon departs tonight, the issue will be moot.

Wearing a clean surplice and a pure white laced stole, he led Bishop, Halloran, and VanRoo to the third floor bedroom. The boy had eaten well and was reading comic books when they entered. The moment he saw the men his eyes began to roll back. Bowdern wasted no time: PRAECIPIO TIBI...he commanded. Ritchie began swinging his legs in the air, a quick-step march to nowhere. His eyes, warm and glistening wet, beamed at Bowdern. Suddenly he stopped his swinging and rolled off the edge of the bed into Bowdern's arms.

VanRoo moved in to steady the boy and place him back upon the bed. EXORCISAMUS TE...Bowdern cried: alert to the Demon's cunning ways, thanks again to Heidi, he kept up the prayers. The prayer was a warning to the seductive Demon whose proud head, when it was a serpent, had been crushed under the foot of the Mother of God at the moment of her Immaculate Conception. The serpent's sly ways, Mary's purity—how often he had preached that the virgin daughter of Israel had triumphed over the sordid and slanderous ways of the flesh. May the Blessed Mother shield this innocent boy from the Demon who would steal his innocence and make lewd display of the vessel that the Apostle urged to be kept and held in honor. He lifted the vial again and poured water over the body that lay soft and compliant upon the bed. Then he prayed through the night, finally saying AMEN as if it might be his last breath.

In the morning he met Michael on the stairs to the third floor. God bless this loyal servant, who had been up all night scrubbing the walls and floor of the bedroom, and setting up a new bed he had borrowed from Verhagen. After all the abuse this man has taken! Peering inside the room, he saw that Ritchie was awake; he asked if he was ready for breakfast. The boy shook his head. Michael came in to pull up the shade. Ritchie stared at Michael as if he had never seen the man. Strange, how the boy has no memory of the night. But the boy should eat—what about some juice? Again, Ritchie shook his head. Perhaps the boy doesn't want to take anything from the hands of the housekeeper—something strange there.

In the late afternoon, Bowdern took a nap. When he awoke he struggled to remember a vanishing dream in which a voice called his name—he remembered only that. Who? Jesus? The nameless Demon? Yes, he still needed to know the Demon's name. Even if the X meant ten days, he didn't know the Demon's name. No sign was given...unless it came in his sleep. Sleep! He should not sleep so close to Holy Week; in Gethsemene the disciples slept—to their everlasting shame. Those three—Peter, James and John—did not share their Lord's agony because their eyes were heavy. Peter's dream—if he dreamed—must have recalled the Lord's words from earlier in the evening, that Peter would deny him thrice. The three of them may have dreamed that the sheep will be scattered when the shepherd is struck. Those words—heavy enough to shut the eyes of tired men—were almost the last words they heard from the Lord's lips before they fell to the ground. Bowdern rose from his bed quickly. His job was not to dream, but to act.

Bishop called him that evening: Ritchie was quiet all day, and was asleep in bed. And Frederick was talking about going back to Maryland. But Bowdern stayed close to the phone. Sunday, after the morning masses at Xavier, Bishop called to report: Ritchie was awake, passed a good night, was reading comics and playing monopoly with Eleanor. Bowdern called Bishop to the rectory; he wanted to go over the notes that his friend was taking; he was looking for something, anything that would pass as a sign. He held on to the notes during the week and studied them. No sign—nothing.

Thursday evening at 11:30 he picked up the phone in his study and heard Klara's hysterical, demanding voice. Why would she not call Bishop? She answered the question without his asking. Ritchie complained about his feet, she began, which were first cold then hot, and he begged everyone to come up to his room and he began marking on a bedsheet. Klara's voice was cracking, but she continued: he read his own words from the sheet, which nobody else could see, and the words were like this:

I will stay 10 days, but will return in four days
If Ritchie stays (gone to lunch)
If you stay and become a Catholic it will stay away.
Klara Hipp
God will take it away 4 days after it has gone 10 days
God is getting powerful
The last day when it quits it will leave a sign on my front
Fr. Bishop—all people that mangle with me will die a
terrible death.

She was right; best leave Bishop out of it. He called VanRoo and the two men drove to the house.

Ritchie's room was littered with paper. The boy himself was sitting up in bed, pencil in hand, scrawling furiously on a note pad, flinging the pages to the floor. Eleanor handed him one of the papers: Bowdern read:

I will speak the language of the persons. I will put in
Ritchie's mind when he makes up his mind that the
priests are wrong about writing English. I will, that is
the Devil, try to get his mother and dad to hate the
Catholic Church. I will answer to the name of Spite.

Eleanor said that most of the pages were crumpled and hard to read; but on some she made out the names "Pete" and "Joe," and Richie had called out those names as he wrote. She didn't think he knew anyone with those names.

So the Demon gives me his name—Spite! Where in the
bible did I come upon that word? But he speaks in
English—can I trust him?

Ritchie turned to him and demanded a pencil. Bowdern shook his head and began to pray. But Ritchie pressed him repeatedly for a pencil—the one that Eleanor gave him would not do, he had to have one from Bowdern. No, thought Bowdern; Heidi warned me—I must pray. Acting on an impulse, however, Bowdern nodded to VanRoo, who gave the boy a pencil. *The Demon has spoken, given me his name. Will he give me the time of his departure?* His hopes dashed that the Demon would depart on the tenth day, Bowdern hoped for a new date. THOU SHALL TELL ME BY SOME SIGN OR OTHER THY NAME AND THE DAY AND HOUR OF THY DEPARTURE! Ritchie grabbed a fresh piece of paper and wrote X on it—four times. Finally, after hours of scribbling, he reached for his pillow and fell asleep.

When he returned to the rectory, he reached for his bible and thumbed through the gospel texts. Where was the word "spite" used? He had just read it as part of his Holy Week meditations: the marker was still in its place, at *Luke 18:32:* Jesus plans his entry into Jerusalem and tells his disciples that he will be treated spitefully, scourged, and put to death, and rise on the third day. Yes and he realized it was Satan who delivered Jesus into the hands of his enemies who would so treat him. He shuddered—what befalls the master befalls the disciple. If so, would he rise again with his Master? Jesus promised deliverance to his followers; what did the Demon predict? God is getting powerful, the writing said. So then, when will it depart? The four X's forty days of Lent? Lent would be over on Easter Day—April 17. But the Demon also said four after the ten. That would carry through to Tuesday of next week. Is it the Demon's decision when he will depart? Or God's? But God gives no sign. No: God does give signs—He gives the Scripture. He took his bible into the nave of the church and read the passion story from the gospels. Something in the familiar text struck him, something he needed to remember:— Jesus predicts he will be treated spitefully by his enemies who await him in Jerusalem. He engages the enemy in an argument about baptism: John's baptism, he demands to know, was it from men—or from God? Then Satan enters Judas Iscariot. The end is determined: Jesus will suffer and die. But first, Jesus takes the disciples to the garden of Gethesemene where he prays in agony; his sweat becomes like great drops of blood falling down upon the ground. The disciples sleep. Jesus is alone—except an angel from heaven stands by his side.

Baptism, Satan; the Garden, the angel. Nothing here to tell when the Demon would leave: no sign. Yet, he thought, baptism itself is a sign; all sacraments are signs—God's signs. He leapt to his feet and dashed back to his study, his cassock swishing as his legs pumped inside its folds. In a notebook—he knew where, in among texts and preaching notes—something a wise Jesuit said in a Holy Week meditation. There!...behind some folders–his notebook. He read: "Baptism is an exorcism. The candidate for the new life in Christ must renounce the Devil and pass through this purging water." Yes!...and something else...here!.. "When Jesus kneels to pray in the Garden he deals with Satan a second time. First, Jesus was baptized in the Jordan and the spirit drove him out among the wild beasts where Satan tested his resolve to begin his work. But angels lifted him up; he did not fail. Finally when Jesus comes to Jerusalem to finish his work he speaks of baptism, that it is from God; he then crosses the book Kidron and prays. Satan is there, listening. Jesus sweats blood that falls heavily to the ground. By his side there appears an angel. This is where the matter will be settled, in the Garden; his bloody sweat moistens the soil in which grows the cross of calvary." It was clear: Jesus passed through the waters, was tested, and entered the Garden where God gave the sign. Now, he and Ritchie must pass through those waters and enter the Garden. Satan is there already, but God will send His holy angel. That will put an end to the struggle.

An angel by the Lord's side! By Bill Bowdern's side! This will be the sign, a sign not from the Demon but from God. He picked up the phone with sweaty hands; he would call Ray Bishop, the diplomat—this time they will not fail. As for the X, they will begin the count of ten from the day Ritchie accepts Holy Baptism.

After he spoke to Ray, he called Heidi. This priest, a college chaplain, was a learned man, and a great resource; what was more, he knew a psychiatrist, the one who issued strange warnings. He would like a talk with that doctor. Heidi agreed, reluctantly. The man is an atheist, Heidi told him—Hoffman is his name—but he knows about mental illness, and a lot about priests—too much. He let Heidi's remark pass; he wanted only to consult Hoffman about Ritchie's sexual exhibitions.

Hoffman returned the call later that evening: the boy is pubescent, he said, and something about priests—the black outfit, the black cassock? —arouses fears and sexual impulses. All on the unconscious level. But, Bowdern protested, why priests? Why black? Hoffman responded: Black is the color of concealed things and death. Then the doctor asked: Who else has been a disturbing factor in the boy's life? Well, there was Aunt Ilse, Bowdern remembered; he related what he knew about the Ouija game. Hoffman replied: That game can spring things loose in the unconscious. Then he asked: When Ilse's body was displayed at her wake, was she dressed in black? What about the casket cover or altar hangings? How much did the boy see? Bowdern was not sure: why? he asked. Hoffman spoke softly: Because priests dress in black; something was transferred from Ilse to the priests, and this caused a regression. The boy is hyper-intuitive and paranoid.

Baptizing the boy, he added, could provoke a combat; your weapon is water, his is urine. And his is as holy as yours—no offense, please, but urine is a sacred scent; some primitive peoples believed rain is a god's urination. It can be used to attract a friend or repel an enemy. How do you think the boy uses it? Bowdern remembered too well the putrid air in the bedroom; it did not attract him. But, Hoffman went on: small children will urinate on each other; it's playful and leads to erotic deeds. At that Hoffman hand no more to say. When Bowdern hung up, he was left with an understanding of where Heidi got his story about the water-test. Psychiatry has no power to save. God does. The baptism is on—the minute Ray and Eleanor gets the family's permission.

Friday morning Ray called the rectory. Klara threw a hissy fit, he said, but Eleanor and Frederick prevailed. They can bring the boy to the church tonight. Bowdern glanced at the calendar: April 1. No conflicts. Good...tonight at eight.

Shortly before eight he pulled a laced white surplice and golden stole over his black cassock, lit a cigarette, and stood on the broad steps of Xavier church. Crocus had come up and a light breeze stirred; people were strolling in the evening warmth. Inside, water and special oils from the ambry were in place. Never had water and oil seemed so potent, he thought: blessed by the bishop each year, they were clean—no evil spirits dwelt in these waters. Holy water was his weapon, and he had an angel by his side. He was ready.

It was half-past eight. *Where are they?* He turned his back to the breeze and cupped his hands around a match as he lit another cigarette. Suddenly he heard a car's tires screeching as it rounded a corner at the far end of the Boulevard. He spun around—it was the DeSoto, speeding toward him. *My God, Fr. Steiger was almost killed by a car.* But the car skidded to a halt in front of the church, two wheels on the curb, its radio blasting static. The doors flew open: Eleanor and Klara spilled out of the front; Werner and Frederick dragged Ritchie from the back and pinned him against a lamppost. The car's engine was off, but the static grew louder. *Why didn't Eleanor turn off the radio?* Flipping his cigarette into the breeze, he turned to open the church doors so the men could drag Ritchie inside. The radio spoke: **you son of a bitch**...Ritchie's mouth was a slit; he stared at him in silence. From behind, the radio blared: **so you think you are going to baptize me!** Eleanor shrugged helplessly, the car keys in her hand. *She did turn off the radio!* Over the static, the voice had another message: **you think you will drive me out with holy communion. Ha! Ha!**

No, not in the church—the Demon will follow Ritchie into the church. Desecration! But the third floor bedroom—yes, he could baptize the boy there, with water from the bath. He called to the men and pointed to the rectory. They led Ritchie, his arms twisted behind him, into the house. Ritchie howled; his eyes bulged, veins stood out on his neck—huge bulbous veins, deep purple—and his face broke out in red scratches that could have been made by a claw. The men shoved him up the stairs. But in the bedroom they tired and lost their grip: Ritchie got one arm free. Eleanor burst into the room in time to help. He filled a pitcher with water from the bathroom and stood over the bed. Ritchie spat and tried to loosen his trousers—he knew why. He would act fast.

DO YOU RENOUNCE THE DEVIL AND ALL HIS WORKS? he demanded. *But who will make the responses? A proxy, I need a proxy. Michael!—he is in the sacristy. How will I send for him?* Suddenly Michael appeared in the doorway. Ritchie howled. Bowdern repeated DO YOU RENOUNCE THE DEVIL AND ALL HIS WORKS? Michael placed his hand on Ritchie's brow. Ritchie hissed and reached again for his trousers, but Eleanor yanked his hand away. Lifting the pitcher with one hand and holding the crucifix with the other, he uttered the question a third time. Ritchie spat. *If only he will be still for a moment, I can accept the proxy's response as his and I will pour the water.* Ritchie thrashed and kicked; he could squirm loose in a minute. *I must do it now.* EGO TE BAPTIZO...he uttered, as he poured the water over Ritchie's head. Ritchie exploded.

Breaking free of his captors, Ritchie rose up to hurl his body at Michael, his fists aimed at the man's midriff. But Michael's long arm was against his brow and the fists flailed in air. Thwarted, the boy retched and directed the torrent at Michael's face. He hit his target. When the men pulled him back to the bed, he lifted bent knees high and defecated.

Bowdern could not be sure the baptism took hold; he waited for a right moment to repeat the water and the words. But how long could they endure the dense air? And Ritchie was screaming at Michael and striking the air with whiplash strokes of arms and legs. How long could the men hold up?—they were at their limits. And the women, they were still shaken by the wild ride down the Boulevard. Only Michael stood calm, serene, his arm still outstretched—does nothing perturb him? Michael—the man put himself in the thick of it all and doesn't flinch, doesn't bat an eye. Yet he has been the sole object of the Demon's fury. *Did the Demon use us all to lure my housekeeper?*

He was thinking too much; his job was to act. He prayed God would give strength to the men and to himself, then he began the Apostle's Creed; Michael joined him. At the end of the creed, Ritchie quietly collapsed upon the bed and sighed: "I renounce Satan and all his works," he whispered. Michael turned to Bowdern and nodded: Bowdern poured more water over Ritchie's forehead and repeated the sacred formula: EGO TE BAPTIZO, IN NOMINE PATRIS, ET FILIO, ET SPIRITU SANCTO. Michael added AMEN. There—it was done. It mattered not if Ritchie exploded again. Whatever he did now, he did as a Catholic.

In the morning he sat quietly in his study, the door open into the hallway so he could listen for sounds from above. Ritchie should be asleep, his father next to him on the divan. Shortly before nine, Father Joseph McMahon tapped lightly on the door and entered; Bowdern liked "Father Joe," and needed him to replace Halloran and VanRoo, who were combat weary. Another priest, John O'Flaherty, would join them soon. The two men spoke softly about how to prepare Ritchie for holy communion. First, an examination of conscience, said Joe; the boy must confess any disobedience to his parents, any immodesty in thought, word, or deed. Bowdern flinched. Father Joe had yet to behold the boy's talent for immodesty. But of course, that was the Demon's doing. He turned in his swivel chair and stroked his chin: this needed thought. It might be best to give Ritchie a conditional absolution and have him confess his sins later, when the Demon was gone.

O'Flaherty arrived at ten. The three men plotted their move. Bowdern explained that Ritchie was prone to "seizures," but he prayed silently that the Demon had fled the baptismal waters and Ritchie would make a routine confession and first communion. He would leave his housekeeper out of this: Ritchie hated the sight of Michael. He had already placed five consecrated wafers from the tabernacle in his pyx; no need to wait. With a prayer on his lips, he motioned for the two priests to follow him to the darkened third floor hallway. Frederick had left; the boy should be alone. *Will he be asleep?* Gently he pushed the door open. A broken crockery basin was on the floor by the window; the overhead light bulb was missing. Ritchie was awake and staring at him—a familiar stare, it meant trouble. *Conditional absolution, I'll do it myself.* He locked the door; then ducking into his surplice and purple stole he faced Ritchie and pronounced EGO TE ABSOLVO.

He opened the pyx and held up a consecrated wafer. BEHOLD THE LAMB OF GOD, he said, as he looked down upon the figure prone upon the bed. *Will he open his mouth?* How intimate a moment, he thought, between a person and his Lord, when he opens his mouth. It is also an intimacy in the presence of the priest, and a trust—to open wide that orifice. His parishioners trusted him with open mouths and extended tongues. What would Hoffman say about this intimacy? But it didn't matter now; he had here a different species of communicant. He moved close, the wafer in his hand. Father Joe reached in with a linen cloth to hold under Ritchie's chin.

There...he touched the lower lip with the wafer; the mouth opened, the tongue lolled out. THE BODY OF OUR LORD JESUS CHRIST...he said, as he placed the wafer upon the tongue. *His tongue is cracked and dry; can he salivate?* The wafer remained in place for a second, then fell out into the cloth as the tongue retracted. Suddenly Ritchie sprang to his feet and began to whipsaw his arms as if caught in a gale; then he jumped from the bed and sprinted past O'Flaherty toward the door. The door was locked.

The three men and the boy faced each other. Bowdern read fear in the boy's eyes. He put the pyx down, stepped away from the bed– the two priests moved with him—and began to pray: OUR FATHER...he began. O'Flaherty, as if on cue, preached a homily about Our Lady of Fatima; it was the first Saturday of the month, he said, when many churches, including Xavier, honored Our Lady with special services. They recited the rosary. Ritchie stood still, clasped his hands, and listened attentively. *Does he remember the story of the three children?* Slowly, Ritchie moved back to the bed; he got in, and opened his mouth.

He took a fresh wafer from the pyx and placed it on the dry tongue: Ritchie gagged and spit it out. *Is he resisting communion? Or is it the dry mouth?* He asked O'Flaherty to get water from the bathroom. Father Joe held Ritchie's head as O'Flaherty put the cup to his lips. With moistened tongue, Ritchie took a third wafer, but he scraped it off with his upper teeth. Bowdern was worried: the boy's eyes glazed over and his feet took to tapping a beat as if marching off to some distant war. He signaled to O'Flaherty who launched into another recitation of the rosary. After several decades of prayers, he offered a fourth wafer; it dropped onto the cloth. But the feet stopped their beating. The room was quiet. One more effort—it was almost noon; he threw open the window and flooded the room with light. A fifth wafer...*if this fails I will pick up the Rituale and admonish the Demon*...he took the fresh wafer in his hand and held it to Ritchie's lips. The tongue protruded. He placed the wafer on the tongue, in as far as he could. Ritchie flicked his tongue as if to reject it, but the wafer was trapped behind his teeth and he swallowed it.

Sunday, after the early mass, Bowdern got a call from Bishop: Klara reported that Ritchie had broken out in a strange rash and had attacked her sister-in-law, Werner's wife. He would be eating ice-cream in the kitchen, as normal as any boy in the world, then erupt in a storm of violence. The men were trying to hold him down right now. It appeared that they were needed at the house—if Klara would let them in—to begin the exorcisms all over again. Ritchie was worse than ever.

After the last morning mass, Bowdern went to his study where Michael brought him his usual light breakfast. He pushed it aside. The look on Michael's face...was he offended? Michael was staring at him...oh, yes, the stiles, the loose skin, the hollow face; he was losing weight, and Michael was showing his concern. The *Rituale* required fasting in difficult cases, he explained, and he will fast on bread and water alone. He picked up the phone and called Bishop: they would not return to that grim house, he told him; they will take him back to the Alexians' fifth floor restraint room.

But it would take time to persuade Klara. Making Ritchie a Catholic had made things worse, she argued. So he would return to the house that evening, along with Bishop, O'Flaherty, and Michael. He worried about Ritchie's antipathy toward the housekeeper, but he needed Michael's strong arms. They arrived at seven-forty. There was Richie in the living room in his underwear, waiting for them...or was he waiting for Michael? —for the housekeeper was immediately the object of the boy's fiery glances.

He waited patiently as Ritchie dawdled over a dish of ice-cream. Finally the boy finished, tossed the dish aside and bounced upstairs and into bed with peals of wild laughter. Bowdern followed him. *It's a game: he teases and flirts with me.* PRAECIPIO TIBI...he thundered, in no mood for play. DICAS MIHI NOMEN TUUM, DIEM, ET HORAM EXITUS TUI, CUM ALIQUO SIGNO...Ritchie flung the words back into his face **dicas mihi nomen tuum, diem, et horam**...*It's a child's game: I'll tell you my hour, you tell me yours.* But the game turned ugly: **stick it up your ass,** Ritchie screamed, as he ripped off his pajama bottoms and repeated **diem et horam**. Bowdern gasped: at the words **diem et horam** three red welts rose up in parallel streaks on his thigh; they reformed as an **X**, then the number 18. Ritchie rolled over and cried **please, I can't stand it. I'm going crazy.**

In his study later that evening, he pondered the number 18— why not 17? Easter Day will be April 17. What did 18 mean? Thursday the Demon had said something about four days after ten days—the scribbling on the bedsheet. That's fourteen days; two weeks from today: Passion Sunday to Easter Day, exactly two weeks. But no—he was deceiving himself—the number was 18. He called Heidi.

It is the mark of the beast, Heidi stated. The infamous number of the Apocalypse, 666, in series is three sixes—there is your 18. The Demon loves to parody the sacred number three, and he does that here. The three sixes, and the three scratches, prove his childish, contrary nature: the number three flourishes in our religion, so the child has to imitate us, have his own threes. The Demon knows we are entering Holy Week, and Jesus—who was an exorcist, remember (there is your X!)—during that week was condemned at the third hour, nailed to the cross at noon, and he died at three. And the dragon, beast, and false prophet are his unholy travesty of the holy triad, which is God himself, Christ, and his servants. The Demon— Satan—aspires to be a false God; the beast a false Christ; the second beast a false servant. You, Father Bowdern, are a third of the divine triad—a servant of Christ. Our demonic counterpart therefore is a biblical beast. You must trust in prayer.

By Thursday he was well into his fast and feeling faint; the phone was ringing, but he let it ring. Each evening he had gone to the house the outcome was the same: fatigue, despair; and he still had to face the rigors of holy week. Who was calling? The New Testament was on his lap, his mind focused on the holy week reading. The pages were crowded with threes: Three times Jesus comes to Jerusalem before he enters it for Passover; three times he tells his disciples to watch; three times Peter denies Jesus; three times Pilate tries to release him. Jesus is accused of plotting to destroy the temple and raise it in three days. Jesus' promise to the centurion that he will be in Paradise is followed immediately by three hours of dark. The dark before the dawn? The profusion of threes near the end of the gospel, do they signify a nearing of the end—Easter? Jesus uttered the words: "He who endures to the end will be saved." He needed to cling to this hope. His arm inched toward the noisome phone: it was Bishop; Ritchie was acting up, could they go over soon? *My God, it's not even dusk...*

Ritchie was nude on the bed, his chest heaving. Bishop said there was a struggle earlier, as Frederick and Werner had labored through the late afternoon to restrain him—the men were collapsed about the bed, panting. Klara stood in the doorway, gaping. A number! The number 4 stood out clearly on his stomach, etched in red. Blood-streaked lines ran down one thigh in the shape of a claw. As Bowdern and Klara stared, the words **hell** and **spite** jutted up on the other thigh.

Spite and **hell** he had seen before—the Demon's name and address. The claw-like blotch he had seen before. The number four, too, he had seen and pondered—**God will take it away four days**... **The last day when it quits it will leave a sign on my front,** scrawled on the bedsheet. The *Rituale* warned him against conjecture: but he was human, he had to wonder if the number was a sign of the end. He opened his *Rituale* to begin the prayers. As he opened his mouth to utter the first command, a voice like the shout of a drill sergeant he knew during his combat years filled the room: **I will not go until a certain word is pronounced, and this boy will never say it.** Ritchie was stiff limbed upon the bed, his mouth tightly closed. Klara shrieked and fled the room.

When he met with Bishop, VanRoo, Halloran, Father Joe and the others Friday morning, he knew they would be shocked; he was lightheaded and full of fantasy. He ranted on about numbers, the end, Easter. They were used to crisp logic from him, he knew; they would take this to be mumbo-jumbo; they would worry about him. But he found he could no longer keep his thoughts to himself; these were his friends, fellow priests—he depended on their loyalty. He was a loner, had been for so long; but he couldn't go on like this, alone. He needed help. The Alexians—they had helped before; they would help again. He called Brother Cornelius.

After his last Palm Sunday mass he collapsed in a soft divan, lit a cigarette, and listened to Michael chide him about his fast. The housekeeper went on to remind him that every year, three days before Palm Sunday, he cleaned and polished every stick of furniture in the rectory, washed the windows inside and out, and made the rectory glow. He had done that. Now, if

Father is pleased with his work, he will work on the grounds. As he spoke, he had a way of glancing upstairs—he was clearly relieved that Ritchie was in the hospital, and no longer in the third floor room where he had made monumental messes. Bowdern wondered if he had thanked the man for his extra work? Sometimes he forgot to thank those who helped—who did their share of the common work. Michael was a good man. And, thinking of Michael—he had not yet taught the Michael prayer to Ritchie; and there was a Michael statue at the hospital—it should be placed in the boy's fifth floor room.

At seven thirty he met Bishop, O'Flaherty, and VanRoo at the hospital. Ritchie had been there only a few hours, Brother Cornelius said—so far untroubled. The four men took the cranky elevator to the fifth floor. The brother who stood outside the restraint room unlocked the door warily. Inside, Brother Bruno was chatting with Ritchie; cards and comics littered the bed and floor. Ritchie looked up and smiled at Bowdern. Seeing the Michael statue between palm fronds on a table near the bed, Bowdern began by reciting the great prayer Pope Leo composed on his knees to the mighty archangel. Ritchie moved his lips as if in response. After four hours of the rosary and other prayers, Bowdern decided to risk giving holy communion. He opened the pyx and held up a wafer. Ritchie's eyelids were drooping, but he opened his mouth and exposed a moist tongue. *Today Ritchie has been a good Catholic*, Bowdern thought. As he left, he warned the brother on duty to keep a watchful eye during the night.

Monday at noon Michael placed a heavy package marked "Fragile" on the desk in the rectory study. Bowdern was disinclined to bother with it; he was scurrying about with his hat and coat on, off to make his pastoral rounds. But Michael called out the name of the sender: Father Hermann Heidi of New York City. At that, Bowdern turned around and opened the package. It contained two large albums of phonograph records, Volumes I and 2 of Handel's *Messiah*—unexpected but appropriate for Holy Week. He would have little time to play the records, but a note from the sender caught his attention:

I hope this music will inspire and sustain you during your ordeal. It is an unusual recording—you will discover why. The Demon's signs and deeds are nothing compared to the greater glory of God's works. Look for signs, yes, but remember all signs and numbers are God's. The Satan thinks, in his ignorance, that the signs are his, but he is wrong.

Satan is always wrong. His notion that if you know his name or the names of his demons you control them, is his perverted understanding of the mystery of God's name: God revealed His name. I AM WHO I AM, to Moses, so Satan imitates God, pretending his name too is a sacred revelation.

God's name gave great power to Moses. But Moses had to be
tested. Five times Moses tried to slip away from God's call—read
Ex. 3:11: 3:13: 4:1: 4:10 and—his last resort—4:13. I am sure
Satan was behind this tempting. But Moses became the nation's
greatest hero, and turned Satan's five into a holy five, the
Pentateuch.

Trust God. You will not drive Satan out by guessing at his names
and signs. The real meaning of all signs resides in the mind of
God—we cannot read the mind of God, neither can Satan. But
God will send his angels to help you.

Heidi's words were enigmatic: What was unusual about the
recording? What did he mean by Satan's signs that are really God's
signs? He shrugged and went about his duties: let the theologians
wonder at such mysteries. He was a simple priest; his job was to
return to the hospital and pray. Yet, it disturbed him that as yet he
had neither seen nor heard a certain sign that the Demon had loosed
its hold and fled from this corner of the earth.

In the evening Halloran drove Bowdern to the hospital where the
same four priests joined him. There was Ritchie with Brother Bruno
again, chatting sweetly, playing rook. He took his place at the foot of
the bed, opened his *Rituale*, and began the prayers. The priests
circled the bed, adding an Amen chorus to his words. Slowly, Ritchie
moved his lips, as before. As they began the second decade of the
rosary he screamed and grasped his chest. Bishop loosened the boy's
gown and exposed a red blotch. Bowdern had seen it before; he knew
what to expect. PRAECIPIO TIBI...he intoned. The blotch took the
form of four letters: EXIT, and an arrow slit his skin toward his penis.
The EXIT mark faded, and reappeared on his thigh; it faded again,
and returned on his opposite thigh as if tracing a triangle, the boy's
penis at the center. *Three times the Demon speaks to me—will he exit
through the boy's penis?* Ritchie howled in pain and grasped his
swollen member: *it stings*, he cried. Urine gushed through his fingers,
flooded the bed clothing, and poured over upon the floor.

Brother Bruno called in kitchen help to assist in the cleanup, and
an hour later Bowdern returned to the room. Ritchie was playing
cards with Brother Bruno and the others. Bowdern moved close to
the bed and reached for the pyx: *If the Demon is gone, we shall
celebrate with the holy communion.* He reached for a wafer. Ritchie

erupted: he thrashed about, cursed, and issued a stream of spittle that caught him directly in the face. Brother Bruno rang a bell and several brothers rushed into the room: soon Ritchie was looped inside restraint belts. Again he reached for a wafer and held it close to Ritchie's face. In an instant Ritchie got his left arm free, snapping the belt, and ripped open his gown; his body curled upward and the letters **HELL** stood out like a fresh hot brand on his tender skin. THIS IS THE BODY OF OUR LORD JESUS CHRIST...he said. Ritchie slumped upon the bed, his mouth open. A brother replaced the snapped belt. *He must be receptive now. I will place the wafer in his mouth.* He leaned in with the wafer, the laced sleeve of his surplice lightly touching the boy's restrained left arm. The new arm belt snapped...its buckle flew against the far wall...the backhanded blow struck him square in the testicles...Oh! he cried, as he fell to the floor in a faint.

The next morning, having declined tea and toast for breakfast, he made his way to the Xavier sanctuary and dropped to his knees. The 22nd psalm was running through his head, as it did every Holy Week. The Psalm troubled him. Jesus alluded to it when he hung from the cross: the words were now his own: "My God, my God, why hast thou forsaken me?" he cried. How terrible that the Lord's tongue cleaved to his jaws; that he was forsaken and abandoned; that his strength was died out and sucked up; that he, the lion of Judah, was at the mercy of dogs and lions and jackals and the horns of wild oxen. Well, the Lord and Bill Bowdern had this in common: his own strength was like a potsherd—dried up and sucked out. And something else was sucked out, something of his essence—what was it? The Demon said—speaks the language of persons: yes, it speaks like a person but it is not—it is a beast who sucks at the human breast and leaves a man bare blood and bones —no spirit, no will, no life, no hope.

No hope? Had not the Demon pointed to its **exit**? Yes, but the Demon is a master of frauds and deceits. Signs come not from the Demon, but from God, remember? Yes? —well, what sign came to Jesus upon the cross? Where was his angel? "I am a worm and no man," said the psalmist that he quoted, as his life's blood gushed from his wounds and spilled upon the ground. He read the psalm again—to the finish. For the first time, he heard it—the sermon from the cross.

The sign came not to the Lord but from the Lord: his parted lips moved slowly as he read the words that had eluded his thick skull. "Save me from the lion's mouth," the psalmist went on: then "God hast not despised nor abhorred the afflicted, neither hid his face from him. Your heart shall live forever...They that go down to the dust will...live and serve him." It was a triumphant ending. It told of a new race to be born, a race of the righteous. He rose from his knees, made the sign of the cross, and hurried back to his study; he had another thought.

When the Lord hung there, two men flanked him. One was a thief, but never mind that. Jesus was not alone, he was in the right place, among people who sin and suffer. The three of them hung there together. He, Bowdern, was one among three: how often had two fellow priests been at his side as he read the prayers? Often. Always. They too had prayed and suffered. As he did. As Jesus did. Yet he had gone up against the foe as if he were alone, a solitary Samaritan who acted as if he were God. He upbraided himself: he, a Jesuit, should know better; a Jesuit is a member of a community; a soldier is part of an army. His pride needed to tumble. He called Widman and asked him to give holy communion to Ritchie. Then he limped into the kitchen for tea and toast.

Brother Rector Cornelius called on Wednesday to report that Ritchie was well behaved during the day, except for minor "spells" of moodiness, and he opened his mouth wide for Father Widman each morning, he added. So he has received communion. Therefore Brother Cornelius had an idea: why not let Ritchie stroll about the grounds and help the brothers with their chores? And if all went well, maybe a brief trip off the grounds. Bowdern agreed: the Demon fled the light of day; the trip should be safe.

Yes, he would accept the brothers' help. And Halloran could go along with a seminarian friend to escort Ritchie on that little trip off campus. And at Xavier, even though Holy Week was upon him, he would not try to do it all by himself. His job now was to accept help from others and to learn patience. Feeling better about it, he picked up to phone to call Heidi.

Having thanked Heidi for the Messiah album, he discussed with his educated friend the fact of Ritchie's normality during the day: what is it about light that scares off the Demon? The Demon reigns at

273

night, said Heidi; he is called the "Prince of darkness." His avowed enemy is Michael, who is the "Prince of light." The Apocalypse speaks of a destined and furious encounter between the two: night shall be no more and the dead shall rise up from the waters. Heidi read from the text, at chapter 20: the seer has three visions of the end– –the binding of Satan, the reign of Christ, and the last judgment. And who is the angel who shall stand in the sun just before Satan is bound? Heidi asked. Michael, surely. Bowdern replied—the archangel to whom he had prayed those long nights, and whose image still stood in the fifth floor room where so often Ritchie had been wrapped in leather straps.

The strong man bound! Heidi reminded him of the story: early in the Lord's ministry, malicious scribes accuse him of being in league with the prince of demons, because the demons show complete abasement toward him—who but their master would they thus obey? The Lord's reply is an exercise in logic and allusion: if Satan drives out Satan, then he is a house divided. Yes, said Heidi, and this is a sign that his reign is near its end. And more: if a strong man's house is plundered, someone who has power has bound him first. Heidi paused: you have that strong man in your grip, in that fifth floor restraint room—you plunder Satan's house when you pray for the power of God's name to bind him. Michael stands in the sun: Satan's reign is near its end.

Bowdern's mind raced—he recalled another strong man bound. Holding the phone in one hand as Heidi went on about signs of the end, he reached for his bible and fingered his way through Mark's early chapters...there! he found it—chapter five—and related the story to Heidi—for once he could explain something to his learned friend. Jesus crosses the sea, the boat pulling against a mighty wind, but he says to the storm, "Peace!" And to his disciples "Why are you afraid, have you no faith?" Heidi picked up at once: Yes, Jesus has mastery over the wind and waters, as did God in the first days of creation. Bowdern persisted: he read slowly, his lips parted: Jesus arrives in the land of the Gerasenes. The moment he steps out of the boat a wild man rushes at him from among the tombs where he lived, where the local folk had often tried to bind him but he wrenched apart the chains, and the fetters he broke in pieces. Jesus speaks: "Come out of the man, you unclean spirit," he says, and he demands the Demon tell his name. **Legion**, says the Demon. At that the pack of demons take refuge in a herd of swine, and they all perish in the sea.

The entered the swine, Heidi remarked, because swine are unclean animals, as they are—unclean spirits, unclean animals. And they perish in the water. Yes, they entered Ritchie, too; he is no swine, but they turned him into an animal, an unclean creature that arouses fear and contempt. But Ritchie submitted to the waters of Holy Baptism––now he is clean. Water!—one may perish in it, one may be saved in it. We must pray the sacrament was valid. Bowdern's thought turned practical: he had agreed with Brother Cornelius that Ritchie could be let out of his restraint room and roam about the campus—even take a trip down the Mississippi river bluffs. Had he made the best decision?

Walter Halloran checked the rear view mirror. He had aimed it so that the boy's face and upper body would be in his sight; any move the boy made would be spotted instantly and he would stop the car. But when Ritchie got settled in the back, Halloran realized that he could not see the boy's hands behind the seat—his hands were below the mirror's range. If he should make a fist or grab his neck from behind, he would be unable to pull over. Then what?

That fist!—the fist that slammed into his nose and broke it...where did he get that power? That's why he had Barney Hasbrook in the back with the boy: a strong, stocky seminarian, Barney was handpicked for this job; and he had been warned, just in case. The car passed through the wide swinging hospital gate and onto the main highway, where he turned south. In half an hour they would arrive at the retreat house that overlooked the river. Ritchie, in the back, said nothing; he pressed his head to the window and stared out. Halloran, driving slowly, called attention to the terraced lawns of the large estates that lined the river road, the gardens, the early blooming flowers and their smells. The boy was always good by day—he knew that—but still he prayed that this fresh spring morning would tame whatever notions Ritchie might harbor in his strange heart.

In the mirror, he caught a glimpse of Ritchie squirming and gazing about, his eyes roaming for some new object. Their eyes met in the mirror and locked. The boy didn't blink. Halloran lowered his eyes and began the rosary: the boy and Hasbrook joined in: Holy

275

Mary, Mother of God, pray for us...at the hour of our death. After a few decades, Ritchie asked what they would do at the retreat house. It's called the White House, Halloran explained: a quiet place where priests and others rest, study, and pray; it overlooks the grand Mississippi river—they will see it in a minute, to the east. And at the house the three of them will make the stations of the cross, which shows how Jesus, who loved us, went to his death.

As the car climbed a gentle curve along the spine of a ridge, slivers of sunlight reflecting from the waters below reminded him of a Protestant hymn he heard at a friend's funeral: "Shall we gather at the river, where bright angel feet have trod: With its crystal tide forever, flowing by the throne of God?" Soon they would see the White House, situated between a small forest and the river bluffs...there, the evergreens, just ahead; and, visible through open patches of sun-lit forest, the great stone carvings that depicted Jesus' death march, the stations, standing tall; there he would teach Ritchie how to genuflect, make the sign of the cross, and act like a good Catholic.

He turned into the driveway, parked near a path that led directly up to the stone figures, got out of the car and planted himself in front of the rear car door; as Ritchie stepped out, he put an arm on the boy's knobby shoulder and began to lead him up the path. Ritchie slipped out from under the arm, and walked between the two, lagging but not resisting. The first station was just ahead, atop a hillock that overlooked the river.

Halloran bent his knee and crossed himself in front of the plinth that read: I Jesus Is Condemned To Death. Hasbrook pointed to the ground where he would drop his knee, and nodded to Ritchie, who bent his own knee, stiffly. On his feet again, Halloran told Ritchie that the fourteen statues they would visit were prayer stations, where people could follow Jesus on his way to the cross. Jesus, he said, was taken away by wicked men to his suffering, and Catholics all around the world followed him prayerfully during this special week. Ritchie stared at the life-like image of Jesus standing before Pilate. Pleased, Halloran said the prayers and moved on to the second station. Ritchie followed.

Ritchie's eyes bulged when he saw how Jesus suffered. Good, thought Halloran—he understands what Holy Week is about. Soon Ritchie was genuflecting and crossing himself like a bishop. He smiled at Hasbrook–things were going well. At the ninth station—Jesus Falls For The Third Time—he thought Ritchie looked tired; after all, he's going through an ordeal. They should rest before going on to the station marked X.

They sat down on the grass and chatted. Looking eastward, Halloran pointed to the dusty flatlands across the river, where barns and fences studded the horizon: that was not Missouri over there, it was Illinois, he told Ritchie, and the river is the Mississippi—all Indian names, he believed. Ritchie shaded his eyes from the morning sun and squinted at the next statue. That station, Halloran said, will read: Jesus Is Stripped Of His Garments. They got up and stood before the immense depiction. The wicked men took away Jesus' clothes, Halloran said, because they had no respect for his body.

He faced the statue and began to recite the prayers. A commotion off to his side caught his attention. Hasbrook was struggling to grab the boy around his waste...why? Ritchie's breath hissed through his teeth, and he pumped his legs to get free of Hasbrook. In a flash he was gone. Hasbrook fell forward and perched helplessly on knees and elbows as he watched the boy speed up the slope to the cliff.

Halloran threw down his prayer book and started up the slope. There were rows of dense hedges and small saplings lining the bluffs before the ground fell off precipitously; he could see nothing beyond: he knew it was straight down after that. Could he catch up?...he trailed by only a few steps but he was losing wind already...he had a chance if the boy got tangled in the clumps of brush ahead. But now he was out of breath, the boy was far ahead. He heard Hasbrook laboring behind him...no help there, he's too slow. The boy plunged into the hedges and disappeared...where is he?

The boy's shoe!...over there—it came off. He can't be far. Just ahead, from behind the last of the hedges, Ritchie stood up...he stumbled with his shoe: he limped toward the edge. Halloran gulped air and lunged. The river came into majestic view. A second more he needed, only one second...he grabbed the boy's shirt from behind. It ripped. The boy stumbled and went down again. Halloran on top of him. Hasbrook lumbered up at last and the two men pinned Ritchie to the earth.

Bowdern sat at his desk, legs crossed under his cassock, gazing at Halloran and Joe McMahon through a cloud of smoke. What made Ritchie bolt and run for the river? he asked. Halloran shrugged and rolled his eyes at the ceiling. Joe said that maybe Ritchie's baptism wasn't valid; or maybe the conditional absolution hadn't washed away his sins, so he wanted to jump in the river to cleanse himself, in some perverse, idiotic way. Bowdern shook his head: - that kind of thing Hoffman might have said, he thought. Or—McMahon fingered through the office bible and read from Mark's Gospel—maybe Ritchie wanted to drown the Demon in the water, like the demons who entered the swine and then perished in the sea. Again, Bowdern shook his head.

Joe turned to the Apocalypse. The angel reveals a great truth, he said—see here in the 22nd chapter: Then they showed me the river of life,...and...Blessed are they who wash their robes... Why hasn't the angel come to help Ritchie? It's because of sin; the boy hasn't washed in the river, he hasn't confessed. That's what gives the Devil his power. The Devil has no power greater than any human's power to resist him—we know that. But the Devil's power is parasitical; he sucks on the sins of our species. When we sin, we invite him to the feast. Bowdern smiled: Joe was reciting from the same lecture notes he often used for his own homilies. But, he asked, what sin has Ritchie committed? Joe ignored him: Our sins give substance to the Devil's lies before God's throne, he added; God will not send his angel until the boy has been purged of his sins.

Bowdern rose and vested for mass. At the altar he reflected upon Joe's words: if sin delayed the angel, whose sin was it? Ritchie's? Or his? He had purged himself...confessed his sins...fasted...prayed...what more...? At the consecration, he lifted high the chalice of the Lord's blood: at communion he chanted, Behold the Lamb of God, as he held the blessed bread in his hands. He wondered why the Lamb would delay the coming of the angel, he who offered himself as a full, perfect, and sufficient sacrifice for the sins of the world. Could it be the Lamb did more on the cross than he does from heaven? No! The fault is on earth. What was it Heidi intimated? Or Hoffman?—some stain that water won't take away— or blood, either. All men sin. Even priests.

278

The thought of priestly sin nagged at him all the way to the hospital, but he shucked it off when he got off the fifth floor elevator and saw the brothers on duty outside Ritchie's room. He felt holier in the presence of such men. In their ankle-length cassocks and scapulas they shielded Ritchie, and others, from deadly sins and offenses. Brother Cornelius let him in: there were Ray, Walter and Joe, waiting for him to begin the prayers. Ritchie was laid back on his pillow, eyes open, a glad smile on his lips. What sin beset that frail soul? He sprayed the room with the holy water, opened his *Rituale* and began the Litany of Saints.

He intoned, HOLY MICHAEL PRAY FOR US...Ritchie whipped around and exposed his backside to him, then just as quickly his head spun back to face him—so fast it seemed he was grinning at him from the back of his head. Bowdern had not seen this before; he sensed new menace. Ritchie's grin was now a leer, his face ghostly white. Suddenly a voice sounded from all corners of the room: **God has told me to leave at eleven tonight**, it said, **But not without a struggle**. His breath stalled in his throat. The same voice, he was sure; but deeper, as if from the basement of the building.

He prayed, but the room turned cold; his tongue stiffened in his mouth and his fingers snapped and chaffed against the stole and book. The others began to quiver. Brother Cornelius threw capes and blankets over their shoulders. Then, from the basement again and echoing down the corridor, the voice sounded: **Fire! Fire!** *The trickster!* Soon he heard cries of alarm, stamping feet, fists pounding on metal, doors slamming; the brothers would be hurrying the patients out of their cells.

It must be close to eleven: he dared not look at his watch; that would be a sign of his fatigue. He felt faint. *Who could fault him if he passed out, dropped to the floor?* A bell tolled from a church close by; it tolled a familiar hymn tune, reminding him of Holy Week and Easter—if it will ever come. He prayed on...**Bong...Bong...** ...sounded inside the room; Ritchie's lips were moving, his arched body swaying in rhythm. *He parodies, as before! He ridicules Easter; he says Easter is folly, he will never leave.*

Thursday he found a message on his desk: his brother Edward called to remind him of their annual Easter dinner. My God, he thought, Ed is a doctor! He will see I've lost fifty pounds—and the stiles, and the skin that hangs from my neck. And what will I order for dinner: bread and water? He pondered this into the evening when he made his way down the Xavier center isle toward the chapel of repose: he carried the Blessed Sacrament in a gold and silver monstrance. God forbid he faint and drop the blessed host. He was weak:—but so was the Demon. Ritchie's spells last night were intermittent: vicious but in spurts. Mostly blather and bluff; no urine, no feces. The foul thing was drying up. But so was he.

He needed his friends, Ray, Walter, and Joe—he could hardly stand up straight without them. Tonight he would let them recite some of the principal prayers; maybe they could work in shifts. He was tired of being the Samaritan of St. Louis—the bishop was right, he needed help. But not from Michael: the Demon detested Michael. *Why? The name?* In the Apocalypse, the angel Michael will come with a key and chain to bind the Demon for a thousand years; then the book of life shall be opened, the sea shall give up its dead, and the angel will throw the Demon into a fiery sea that will burn forever.

A fiery sea! Of course!— the Demon cried **Fire! Fire!** in terror. He reads the Scripture, like I do. He knows his destined end. He fears holy water because it stings like fire. He gets weak; his end is near.

Friday at noon he made his way to the Xavier sanctuary and grasped the pulpit rails with both hands. He steadied himself and gazed out upon the large congregation that had come to hear him preach the three hour service of the Lord's passion. They must be gaping at the sight of him—the sunken face, the skin hanging from his neck. In the pulpit at last, he gripped the small carved figure of St. Peter on the newel and with his other hand he tapped the mike—he would need amplification. Many times he had preached on the dying Lord's seven last words: he began with "My God, my God, why hast thou forsaken me?" But the words were dry on his parched tongue; he was withered like the potsherd of the psalmist.

But his spirit rose up and the words came: *Peter the apostle was among the first to forsake the Lord:— An apostle, he began as an apostate. He slept in the Garden while the Lord went aside and prayed. Later, as he warmed himself by a fire, he denied the Lord three times. After Easter—a day or two—the runaway disciple was fishing in the Sea of Galilee. All night he had fished, but caught nothing. At the break of day, Jesus came and called to him. Peter failed to recognize him; but as the sun rose higher, Peter and the others recognized their risen lord at last. Three times Jesus came to them, before they opened their eyes to him. How long before our eyes open; how long the night of our waiting! But if it is the dark before the dawn, the sun is soon to rise.*

When the service was done, he set the alarm in his bedroom and lay down; he would get up in an hour or two and go to the hospital. As he groped for rest, his words from the pulpit turned against him and oppressed him. Why, he wondered, did Peter forsake his dying Lord? Obvious: he feared the power of Pilate and the others. Why did he go fishing? He went fishing because that was his business. But at night? That is strange: Jews believed those waters were infested by demons—to put out at night must have been a terror. He feared Pilate so much that he hid in the dark. Who did Ritchie fear, that he hid in the dark? What is this dark?

Why is Ritchie worse at night? If only his words could have reached the boy, to tell him not to fear the night. God rules the day; God rules the night. Finally, unable to sleep, he got up and roamed about in his study. Messages cluttered his desk—one was from Brother Cornelius: Ritchie had a beautiful day, the note said; he listened to the service broadcast from the cathedral, and was deeply touched by Jesus' words to the thief that this day he would be in Paradise. He picked up the phone and called the hospital. Cornelius answered: Ritchie closed his eyes after talking about the thief in Paradise, he said, and fell asleep; he is still asleep, a fine, natural sleep. No need for Bowdern to come.

Saturday morning he rose early and knelt before the bare marble altar. The sight of it—the nude marble slab, its great tapestry frontal stripped away—told of a world bereft of its God. The chaste morning light, which so often quickened his spirits, today exposed a scourged interior. He prayed in hushed silence, as if in God's tomb. Only blue trails of incense that hovered in the apse reminded him of prayers to a redeemer God. Xavier was in mourning.

Brother Theophane stood outside the fifth floor restraint room, where he had been posted during the night; his prayer book was open, his lips moving in silent homage to the sacred words. He heard the creaky machinery of the elevator and looked up from his prayers. Father Seraphim Widman stepped off the elevator and passed down the corridor carrying a golden pyx. An acolyte marched ahead, ringing a sanctus bell. At each cell they stopped and Widman chanted, <u>The Lord is Risen</u>, to which the acolyte answered, <u>He is Risen Indeed, Alleluia</u>. Widman then reached into the pyx with his right hand and held out a consecrated wafer, slipping it through the barred opening in the cell door. Soon he would come to Ritchie's cell. Theophane knew that twice before Widman had given communion to Ritchie and nothing had gone wrong. There had been three days of peace: Holy Thursday, Good Friday, and Holy Saturday—the day when baptizands renounced Satan and all his works. On this holiest of days, God would tolerate no evil.

Theophane opened the door as Widman approached, and stepped aside to let the priest enter. The table was prepared for communion: a lavabo bowl, a linen purificator and a crucifix were set beside a statue of an angel, along with a book of post-communion prayers for Ritchie to read after he had received the Blessed Sacrament. He knelt and crossed himself. After Ritchie, he would receive the host. He looked up as Widman placed the pyx on the table near the statue. Standing over Ritchie, Widman uttered the Easter salutation: <u>The Lord is Risen</u>. Theophane and the acolyte answered, <u>He is Risen Indeed, Alleluia</u>. Ritchie said nothing.

Ritchie is sleepy, he needs a little nudge, Theophane thought. He sprang to his feet and pressed on Ritchie's cheeks to open his mouth. Ritchie's eyes narrowed, but his lips parted. Widman placed the host on the tongue and stepped back. The men recited a prayer and turned to the door. Theophane held it as the two filed out. Tired of standing, he decided to sit in a chair facing the thick glass window, his back to the bed, and opened his prayer book to finish the daily office. Before he could turn to the proper page, the book sailed out of his hands: its pages flapped as it flew across the room and shattered the window. He gaped at the sight. The book's spine was exposed, its cover bent shapeless. Shards of glass littered the floor.

He turned. Richie was up against the locked door struggling to push it open. It didn't give. Ritchie turned to face him. Theophane knew what do—he had done it hundreds of times with violent patients: he reached out to spin the boy around and pin his elbows behind his body. But Ritchie grabbed him by his cowled cloak and ripped it off, snapping his head and wrenching his arm. Stunned, he could only stare as Ritchie shook and twisted the garment, threw it to the floor, stomped on it, and finally, doused it in spit.

After the last Mass, Bowdern picked up the messages that Michael had organized for him on the desk. An urgent call from brother Cornelius: Ritchie had desecrated Brother Theophane's holy garb, and later in the morning, a deep voice had been heard coming from his cell: **I will not let him go to mass. Everyone thinks it will be good for him.** Yet Ritchie had taken holy communion; and he had not attacked the brother; only the garment was the object of his wrath. He had no time to ponder it: he would have dinner with Ed, and go directly to the hospital, as soon as he could shake loose from Ed's probing questions.

At the diner Bowdern ducked the issue of his fasting by ordering one boiled egg, toast and coffee, but he could not avoid his brother's questions about his health. Finally, he put him off by agreeing to get a check-up later in the week—if he had time. As he made small talk with his brother and listened to medical bulletins, he meditated upon the message from Cornelius. Odd. A daytime incident and not demonic—no overpowering strength, no violence. Could the Demon be gone? It was Easter Day, the 17th. Yet, he remembered that Peter's Easter Day came a day or two late and at night. He would go to the hospital and stay as long as needed. For now, he would honor his brother with lip service.

He arrived at dusk. The brothers were still chanting their evening prayers in the west wing chapel; he slipped into a pew and added his prayers to theirs. When the prayers were over, Brother Cornelius took him by the sleeve and led him aside into an office, where he addressed him with wavering gaze and unsteady voice. Ritchie had made slurs against the character of some of the brothers, he said, and the community was perturbed. How could the boy say such things? How could he know? Of course, they could not be true. And in the afternoon Ritchie had gone into the cloister yard to play ball with Brother Emmet—the two always got along—but Ritchie hit him in the face and knocked him against the wall. If several brothers had not rushed over to help, Ritchie might have killed him.

Ritchie was strapped into his bed, Cornelius explained, as he escorted Bowdern into the elevator to the fifth floor. In the corridor two large brothers in cowled garb stood outside the restraint room. Cornelius pointed to the door: the lock was broken and a temporary bolt hammered into place. Yes, Ritchie tried to escape, Cornelius said. Bowdern slipped his gold and white stole over his starched surplice—at last Ritchie will see the color of Easter—and entered the barely lit room. Two other brothers, wearing only cassocks, were standing in the far corner. Ritchie was strapped to the bed frame, as Cornelius had said, but with extra straps around his wrists and ankles. His eyes were closed, his head tilted to the side, his body limp. Suddenly the voice spoke out of nowhere: **I will have Ritchie awake and ask for a drink of water**, it said.

Ritchie's eyes brightened; he turned toward Bowdern, his mouth split in a wide full-toothed grin, and politely asked for a glass of water. *What is this?* Bowdern wondered, *Is there no end to his power? Has he taken the boy away forever?* He nodded to Cornelius, who fetched a cup of water and a straw and held it to Ritchie's lips. He drank the water, thanked him and the Brother, and turned his head to the wall. Bowdern picked up his *Rituale*—PRAECIPIO TIBI...he began. Ritchie turned to face him; his eyes slowly thickened and whitened with a filmy gauze; his body heaved and strained against the straps; finally, he began to wail through locked lips. Bowdern dropped his book and clamped his hands over his ears. The brothers wrapped their cowled hoods or scapulars around their heads and pressed them to their ears as they fled the room. Bowdern, on his knees, tried to pray. No words came. The wail rose to a crescendo, persisted, then sank into a hollow depth. At last the room was silent.

A brilliant sun streamed through the blinds Monday morning and woke him before the alarm. At the pre-dieu he offered up his rising prayers: the Salve Regina, the Anima Christi—the Anima seemed fresh and appointed: Soul of Christ sanctify me, Water from Christ's side wash me, enter my veins. But his mind didn't settle easily into the day's prospects; instead it raced back to a spate of notions that seemed to lead nowhere: priestly sins, disciples fleeing into the night, the need for a sign. After a biscuit and water breakfast, he locked himself in the study and rummaged for answers. Peter at sea, at night...the Lord came to him and gave him Easter peace at last. When? A day or two after Easter? The large office bible rested on a stand near the window; his hands quivered, his knees buckled, but he got up and opened its pages to John's Gospel. Jesus, the evening of the day of his rising, passes through shut doors where the disciples are huddled in fear, and he says "Peace be with you." Bowdern read on: Eight days later Jesus again passes through shut doors and says "Peace be with you." The second revelation. Eight days later. Eight days.

He fell back into the recliner and pondered the matter. What folly—he was looking for signs again. Yet,—he picked up his small *New Testament*,—Jesus did many signs in the presence of the disciples. John recorded those words and placed them just before the third revelation. Peter needed a sign, a special sign, because he needed to be redeemed. And he got it. That event sealed something, finished it off.

Jesus finished his work on the third day, when he rose. God finished his work after seven days and rested. When will Bill Bowdern finish his work and rest? He was neither God nor Jesus; he was not given to know.

Resolved that he would return to the hospital that night, he planned an afternoon nap. He called two younger priests assigned to him and asked them to do his pastoral rounds today: Easter communions for the home bound, a house call—the husband was a drunkard, and a domestic spat. He would break these youngsters in right. Now, for Heidi's gift. He placed the records on the spindle and leaned back. <u>A voice crying in the wilderness</u>, sang the tenor, <u>Make straight the way of the Lord</u>. How wonderful: Handel's music always refreshed his spirit.

The album cover rested on his lap. As the record changer paused to drop a second record onto the spinning turntable, he glanced down at the artwork. Four circular portals revealed four cathedrals, joined by four points of a cross in the center; the names of the artists were listed in a column below one of the portals. Something was wrong. His eye ran down the list of names again: there, at the bottom of the list, the album's catalogue number—ML 666. *The mark of the beast.*

What did Heidi say? Where is the note? In the desk drawer. He read:

> It is an unusual recording—you will discover why. The Demon's signs and deeds are nothing compared to the greater glory of God's works. Look for signs, yes, but remember, all signs and numbers are God's. The Satan thinks, in his ignorance, that the signs are his, but he is wrong.

The records dropped onto the turntable one after another. The soaring choruses—<u>For unto us a child is born</u>; <u>Behold the Lamb</u>; <u>Alleluia</u>; <u>Blessing and Honor and Glory and Power be unto thee</u>, <u>O Lord</u> – entered his soul and swept away all doubt about the signs. The blemish on the cover—no doubt the work of a prankster at Columbia Records—is nothing compared to the beauty and power of Handel's music, music written in the bleakest dark, for the composer, he remembered, was blind. At the <u>Amen</u> Chorus he knew that it was not the beast but the Lamb who has sealed Ritchie's destiny. And his own.

He called Cornelius in the evening, after the brothers had finished their chapel prayers. The Brother related that Joe McMahon came by in the afternoon to teach catechism, then Widman came to give communion, but Ritchie spit it out, and a cruet of lavabo water went flying across the room. But they heard a faint voice say, "I can't." Widman held up another wafer. The faint voice said, "I wish to receive you in holy communion." Bowdern felt a rush of excitement. This was different, new.

The Brother went on: Widman still couldn't get it in his mouth, his lips were closed tight. So Widman said the prayers of a spiritual communion. Then that voice again, but not so loud this time. **One devil is out**, it said. **Ritchie must make nine communions, then I will leave**. Widman tried to administer nine more communions, but Ritchie failed to utter even the short form, I wish to receive you. Then, Cornelius added, the voice said **That isn't enough. He has to say one more word, one BIG word. He will never say that word, I won't let him**. But Bowdern was not impressed. It didn't matter what the Demon said; what mattered is God's will, and God's alone.

O'Flaherty drove him and Ray Bishop to the hospital at seven. He stepped from the elevator...there was Klara in the corridor whispering to some of the Brothers. Usually she came and left in the morning, but her reddened eyes and drawn face told him that she had been here for a long vigil. She was waiting for him. She expected the Demon to depart yesterday, Easter—but it did not. What will she say to him? He knew.

They sat on a cot in an empty cell and talked. The light thrown by a corridor bulb picked up an odd expression in her eyes. He eÿÿxpected wrath; he read despair. She was terrified, she said, that she had lost her son forever. She began to weep. He put sown his vestments and held her head to his breast.

Brother Cornelius pulled on the metal door and stood back. Bowdern wrapped himself in his festive stole and nodded to his companions. Inside, heavy breathing broke the silence, body odor thickened the air. The three priests circled the bed. PRAECIPIO TIBI...he began. When he finished the first of the commands, he remembered the Michael prayer; he reached for the statue of the angel that Cornelius had placed on the table. The golden haired angel held a burnished shield and fiery sword under the canopy of his immense wings. He held it to Ritchie's face and spoke in English: ST. MICHAEL, he prayed, DEFEND US IN BATTLE, BE OUR PROTECTION AGAINST THE WILES AND WICKEDNESS OF THE DEVIL...CAST INTO HELL SATAN AND ALL EVIL SPIRITS... The bed began to shake, then it rose from the floor until Ritchie's head was level with Bowdern. His face was darkly furrowed, his neck a knotted rope. The bed hovered, then crashed to the floor.

Bowdern began the second set of prayers. He faced his companions and intoned: Dominus Vobiscum.

Before the men could respond, Ritchie erupted: **I see bad men in hell**, he screamed; **they use bad words and do bad thing**s. With a sweep of his right ar*m–how did it get loose?*–he tore at the straps that bound his left arm and severed them, then began tugging at the straps around his waist. Four Brothers instantly rushed upon him.

Dominus Vobiscum, Bowdern repeated. Et Cum Spiritu Tuo, the priests and brothers answered.

Ritchie arched his body against the straps, pivoted toward Bowdern, and spat. He missed. *Or did he?* Bowdern instantly withdrew the Michael statue; the angel's winged torso was covered by gobs of mucus.

Bowdern reached over and traced the sign of the cross on Ritchie's forehead, as he said: IN THE NAME OF THE FATHER, AND OF THE SON, AND OF THE HOLY GHOST.

Ritchie's jaw went slack. His mouth hung open, showing gums and throat. His chest heaved with violent contractions.

From the open mouth came a new voice, rich, resonant, a voice from the four corners of the earth.

"SATAN! SATAN! I AM SAINT MICHAEL AND I COMMAND YOU AND THE OTHER EVIL SPIRITS TO LEAVE THE BODY IN THE NAME OF **DOMINUS**. IMMEDIATELY! NOW! NOW! **NOW!**"

Bowdern dropped to his knees. *Dominus—the word? Or a cruel trick?*

The foot of the bed began to rise. Four brothers rushed to clamp down on the bed and Ritchie in it. He writhed under their grip, wagged his tongue and hissed at them. With his free arms, he slashed at two brothers, knocked them from the bed, and bent forward to pull at the leg straps–in a minute he will be free. Bowdern grabbed one of Ritchie's feet: *God, it's like ice.* Brother Cornelius raced down the corridor and rang a bell—in moments several brothers and kitchen help dashed in and worked in shifts as they struggled to keep the boy on the bed and secure the straps on his upper body. Bowdern felt the boy's eyes fixed on him—an unwavering glare that held him like an invisible cord: he could not move, he could not pray.

Finally Ritchie closed his eyes and collapsed with a shudder. No one spoke. It seemed that no one would ever speak again in that silence. Finally Ritchie opened his eyes; they were bright and clear. Then he said softly, "He's gone."

He sought solace in the semi-darkness of a small oratory just off the study, where the steady light of altar candles often foretold an end to the world's foolishness and an abiding peace in a more sane world to come. But tonight his spirt wilted at the thought he had been taken for a fool. Of course the Demon could mimic an angel; he is the father of lies and deceit. The *Rituale* warned the exorcist not to desist until he sees signs of deliverance. There was no sign.

Michael tapped on the study door —*Michael is still here?...it is almost midnight*—an urgent call from the hospital. He urged Michael to get a night's sleep, then picked up the phone. It was Joe McMahon.

"Did you hear the noise?" McMahon asked.

"How is Richie?"

"The noise like a firecracker...you must have heard it—were you awake?"

The hospital is miles away, how could I hear a firecracker?...who cares? "How is Ritchie?" he demanded. "What's he doing?"

"He read comics for a while, then fell asleep."

"Do you need me?"

"No. Bill, it's over. Praise God. Get some rest."

He hung up slowly and returned to his oratory. Why, he wondered, was he denied a sign? Was he perverse like those who demanded a sign of Jesus, to be told that no sign would be given save the sign of Jonah?

In the morning he called Brother Cornelius to ask how Ritchie passed the night. Just fine, the Brother reported. He was out of his straps, in a guest room in the new wing, chatting away with the brothers. Word of his deliverance had spread through the hospital and since dawn the brothers—Widman gave him communion—had been filing in and out of the room marveling at the miracle. Oh, he had a dream, a glorious dream. A wonderful man came to him, he said, who looked like an angel; the man stood in a bright light and had long flowing hair and a white gown. He held a shining sword in his right hand, and with his left he pointed down to a cave where the Devil stood, with flames all around him. The Devil laughed and attacked the angel, but the angel looked straight at Ritchie, smiled, turned to the Devil and said "Dominus." At that, the Devil ran back into the cave with the other devils. The angel barred the cave and put a sign over the entrance. The sign said: S P I T E.

No: the Demon is a thief: he took the word Dominus from the priest's greeting to his companions; he took the angel figure from the Michael statue that he held up to Ritchie's face. No: a sign had been given, but not from God to the exorcist; it was from the Demon to his victims. And he, Bill Bowdern, was the intended victim. He told Cornelius he would be back that evening and they would pray again.

At noon he accepted tea and biscuits in the study as he poured over some texts. Dominus, he read, meant Lord, Master. Dominion is the right and power to rule. This power is from God, who gave it to Adam so that men could rule over the fish of the sea, the fowl of the air, and over the beasts of the earth, and over every low thing that creeps over the earth. And God gave Adam the power to name these creatures. Something new stirred in the back of his brain. He called Ray Bishop. He had almost forgotten that Ray, an obsessive note-taker, kept a diary—he wrote down every word the Demon said. Even when Ray wasn't present, he spoke to those who were. Ray brought the diary. Bowdern read it with trembling hands.

He remembered most of what Ray had recorded, but he was surprised to come upon the names Joe and Pete. He looked up at his friend. "Who are Joe and Pete? he asked. Ray shrugged.

"The Demon reads the bible," Ray said. "Joe and Pete must be St. Joseph and St. Peter."

Bowdern corrected his friend: "He doesn't have to read it—he remembers. And Joseph might be the patriarch who was slain by a wild beast—so his brothers told their father—and who rose to power over man and beast."

Ray was puzzled. "What of it," he asked.

"I'm no theologian," Bowdern admitted, "but I have my thoughts. Peter calls the Devil a roaring lion." And—he opened his office bible to *Acts of the Apostles*—he read to his friend the tenth chapter: Cornelius sends three men looking for Peter, whom they discover on a rooftop in Joppa, the great seaport; the apostle has just had a noon-time trance in which he saw a sail containing many animals and he heard a voice saying, "Rise Peter, kill and eat"—the great command from heaven.

He could think for himself; no longer did he need Heidi to explain things—or confuse the issue; and he had his friend Ray. And he knew the words the Demon feared: <u>Dominus</u>, Lord; <u>Deus</u>, God. God gave dominion to Adam so man could rule over the beasts and the ancient serpent. And he knew the Demon's name—S P I T E—if the dream was to be believed. He had that—if no sign. As it grew late he let Ray return to Verhagen, while he remained alone in the study. He played the second album of *Messiah* again through to the great AMEN Chorus. The number 666 was no distraction.

At dark, he strolled over to Xavier to pray. From the street he noticed that the lights in the church were on, but dim. The Jesuits would be there; they often came at night to recite the last two offices of the day, vespers and compline. He hesitated on the broad steps of the church. Something stirred inside him, distracted him. He lit a cigarette. When the Jesuits finished their office, he would go inside and be alone.

As he drew deeply from the cigarette, he sensed a shift in the wind. It was gusty. He gazed lazily down Lindell Boulevard. The high branches swayed silently overhead. Behind him, the church door opened abruptly. A young Jesuit brushed against him as he ran down the steps and disappeared around the corner. Then he noticed his shadow on the steps. *At night?*

He stomped on his cigarette and threw open the door. The light was almost blinding—a natural light, like a sun. The Jesuits were in disarray: some were kneeling in the pews, others standing about in clusters, speaking in hushed tones. All were looking up, except one who was prostrate before the high altar, his arms spread out to make a cross of himself.

They had seen the angel—he knew without asking.

***

Author's Postscript

In the days and years to come, Father Bowdern would hear them tell over and over about that night at Xavier, how real the angel was, as it—he—(they couldn't decide) appeared, first over the font then over the altar. Any closer and they could have touched him. They described him in detail: long flowing hair, the sword— a perfect match for the figure in Ritchie's dream.

Of course, he had been seen standing outside smoking. Sometimes the Jesuits would chide him: if only he had come in, he too would have seen the great Archangel Michael. Yet, he had no sense of loss. What they had seen inside the church, the angel's face itself, was stirring in his spirit, deep within. He had entered Ritchie's world—he knew.

291

CHAPTER FIVE

The Tree of Life (Conclusion)

THE TREE OF LIFE
(Author's Conclusion)

Thomas Allen, the author of *Possessed: The True Story of an Exorcism*, says that there is something of the fable about an exorcism. He is right: a story is being told that throws a veil over the face of the truth. He seems to imply—and I agree—that the fable is the medieval church assumption that a "possessed" person is one who has been assaulted and taken over by a demon or by the Devil himself. In my meditation (Chapter Four: "The Trap" and "The Sign") I pull back the veil and expose the face of our ancient enemy. He is no supernatural being— he is *Dinofelis,* the beast who stalked us in the short and tall grasses of the African Pleistocene, who embraced us in his jaws, and who stamped upon us and our genes the knowledge of our mortality and the fear of the demonic. We now know him to be natural—but our ancestors worshiped him as an awesome deity, and he occupies this status today in our desperate dreams and our ancient liturgies of worship and war.

The beast occupies the theater of our worship, where the fable is told again and again. In *Genesis*, we read of a paradise garden where our first parents encountered the beast in the form of a low lying serpent in the midst of two planted trees. God had offered Adam and his mate the fruit of the Tree of Life. If they eat of this fruit, God tells them, each day will be an eternity of delight. But Adam has a rival for this high status, the serpent who slithers through the grass and who seduces the woman Eve away from the Tree of Life and tempts her to eat the fruit of the other tree. The other is the Tree of Knowledge of Good and Evil—so-called by the biblical editor, who pinned a moral tale to the original story. If we peer beneath the moralizing, however, we see that the other tree simply stands in stark contrast to the first; it is the Tree of Death. The couple eat of this tree. Banished from the paradise garden, their return is forbidden by brandished angelic falchions. They must toil in a barren soil, suffer, die and return to dust forever. As the curtain rings down on this primal scene, the Tree of Life stands alone in the center of the garden; its fruit may be had by the victorious beast; he and his progeny will live forever.

The editor of the bible story has all but concealed the question that hung over the Pleistocene grasslands—who shall win the contest between man and beast for prime place and immortality for the species? The original form of the bible story, however, makes the issue clear: the Sumerian hero Gilgamish wished to be eternally young, and was given a sacred plant that would confer this gift; but while he bathed in a deep well, a serpent made off with the plant, leaving the hero to bemoan his mortality. Myths from other parts of the world abound that tell of men and beasts as rivals for immortality: the Nandi people of East Africa tell how a dog once came to their fathers and told them about a river in which they may immerse themselves and after three days rise up immortal; but the people ridiculed the dog, whereupon the dog turned against the people and denied them the divine gift. Many other myths connect the death of humans with the deeds of animals. (The partial obscurity of the primal issue in the bible is the overlayment of legalistic morality: the biblical editor's drumbeat of obedience to Jewish law turned the tree of death into the tree of knowledge of good and evil. But the issue of Life is brought to the fore again in the New Testament, where the parable of the Good Samaritan treats of this very matter, how Life has been obscured by pharisaic moralism: "Master, what must I do to inherit Life?" The reader is referred to Chapter Three, "A Certain Man.")

Life is the question that hangs over the St. Louis exorcism. It is partially obscured by the well meaning clerics who wanted Ritchie to make a confession of his sin and become a good practicing Catholic. But at its core is the ancient struggle for immortality. "Ritchie," has been attacked by an enemy and left for dead: the enemy is the predator beast, who arises in the boy's unconscious mind and takes on objective reality.

"Possession" is a dissociative phenomenon: Ritchie at times is a normal, although introverted, boy who reads comic books and plays board games. At other times he is the very serpent who has attacked him. In primitive societies, and in infantile mentality, the individual is fused with the beings and realities of his family and tribe. No distinction exists between "I" and "It" or between "I" and "You." The child is at one with his mother; he is at one with his tribe; he is at one with his deeds; he is at one with his opponent. (In such societies, in order to exorcise an animal, the man becomes the animal or draws the animal: this identification is no fiction of an artist's imagination; it is a matter of pre-rational absorption in the dynamics of a unitary realism, a numenous, magical whole.) Ritchie succumbed to a threat that took him back to the Pleistocene, and in this neurological state he faced his adversary as an aspect of himself. In his identification with the beast adversary, he was both the devouring beast and the victim. As devouring beast, he attacked himself; as victim, he imitated the beast to protect himself from the beast and those whom he perceived to be in league with the beast—predators, real or imagined, such as Rev. Schulze and Father Bowdern.

　　Ritchie was first threatened in his own home—possibly by Aunt Ilse, whose Ouija game tipped him toward dissociation and regression. His home became a lair for the beast, who attpted to drive out the competitors by psychekinetic means. Schulze made the mistake of inviting the boy to his home, where the boy sensed danger by the proximity of the pastor's bedroom-lair (our instinctive animal nature is more astute in threatening situations than is the nicely developed brain), converting him into the beast again, which precipitated another psychokinetic volley.

Bill Bowdern came into this amphitheater of psychic reality bearing his own myth—that of the hero. The hero myth is universal in human experience: a wanderer or warrior struggles with a beast that threatens to destroy him or others; he overcomes the beast (or is killed by it, but returns to life) and saves his fellows from devastation. The hero's adventure often begins with a call to leave his family and fellows to pursue a new career fraught with obstacles and dangers. Often, in hero stories from around the world, the hero finds helpers, or is fortified by waters and magical numbers. The mythic resonance of Jesus' life explains the wonder and romance of it: he left his home, he bathed in baptismal waters, he encountered Satan, he received aid from angels, he performed miracles, he sacrificed himself upon the cross, and on the third day he rose a conqueror. Bowdern, like his master, left behind the comfortable religiosity of the Xavier sanctuary and entered the lair of the beast. Significant, too, is the fact that he entered Klara's Lutheran world where he was treated as an outsider (Again, refer to Chapter Three, "A Certain Man.") and he came near to losing his life.

Psychologically, the hero matures by means of his deeds—from the depth of his psyche he hears a summons to break the bonds of infantile dependency, and strive for liberation and self-distinction by certain actions or rituals. Everyone receives this summons to break away, to withdraw from the familiar past and release new energies for new tasks. Bowdern heeded the summons. He made the honored passage by casting off the shackles of his prideful self-esteem ("Samaritan of St. Louis"—he never missed a wake) and his formulaic spirituality (I conjecture, based on Allen's biographical remarks and what I may assume was true of a Jesuit in the 1940's— that he was true to the church's dogmatic traditions). At some point, I believe, he realized that the creeds and prayers didn't work, that something else was needed—this is why he called Heidi. What was needed was Bill Bowdern himself, his authoritative presence as a full human being. Bowdern needed to pass through the baptismal portal more than Ritchie.

Fatigue and fasting brought him to the breaking point. Like an athlete or warrior who pushes himself to extremes, he learned that man is mortal and life is short. This learning compressed and intensified his life and gave it an urgency, an immanence, and the need to strive to finish his work. William James of Harvard said that this experience of hardship and pain can initiate a man into a more profound way of handling the gift of existence. And it initiates a man into a new sense of time– *timelessness*; like certain primitive peoples who have one word only to cover past, present and future, his psychic dwelling is above those states that for us define limits. Albert Einstein reflected on this subject from a different perspective when he wrote about a friend who died: "Now he has gone a little ahead of me. This is of little significance. For us believing physicists, the separation of past, present and future has only the meaning of an illusion." Bowdern, as journeying hero, came to a crisis that honed his life down to one task; he struggled to decipher the end of it in time, and in so doing he projected a numbers scheme upon the "demon": the end came when he despaired of ordinary time and entered the timeless center of his own psyche.

But the journey to the center is a deeper matter than a search for personal maturity and renewed energy for the tasks of life; it is a return to the source and center of all being. It is a fearful journey the hero makes—strange thoughts and visions may overwhelm him; it will seem God and His angels are against him, when, like a new Adam he puts forth his hand to eat of the Tree of Life (*Genesis 3:22*). Of course, it is his own psyche he explores: not just his personal ego, but the psyche that opens up onto the world's psyche, whose deep roots are at the base of nature. There is more to the psyche than we know. Immortality—for the hero himself and his fellows—is the issue. "Master, what must I do to inherit Eternal Life?"

As he journeys to the center, the hero may cross a river; or he comes upon a deep and beguiling pool; or a raging sea. God threw Jonah into the water where he was devoured by a sea monster. For three days in the belly of the beast he journeyed from west to east, from the setting of the sun to the rising of the sun. His night sea journey translated him from the realm of death to the realm of Life.

Water issues from the habitation of the Most High, says the psalmist (*Psalm 46*), where there is a river that makes glad the city of God. Jerusalem was desperate for water; it is the Jews' desert image of salvation. First the psalmist tells of waters that rage and foam; then he speaks of other waters, and he asserts that God will succor his people. God is in the midst of the waters—the psyche—to be seen at the break of day. The search for water, the crossing of water, the descent into water, is a mystical allusion to the hero's night passage to the city of God, the center and source of his being, the center and source of all being.

Water is the source, the font, the original substance: all life on the planet came up from the oceans many billions of years ago. It signifies our biological birth and our spiritual rebirth. On Holy Saturday, the second of three savings days of Holy Week, the priest processes to the baptismal font singing, "As the heart longs for flowing streams, so longs my soul for thee, O God..." (*Psalm 42*). At the font he prays, "...to the end that a heavenly offspring...may emerge from the immaculate womb of the divine font, reborn new creatures..." He holds his hand over the water and prays that Satan be cast from it; he makes the sign of the cross and sprays the four quarters of the world; he breathes three times over it, and plunges a candle three times into it, each time to a greater depth, as he prays, "Make the whole substance of this water fruitful for regeneration." Popular opinion holds that baptism is a washing away of original sin; but in the mythological realm, baptism is a cluster of themes that

297

center about our origins, the hero's discovery of his source, and the promise of his rebirth. "You must be born again," said Jesus to Nicodemus, and he added, "Except a man be born of water and the spirit, he cannot enter the kingdom of God."

The hero searches for rebirth when the old course makes him forlorn and heavy laden. He looks for a hidden light, he listens for a distant voice, that sets him on a new course. If he persists, he begins to hear within himself a cadence, a passage of harmonic and rhythmic tension that yields to a new tempo, a new harmony, and he arrives at a new theme. The analogy from music theory is apt, I believe, for the wise Pythagoras, in his *Golden Verses*, spoke about a high and holy heaven, the invisible core of the world, a harmonic unity of voices and numbers that existed before all creation. Pythagoras heard the sacred sounds when he invented a single stringed instrument and discovered that simple proportions of measurement made for consonant and pleasing tones. The whole world is based upon these numbers and harmonies. However, Pythagoras warned that only those who will make the difficult and rigorous ascent will come to this place where the tones lead us. And the world weary came to him in great numbers. (When the spent and bereft Bowdern arrived at the brink and crossed the waters into the unconscious source of his being, Christ, he heard the music of the spheres, and his world blossomed into sounds and numbers that signified that he had come close to his Christ.)

To our western ears, harmony depends upon the number three—the triad. A three note chord built on intervals of thirds, it is as natural as the air and the clouds and the colors of the rainbow. The three tones of a basic triad are derived from the first five tones of the overtone series – a fact known to our art and science, and inherent to our aural experience of nature. Great symphonies—cathedrals of tones—depend on this basic fact. Then there is the simple triplet: three notes in a series. Schubert, in his C Major Symphony of 1828 introduces the finale with a triplet fanfare that sets us spinning and marching along like heros: a pause—then the horns, reiterating four D's, start off again and we are treading on air as the elemental force of the music bears us to some nameless realm. Beethoven summed up the magic of triplets in his last piano sonata, the Opus 111, where the three becomes a five. This piece moved Thomas Mann to reflect, in his Doctor Faustus, "...only three notes...a quaver, a semi-quaver, and a dotted crochet, to be scanned as, say, *heaven's blue,* or *lover's pain,* or *fare thee well,* or *meadowland*—and that is all. But this mild utterance...will undergo vicissitudes, struggles, will enter into dark night and dazzling flashes, crystal spheres, where coldness and heat, repose and ecstasy, are one and the same. Finally the melody, D G G, acquires a C and a C sharp before the D. Now it scans as, say, *O thou heaven's blue, greenest meadowland, fare thee well for aye.* The C sharp redeems all; it makes the melody consoling, reconciling all conflict and opposition...justifying the dark night." Mann seems to say that, in this music, a great gulf exists between bass and treble, right hand and left, which brings on a crisis that cannot be resolved by any earthly means. But the great melody, when it scans with five notes, bestows an infinite grace, a peace beyond understanding: instead of three, we read, *great was God in us; now forget the pain; Dearest Butterfly.* We have come to the center of the mystic cross, where the Redeemer's outstretched arms embrace all and reconcile all opposition; where all is harmonized in a wondrous world of Peace and Love.

Our nominalist science has educated us out of the notion that numbers are magical, that they have souls, that they speak to us. But the psychological import of numbers works deeply to influence us in ways we hardly suspect. Carl Jung states that numbers are the most primitive archetypes, that they spring from the unconscious aspect of the psyche, a trove of hidden treasure. The number one—in the qualitative and psychological sense—is the original unity that existed before all else. Jung calls it the uroboric state, using the image of the snake that forms a circle to bite its tail. The number two reflects a split in the uroboric state and the emergence of opposites. Three represents a power that mediates and reconciles the opposition implied in the number two.

Alfred North Whitehead in his essay, "The Rhythm of Education," speaks of threeness as a character of a person's learning and growing. First, he says, there is the stage of "romance," the emotional excitement of discovery. Then there is the stage of precision, where breath and totality are subordinated to exact formulation and intellectual analysis. The third stage he calls generalization, a synthesis of the first two stages, a return to the wide ranging poetic intuiting of the world, with the added advantage of a classified idea and relevant technique. Many others see "threeness" in human life. Freud speaks of oral, anal and genital stages of maturation, and he analyzes the mind in terms of ego, id, and superego. Eric Berne speaks of adult, child, and parent ego-states. And of course, Hegel's thesis, antithesis, and synthesis come to mind. Many of these states or stages exist or operate on the conscious plane, but may be sculpted and driven by invisible forces within the psyche that have the indwelling threeness. Edinger, the Jungian student, writes about deeper levels of growth: in his essay "Trinity and Quaternity," he depicts the transforming powers of death and rebirth as a threefold act of spirit: three days is the symbolic duration of the night sea journey, he says, for Jonah was three days in the belly of the whale, and Christ, who was crucified between two fellow humans, was three days in the bowels of the earth.

Mystical traditions abound in threeness. Tao means "the way" and it is a middle ground between opposites. The *Tao Te Ching* of Lao Tse relishes the fluid motion of life in these words:

> Life, when it came to be,
> Bore one, then two, then three
> Elements of things;
> And thus the three began-
> Heaven and earth and man-
> To balance happenings.

And how often we find in fairy tales—and in even in our dreams—that a hero or heroine is given a task or goal, and on the way or at the end, there is the number three. In one story a sick, world - weary king desires the "water of life," and "three golden hairs from the head of the devil." In an Iranian story, Prince Hatim is trapped in mysterious waters; he is told that the waters conceal a wondrous diamond that will restore the dead to life; the hero is allowed three chances to kill a large bird with a golden bow and arrow; he kills the bird on the third attempt and the dead return to life. The more familiar tale of beauty and the beast tells of a young woman, youngest of four daughters, who, after a beast has threatened to punish her father three months after the theft of a rose, goes herself to the beast's enchanted castle after three months, whereupon the beast is transfigured, and the young woman becomes the bride of a marvelous prince.

(Over against the sacred three, an "unholy three" appears in the Christian Apocalypse: the Dragon, the beast, and the false prophet. And when the whoring Babylon falls and becomes the haunt of foul spirits, the kings who committed fornication with her, together with merchants and seamen, send up a threefold dirge. Lower powers are capable only of brutish imitations and repetitions of heavenly sights and sounds; but they use these imitations to deceive the gullible on earth.)

The number three conjures up powers that are not yet perfect, that clamor for a redeeming motion. In the first chapter, "The Fourth Watch of the Night," I conjectured that the evangelists used three to indicate the search for God, and four to indicate God Himself. Of course, in mystical literature and in unconscious processes, both numbers convey the aspect of divinity. Yet, Jung saw four as the crucial aspect of totality images; when speaking of the Christian doctrine of the Trinity, he asked the question that the alchemists asked, "Where is the four?" He felt the need to incorporate the neglected human factor, with our instinctive and earthy natures, so long ignored by western religion, into the Godhead to fill out the whole. Both humanity and Godhead clamor for perfection. Another Jungian, Gerard Adler, agrees: while the Trinity expresses Godhead in a complete structural sense, he says, the fourth element of human realization needs to be added; three characterizes the self-manifestation of God, four has a human quality: "In this case," he says, "the four may itself represent a factor of uncertainty and new movement." So, then, these numbers speak of God, and at the same time our need to incorporate Him into our lives and ourselves into His.

Following Jung's insight about the numbers three and four, Jung's disciples singled out, in their observations of psychological products, images of the Quaternity. Analytical psychology venerates the number four as it is found in dreams, primitive drawings, myths, and—in the *New Testament*—the four evangelists, and the four living creatures of the *Apocalypse*. In Mark's *Gospel*, the fourth healing miracle takes place as four men lower a corpse-like figure through a portal to Jesus standing, we may imagine, in the center of the opened space to great him and restore him to the Life with God that Adam lost. The number four signifies Godhead and our inclusion in Godhead.

(But our dark side abhors the penetrating shafts of divinity: over against the venerated four, the *Apocalypse* describes the dreaded four horsemen.)

The number five is consciously used by biblical authors to convey the power of God's will. The *locus classicus* for the power of five is *The Book of Daniel*, where a simple numerology based on four plus one over is revelatory for God's chosen people. Mark understood this pattern and put it to use in his gospel narrative. In Luke, Pentecost expresses the power of the Holy Spirit. The basis seems to be the five books of Moses.

The number seven stands tall in *The Revelation of St. John the Divine*, where (12:7) the seer tells us "There was war in heaven..." The number seven is redemptive: seven churches, seven lamp stands, seven beatitudes, seven seals, seven stars, seven angels, seven trumpets, seven spirits of God, and the seven horns and seven eyes of the Lamb. Its literary pattern is based on three series of sevens. The Chaldean system of astronomy gave names to the seven days of the week from the names of the seven luminaries. John takes his readers on a seven day spiritual voyage under the stars from the first day to the Sabbath. Jesus himself is revealed as the true fruit of the Tree of Life, which man may eat and be restored to his original state. But again the near presence of a beast spawns evil numbers: God's wrath is poured out from seven bowls; and the beast with seven heads comes up from the sea during the war in heaven, when Michael and his angels fight against the dragon. The *Apocalypse* epitomizes the theology of primitive groups and societies who believed that the gods fought among themselves and presided over human wars to achieve their victories. The negative imagery of the *Apocalypse* is that of a bestiary; its message is that the saints will be delivered from the beast and his evil dominion.

The archetypal images are liquid and shifting; numerical reality often flows into other images. The circle ("mandala") and the square are geometric embodiments of the numenosity of numbers that impact us with syllogistic power. Their scriptural manifestation begins in the garden of paradise, a spacial enclosure (from the Persian: *pairi*, "around," and *daeza*, "wall," thus a circular walled-in space) in which a figure at the center unites four cardinal points. It is the Tree of Life that stands at the center. In the new garden, Gethsemene, it is the Christ who stands at the center. This garden, too, is an enclosure; its symbolic space is defined by the overlooking temple that has replaced the Tree of Life and made of it a Tree of Death; and the flowing waters of the brook Kidron, the water through which man must journey on his way home to Paradise. As the new Adam, Christ deals with Death, as did his prototype: he confronts those who would lead him away to the cross; he has with him the inner three disciples, and they are soon joined by a fourth, one who bears the character of all sinners and evil men who require redemption—Judas Iscariot. Yet, the garden is also his passage to his third day rising, when he will bestow Life. He embraces these opposites, he is the mediator of mankind. Even on the cross—especially on the cross—he remains inside his mandala and, suspended between a thief consigned to hell, and a second sufferer whom he will call up to Paradise, he mediates between opposite types of humanity. The wood of the cross becomes a Tree of Life.

When Bill Bowdern and his helpers circled Ritchie's bed, they may have set up a psychic field of influence. I use this term advisedly—it would have pleased the eminent William James, who compared the unconscious aspect of psyche to the "field" concept in physics. In this charged atmosphere, whether it pleases us to call it a mandala or a field, numbers materialized on the body of the "victim." Bowdern tried to decipher these numbers as messages from the "Demon," but they came from his own unconscious, or they welled up from the common deep. They were soterial–"X" as "ten" (Pythagoras added the numbers one, two, three and four and considered the total a sublime expression of the universe—the *tetractys*, or the Roman numeral X.); or: **X**avier? GOD at **X**avier? (Bowdern's feverish prayers and meditations charged the Xavier sanctuary; it is a pity he did not see Michael, who, together with Christ and the Samaritan, is an image of the highest elevation of the human spirit.)

All the saving numbers and signs that took shape on Ritchie's body or emitted from his mouth came as projections from Bowdern's Higher Self. Even the Demon's name, "Spite," emerged from Bowdern's Lenten reading in the Xavier sanctuary of the text in *Luke*

18:32, where Jesus goes against demonic forces that treat him with spite. The sanctuary of a liturgical church, with its sacred site at the center, is itself a manifestation of the psyche and the Self. "X," therefore, reflected the Xavier sanctuary, where Bowdern read his bible, preached, and prayed.

I believe that Bowdern's maturation and purity of heart transformed the bedroom-lair into a timeless, numenous sanctuary of saving signs and numbers. In this sanctuary the three priests and the boy-victim participated, for moments at least, in the psycho-physical unity that underlies all phenomena; not that the physical is the outer garment of the spiritual, as some mystics have proclaimed; but that the physical and the spiritual are in reality a seamless garment. In this sanctuary, the mind and the body, the thought and the act, the doer and the deed are one. Three becomes four; the believer and his God, no longer opposed, become one. Here, as Jesus said, faith moves mountains; all prayers are answered. Bowdern stood there in the midst of it and, like his Christ in Gethsemene, he prayed. His prayers evicted the "Demon."

The third eye opens upon this sanctuary—let us call it paradise—and finds the first home and ultimate refuge of the spirit. At the center stands the Tree of Life. We shall again eat of the fruit of this Tree. (*Revelation 2:7*) Four streams of water flow from it to nourish the four quarters of the world. "Mary" is here. She has passed through the cavernous jaws and the portal where angelic falchions no longer forbid entry. The five nuns who perished in the Thames, they too are here; they understand why God's winds cast them into the sea.

FINIS

SELECTED BIBLIOGRAPHY

(The interested reader may turn to these books and other books by these authors for more reading on the subjects covered by The Fourth Watch of the Night)

1. Allen, Thomas. *Possessed: The True Story of an Exorcism.* New York: Doubleday, 1993.

2. Amorth, Gabriel. *An Exorcist Tells His Story.* San Francisco: Xavier Press, 1999.

3. Boehme, Jacob. *Signature of All Things; of the Supersensual Life; of Heaven and Hell; Discourse Between Two Souls.* Kila, Montana: Kessinger Publishing, 2002.

4. Bucke, Richard M. *Cosmic Consciousness*: *A Study in the Evolution of the Human Mind.* New York: E. P. Dutton and Co. 1901.

5. Campbell, Joseph. *Myths to Live By.* New York: Bantam Books, 1988.

6. Campbell, Joseph. *The Hero with a Thousand Faces.* Princeton: Princeton University Press, 1949.

7. Campbell, Joseph. *The Masks of God, Vol.* 1. New York: The Viking Press, 1970.

8. Cuneo, Michael W. *American Exorcism: Expelling Demons in the Land of Plenty.* New York: Doubleday, 2001.

9. Canetti, Elias. *Crowds and Power.* New York: Continuum, 1962.

10. Davies, J. G. *He Ascended into Heaven.* London: Lutterworth Press,1958.

11. Ehrenreich, Barbara. *Blood Rites: Origins and History of the Passions of War.* New York: Henry Holt and Company, 1998.

12. Farrer, Austin. *A Study in St. Mark*. London: Westminster: Dacre Press, 1951.

13. Farrer, Austin. *St. Matthew and St. Mark*. Westminster: Dacre Press, 1954.

14. Goulder, Michael D. *Type and History in Acts*. London: SPCK, 1974.

15. Heron, Laurence Tunstall. *ESP in the Bible :The Psychic Roots of Religion*. Garden City, New York: Doubleday and Company, 1974.

16. Huxley, Aldous. *The Doors of Perception*. New York: Harper and row, 1990.

17. Jung, Carl G. Ed. *Man and his Symbols*. (Essays by M.L. von Franz, Joseph L. Henderson, Jolande Jacobi, Aniela Jaffe. Introduction by the editor.) Garden City, New York: Doubleday and Company, 1974.

18. LeBar, James J. *Cults, Sects, and the New Age*. Huntington, Indiana: Our Sunday Visitor Publishing Division, 1989.

19. Lorenz, Konrad. *On Aggression*. New York: Bantam, 1966.

20. Martin, Malachi. *Hostage to the Devil*. San Francisco: Harper Collins,1992.

21. Montgomery, Sy. *Spell of the Tiger: The Man-Eaters of the Sundarbans*. Boston: Houghton Mifflin, 1995.

22. Motyer, S. "The Rending of the Veil: A Marcan Pentecost. " *New Testament Studies* 33 (1987).

23. Nicola, John J. *Diabolical Possession and Exorcism*. Rockford, Illinois: Tan Books, 1974.

24. Ouspensky, Peter D. *A New Model of the Universe: Principals of the Psychological Method in its Application to Problems of Science, Religion, and Art.* New York: Vintage Books, 1971.

25. Pagels, Eileen. *The Gnostic Gospels.* New York: Random House, Inc. 1989.

26. Peck, M. Scott. *The People of the Lie: The Hope for Healing Human Evil.* New York: Touchstone, 1983.

27. Peck, M. Scott. *The Road Less Traveled: A New Psychology of Love, Traditional Values and Spiritual Growth.* New York: Touchstone, 1978.

28. Zaleski, Carol. *Other World Journeys: Accounts of Near-Death Experience in Medieval and Modern Times.* Oxford: Oxford University Press, 1987.

SOURCES

Father James LeBar of Hyde Park, New York, numerous interviews by author covering the period of May 1992 to January 2001

The Reverend Dr. Arthur McGill, of the Church of Canada. Lectures in Memphis, Tennessee.

Weller, Phillip T. *The Roman Ritual.* Milwaukee: The Bruce Publishing, 1952

About the Author

Carter J. Gregory, B.A., M.Div., S.T.M. is an Ordained Minister of the Episcopal Church and a psychotherapist, who searches religion and psychology for signs of transcendence in human life. In his pastoral and clinical work he strives to rescue religion and scripture from the court house of legalistic and literalist readings, so that people can find their true spiritual roots. As a clinician for hospitals in New York state, and as a therapist in private practice, he brings his professional and spiritual resources to bear upon the needs of his clients. As a public speaker for schools and hospitals, he is noted for his emphasis on human development and spiritual growth. He lives in Dutchess County New York.